From the Library of

Gary Smith

ALSO BY LAURA JOH ROWLAND

Shinjū

BUNDORI

BUNDORI

A NOVEL OF JAPAN

LAURA JOH ROWLAND

VILLARD • NEW YORK

Library of Congress Cataloging-in-Publication Data
Rowland, Laura Joh.
Bundori / by Laura Joh Rowland.
p. cm.
ISBN 0-679-43423-2
1. Japan—History—Genroku period, 1688–1704—Fiction. I. Title.
PS3568.0934B8 1996
813´.54—dc20   95-4826

Printed in the United States of America on acid-free paper
2 4 6 8 9 7 5 3
First Edition

In memory of my grandparents:

Day Hung and Susanna Joh
Gow Sing and Quon Gin Lee

EDO

GENROKU PERIOD, YEAR 2, MONTH 3

(Tokyo, April 1689)

PROLOGUE

As the hour of the boar approached, the great city of Edo lay shrouded in a heavy mist that blurred the darkness and muffled sound. A thin spring rain pattered onto the tile roofs of the Nihonbashi merchant quarter, puddling the narrow streets. Yellow lamplight glowed faintly behind the wooden lattices and paper panes of only a few windows; smoke from charcoal braziers rose to mingle with the mist and thicken the air still more. Although the city's many gates had not yet closed, blocking off passage from each section to the next, the streets were already as deserted as if midnight—nearly three hours away—had already arrived.

The lone stalker emerged from the shelter of a recessed doorway in a row of shopfronts whose sliding wooden shutters were closed tight against the hostile weather. The dank chill penetrated his cloak and seeped between the plates of the armor tunic beneath it. Cold moisture gathered under his wide-brimmed hat and inside the iron mask that covered his face. His body, already tense with anticipation, began to shiver. With each shallow breath, he inhaled and exhaled air that smelled of damp wood and earth and the fishy taint of the Sumida River. Keeping to the shadows beneath the roofs' overhanging eaves, he moved sideways, stealthily, until he reached the next doorway. There he paused, all his senses alert for the first sign of his prey.

Moments passed. The night noises—voices from inside nearby houses, distant hoofbeats, the clatter of the night-soil carts making their way toward the fields outside town—gradually ceased as Edo prepared for the closing of the gates and the captivity it would endure until dawn. Quivering with impatience, the stalker peered down the street. His fingers traced the flat guards, shaped like human skulls, of his swords. Would the enemy appear tonight? Would he at last achieve the goal postponed for so many years?

The mist allowed him to see no farther than ten paces in any direction. To his right, he could barely discern the murky glow of a torch that lit the gate at the street's end. The night seemed empty of all movement and presence save his own. Frustration mounted; blood lust consumed him in waves of hot desire. As he waited, his fevered mind projected images at first vague, then more distinct, against the mist's dense blankness. If he squinted—there, just so— he could imagine himself back through the years to that time about which he'd heard so much that he knew it almost as well as his own. The time of constant and glorious civil war, before the village of Edo had burgeoned into a city of one million inhabitants; before the first Tokugawa shogun, Ieyasu, had subjugated his rivals and imposed peace upon the land.

The time of the greatest warlord who had ever lived.

≈

Kiyosu Fortress, one hundred and twenty-nine years ago. A merciless summer sun blazed down upon the two thousand samurai sheltered within the wooden walls of the stockade. The stalker, though among the humblest of the foot soldiers, felt the unease that permeated their pitifully small army. This day could mean victory and life—or defeat and death—for them all.

"He's coming!"

The words, whispered from one man to the next, passed through the ranks. Along with his comrades, the stalker knelt and bowed, arms extended, forehead to the ground. But he couldn't resist a quick glance upward as their feared and beloved lord passed.

Oda Nobunaga, lord of Owari Province, with ambitions of someday ruling the entire land, was resplendent in a suit of armor made from hundreds of metal and leather plates tied together with blue silk cord and lacquered in brilliant colors, and wearing a black iron helmet crowned with a pair of carved golden horns. He rode a magnificent black steed. His expression grave, he dismounted to confer with the three generals who accompanied him into the whitewashed wooden fort.

Another whisper swept the ranks: "Marune has fallen!"

Dread paralyzed the stalker. He gasped with the others. With the capture of Lord Oda's frontier fortress, nothing stood between them and the enemy Lord Imagawa's troops, twenty-five thousand strong, who were advancing on them even now. They were doomed. But his fear for Lord Oda overshadowed that which he felt for himself.

The sound of footsteps jolted him back to the present. Relinquishing his lingering terror and the image of the imperiled fortress, he looked into the street. Out of the mist to his left shuffled an elderly samurai, with the customary swords, one long and one short, at his waist.

The stalker savored the heady rise of excitement as he grasped the hilt of his own long sword. Trembling, he waited for the man to draw nearer. He focused his thoughts on the confrontation ahead. But a part of his mind leapt backward to that morning long past.

The fortress gates opened to admit two panting scouts. "Imagawa's army is in the gorge outside Okehazama village!" they cried, hurrying to convey the news to Lord Oda.

Almost before the stalker or his comrades could comprehend the significance of this information, they were on the march. All two thousand of them, so few compared to the massive force that awaited them, mounted and on foot; first banner-bearers, gunners, and archers, then the swordsmen and spear-carriers, with Lord Oda and the generals bringing up the rear. They sweltered in the heat that baked the hills and rice fields.

Midday came. At last they stopped behind a hill just short of the gorge and waited for the command to act. From inside the gorge, the stalker could hear voices raised in drunken laughter and song. Imagawa's troops were celebrating their earlier victory. He listened and waited some more. A tense hush gripped the hillside and held him motionless, afraid to breathe.

Suddenly a mass of dark storm clouds boiled up out of the west, hiding the sun. Lightning split the sky; thunder shook the earth like the beat of a great war drum. The first raindrops pelted the earth. As if on this signal from the heavens, Lord Oda raised his great gold war fan and brought it down again, cleaving the air in a decisive motion. The conch trumpet blared the order:

Charge!

In one movement, they rose and ran toward the gorge. Great sheets of rain lashed the stalker as he struggled against the wind. Ahead of him, the first rank had disappeared into the gorge. He heard the boom of gunfire and the startled cries of Imagawa's army. Then, his heart pounding louder than the thunder, he skidded down the slope and into the swirling chaos that filled the gorge.

The storm had driven Imagawa's men to seek shelter under trees. Now they scrambled to load drenched and useless arquebuses, groped for bows, spears, and swords lost in the mud. But it was too late. Oda's troops fell upon them, slaughtering them by the hundreds. The clash of steel blades echoed up and down the gorge. Guns roared, emitting clouds of black smoke. Arrows sang through the air to strike flesh with meaty thumps. Screams of death agony echoed the attackers' murderous shouts. The metallic scent of blood overpowered the summer smells of sweat and rain. Into the raging battle rode Lord Oda. Sword raised high, he made straight for Lord Imagawa, who stood alone and unprotected. One expert slash of Oda's sword, one triumphant yell, and Imagawa lay dead.

Wild with ardor and admiration, the stalker drew his sword and plunged into the melee. "Lord Oda, I offer my life in your service!"

Now the old man had almost reached the doorway. The stalker could hear his wheezy breaths. His sword, already drawn for that battle long past, was in his hand. A fierce eagerness burned inside him as he slipped from the shadows to block his prey's path. The man uttered a whimper of surprise and stood still, one hand lifted in a gesture of greeting, or entreaty.

The stalker raised his sword in both hands and swung it in a swift, sideways arc. The blade sliced cleanly through the old man's neck. It severed his head, which hit the ground and rolled a few paces before coming to a halt faceup in the muddy street. A great gush of blood, black in the dim light, spewed from the neck as the body crumpled and fell.

Filled with the sweet fire of conquest, the stalker beheld the carnage that lay at his feet. He saw the remains of his present-day enemy; he could also see the fallen bodies of dead and wounded soldiers in the gorge. He longed to stand there and play out in his mind the short remainder of the Battle of Okehazama.

But he must not let his fantasy make him forget where—and in what time—he was, or the danger of remaining at the scene of a murder he'd just committed. Besides, he had much work to do before the gates closed. Sheathing his sword, he picked up the severed head and tucked it under his cloak. Then he hurried away through the misty streets and alleys.

The returning troops swarmed into Kiyosu Fortress on a wave of riotous excitement. Cheers and laughter rattled the stockade walls. Glee replaced the morning's despair. The Battle of Okehazama had ended moments after it began—with Oda the victor. Lord Imagawa was dead; those few of his troops not killed in the gorge had fled in panic. Mikawa, Totomi, and Suruga Provinces belonged to Oda now, and the way was cleared for his march on Kyōto, the capital. The celebration would last through the night, with much drink, song, and revelry. But first would come the solemn ritual to mark Lord Oda's brilliant triumph.

Alone in a cramped room lit by a single guttering oil lamp, the stalker knelt and unwrapped the severed head. Tenderly he washed his bloody prize in a bucket of water and dried it with a clean cloth. Beside him sat a square board with a sharp iron spike thrust up through the middle. He mounted the head on this contraption, grunting with the effort as he forced it down upon the spike. At last the point penetrated the brain, and the neck was flush with the board. Carefully he combed the wispy gray hair and tied it in a pigtail with a piece of white string. He applied rouge to the pale, wrinkled cheeks to restore the color of life, and buffed the bald crown. He prodded the eyeballs with his fingers until they gazed downward in the manner considered most auspicious. Lighting a stick of incense, he waved it around the head to sweeten its odor. Finally he added the most important touch: the white paper label inked with black characters that explained the purpose of his deed. This he fastened to the dead man's pigtail. Then he stood and surveyed his work. His heart swelled with pride as he gazed upon the head.

His *bundori*. His war trophy.

On the ramparts of Kiyosu Fortress, banners swayed in the evening breeze beneath the setting sun's red globe. War drums boomed; singers' chants rose to the heavens. Flaring torches lit the yard inside the stockade, where Lord Oda Nobunaga, still clad in full armor, sat on a stool, flanked by his generals. Arranged in ranks before him knelt his troops. Lord Oda nodded solemnly, ordering the ceremony to begin.

From the fort came a procession of samurai. Each brought a mounted head, which he placed at his lord's feet, then bowed before returning to the fort to fetch another. The stalker was fourth in line. His spirit soared skyward with the chants and drumbeats; he could scarcely contain his joy. Today he'd distinguished himself in battle by killing forty men singlehandedly. His reward: a place of honor in the procession and the recognition of his lord and peers.

This is only the beginning, he thought deliriously. He envisioned the future, seeing himself first as a commander, then as a general. And, when his end came, he would die in the glory of battle, paying his lord the ultimate tribute: his life.

Now it was his turn to pass before Lord Oda. Squaring his shoulders and looking straight ahead, he stepped forward, his *bundori* extended in both hands.

Outside the mist had thickened; the rain continued. Bent under the weight of the large basket on his back, the stalker hurried through the empty streets toward the resting place he'd chosen for his precious trophy.

"Hurry home now," a night sentry called to him as he slipped through a gate. "Almost time for closing."

The stalker ignored him. He must place the *bundori* where everyone could see and admire it and know the great deed he'd done. His time was rapidly slipping away; every moment increased the risk that someone might stop him. Yet he felt no fear or anxiety—only a yearning for completion.

Quickly he scaled the rungs of a ladder that climbed up a shop's wall, above roof level to the platform of a tall, rickety wooden firewatch tower. The mist enfolded him, obliterating his view of the city below. He opened his basket and took out the head. His mind populated the night with shadowy figures and filled the dripping silence with drumming and chanting. He placed the head carefully on the platform and bowed deeply.

"Honorable Lord Oda," he whispered. An almost sensual satisfaction overwhelmed him. "Please accept this, my first tribute to you."

Then he shouldered his basket and descended the ladder. Head high, he started homeward, feeling as if he'd slain not just one man but a legion of enemy soldiers, all the while dreaming of future victories.

In the vast, deep pond at Edo Castle's martial arts training ground, Sano Ichirō trod water furiously, trying to stay afloat. The two swords and full suit of armor he wore—tunic and shoulder flaps made of leather and metal plates, chain-mail arm shields, metal leg guards, helmet, and mask—threatened to drag him to the bottom. In his left hand he held a bow; in the right, an arrow. His lungs heaved with the effort of keeping these and his head above the water. Around him bobbed other samurai, fellow retainers of the shogun Tokugawa Tsunayoshi, attending this morning's training session to practice the skills they would need in case they ever had to make war in a river, a lake, or at sea. At the pond's other end, more men fought a mock battle on horseback. Their movements churned the pond. A big wave washed over Sano's head. Water, foul with mud and horse droppings, gurgled into his helmet and mask. He gasped, spat, and barely managed to gulp a breath of air before the next wave hit him.

"You, there!" the *sensei* yelled from the bank of the pond. A long pole rapped sharply upon Sano's helmet. "Body straight, legs down. And keep that arrow dry! Wet feathers don't fly straight!"

Mustering his strength, Sano gamely tried to follow the orders. His legs ached from executing the circular kicks necessary for maintaining an upright position. His left arm, recently wounded in a sword fight, throbbed; the other arm had gone numb. Each painful breath felt like his last. And he was freezing. The uncertain spring weather hadn't warmed away the pond's winter iciness. How much longer would this torture last? To take his mind off his physical distress, he squinted upward at his surroundings.

Man-shaped straw archery targets dotted the grassy space beside the pond. To Sano's right loomed the dark green pines of the Fukiage, the forested park that occupied the castle's western grounds and surrounded the training area. On his left, he could see the stands of the racecourse, from which came shouts, cheers, and hoofbeats. In the distance directly ahead of him rose the high stone wall that surrounded the inner castle precincts, where the shogun, his family, and his closest associates lived and worked in luxurious palaces.

Sano kicked harder to raise himself an infinitesimal distance higher above water level. The brilliant sunlight made dazzling jewels of the droplets that sprayed his eyes. He blinked them away and tilted his head back to look up at the castle keep: five splendid stories of whitewashed walls and multiple gleaming tiled roofs and gables that soared against the blue sky. A visible symbol of the complete and overwhelming Tokugawa military power, Edo Castle filled Sano with awe. After two months of living within its walls, he still couldn't believe that it was home to him now. Even less could he believe in the fantastic series of events that had brought him here.

The son of a *rōnin*—a masterless samurai—he'd earned his living as an instructor in his father's martial arts academy, supplementing his family's meager income by teaching reading and writing to young boys. Then, just three months ago, through family connections, he'd attained the position of *yoriki,* one of Edo's fifty senior police commanders. He'd lost that position, suffered disgrace, dishonor, and physical agony, solved a puzzling murder case, saved the shogun's life—and ended up as Tokugawa Tsunayoshi's *sōsakan-sama:* Most Honorable Investigator of Events, Situations, and People.

The appointment was an undreamed-of honor, but Sano's move to the castle had created an enormous upheaval in his life. Cut off from everything and everyone he knew, he'd found himself adrift in a strange landscape filled with unfamiliar faces, swamped by new and confusing regulations and rituals. The training pond wasn't the only place where he had to struggle to keep his head above water. But the changes in his life hadn't stopped there. His father, whose health had been poor for many years, had died just fifteen days after Sano had left his family's house. With a sorrow still fresh and raw, Sano remembered his father's passing.

Kneeling before his father's bed, he'd pressed the old man's withered hand to his chest. Through the grief that swelled his throat, he tried to express the love and esteem he felt for his father, but the latter had shaken his head, demanding silence. "My son . . . promise . . ." The cracked voice faded to a whisper, and Sano leaned closer to hear. "Promise me that . . . you will serve your master well. Be the living embodiment . . . of Bushido. . . ."

Bushido: the Way of the Warrior. The strict code of duty, honor, and obedience that defined a samurai's behavior, during battle and in peacetime, which he mastered not once and for all, but through confronting the innumerable challenges it presented throughout his life.

"Yes, Father, I promise," Sano said. At whatever cost to himself, he would strive to mold his independent, unruly spirit to Bushido's tenets. This deathbed promise was the most serious obligation he'd ever owed his father; it must be fulfilled. "Please rest now."

With another shake of his head, his father continued. "The aim of a samurai . . . is to perform some great deed of bravery or loyalty that . . ." He took several slow, painful breaths. "That will astonish both friend and foe alike, make his lord regret his death, and . . ." A coughing spell stopped him.

"And leave behind a great name to be remembered for generations to come," Sano finished for him. The lesson was one of the many aspects of Bushido that his father had taught him in childhood, indoctrinating him with this philosophy, which had evolved over the course of six hundred years.

"Promise . . ."

Sano gripped his father's hand tighter, as if to physically keep death from claiming him. Tears stung his eyes. He knew it grieved his father that the miraculous deed he'd already performed for the shogun must remain forever a secret. "Father, I promise I will secure our family's name a place of honor in history," he said.

Satisfied, his father relaxed and closed his eyes. Shortly afterward, he lapsed into the final throes of death.

Sano felt as though his father's passing had removed the foundation of his life, his link with his heritage, the font from which his strength and courage flowed, and the inner compass that guided him. Bereft, unsure of himself, he longed for his father's presence. Still, the promises he'd made hadn't seemed rash or extravagant then. As *sōsakan,* he would have countless opportunities to distinguish himself.

Now, however, Sano despaired of ever fulfilling the promise. For the entire two months since his arrival at Edo Castle, Tokugawa Tsunayoshi had completely ignored him. Sano had seen his new master only from a distance during formal ceremonies. Instead of solving problems of vital national importance, he was now a clerk in the castle's historical archives. He spent his excess time and energy on the one avenue of Bushido open to him: martial arts training for a war that might not come in his lifetime. He seemed destined to become one of the government's countless bureaucrats, who did trivial work in exchange for generous stipends—a parasite, fattening off the Tokugawa wealth.

"Ready! Take aim!"

The *sensei*'s voice interrupted Sano's thoughts. At last the exercise was nearing its end. Exhausted, Sano aligned his body with one of the straw targets. His heart hammered in protest inside his chest. His armor and weapons now weighed as much as the Great Buddha statue of Kamakura. Every part of his body ached; his stomach churned, sickened from overexertion. He raised his bow and fitted the arrow to it. Despite his frantic kicks, his head sank below the water. Blindly he aimed.

"Fire!"

Sano let his arrow fly. Without looking to see where it landed, he swam to shore. He no longer had the strength to care how well he'd performed the exercise. He couldn't determine how he might become the ideal samurai and confer everlasting honor upon his family name. All he wanted to do was rest, on dry land. Dripping and shivering, he heaved himself onto the bank, where he lay motionless on his back, eyes closed. He was dimly aware of the men around him, some resting, others talking while they removed their armor. The sunlight warmed him. Then he heard footsteps approaching. Someone stood at his feet, blocking the sun. Removing his mask, Sano raised his head, expecting to see the attendant who helped him in and out of his armor.

Instead he saw two of the shogun's senior officials. Dressed in colorful flowing silk robes, oiled hair tied in sleek looped knots, crowns freshly shaven, they gazed down at him in mild disdain.

"*Sōsakan-sama?*" one of them said.

Sano struggled to his feet. "Yes?" Water ran out of his helmet and armor. He bowed, feeling uncouth beside their elegance.

"The shogun wishes your presence at once, in the No theater," the other official said.

Sano's heart leapt. After two months of silence, Tokugawa Tsunayoshi wanted to see him! "Did he say why?" he asked eagerly. Already yanking at the fastenings of his armor, he beckoned the attendant to come and assist him.

Both officials shook their heads gravely, bowed, then turned and walked away.

With the attendant's help, Sano shed his armor. In the dressing shed he removed his wet garments, rinsed in clean water, and wiped himself with a towel. He donned his everyday clothing: long, full black trousers, a dark red kimono stamped in gold with the triple-hollyhock-leaf Tokugawa crest, and a black surcoat bearing his own family crest of four interlocked flying cranes. He sat impatiently while the attendant dried his shaven crown and re-knotted his hair. Finally he fastened his two swords to his sash.

Maybe the shogun had a task for him to perform, Sano thought, one by which he could fulfill his promise to his father. Anticipation rose in his chest. He fought it down, cautioning himself that maybe the shogun, as a courtesy to the man who had served him well, merely planned to bestow a moment of attention on him before consigning him to oblivion thereafter. But he couldn't help hoping otherwise.

On his way to the gate that led from the training grounds to the castle's inner precinct, he glanced toward the archery targets. The other men had already collected their arrows. Only his remained. Sano looked away. Sticking up out of the grass an arm's length short of the target, it did not seem an auspicious omen.

A battery of armed guards recorded Sano's name in their log, examined him for hidden weapons, and finally let him through the inner precinct's iron-banded gate. Once on the other side, he followed a circuitous stone passage that ran between parallel stone walls topped with continuous lines of whitewashed guardhouses. He circled the perimeter of the inner precinct to its eastern side, where the shogun's palace lay. The passage gradually ascended, following the contours of the hill upon which Edo Castle perched. Every few hundred paces or so, Sano came to a checkpoint. There other guards inspected him before letting him past yet another gate. Through the windows and gunholes of every guardhouse, he could see more men on duty; still more patrolled the passage or escorted visitors and officials. Even in peacetime, with the chance of a siege remote, no one moved unwatched through the castle. Sano couldn't get used to the constant surveillance. He sometimes thought that Edo Castle, for all its splendor and elegance, was nothing but a huge prison.

On a day like this, however, it was a beautiful one. A fresh spring breeze swept down from the mountains to whisper through the pines that swayed above the tiled roofs of the guardhouses along the inner walls. Through the windows of the outer ones, Sano caught occasional glimpses of Edo, spread across the plain below. A haze of pale foliage added brightness and life to the city's drab brown thatched or tiled roofs. Cherry trees, in full blossom now, spread rosy clouds over the banks of the many canals, formed solid bands of radiant color along the broad, muddy Sumida River, and turned the hills beyond the castle into a breathtaking wash of pink and green. Their fragrance scented the air with an elusive, poignant sweetness. In the distance, high above the city to the west, rose Mount Fuji's serene, snowcapped peak. Sano hurried on his way. Another time he would savor the beauty of the castle. Another day he might grow comfortable within its walls.

"Wait, if you please, Sano-*san!*"

The call, accompanied by hurrying footsteps, came from behind him. Sano turned and saw Noguchi Motoori, his immediate superior, huffing and puffing along the path. He waited, then bowed in greeting when Noguchi reached him.

Noguchi, Edo Castle's chief archivist, perfectly fit Sano's picture of the samurai-turned-scholar. His loose trousers and surcoat covered a short body gone soft and pudgy from lack of physical activity. The two swords at his waist seemed like unnatural appendages for a man so awkward and hesitant in his movements and so disinclined to quarrel, let alone fight, with anyone. About fifty years of age, Noguchi had small, vague eyes set in a round, childlike face. When he frowned, as he did now, the wrinkles in his forehead climbed all the way up to his shaven crown. Sano had liked Noguchi from their first acquaintance. The man was kind, helpful, and tolerant, and shared his love of history. Yet Sano, upon assuming the position in which he hoped to make his fortune, had craved a harsher taskmaster.

"Oh, my, I am glad I caught up with you," Noguchi said, panting.

Hiding his impatience, Sano slowed his pace to match Noguchi's. He must spare a few moments' courtesy for his superior.

"You will be pleased to know that your marriage negotiations are proceeding quite satisfactorily," Noguchi continued. "The Ueda have agreed to a *miai*—a meeting, so that you and Miss Reiko and your families can become acquainted."

The news did please Sano. "Your efforts on my behalf are much appreciated, Noguchi-*san*," he said, offering the formal but heartfelt expressions of gratitude dictated by convention.

Sano, single at the advanced age of thirty-one, yearned for a wife and family—especially a son, who would carry on his name. He also harbored a romantic, albeit unrealistic wish for the emotional intimacy that an arranged marriage might, but wouldn't necessarily bring. He hadn't yet married because his father, eager to improve the family's economic and social status, had refused to let Sano take a wife of their own class, instead sending proposals only to daughters of wealthy, high-ranking samurai affiliated with major clans. All the proposals had been rejected. But now, with his advancement, Sano found his prospects much improved. And Noguchi, acting as his go-between—as a samurai's superior often did—had done well by him. Ueda Reiko's family were hereditary Tokugawa vassals, her father the south magistrate of Edo and a very rich man.

"If all goes well with the *miai*," Noguchi said, "why, then, very soon—after the period of mourning for your father is over, of course—I shall have the pleasure of attending your wedding. Oh, my."

He smiled, but his frown-wrinkles slid higher on his head. Sano waited, sensing that the archivist had concerns unrelated to the marriage negotiations.

Finally Noguchi said, "Sometimes it is possible to convey, without actually saying in so many words, that although you would be glad to perform a task, your time might be spent more profitably otherwise."

He'd switched from direct speech to the circumspect style used by many members of the refined upper classes. Watching Sano closely, he continued circling his point. "It is also possible to leave the impression that a task would be better given to someone else. Without, of course, casting any doubt upon one's own willingness or ability. Even not knowing the particular circumstances, I believe that a clever man might manage to bring others around to his own point of view, without risking censure or loss of face."

Sano was utterly mystified. "Yes, I see," he said, but only because Noguchi was looking up into his face and leaning against him as they walked, the pressure of his body an unspoken plea for understanding.

Noguchi bobbed his head for emphasis. "And of course, you will remember that His Excellency is a very busy man. Small matters must inevitably slip from his memory now and then. But this is not an entirely bad thing." His earnest gaze held Sano's as they reached the gate that led to the palace precinct.

Now his meaning became clear to Sano. Many officials, Noguchi included, were so afraid of disgracing themselves or getting in trouble that they went to great lengths to avoid doing anything, good or bad, that would draw the shogun's notice. They wouldn't openly advise their subordinates to ignore a direct order. But Noguchi, having evidently heard that the shogun had summoned Sano—although not the reason—was telling him to use every means available to escape whatever task given to him. Or, failing that, to wait before acting, in hopes that Tokugawa Tsunayoshi would forget about it. Sano understood, but couldn't share Noguchi's attitude.

He waited until they'd cleared the checkpoint and entered the palace garden. Then he said, "I appreciate your concern, Noguchi-*san,* but whatever our lord orders, I must do, without evasion or delay."

Noguchi gasped at Sano's bluntness. "Oh, no, I never meant to imply that you should disregard a command from His Excellency!" he blurted. Then he clapped a hand over his mouth and looked around to see if anyone was listening.

The palace garden wore its full spring glory. Guards patrolled white gravel paths that wound through a fresh green lawn studded with flowering cherry and magnolia trees. Gardeners swept the paths and tended azalea bushes bright with red blossoms. Officials and their attendants strolled the garden, their brilliant garments adding more color to the scene. Still more officials lingered outside the palace, a low, vast building with whitewashed plaster walls, dark wooden doors, beams, and window lattices, and a many-gabled roof of gleaming grey tile. Sano knew why Noguchi feared eavesdroppers: even a hint of disobedience or disloyalty could be interpreted as treason and punished by exile or death. Edo abounded with spies and informers, many within the castle itself. Any of those officials or servants could be a *metsuke*—one of the shogun's intelligence agents—or simply someone eager to advance himself by discrediting his colleagues.

"I was merely giving you the benefit of my experience," Noguchi finished in a loud whisper.

Sano couldn't follow the advice, coming as it did from someone seeking only to live out his remaining years in peace. But Noguchi meant well. "Yes, I know. Thank you for your advice, Noguchi-*san.* I'll keep it in mind."

They reached the palace entrance. After they'd made their farewells, Noguchi shook his head and said in parting, "Young men. You are all so rash and impetuous. I hope you will not come to regret your actions, Sano-*san*." Then, more cheerfully: "Well, *gambatte kudasai!*" Do your best, and good luck.

Sano gained admittance from the guards posted at the palace's massive, carved door. As he removed his shoes and hung his swords in the huge entry hall, he thought about Noguchi's warning and felt a twinge of trepidation. He had much to learn about life at the heart of the Tokugawa *bakufu*—the military government that ruled the land. Would he be making a mistake by trying to do his duty to both his lord and his father? The idea seemed fantastic. He walked along the polished cypress floors of the corridors that led through the building's outer portion, which served as government offices, trying to shed his unease. But his heart was racing, and his hands turned clammy with nervous sweat. Reaching the heavily guarded doors that led to the No theater, he paused, bracing himself for his encounter with the nation's supreme military dictator.

"*Sōsakan* Sano Ichirō, to see His Excellency," he said to the guards.

They bowed, slid open the doors, and stood aside to let him enter. Swallowing his apprehension, Sano went in.

He found himself standing on a veranda overlooking a huge gravel courtyard bordered by rows of pines. Ahead of him to his left stood the No stage, a raised wooden platform with a roof supported on four pillars, which faced right. Seated at the rear of the stage, three drummers and two flutists played a solemn, archaic melody. Under a small potted cherry tree at center stage lay an actor dressed in the striped robe of an itinerant monk, presumably asleep; the chorus and other actors sat in the wings. Sano turned his attention to the man he'd sworn to serve.

The sliding doors of the building opposite the stage stood open. Inside, Tsunayoshi, the fifth Tokugawa shogun, occupied a dais. Seated upon piled cushions, he wore an opulent silk kimono patterned in shades of gold, brown, and cream under a black surcoat with broad padded shoulders, and the cylindrical black cap that marked his rank. He held a closed fan. He was smiling, nodding his head in time to the music. Tsunayoshi, Sano had heard, enjoyed No above all the other arts he patronized. He seemed unaware of the bored expressions of the ten retainers who, forced to watch with him, knelt on either side of the dais.

Sano felt a touch of surprise when he looked at Tsunayoshi, whom he didn't remember as looking quite so small or benign, or so old for his forty-three years. He had to remind himself that this was the descendant of the great Tokugawa Ieyasu, who, less than a hundred years ago, had triumphed over many warring clans to bring the country under his control. And Tsunayoshi himself commanded the authority he'd inherited. His word was law; he held the power of life and death over his subjects.

A young actor carrying a sword came down the bridgeway that led from the curtained door of the dressing room. He wore a long, flowing black wig, tall black cap, gold brocade robe, and broad, divided scarlet skirt. Taking up a position at the left front of the stage, he performed a slow, stylized dance and sang:

> *"Driven by my worldly shame,*
> *In ghostly guise I come*
> *To the place where I died,*
> *Taking the shape I had*
> *When I lived upon the earth,*
> *To tell this sleeping monk*
> *My tale of long ago."*

Sano recognized the play as *Tadanori,* written almost three hundred years earlier by the great dramatist Zeami Motokiyo. Tadanori, lord of Satsuma, had been a poet-warrior of the Heike clan. When the Imperial House compiled an anthology of great poetry, they included one of Tadanori's poems unsigned, because the Heike were regarded as rebels. Tadanori died in battle, lamenting the exclusion of his name. In the play, his ghost tells a traveling monk his sad story so that his fame as a poet need not be forgotten.

> *"My poem, 'tis true, was chosen for the Great Book,*
> *Alas! Because of my lord's displeasure,*
> *It does not bear my—"*

The shogun rapped loudly on the dais with his fan. The actor, halted in midverse, stumbled in his dance.

"Not like that," Tokugawa Tsunayoshi shouted. "Like this!" He sang the lines himself, in a high, reedy voice at odds with his exalted status. Sano failed to see any improvement over the actor's rendition, but the rest of the audience murmured in approval. "Never mind, ahh, you are dismissed. Next!"

The actor slunk off stage. The music resumed, and another actor started down the bridgeway. Now Sano understood that this wasn't a performance given by the shogun's troupe of professional actors, but an audition for amateurs, those among the Tokugawa vassals and daimyo clans—families who governed the country's provinces—who curried favor by catering to their lord's taste in entertainment. A sudden awful thought occurred to Sano: Did Tsunayoshi want *him* to audition? His visions of performing some feat of great courage began to fade, and he took an involuntary step backward. Then the shogun beckoned.

"Ahh, *Sōsakan* Sano," Tokugawa Tsunayoshi called. "Approach." To the actors and musicians: "Go away until I call you."

The men on stage bowed, walked down the bridgeway, and disappeared into the dressing room. Sano, self-conscious before the curious gazes of the watching officials, crossed the courtyard and knelt before the dais.

"I await Your Excellency's command," he said, bowing with his forehead touching the ground and his arms extended straight in front of him.

"Rise," the shogun ordered, "and come closer."

Sano did. He locked his knees to still their trembling as Tsunayoshi studied him. Risking a direct glance at the shogun, he wasn't surprised to see lack of recognition in the mild eyes, or puzzlement creasing the thin, aristocratic face. If he'd forgotten Tsunayoshi's features, so must the great dictator have forgotten his.

"Well, ahh," Tsunayoshi said at last. "You seem an able-bodied and able-minded samurai, just right for the task I have in mind. In fact, I cannot think why I have not utilized your services thus far."

He looked around at his attendants, who offered noncommittal murmurs.

"However, I shall do so now," Tsunayoshi said. "Kaibara Tōju was murdered last night. His head was severed from his body and mounted like a, ahh, war trophy."

The nature of the crime shocked Sano, as did the victim's identity. The taking of trophy heads was a war tradition, not normally practiced in peacetime. Kaibara Tōju was a *hatamoto,* a hereditary Tokugawa vassal—one of many soldiers whose clans had served the shogun's for generations and held time-honored positions in his vast empire. But neither piece of news disturbed Sano as much as his heart-sinking realization that the shogun was going to ask him to investigate the murder. Too many lives had been ruined or lost during his first and only other case. But Sano's interest stirred in spite of himself. A not wholly unpleasant surge of fearful anxiety made him feel more alive than he had in months. Without his realizing it, his short-lived police career had given him a taste for danger and adventure. And he'd always had a yearning to seek and find the truth. Lately he'd had no chance to satisfy either desire. But now . . .

"The *bundori* was found, ahh—" The shogun paused, frowning in an obvious attempt at recollection.

"On a firewatch tower in the Nihonbashi pharmacists' district, Your Excellency."

Silk garments rustled as the shogun and his retainers turned toward the sound of a man's voice that came from within the building. Following their gazes, Sano saw Chamberlain Yanagisawa Yoshiyasu standing behind the dais. His curiosity roused at the sight of this man, about whom he'd heard much but seen only once before.

Yanagisawa's combination of height, slimness, graceful carriage, and sharp, elegant features added up to a striking masculine beauty. The keen intelligence of his expression drew attention away from his brilliant, fashionable robes and kept it on his face. Rumor said that Yanagisawa, now thirty-two years old and Tsunayoshi's protégé since his twenties, had been and still was the shogun's lover. Whatever the truth, Yanagisawa supposedly had much influence over *bakufu* affairs.

Now Yanagisawa knelt beside the dais, in the place of honor

nearest the shogun. The retainers' obsequious bows and the haste with which they made room for him testified to his power.

"Your Excellency," he said, bowing to the shogun.

Tsunayoshi smiled in greeting. "Ahh, Chamberlain Yanagisawa." His voice held a hint of relief, as though he welcomed the arrival of someone more knowledgeable than himself. "We were discussing last night's unfortunate incident. I have decided to give the task of apprehending the, ahh, murderer to my new *sōsakan*."

Yanagisawa glanced at Sano. His eyes, large and liquid and enhanced with thick, slanting brows, looked black even in the sunlight, as if the pupils were permanently dilated. The hostility in them pierced Sano to the core. What could he have done to offend the chamberlain?

He'd sensed a heightened alertness about the others, including the shogun, when Yanagisawa appeared. Now the tension slackened as Yanagisawa said suavely, "A wise decision, Your Excellency."

The shogun seemed pleased to have his chamberlain's approval, and the retainers grateful that no conflict had arisen. Chests heaved sighs of relief; bodies relaxed more comfortably on the cushions. Sano's own uneasiness subsided. Yanagisawa sounded sincere, despite that first malevolent glance. He even favored Sano with a smile that lifted one corner of his finely modeled mouth.

Tsunayoshi turned to Sano. "This murder constitutes an, ahh, act of war against the Tokugawa clan. The offender must be caught and punished promptly. We cannot let him get away with such a heinous affront to our regime, or let the daimyo think us vulnerable to attack. Therefore I am granting you the full cooperation and assistance of the, ahh, police force. All the necessary orders have been given.

"In addition," the shogun continued, "you will have the services of the castle's chief shrine attendant, a mystic who has the power to communicate with the spirit world. I have ordered her sent directly to your residence. Now, *Sōsakan* Sano, go and begin your inquiries at once. Report to me in my chambers this evening to inform me of your, ahh, progress." He waved his fan in dismissal.

Sano bowed deeply. "Thank you, Your Excellency, for the great honor of being allowed to serve you," he said, hiding his surprise and skepticism at the mention of the mystic. Never had he heard of one assisting in a criminal investigation—it wasn't standard police procedure—but he couldn't challenge the shogun's decision. "I shall do my humble best."

He would have gone on to express his appreciation for the assistance granted him, but the shogun's gaze wandered toward the stage. Obviously he was eager for the auditions to resume.

"Many thanks, Your Excellency," Sano repeated, turning to leave the theater.

He fought to keep the bounce out of his step, and his exuberance from erupting in an unseemly smile. Earlier this morning, his hope of distinguishing himself had looked minimal. Now he had a chance to prove himself a worthy practitioner of Bushido; to perform an act that could earn his family name a place in history. A chance to experience excitement and danger, and, even more important, to find truth, deliver a criminal to justice, and possibly save lives. Furthermore, with such a wealth of resources at his disposal, success seemed almost assured. Self-confidence flowed through Sano in a warming rush. The assignment offered great potential rewards at small risk.

As he left the palace and stepped out into the bright spring morning, Noguchi's warning and Chamberlain Yanagisawa's initial hostility made only a small dark shadow in the back of his mind.

The way to Sano's residence led down the hill through another series of passages and guarded checkpoints, over a bridge that spanned the castle's inner moat. From there, he passed through another gate into the Official Quarter, composed of the office-mansions of the shogun's chief retainers and highest officials.

Sano entered the quarter, experiencing his usual disbelief that he actually lived there. Splendid estates lined the roads, each surrounded by two-story barracks with whitewashed walls decorated with black tiles laid in diagonal patterns, and rows of barred windows. Roofed gates with twin guardhouses punctuated the long expanses of black and white. Past them moved a stream of well-dressed officials and their attendants, ladies in palanquins carried by strong bearers, servants and porters, bands of samurai both mounted and on foot. Sano exchanged brief, formal bows with his colleagues, most of whom he knew only slightly, then stopped before his residence. There the two guards bowed and opened the gate. He passed into a paved courtyard. The empty barracks, meant for retainers he didn't yet have, loomed around him. A high wooden fence enclosed the main house. With the reluctance he always felt upon arriving home, Sano walked through the inner gate.

From atop a high stone foundation, the house, a huge, half-timbered building with a heavy brown tile roof that spread deep eaves over a broad veranda, seemed to repel rather than welcome him. Dark lattices covered the windows; wooden steps ascended to a protruding entrance porch. Sano entered, remembering the day he'd moved to the castle.

When he'd protested that the house was too big for one man, and its stable of horses unnecessary, the official who'd welcomed him had said, "If you refuse that which His Excellency has bestowed upon you, he will think you ungrateful."

Sano had acquiesced and taken possession of the house. Now it swallowed him up in its vast, hushed space. He left his shoes in the entryway. Then, resisting the urge to tiptoe, he walked down the corridor and into the main hall.

"Has the shrine attendant sent by His Excellency arrived yet?" Sano asked the manservant who greeted him.

"No, master."

Sano grimaced in annoyance. He would rather begin his investigation by examining the murder scene, where vital evidence might be lost if he didn't get there soon enough. He could ill afford to wait for some elderly woman to hobble over from the shrine, and he felt a strong resistance toward the shogun's plan. He didn't share Tokugawa Tsunayoshi's superstitious belief that communication with the spirit realm would reveal the killer's identity. Practical means would more likely provide the answers. But the shogun had as good as ordered him to consult the mystic. For the first time, Sano suspected that his new position, for all its prestige and authority, might have constraints that would make solving a murder case harder instead of easier.

The servant was waiting for his orders. Sano, realizing he was hungry, said, "I'd like a meal now." With much work ahead of him, he didn't know when he might get another chance to eat. He could do so while he waited for the mystic.

"Yes, master." Bowing, the servant left the room.

Sano knelt on the dais and surveyed his new domain with customary awe and discomfort. Fine tatami covered the floor. A brilliant landscape mural decorated the wall behind him. Sliding doors stood open on both sides of the room. Through them to his left, he could see past the veranda to a garden of flowering cherry trees, mossy boulders, and a pond. Sunlight shone upon the teak-wood shelves, cabinets, and desk in the study niche, and lit the scroll and the vase of lilies in the alcove. On the right, he looked across the corridor to his bedchamber, where a maid was dusting the lacquer cabinets and chests. Faint sounds told him that other servants were at work in the kitchen, the bathchamber, the priv-ies, the six other bedchambers, or the long corridors. But to Sano the house seemed empty, unlived-in. With his books and clothes stowed away in cabinets, nothing of him showed, except for the Buddhist altar in a corner of this room, where incense burners, a cup of sake, and a bowl of fruit stood before his father's portrait. Accustomed to close quarters, he couldn't expand to fill the house's space. Neither could he relax in its grandeur.

He'd lived for most of his life in a crowded Nihonbashi neigh-borhood, in the small house behind his father's martial arts acad-emy, with his parents and their maid Hana. The four tiny rooms had walls so thin that they could never escape one another's sounds, or those of the city outside. His rooms in the police bar-racks had been larger but just as noisy. The relative silence of his new mansion unnerved him. But even worse than the silence was the loneliness.

After his father's death, he'd brought his mother and Hana to live with him, but his mother hadn't taken to life at the castle. Afraid to go outside, afraid of the sophisticated neighbors and ser-vants, she'd refused to leave her bedchamber. When Sano tried to comfort her, she just stared at him in mute misery. She couldn't eat or sleep.

After ten days, Hana said to Sano, "Young master, your mother will die if she stays here. Send her home."

Reluctantly Sano had complied, regretting that he couldn't share his new affluence with his mother. His loneliness worsened after she and Hana left. He spent as much time as possible at the train-ing grounds, in the archives. He went to parties given by the shogun's other retainers, who didn't understand why their lord had promoted him, because circumstances prohibited them from knowing. Consequently they resented him, even as they courted his favor. But after martial arts practice, work, and recreation ended, there always came that dreaded moment when he must return home, alone.

Perhaps a marriage with Ueda Reiko would fill the emptiness in his life. Sano hoped the *miai*, that first, most important formal meeting between their families, would go well.

A maid entered and placed a tray laden with covered dishes before him. He ate vegetable soup, rice, grilled prawns, sashimi, pickled radish, quail eggs, tofu, steamed sweet cakes—all tasty, prettily arranged, and in abundant quantity. Whatever he disliked about life at the castle, he couldn't complain about the food or service. He was just finishing when he heard footsteps in the corridor. Looking up, he saw a woman, escorted by his manservant, enter the room.

"His Excellency's shrine attendant," the servant announced.

Sano had never visited the Momijiyama, the Tokugawa ancestral worship site in the castle's innermost precinct. He'd therefore based his notion of its attendant on the old crones who tended the peasants' Shinto shrines in the city. Now he felt a jolt of surprise when he looked at her.

She was tall, perhaps his own height, and probably near his age. Her face was bare of white makeup, yet very pale. A spray of rare freckles dotted her cheeks and the bridge of her long, thin nose. Thick glossy black hair, which glowed rust-brown in the sunlight, was piled neatly on her head, except for one long strand that had escaped the combs to lie against her neck. She had a square jaw, its uncompromising shape repeated in the set of her shoulders and in the strong, blunt-fingered hands she placed on the floor as she knelt before the dais and bowed.

"I am Aoi," she said.

Her voice had the rich, vibrant tone of a temple bell; it resonated pleasurably through Sano's body. When she sat back on her heels to face him, her movements had a natural grace that softened her body's angularity. Somehow she made her simple cotton kimono—pale blue printed with white clouds and green willow boughs—look more elegant than a fine silk robe on a slimmer, daintier figure. Sano thought that many men might consider her plain, a far cry from conventional standards of feminine beauty. To him, she was one of the loveliest women he'd ever seen.

Unflinchingly, she held his gaze for several heartbeats. Her eyes were a strange, luminous light brown, Sano noticed. Then she flashed him a brief smile. His breath caught as dimples wreathed her face, transforming its somber beauty into something mercurial and mysterious.

"His Excellency has explained that you're to help me investigate the murder of Kaibara Tōju?" Discomfort stiffened Sano's manner. In his world, convention kept men's and women's work separate. All the *bakufu* officials, secretaries, and clerks were male. Gone were the days when samurai women rode into battle beside their men. The novelty of the situation hadn't troubled or even interested him when he'd imagined the shogun's mystic as old and matronly. But to consult and collaborate with such a young, attractive woman . . .

"Yes. The shogun has explained."

Sano had never seen anyone so serene, so self-possessed as Aoi. And she exuded a subtle but unmistakable aura of power. On some primitive level, he, like the shogun and even the most modern and sophisticated of other men, believed in the ancient myths and legends, in powers beyond human comprehension, in the existence of ghosts and demons. As he looked at Aoi, his skepticism wavered. Perhaps she really could command the spirit world. A tinge of atavistic fear added to Sano's uncertainty. Such power set her outside society's rigid class system, where a peasant must automatically defer to a samurai. Not knowing exactly how to address Aoi, Sano took refuge in brusqueness.

"So. Do you think you can identify the killer?"

"Perhaps." She lowered her eyes, inclining her head in a slow nod. Evidently a woman of few words, she showed no intention of helping the conversation along.

"How?" Sano asked, resisting the nervous urge to fidget.

Aoi's gaze met his, its candor somehow more alluring than coy flirtatiousness. "I'll perform a ritual. To contact the spirit of the dead man. Perhaps we may see the killer through his eyes. What he knew, we can know. From him. If the spirits are willing." Her strong hand turned palm up in an eloquent gesture that conveyed the uncertainty associated with such a venture, as well as the miracles possible.

"I see," Sano said, intrigued by both the idea of taking a short-cut to the truth and the prospect of seeing Aoi again. But the murder scene awaited him, as did witnesses, and possible suspects among Kaibara's family and friends. The painstaking, earthbound search for information must come first. "I'll come to the shrine tonight."

"Tonight. Yes." Taking his words as a dismissal, Aoi bowed again and rose, adding, "For the ritual, I'll need something that belonged to the victim. To establish a link with his spirit."

Sano nodded. "All right."

And she was gone, as unobtrusively as she'd come.

Sano gazed thoughtfully after her, wondering whether her ritual really might lead him to the killer. Then he called the manservant and ordered his horse brought to the gate.

As he left the house, he felt a surge of anticipation that had nothing to do with his assignment. For the first time, he found himself looking forward to night at the castle.

3

East of Edo Castle and crammed into a narrow piece of land between the great daimyo estates and the Sumida River, the Nihonbashi merchant quarter bustled with commerce. Along the narrow,
winding streets, open storefronts displayed their wares: oil in one
sector; sake, pottery, baskets, metalware, and soy sauce in others.
The smells of charcoal smoke, cooking, and sawdust from work-
shops behind the stores mingled with those of privies and horse
manure in the streets. Merchants sat on the raised floors of their
establishments, haggling with customers or shouting come-ons to
the crowds:

"The best soy for the lowest price, here!"

"High-quality baskets, come in and see for yourself!"

Beggars shuffled through the throngs, holding out their bowls
for alms. Shrieking children careened underfoot. As Sano rode
toward the scene of Kaibara Tōju's murder, he edged his horse
sideways past shoppers. But when he neared the pharmacists'
street, he saw that ordinary business there had ceased. In the
shops, proprietors and customers ignored the merchandise to
stand in the doorways, talking excitedly. Sano could guess why,
but the sight that greeted him when he turned the corner surprised
and disturbed him nevertheless.

A huge, unruly crowd had congregated in front of the largest pharmacy. Exciting news traveled fast in Edo. It was only a few hours after Kaibara's body had been discovered, and already mounted samurai, craftsmen in dirty work clothes, and peasants carrying parcels on their backs craned their necks to view what must be the murder scene. Cries of "What is it? Let me see!" clamored. Newssellers distributed hastily printed broadsheets, making sure that word would soon reach anyone who didn't already know what had happened.

"Read about the Bundori Murder!" they shouted.

So the case already had a sensational name that would increase its notoriety. Sano sensed a contagious atmosphere of fear, horror, and excitement. The shogun had been most concerned about the murder's political ramifications, but Sano saw another reason for catching the killer quickly: the possibility of mass panic among the townspeople. Where were the police? Why hadn't they taken steps to control the crowd, or protect valuable evidence? Sano hastily dismounted, secured his horse to a post, elbowed his way through the crowd—and stopped short.

A group of men leaned idly against the shop wall, surveying the commotion. One, a samurai in his late forties, wore an elaborate armor tunic over a rich silk kimono and flowing trousers, a surcoat bearing the Tokugawa crest, and a lacquered helmet. With dismay, Sano recognized a former colleague and adversary: *Yoriki* Hayashi, the senior police commander who'd helped arrange his expulsion from the police force. Two of the other men were *doshin*—patrolling police officers. Each had the short hair of a low-ranking samurai, wore a single short sword at his waist, and carried a strong steel parrying wand with two curved prongs above the hilt for catching the blade of an attacker's sword: the *jitte,* standard *doshin* equipment. Their assistants, peasants armed with clubs and spears, stood beside them. But surely the police, experienced in criminal procedure, hadn't waited for his arrival to begin work?

Reluctantly approaching his old enemy, Sano bowed and spoke with forced politeness. "Good morning, Hayashi-*san*. Why are your men just standing there instead of restoring order or investigating the murder?"

Hayashi's thin, pinched face stiffened with dislike. *"Sōsakan-sama."* His voice oozed supercilious courtesy, and he bowed mockingly. "So you have descended from your lofty situation"—he raised his eyes toward the castle—"to these squalid environs." Where you belong, his tone implied. "But why do you expect us to do your work?"

A stab of foreboding pierced Sano's annoyance at the insult. "The shogun has placed me in charge of the murder investigation," he explained, "but with the full cooperation of the police."

Hayashi smirked. "I've received no orders to that effect." Despite the evil relish with which he uttered the words, they carried the ring of conviction. "My instructions were to leave the case in your capable hands."

He started down the street, motioning for his men to follow. The crowd withdrew to let them pass. Sano realized with alarm that the shogun's orders had become garbled during their passage through administrative channels. Without the necessary clearances, he had no right to commandeer police manpower. But he couldn't afford to wait for them. The killer's trail was already growing cold.

"I insist on your cooperation, Hayashi-*san*." He blocked the *yoriki*'s path and looked him straight in the eye.

Hayashi's nostrils flared in anger. *"Okashii*—ridiculous! Now get out of my way." His eyes shifted craftily.

Sano knew Hayashi didn't want to yield, especially in front of his subordinates and the townspeople, but he also didn't want to risk the possible consequences of disobeying the shogun's favored retainer. Sano wasn't sure how far his new authority extended, but he pressed his advantage. "We've much work to do. Let's get started."

Face taut with fury, Hayashi jerked his head at one of the *doshin*. "Tsuda. See that the *sōsakan-sama* gets the assistance he needs." Then he stalked down the crowded street toward his richly caparisoned horse.

Sano's relief faded when he recognized Tsuda as the *doshin* who'd once helped frame him for murder. Now Tsuda's prominent jaw jutted out farther as he shot a resentful glance after the departing Hayashi. He clenched his *jitte,* as if longing to use it against both Sano and the superior who had shifted an unwanted burden to him. Then his face relaxed in a grin no more reassuring than his usual sullen expression.

"You, Hirata," he said to the other *doshin*. "Assist the *sōsakan-sama*." His tone made the title an insult. He fixed Sano with a triumphant leer.

Hirata stepped forward. In his early twenties, he had a wide, innocent face, an earnest gaze, and the stocky body and suntanned skin of a healthy peasant. His three assistants, all men even younger than he, clustered around him.

Sano's dismay must have shown on his face, because Tsuda guffawed, evidently not caring if he offended. "Investigate all you want," he said. "But don't bother looking for the dead man's remains. They're already on their way to Edo Morgue." He kicked the ground in a derisive gesture, laughed again, ducked his head in a perfunctory bow, and left with his assistants.

Sano looked down at the spot Tsuda had indicated. His spirits plummeted lower when he saw that the street's packed earth was damp and freshly scrubbed. This must be where Kaibara Tōju's body had fallen, yet no trace of it remained—no clues, if any had existed, and nothing for him to give Aoi for her ritual. He had a field of suspects that potentially encompassed all Edo's citizens, and until the shogun reissued the orders to the police, he had no help other than four young men with probably no more expertise than he. Remembering his earlier optimism, Sano couldn't believe his investigation had begun so badly. Duty, however, demanded his immediate best effort; justice and honor awaited his service.

Cupping his hands around his mouth, Sano shouted, "Attention!" The crowd quieted; heads turned his way. "Will the persons who discovered the dead man's remains please step forward." If they hadn't already left the scene!

To his relief, two men and a woman emerged from the crowd. They immediately fell to their knees and bowed, mumbling, "Honorable Master," over and over.

"Rise," Sano said, embarrassed by their lavish display of respect. Peasants always deferred to samurai, who could kill them and earn no more punishment than a reprimand. But since he'd begun wearing the Tokugawa crest, the courtesies shown him were more than a man of his humble origins could feel comfortable receiving.

To Hirata, he said, "Clear the street if you can, while I interview the witnesses." More gawkers had swelled the crowd; some, with tattooed arms and chests, looked like hoodlums. In rowdy Nihonbashi, any incident could spark a brawl, which was the last thing he or the city needed.

With unexpected efficiency, Hirata and his assistants began dispersing the crowd. Sano turned to the witnesses. Two were an old peasant couple, huddled shoulder to shoulder, who looked enough alike to be brother and sister—both small, thin, and bent, with missing teeth, gray hair, and age-spotted skin. They wore identical dark blue kimonos and straw sandals, and the same pattern of wrinkles lined their faces. The other man was some twenty years younger, thickset, with flabby jowls and short hair that stood up in a cowlick. His bamboo-handled spear and leather armor tunic marked him as a sentry, one of the civilians who manned Nihonbashi's gates.

Sano addressed the old man. "Your name?"

"Tarō, master. Proprietor of this pharmacy." He pointed at the shop. "My wife and I found the body."

"And you?" Sano asked the sentry.

"Udoguchi," he whispered. Obviously distraught, he kept rubbing his hands on his short gray kimono. "I found the head."

Despite Hirata's efforts, an audience had gathered around them. Sano turned to the old man. "May we talk inside your shop?"

After exchanging awestruck glances with his wife, the proprietor nodded. "Of course, master." He lifted the indigo cloth that hung from the pharmacy's eaves and extended halfway to the ground. Sano entered.

The pharmacy's layout fit the general pattern of most Edo shops—a central aisle between raised plank floors, a low ceiling with skylights to supplement the light from the open storefront. It was crammed with medicines: ceramic urns containing plant extracts; trays of dried ginseng root; bins of herbs, nuts, sliced reindeer horn, and various powders; shelves stacked with boxed remedies. Bitter, sweet, sour, and musky scents filled the air. Having taken stock of his surroundings, Sano sat on the edge of the raised floor and bade the witnesses join him.

The old woman spoke for the first time. "Father, where are your manners? We must offer our guest some refreshment!" To Sano, she said, "Master, please honor us by drinking tea in our humble store."

Sano reflected that rank gave him advantages he hadn't enjoyed during his first investigation; namely, cooperation from witnesses. "Very good," he said after ginseng tea had been served and he'd taken a sip. His hosts relaxed and smiled, settling themselves on the floor. "Tarō-*san,* how did you happen to find the body?"

"Well," said Tarō, "when we opened our doors this morning, there it was, lying in a pool of blood in the street." Unlike the sentry, he showed no sign of shock or discomfort. Perhaps he'd seen so many terrible things in his long life that the murder hadn't disturbed him unduly.

"What time was this?" Sano asked.

"Oh, before dawn," Tarō said. "Ours is always the first shop on the street to open in the morning, and the last to close at night. That's why business is so good." He gestured toward the entrance, where Hirata was explaining to some customers that the shop was closed for the moment.

"Did you see or hear anything suspicious last night?"

The couple adopted thinking poses that were comically similar: finger on cheek, eyes narrowed. Then they shook their heads regretfully as the pharmacist answered, "No, master. We work very hard all day and sleep very well at night."

The old woman sighed. "That poor man. Such an awful thing to happen to someone so harmless."

"You mean you knew Kaibara?" This surprised Sano, for what acquaintance could these peasants have had with a Tokugawa *hatamoto* who probably employed servants to do his shopping?

"Oh, yes," the pharmacist said. "Not by name—until today, that is—but since last year, he has walked often in this street. At night, as well as in the daytime."

Now Sano wondered whether Kaibara's murder represented, as the shogun believed, an attack on the Tokugawa, or one aimed specifically at Kaibara, committed by someone who knew his habits and had followed him here last night.

"Did Kaibara say why he came here?" he asked. "And did he come at any particular times?"

The old woman shook her head. "He never spoke to anyone. He would just smile and nod. And we never knew when we would see him. Sometimes every day for a while, then not again for a month. But he always came back." She sighed. "Though he won't anymore."

The necessary check into Kaibara's background was more important than ever now, Sano realized as he turned to the sentry.

"Just a few questions, Udoguchi-*san,* then you can go," he said, noticing that the man looked physically ill, his complexion pasty and his mouth trembling. "How and when did you find Kaibara's head?"

"I was walking home from my post." Udoguchi spoke in a thin, tight voice that sounded squeezed from his throat. "The fog was lifting. I looked up at the sky, and that was when I saw something—" he swallowed hard "—in the firewatch tower. I climbed up to see what it was . . . and I found it." One shaking hand passed over his mouth; the other continued to rub against his clothing.

"Did you see anyone?" Sano asked hopefully.

The sentry shook his head, but in confusion rather than denial. "I don't think so. I—I was so frightened that I don't even remember climbing back down the ladder. All I remember is running through the streets, yelling for help. And people coming out of their houses to see what was wrong." Udoguchi's voice thinned to a thread of sound. "Someone must have called the police, because the next thing I knew, they were there, asking me questions, making me show them the—" He retched.

Watching Udoguchi's hands rub against his clothing, Sano realized he was trying to wipe away the *bundori*'s taint of death, as well as the horror of finding it. He turned to the pharmacist.

"Please bring Udoguchi some water to wash with."

He waited while Udoguchi gargled, then cleansed his hands. Soon the sentry's color returned, and he grew still.

"Then somehow I ended up here, and I saw the body, with all the blood." Udoguchi spoke calmly now, but barely above a whisper. "I told the police I didn't know who killed him."

"Well, I do." The old woman nodded sagely. "It was a ghost. The invisible ghost of a samurai who walks the earth, thinking he's still fighting the battle he died in."

"She's right," Tarō exclaimed. "Who else but a ghost can kill and vanish without making a sound or leaving a trace? And who but a samurai from the old days would make his enemy's head into a trophy?"

Sano stared, appalled. Indeed, eighty-nine years had passed since the warring clans had last taken trophy heads, during the Battle of Sekigahara. And most murders in Edo were straightforward crimes, often with eyewitnesses, plenty of evidence, obvious motives, and easily identifiable culprits. Thus, these ignorant, superstitious peasants had seized on the ghost story as an explanation for something they didn't understand. It would terrify the credulous townspeople, increasing the possibility of mass disturbances. And Udoguchi's response proved its dangerous power.

"Oh, no, oh no," he wailed. "Then it was a ghost I saw last night. I'm cursed. I'm going to die!" His ashen pallor returned; he swayed.

"The killer is a living human, not a ghost." Sano spoke forcefully, throwing the pharmacist and his wife a warning glance. "Here, Udoguchi-*san,* put your head on your knees." He positioned the sentry, waited until the man's gasps ceased and his trembling abated. "Now. Describe the person you saw, and tell me when you saw him."

Sitting upright, the sentry shook his head until his loose jowls wobbled. "He was the last person to pass my gate before closing. I spoke to him, but he didn't answer. And it was so dark and foggy that I didn't get a good look at him."

"Was he fat or thin?" Sano asked patiently. "Tall or short?"

"I don't know, I don't remember. He was samurai—at least I think he had swords. He was wearing a baggy cloak. And a big straw hat, so I couldn't see his face."

Sano's hopes dwindled. Even if the man was the killer, no one could possibly identify him from Udoguchi's description. "Was he carrying anything?" he asked, hoping at least to learn whether the man might have had Kaibara's head with him, thereby helping to establish the time of the murder.

"I don't remember."

"Did you notice anything else about him? Think hard."

But the sentry could recall nothing else about the man he'd seen. Sano reviewed the results of the interviews with frustration. That the murderer was a samurai might be inferred from the manner of killing, but it was dangerous to make assumptions. To have such a poor description of the suspect was discouraging, and the witnesses' stories didn't establish the crime's exact time frame or narrow the field of suspects.

The old pharmacist had found the body before dawn, before the gates opened. This meant that Kaibara had died last night, when he and the killer had entered the street before the gates closed. But Udoguchi had found the head on his way home after the gates had reopened. The killer could have placed the *bundori* on the firewatch tower either last night, or very early this morning. Sano had hoped to discover that the killer had murdered Kaibara, taken the head home, prepared the trophy, and put it in the tower during the relatively short time between nightfall and the closing of the gates—a feat that required he reside in the pharmacists' district. But with the whole night at his disposal, he could have come from anywhere.

"Thank you for your hospitality and your help," Sano said to the old couple. "I must order you not to spread your ghost story; you'll only frighten people." To the sentry, he said, "I'd like to see the tower where you found the head."

Seeing Udoguchi's mouth drop in horror, he added hastily, "You don't have to go back there. Just show me."

"Yes, master." Obviously relieved, Udoguchi accompanied Sano out to the street, where he raised his hand and pointed.

Sano saw the tower rising above the rooftops several streets to the east. As he started toward it, a large procession of curious onlookers followed. All had apparently learned his identity and wanted to watch him work.

"Go!" Beside him, Hirata raised his *jitte*. "Give the *sōsakan-sama* room!"

He and his assistants, though unable to scatter such a large crowd, held it at bay, letting Sano continue to the tower unhampered. Sano realized that he might actually get better—and certainly more willing—service from the young *doshin* than from Tsuda and Hayashi.

He mounted the ladder's rungs. They felt damp, so he was disappointed but not surprised when he reached the square wooden platform and found the boards clean, with a small puddle in the center. A gritty substance crunched under his feet: salt. The townspeople had already washed and purified the tower to remove the spiritual pollution conferred by its contact with death, eliminating all traces of the trophy and the murderer.

Sano braced himself against the poles that supported the tower's roof and gazed out over the houses. In a city made of wood, where the citizens used charcoal braziers for heating and cooking, fire posed an everpresent threat. Hardly a month passed without one, and thirty-eight years ago the Great Fire of Meireki had destroyed most of Edo and taken a hundred thousand lives. The residents kept watch from these towers, ready to ring the bells suspended from their roofs at the first sight of smoke or flame. Today the air was clear in all directions. But last night the fog had made firewatching useless. The killer had chosen his time well, and escaped the scene without leaving a clue. Shaking his head, Sano looked down in dismay.

The teeming streets reminded him that Edo boasted a population of one million, including some fifty thousand samurai. He'd investigated only one other murder, completely unlike this one. How would he ever find the killer? With the possibility of failure and disgrace looming large before him, Sano almost wished he'd heeded Noguchi's advice. Yet Bushido demanded from a samurai unstinting, uncomplaining service to his lord. And his promise to his father demanded fulfillment. Now, more than ever, Sano longed for his father's wisdom and guidance.

"*Otōsan,* what am I going to do?" he whispered.

If his father's spirit heard, it didn't answer. Feeling his bereavement all the more, Sano descended the ladder to find Hirata waiting for him.

"Question everyone in the district and find out if they noticed anything or anyone suspicious last night or this morning," he said. "Watch for men with sword wounds. Conduct a door-to-door search of every building, starting at the firetower and the pharmacy and working outward."

He explained what to look for, then paused, reluctant to trust this young stranger. But he had an important matter to attend to.

"Report to me outside the main gate of the castle at the hour of the dog," he finished, and took his leave.

"*Sōsakan-sama.*"

Sano, already some ten paces down the street, turned to see Hirata still standing by the ladder. "Yes?"

"*Sumimasen*—I'm sorry; excuse me." Hirata's Adam's apple jerked in a nervous swallow, but his voice was steady as he said, "You won't regret letting me work for you." A brave red spot burned in each cheek.

Sano regarded him in surprise. The young *doshin's* manner combined the purposefulness of maturity with youth's brashness. Here was another samurai who saw this investigation as an opportunity to prove himself. Sano felt an unexpected burst of sympathy for Hirata.

"We'll see," he said more kindly. He, of all people, knew that determination could compensate for inexperience.

Flushing brighter, Hirata hurried away, his step jaunty.

Sano retrieved his horse and headed north toward Edo Morgue. Perhaps Kaibara Tōju's remains would yield the clues that the murder scene had not.

4

High above Edo Castle, the keep's gloomy top story echoed with the footsteps of guards patrolling the corridors and stairways below. Afternoon sunlight filtered through the barred windows to hang in thin, dusty shafts in the air. Chamberlain Yanagisawa stood facing a window, his tall, elegant form silhouetted against the alternating bands of light and dark.

"So, *kunoichi,*" he said. A sneer curled the edges of his voice. "What information have you and your spy network managed to collect regarding *Sōsakan* Sano?"

Aoi, standing behind him, flinched at the way he'd addressed her. *Kunoichi:* female ninja; practitioner of the dark martial arts, descended, as legend claimed, from demons with supernatural powers. She didn't object to the term; she was proud of what she was. But Yanagisawa's open contempt started a slow, angry fire in her blood. Deeper than that of a man for a woman, superior for inferior, it echoed that in which the samurai had held the ninja since time immemorial. They despised her people as dirty mercenaries who used stealth, sabotage, covert assassination, espionage, and deception instead of the forthright samurai martial arts. Aoi wondered whether Chamberlain Yanagisawa realized that his class had created the demons themselves. Once peace-loving

Buddhist mystics, the ninja had developed their famed, deadly skills as a defense against the ruling samurai who burned the temples and killed the worshippers in an attempt to destroy what they didn't understand. However, this aversion had never stopped Yanagisawa and his kind from employing the ninja to do work that they themselves considered dishonorable, cowardly, and beneath them.

Like using her to spy on a helpless subordinate.

Swallowing her own contempt for her master, Aoi said, "Sano rises early to practice the martial arts every day. He works long hours in the archives. He eats and drinks moderately." Rigorous training enabled her to purge her voice of all emotion as she related the information reported to her by Sano's servants. "He never goes to the Yoshiwara pleasure quarter, but does visit his old mother. He doesn't gamble, or squander money on trifles. When he attends parties, he always returns home early to sleep alone."

While she spoke, Aoi pictured herself standing at the end of a long line of ninja that began more than two hundred years ago and spanned the long wars that had preceded the Tokugawa regime. She saw Fumo Kotarō, who had aided Lord Hōjō Odawara though secret night attacks on the enemy Takeda; Saiga Magoichi, master of firearms and explosives; and the Hattori ninja, who had established the *metsuke* and served as chief of security at Edo Castle. And always behind the scenes, the women, shadowy figures whose names did not appear in any historical account. Disguised as servants, prostitutes, entertainers—or shrine attendants like herself—they'd acted as spies and assassins, compromising the enemy in ways that male agents couldn't.

But now the wars were over. Most surviving ninja had returned to their secret mountain villages. Some had become criminals or private security guards in the cities. The line of ninja who aided the ruling warrior class in their military and political schemes ended with her. She was an anachronism, serving the Tokugawa under the same threat used against her ancestors: annihilation of their kind. If she refused to obey, the Tokugawa would kill her, then send troops into the mountains to destroy her clan and the other families that comprised their small ninja school. It had happened before; it could happen again. In Japan, families were routinely punished for a member's offenses. Aoi fought her impotent rage, reminding herself that negative emotions are sources of strength, but only if used properly.

"Sano doesn't have a mistress, or force himself on the maids or stableboys," she finished. "From what my informers tell me, he's exactly what he seems: A man focused entirely on his duties. A perfect samurai."

Unlike Yanagisawa, who possessed all the vices and weaknesses that Sano did not. What a despicable creature!

Yanagisawa's silk robes hissed and slithered against the floor as he turned to face her. The bright window backlit him, leaving his face shaded, but Aoi, with her keen vision, saw the anger that rendered his handsome features ugly.

" 'A perfect samurai.' " His mocking repetition issued from between clenched teeth.

Aoi's sharp senses detected the slight turbulence in the air around him, and the faint bitter scent that his body exuded. Both betrayed his overweening fear and hatred of Sano. Focusing her trained concentration upon Yanagisawa, she probed for the reason he would waste such strong emotions and relentless effort on an underling. He had a reputation for ruining early the careers of men who might eventually rise to compete with him for status and power. And Sano, by virtue of having saved the shogun's life, was in a unique position to do so. But Yanagisawa's next words distracted her, masking his motives.

"Two months of surveillance, with nothing to show for it but proof of Sano's good character!" He began to pace the corridor in swift, restless strides. "And now that His Excellency has appointed him to investigate Kaibara Tōju's murder, it is more important than ever to find a weapon to use against him."

Yanagisawa halted in midstep before her. "Are you sure the virtuous Sano has no weaknesses that can be exploited?"

Aoi felt a growing sympathy toward Sano, perhaps because of her hatred for this man who schemed against him; perhaps because Sano's quiet intelligence and modesty made him so different from the typical brutish, egotistical samurai. This sympathy frightened her. She must not let her personal feelings interfere with her mission when so much lay at stake. But just for a moment she envisioned Sano's face, with its thoughtful, wary expression. She remembered the physical attraction she'd felt toward him—which she knew he shared. He was a man she might have liked, under different circumstances . . .

She dismissed the idle fantasy and said, "He's lonely. And loneliness makes people vulnerable."

How well she knew loneliness. As Yanagisawa continued to rant about Sano, the surface of her trained mind captured his words and committed them to memory. On another, deeper level, she relived her life, starting with the day she'd left her native Iga Province.

She saw herself on that misty autumn day fifteen years ago, at age fourteen, a student at the secret academy in the mountains where young *kunoichi* learned combat and espionage skills. She was running a woodland obstacle course of trees, rocks, horizontal poles, and inclined planks, in an exercise designed to incorporate speed, balance, agility, and silence into her body's movements. At the end stood her beloved father: the powerful *jōnin*—high man—of the Iga ninja school. His tragic expression froze her.

"Father, what's wrong?" she asked.

"Aoi, the time has come for you to begin the work you've been trained for," he said sadly. "Today you leave for Edo Castle, to become an apprentice spy."

Aoi hugged herself, buffeted by a desolation as cold as the mountain wind. Her inevitable departure had always belonged to the distant future. But now the future was here.

Her father's eyes reflected her anguish, but he said only, "It is necessary."

Trained in *ninjutsu* since early childhood, Aoi knew better than to ask why. A *jōnin* made all the clan's decisions, based on his superior knowledge of the scheme of totality, and lower members must accept them without challenge. But she'd guessed that the ninja, to ensure their own survival, would always serve whoever stood the best chance of gaining and keeping power. And her father was betting on the Tokugawa. That he would send them his best and dearest young *kunoichi* proved it. Aoi wanted to weep

and rage and refuse, but her training forbade her to do anything
but say, "Yes, Father. I'll go and get ready."

Now Aoi closed her mind to the still-sharp pain of that parting,
forcing her thoughts back to the present.

"Sano must not be allowed to solve this murder case, and he
will not." Yanagisawa laughed, a sound of pure, exuberant enjoyment. "How fortunate that I managed to plant the idea of you in
His Excellency's mind!"

That he would sabotage a murder investigation to serve his own
purposes seemed criminal to Aoi. Why did he wish the case to remain unsolved? Because he wanted to eliminate Sano as a future
rival? Or for some other, even more sinister reason directly related
to the murder? But it wasn't Aoi's place to question her superior's
motives, or to dwell upon what happened to his unfortunate victims. To do so would only make her work less bearable. Fifteen
long years had taught her that.

She'd begun her servitude as a kitchen maid, spying on her fellow servants; desperately homesick, forever isolated from those
whom she befriended in order to learn their secrets; lying awake
in bed until the maids who shared her room fell asleep, then
silently slipping through deserted moonlit courtyards and stone
passages to the Momijiyama.

"Ah, Aoi." Old Michiko's voice crackled like a wood fire in the
great mausoleum's shadowed entranceway. Bent and wizened,
but with bright, youthful eyes, she was a *kunoichi* from Aoi's village. She'd been chief shrine attendant—and commander of the
palace's female spy network—since Tokugawa Ieyasu had
founded Edo Castle. "What have you to report tonight?"

"The nightwatchmen are planning to steal rice from the
shogun's warehouse," Aoi would report. Or whatever other crimes
she'd discovered.

Michiko's answer was always the same. "Very good, child. Your
father would be proud of you."

Now, fifteen years later, the thought of her father still made tears
sting Aoi's eyes. He might accept, but never condone the ruin his
child had wrought: the men and women beaten, or even executed
for petty offenses against the government. As in the past, she
toyed with the idea of failing at the task before her, and sparing

the new victim. Death would provide the release she sought. But to fail was dishonorable, impossible, and unthinkable. She listened closely to Yanagisawa's orders.

Yanagisawa's pacing quickened; the turbulence around him intensified. "You will keep me informed on Sano's progress. But more important, you must mislead him with false spirit messages. Use your intelligence to gain his respect; his loneliness to secure his affection and trust."

Ryakuhon no jitsu: the ninja art of winning an enemy's confidence by pretending to be a comrade. Aoi had perfected this during her first three years at Edo Castle, as she rose from maid to attendant to the women of the shogun's top officials. Her sympathetic manner, knowledge of medicine, and skills as a masseuse made her popular. Instead of the trivial offenses of servants, she reported to Michiko tales of madness, adultery, perversion, and dissipation at the *bakufu's* highest levels. In time, resignation replaced grief; homesickness dulled to a constant but bearable ache. Aoi found a certain fulfillment in exercising her talents. She, like her female ancestors, enjoyed a freedom and mobility greater than that of ordinary women—if only to do her master's bidding. She lived from day to day, focusing on the work at hand, not allowing herself to think of the future.

Just as she must now. She would help Sano just enough to convince him that her intentions were good and her counsel worth heeding. Then she would betray his trust, destroy him, and never think of him again.

"Another idea has just occurred to me." Yanagisawa's intense dark eyes sparkled, lending his face a vibrant charm. Such beauty, wasted on a man so evil. "Perhaps if you seduce Sano and distract him from his work, the shogun will remove him from the case— or even dismiss him for neglecting his duties. And the ruin of his marriage negotiations would be a bonus."

Yanagisawa laughed again. "I dare say I need not tell you how to destroy a man, *kunoichi.*"

Aoi kept her face calm, her breathing steady. But ice crystals formed in her blood at the thought of performing *monomi no jitsu:* finding and attacking the weak point in the enemy's defenses.

At age twenty, she'd begun spying directly upon the shogun's men, entertaining—and bedding—high *bakufu* officials in order to discover their acts of disloyalty and corruption, or to exploit their secret vices until they ruined themselves. She despised their weakness and stupidity; she never thought of the demotions, banishments, or suicides that followed her disclosures. Selective memory erased each victim from her conscience, much the same way that the poisonous herbs she took rid her body of unwanted pregnancies. Until six years ago, when she had destroyed the one man who'd mattered to her.

Fusei Matsugae. An influential member of the Council of Elders when Tokugawa Tsunayoshi had become shogun, he'd encouraged the new dictator's early efforts at government reform and opposed Yanagisawa's attempts to usurp power. His intelligence, integrity, and striking physical appearance had attracted Aoi. In him, she finally discovered a samurai worth her regard. For the first time, she experienced sexual pleasure with a man. Unlike the others who had often treated her with callous disrespect, he was kind. And he somehow satisfied her longing for her father and home.

In the beginning, she'd thought her happiness simply meant that the cruelty of her work no longer bothered her. Seeing Fusei grow infatuated with her, she'd believed her satisfaction purely professional. The sexual ecstasy gave her qualms, which she dismissed in her eagerness to explore a new delight. Never having been in love before, she didn't recognize the danger until it was too late.

Now guilt and self-loathing choked Aoi as Yanagisawa's innuendo conjured up the image of herself and Fusei on their last night together. The dim lamplight of his bedchamber had failed to obscure the signs of his physical deterioration: the lean, fit body gone weak and stringy; the once-keen eyes bloodshot; the trembling mouth and hands. He reeked of the sake that had ravaged him. She could always identify those men with a dangerous affinity for liquor by the unique smell they gave off as it mixed with their blood, and she'd deliberately encouraged Fusei to drink as she charmed him. But that night, she realized that she missed the man he'd once been, and that she loved him.

"No," she whispered, stricken by the sudden knowledge of how much bleaker her life would be when she finished destroying the only person in Edo she cared for.

Seated on the floor, Fusei gazed at her, eyes glassy with drunkenness and incipient dementia. "Perform the ritual, Aoi," he said, his words slurred.

She had often exploited her victims' religious beliefs and filial piety by evoking the spirits of their beloved dead to influence them. It wasn't a trick. The dead did speak—through their possessions, through the minds of living persons who had known them. She need only focus her concentration to hear their voices, then use her excellent acting skill to recreate their personae and manipulate vulnerable men like Fusei. But her heart rebelled against performing the act that would complete her lover's ruin.

"Not tonight, dearest," she murmured, stroking his face.

Fusei ignored her attempts to entice him to bed. With shaky hands, he lit the incense on the altar. "I am losing all my allies," he complained. He couldn't see that his drunken ravings had alienated them, any more than he could see that she was helping him destroy himself. "The whole council has joined Yanagisawa's clique. I don't know how to stop this madness. Aoi, I must have my mother's advice."

Amid the smoking incense burners, he set the sash that had belonged to his deceased mother, then waited in the same anticipation with which he'd once greeted sex.

Go, Aoi wanted to cry, *before all is lost! And take me with you, away from this awful place.* Then she thought of her people, whose lives depended on her continued obedience. Sighing mournfully, she laid her hands upon the sash.

"Listen, my son." She assumed the old woman's raspy voice, and arranged her features in the expression she'd gleaned from Fusei's memory.

"Yes, mother." He leaned toward her eagerly.

"My son, you must take your sword to your enemy."

"No! I cannot!" Fusei's clouded gaze cleared; his mother's message had shocked him sober. "It would be treason!" Then, as he gazed upon what he thought was his mother, speaking through Aoi from the spirit realm, his expression turned resolute. "But if I must, then so be it."

Holding back her tears took every bit of self-control Aoi possessed. "Yes, my son," she whispered.

Two days later, he was dead in a violent scandal of his own making—and hers. Yanagisawa succeeded to the post of chamberlain without further opposition. Night after night, Aoi lay awake, weeping silently, hating herself and the duty that bound her. Then fate dealt her another blow when Chamberlain Yanagisawa summoned her to the keep for the first of many secret meetings.

"Michiko is dead," he said. "From now on, you will command the spy network, reporting directly to me."

The news hit Aoi like a thunderbolt. For years, the lingering dream of freedom had sustained her. She longed to see her father again. And she cherished the wistful hopes that in her own village she might work for good, rather than evil; she might find a man to fill the emptiness that Fusei's death had left in her soul. But now she would never be free. Like Michiko, she would spend the rest of her life in exile, condemned to do work she despised, for men she hated. She wanted to hurl herself through the barred window and onto the ground five stories below.

But the old threat still held. Instead she'd whispered, "Yes, Honorable Chamberlain."

"So, *kunoichi*," the present-day Yanagisawa said. "Do you understand your orders?"

Aoi nodded in resignation. Six long years had passed since she'd driven her lover to his death and broken her own heart. She wasn't a foolish young girl now, but a mature professional who knew how to maintain her detachment. She need not involve herself intimately with Sano and risk more pain. She would sabotage his work so badly that his total destruction would be unnecessary. She could satisfy Yanagisawa without adding another murder to her sins.

A movement outside made them both turn toward the window. Above the palace's rooftops, curving stone walls, shining moats, and green gardens, a hawk wheeled and soared. As they watched, it veered to capture a tiny bird. A shriek of pain, a spatter of blood, and both predator and prey dropped from sight. Aoi winced inwardly.

Yanagisawa contemplated the empty sky for a moment. The voices and footsteps of the patrolling guards drifted up to fill the silence. Then he said, "Will you use the dark forces against Sano?"

Aoi sensed a sudden chill in the emotional climate that surrounded Yanagisawa. His nonchalant manner couldn't disguise his fear of her. The mysterious "dark forces" were simply a combination of heightened perception, sensory awareness, and a thorough knowledge of the human mind and body. Formidable tools, beyond a samurai's comprehension, yet hardly supernatural. But Yanagisawa knew she could kill him—with a poison dart, a concealed blade, or one sharp blow—before he could defend himself or summon help. So far she'd never had to commit an assassination, the last, dreaded resort should all other means of completing a task fail. But she would gladly kill Yanagisawa, if not for the death threat he held over her and her people.

Aoi looked Yanagisawa straight in the eye, and saw that he knew it. His smile vanished. The balance of power between them shifted—but only temporarily. She lowered her gaze and bowed.

"I will use whatever means necessary to achieve your aims, Honorable Chamberlain."

Sano rode through a maze of narrow lanes that grew poorer and drabber as he neared Edo Jail, which housed not only prisoners awaiting trial, but also the morgue, where the bodies of those who died in natural disasters or from unnatural causes were taken. Here the spring sunlight only emphasized the signs of poverty: tumbledown houses with patched roofs and outdoor kitchens; thin, hungry-looking children. The warm weather intensified the smells of garbage, sewage, and poor food.

A rickety wooden bridge led Sano across the rank, stagnant canal that formed a moat around Edo Jail. Before him rose the ominous bulk of the Tokugawa prison, with its high stone walls, multiple watchtowers, and massive iron-banded gate. When he reached the end of the bridge, two guards came out of the guardhouse, bowed, and slid back the heavy wooden beams that barred the gate.

"Come right in, *sōsakan-sama*," they chorused. Two months of his frequent visits had accustomed them to receiving him at this place of death and defilement where no one, especially high-ranking samurai, ever came voluntarily.

As he dismounted and led his horse in the gate and through the prison, Sano reflected upon the changes he'd undergone since his first trip to the jail. Then he'd come reluctantly, on a distasteful errand associated with his first murder investigation. He'd never imagined wanting to return.

Now he no longer needed anyone to escort him through the compound of earthen courtyards and dingy guards' barracks and administrative offices. And he'd almost overcome his ingrained aversion, born of his Shinto religion, to contact with places of death. The proximity of the main prison building, where inmates suffered painful torture and squalid living conditions, and his fear of ritual pollution no longer made him physically ill. Nor did the smell of decay that surrounded the compound like a foul aura. Yet even when they still had, he'd come anyway—not out of professional duty, but to see Dr. Ito Genboku, Edo Morgue custodian, the friend whose scientific expertise had helped him prove that an apparent double suicide was actually a murder. Whose wisdom and kindness had aided his struggle with the conflict between duty and desire, conformity and self-expression.

Now Sano entered a final courtyard near the jail's rear wall and stopped outside a low building with plaster walls and a thatched roof. The door opened at his knock and a short, wiry man with cropped gray hair and a square, stern face came out and knelt on the dirt to bow.

"Mura," Sano greeted him.

He'd also overcome his distaste for this man, an *eta*. The *eta*, society's outcasts, staffed the jail, acting as corpse handlers, janitors, jailers, torturers, and executioners. They also performed the city's dirtiest tasks: emptying cesspools, collecting garbage, and clearing away dead bodies after floods, fires, and earthquakes. Their hereditary link with such death-related occupations as butchering and leather tanning rendered them spiritually contaminated. However, because Mura was both friend and assistant to Dr. Ito, Sano had learned to treat him with a respect not usually accorded an *eta*.

"Is the honorable doctor well, and able to receive visitors today?" he asked.

"As well as ever, master. And always glad to see you."

"Then please secure my horse." As the *eta* rose, Sano removed a flat package from his heavily laden saddlebag and tucked it under his arm, adding, "And unload these parcels."

"Yes, master." Mura's deepset, intelligent eyes flashed Sano a look of understanding as he took the reins.

Sano walked to the door of the morgue, feeling a touch of the old apprehension. He never knew what he would find here. Gingerly crossing the threshold, he held his breath, then sighed in relief.

In the big room, other *eta,* dressed like Mura in short, unbleached muslin kimonos, worked at waist-high tables, tying hemp cords around corpses already swathed in white cotton, cleaning knives and razors and replacing them in cabinets, and mopping the floor's wooden planks. The stone troughs that lined one wall stood empty, drained of the water used to wash the dead. All the windows were open, and the cool draft swept away any lingering odors. At a podium in one corner stood Dr. Ito, a man of about seventy, with short, thick white hair that receded at the temples. He wore his long dark blue coat, the physician's traditional uniform. At Sano's approach, he looked up from making notes in a ledger.

"Ah, Sano-*san*. Welcome." His shrewd old eyes lit with pleasure, and his bony, ascetic face relaxed into a smile as he set down his brush. Walking across the room to meet Sano, Dr. Ito was a living illustration of Tokugawa policy.

Fifty years ago, the *bakufu* had virtually sealed off Japan from the outside world in order to stabilize the nation after years of civil war. Only the Dutch retained limited trading privileges. Foreign books were banned; anyone caught practicing foreign science faced harsh punishment.

But a few brave *rangakusha* like Dr. Ito—scholars of Dutch learning—continued to pursue forbidden knowledge in secret. In a blaze of scandal, Dr. Ito, once esteemed physician to the imperial family, had been discovered, arrested, tried, convicted, and sentenced to lifelong custodianship of Edo Morgue. But this man of great spirit had found a source of consolation in his imprisonment. Ignored by the authorities, he could dissect, observe, and record in peace, with a neverending supply of human corpses at his disposal. He and Sano had begun their friendship over an inquiry related to Sano's first murder investigation.

Sano bowed. "Greetings, Ito-*san*," he said, extending his package. "Please accept this token of my friendship."

Dr. Ito offered the customary thanks and demurrals and accepted the package, which contained writing supplies—the only things he would allow Sano to give him. The first and only time Sano had brought gifts of more substance, his friend had refused them, obviously humiliated to be an object of charity. Now Sano always gave food, fuel, and luxuries to Mura to sneak into the doctor's hut, as he'd done today. All three of them knew about this, but to spare Dr. Ito's pride, no one ever spoke of it.

"And what brings you here today?" Dr. Ito asked, fixing his piercing gaze upon Sano. "Somehow I sense that it is more than just a desire for congenial company."

"The shogun has put me in charge of investigating the murder of Kaibara Tōju, whose head—"

"Was severed and made into a war trophy." Dr. Ito's face grew animated, and his glee seemed out of all proportion to the news. "Yes, I have heard of this murder. And you are to find the killer. Splendid!"

"Maybe not so splendid," Sano said, puzzled. He explained about his difficulties with the police and how the murder scene had provided no clues.

But Dr. Ito, instead of offering sympathy or counsel, just gave him an enigmatic smile and said, "Perhaps you are worrying needlessly, and too soon."

Suspicious, Sano asked, "Why? Do you know something?"

"Oh, perhaps. Perhaps."

Sano would have demanded more information, but the mischievous look in Dr. Ito's eyes stopped him. His friend had little enough pleasure in life; let him enjoy his secret a while longer.

"I'd like to examine Kaibara's remains," Sano said.

"Of course." To the *eta* morgue attendants, Ito said, "Clear the tables. Then bring the body and head that came in this morning. Mura?" He turned to his assistant, who'd just entered the room. "Prepare to assist in an examination."

Mura gave Sano a discreet nod: He'd hidden the gifts. Then he said, "Yes, master," and went to a cabinet for the necessary tools.

The attendants removed the wrapped corpses and soon returned with two bundles, one large and elongated, the other smaller and squarish, both wrapped in rough hemp cloth. They placed these one on each table and withdrew, leaving Sano, Dr. Ito, and Mura alone.

"They've not been washed or prepared for cremation yet," Dr. Ito warned.

"Good." Sano nodded, pleased. Some evidence might remain. But as Mura unwrapped the bundles, Sano steeled himself, anticipating his first sight of the contents. He hoped his last meal had already passed through his system so that he couldn't vomit, as he'd done after his first visit to the morgue. Since then he'd seen many corpses in various conditions, both here and in other, less expected places. But the thought of beholding another still made him queasy.

The last fold of cloth fell back. Sano swallowed hard. Blood caked the corpse's clothes so heavily that he couldn't make out their original colors. It stained the sheathed swords still tucked into the sash, and had coagulated in thick crusts around the cut neck. Sano forced himself to step closer, flinching when he caught the sweet, sickly, metallic odors of blood and decay.

"I suppose there's no point in performing a dissection, because it's obvious how he died," Sano said, relieved to be spared that.

He would never forget the first dissection he'd seen, or the awful sense of uncleanliness he'd experienced while watching a human body cut, mutilated, defiled. But all horror and disgust aside, he had more reason for relief: Dissection was just as illegal as when Dr. Ito had been arrested. Sano doubted that even the shogun's patronage would protect him from the consequences of dabbling in forbidden foreign science. Instead of seeing it as necessary to obeying his orders, the refined, devout Tokugawa Tsunayoshi might be offended enough to exile Sano, or at least decide he didn't need a *sōsakan* of such dubious character. The thought of defying the law and jeopardizing his position terrified Sano. Yet, as in his first murder case, he would do both to satisfy his desire for the truth.

"No, a dissection does not appear necessary," Dr. Ito agreed. He walked around the table, viewing the body from all angles. "But we shall see. Mura, remove the clothes."

Dr. Ito, for all his unconventionality, followed the traditional practice of letting the *eta* handle the dead. Mura did all the physical work associated with Ito's studies. Now he began to undress the corpse.

Sano examined the swords, holding them with his fingertips to avoid the blood. He pulled each free of its scabbard to expose a gleaming steel blade.

"Clean," he said. "He didn't even draw his weapons, let alone cut his attacker." So much for the idea of identifying the killer via telltale sword wounds.

When Mura loosened Kaibara's sash, a small brown cotton pouch fell onto the table. Sano picked it up. Protected by its concealed position beneath the sash, it was free of blood. A white jade *netsuke*—charm—in the form of a grasshopper sitting on a plum dangled from the drawstring. Sano opened the pouch and saw silver coins inside. That the killer had left behind Kaibara's valuables eliminated robbery as a motive. And fortunately for Sano, thieving corpse handlers hadn't braved the blood and gore to find them. He tucked the pouch and *netsuke* inside his own sash.

"I'll return it to Kaibara's family tomorrow," he told Dr. Ito after explaining about Aoi's ritual.

Mura removed Kaibara's cloak, kimono, trousers, and under-kimono, leaving only the loincloth, which was stained with feces and urine: death had loosened Kaibara's bowels and bladder. The clothing had absorbed much of the blood, leaving only the dreadful accretion at the neck and faint blotches on the rest of the body, which was small and frail, with the withered muscles and pale, papery skin of old age.

"Whatever reason the killer had for attacking Kaibara, it wasn't for sport," Sano commented. "The old man couldn't have offered much of a challenge."

"Turn him," Dr. Ito said to Mura.

Sano leaned closer and voiced the obvious. "No cuts or bruises. Killed with one stroke. The murderer must have leapt out of the fog and surprised him."

Ito was studying Kaibara's neck. "Mura, clean the cut."

Mura fetched a jug of water, then rinsed and swabbed until the caked blood loosened; the water washed reddish-brown clots down a hole in the table and through a bamboo pipe to a drain in the floor. The drain gurgled. Sano fought nausea as the cut came clean. He tried to think of the raw red tissue, white bone, and slashed vessels as mere abstract shapes, unrelated to anything human, but an unpleasant sense of contamination crept over him. Though he hadn't touched the corpse, he felt an urgent need to wash his hands.

Dr. Ito must have noticed his discomfort, because he said, "Mura, cover the body."

Having finished cleansing the wound, Mura brought a white cloth from the cabinet and draped the corpse, leaving only the area of interest exposed. Sano's sickness abated. Not having to see the rest of the dead man made looking at the wound easier to bear.

"Thank you, Ito-*san*," he said.

Dr. Ito bent close to the wound, squinting with a scientist's concentration. "No jagged edges on the flesh, or roughness on the bone surface," he said, pointing. "This cut was made with a very sharp blade, in a single motion—swift, sure, without hesitation. And with the necessary amount of force correctly judged. The killer knew exactly what he was doing." His air of suppressed glee intensified.

"Then the killer is a skilled swordsman," Sano said.

"It would appear so."

Sano puffed out his breath in frustration. "Do you know how many men in Edo that description fits?" he asked, thinking of all the samurai who lived in the daimyo estates, and even the castle itself. In peacetime, many had little to do but practice their martial arts skills. "Or he could be a wandering *rōnin*."

Oddly, Dr. Ito didn't seem to share his disappointment. With a dry chuckle, he said, "Your task is a difficult one, but do not lose hope yet. Let us examine the head."

They went to the other table, where Mura was unwrapping the smaller bundle. When Sano saw its contents, awe lifted him momentarily above his worries. He spoke on a sigh of mingled admiration and revulsion.

"A perfect specimen."

He'd read accounts of the head-viewing ceremonies that followed battles. This *bundori* was correct to the last detail. The downcast eyes, the neat pigtail tied with white paper, the square mounting board, the rouged face, the odor of incense—all conformed to the standard specified in classic war manuals. Tokugawa Ieyasu himself would have been pleased to receive such a tribute.

"But this only confirms that the killer is a samurai who knows how to prepare a trophy," Sano said. Morosely he touched the label tied to the pigtail. Then he frowned in surprise when he read the inked characters.

" 'Araki Yojiemon'?"

"I understand that war trophies are supposed to bear the dead man's name," Dr. Ito said. "Perhaps the killer did not know who Kaibara was, and chose another name rather than leave the label blank."

"But why this particular one?"

Araki Yojiemon, Sano recalled, had been a vassal of Tokugawa Ieyasu during the country's Sengoku Jidai—Time of War—more than a hundred years ago. The Araki clan had served the Tokugawa for generations, Yojiemon as a general in the battles Ieyasu had fought for Oda Nobunaga, during that great warlord's drive to conquer the nation. Sano failed to see any connection between Araki Yojiemon and Kaibara Tōju's murder.

"And if the killer didn't know who Kaibara was, what would be his motive for murder?" Sano added. "Why kill a total stranger?"

Dr. Ito shrugged, sharing his bafflement. On a hunch, Sano detached the label and tucked it into his sash beside Kaibara's pouch. He must determine what, if any, significance the label had, and could think of one possible way to do it.

"Have you any advice for me, Ito-*san?*" he asked.

This, evidently, was the moment the doctor had been waiting for. Beaming in triumph, he said, "What I have is important news for you. And if you make use of it, you may not need advice. Mura?"

He nodded to the *eta,* who took from a cupboard a large, covered brown ceramic urn. "Sano-*san,* it is my dubious pleasure to inform you that this unusual murder is not the first of its kind."

"Not the first? What do you mean? How do you know?" Sano looked at his friend in confusion.

Dr. Ito only smiled and, with a wave of his hand, directed his attention to the *eta*.

Mura pushed the urn over to the table. With a sharp knife, he scraped off the wax that sealed the lid. He pried up the lid and set it aside. Then, grimacing in distaste, he plunged his hands into the urn's depths.

Sano gasped when he saw the dripping object that Mura lifted onto the table. Sake, apparently used as a preservative, streamed from a severed male head. An opaque white film clouded the dead man's eyes; his skin had turned grayish-white. In contrast, the prominent wart on his nose had darkened, and the lips had peeled back to expose yellow, overlapping teeth. His short black hair made only a skimpy pigtail.

"No label." Sano spoke through a wave of nausea. "I wonder why not?"

But the head, like Kaibara's, was mounted on a square board, and traces of rouge still adhered to its cheeks. This murder and Kaibara's were unquestionably the work of the same person.

"When did this happen?" Sano demanded. "Do the police know about it?"

But of course they must. How like Hayashi to withhold information from him! Anger boiled inside Sano.

"The head was brought in by the corpse handlers ten days ago, at my request," Dr. Ito said. "And I doubt very much whether the police were informed."

"Why not?" Sano tore his gaze from the gruesome trophy and faced his friend.

Dr. Ito exchanged glances with Mura. "The victim was an *eta*," he said.

"Oh. I see." Enlightenment dispelled Sano's confusion.

The authorities concerned themselves as little as possible with the outcasts; the police didn't bother investigating their murders, no matter how unusual. But for Dr. Ito's intellectual curiosity, the *eta*'s death would have gone disregarded, along with whatever information it could furnish about the killer. Sano felt a rush of gratitude toward his friend, whose assistance and inspiration grew more valuable to him as their relationship progressed.

"Thank you, Ito-*san*," he said.

"Whatever are you talking about?" Dr. Ito feigned bewilderment, but a twinkle in his eye told Sano he understood and appreciated the tribute.

"Mura told me about the murder," he continued. "The man lived in his settlement. Having an unrealistically high opinion of my expertise, he asked me to help find the killer. But unfortunately, there was nothing I could do except preserve the evidence. Unless . . ."

He fixed Sano with a challenging gaze.

"Unless I help." Sano thoughtfully studied the head. "Maybe I can. If the same person committed both murders, then maybe investigating this one will lead me to the killer."

At Sano's request, Mura clipped a lock of the murdered *eta*'s hair and wrapped it in paper for him to carry to Aoi. Then Sano took his leave of Dr. Ito, elated at the new possibilities that had opened up before him, but at the same time disturbed.

Kaibara's decapitation wasn't an isolated incident. The killer had already demonstrated his willingness to kill more than once, for purposes yet unknown, and the Tokugawa *bakufu* was not his only target.

There was a madman loose in Edo, and how many more lives were at stake?

6

cold spring twilight descended upon the Asakusa temple district in the north of Edo. The rooftops of the shrines and temples curved and peaked against a radiant cerise sky. Bells tolled, their harmonious music winging over the western hills, the river, and the city. In the lanes that crisscrossed the district, paper lanterns glowed from the eaves of inns, shops, and food stalls, where pilgrims flocked, seeking food and shelter after their journeys and prayers. Orange-robed priests filed into the monasteries for their evening rites. Voices and laughter rang out; a cheerful serenity reigned.

Through the rippling tide of humanity strode the Bundori Killer. Barely aware of his surroundings, he ignored the noise, the crowds, the welcoming lights. His fellow men threw him uneasy glances, perhaps frightened by his air of grim purpose. Well, let them look. Let them stand in awe of Lord Oda's war hero. He headed for the Asakusa Kannon Temple, which shone like an enchanted fortress amid the lanterns that blazed within its grounds. The first two murders had whetted his appetite for more, and made him yearn harder for the past. Soon he would face another battle, and he must pray for victory.

In the sweltering confines of his lamplit field tent, Lord Oda Nobunaga paced before the generals summoned to this urgent night meeting.

"My traitorous brother-in-law, Asai, has allied himself with Lord Asakura of Echizen," he fumed.

During the ten years since the Battle of Okehazama, Oda had risen to the forefront of military power. He had crushed many rivals and gained an important ally, Tokugawa Ieyasu. He'd seized the capital at Kyōto. At times he seemed invincible and his eventual subjugation of the country a certainty. But the news of Asai's treachery, coming on the eve of his planned assault upon Lord Asakura's territory, drew murmurs of consternation from Oda's generals, among whom the Bundori Killer now numbered.

"Asai controls the passes of northern Omi Province," General Tokugawa Ieyasu said. "He'll ambush our army there before we can reach Echizen."

Bravely the Bundori Killer said what needed saying. "Then we must retreat now, so that we may live to triumph later." As all heads turned toward him, the young upstart, he added, "I will command the rear guard."

And pray that I can fend off Asai and Asakura long enough for my lord to reach Kyōto safely, even if I must die in the effort.

Outside Asakusa Kannon Temple, pilgrims clustered around a huge stone urn full of smoldering incense sticks. Some pilgrims were lame, others diseased. Chanting prayers, they cupped their hands to capture the healing smoke that rose from the vat, applying it to the affected parts of their bodies. The Bundori Killer marched past them to the temple's main entrance. Doves, heavenly messengers of Kannon, goddess of mercy, cooed and fluttered in the eaves. He entered the temple and crossed the hushed, cavernous hall.

The day's worshippers had deserted the temple. Two priests brushed past him, treading silently on bare feet, as he stood alone at the altar. He beheld the many-armed gilded statue of Kannon,

the stalks of sacred golden lotus, the painted murals, the flickering candles and smoking incense burners that bathed everything
in a shimmering golden haze. Then he bowed his head in prayer.

O, Kannon, let my troops crush the enemy forces. Let my victories follow one after another, as a tribute to my Lord Oda.

And then, because he was not so lost in the past that he'd forgotten the duties and dangers of his present-day reality:

I pray, let me destroy those who must be punished for the evil
they have done. And those who dare stand in my way—especially
the shogun's *sōsakan*.

He dropped a coin in the offertory box to speed his prayers to
the goddess, then left the temple. Outside, the sky had darkened;
the crowds had almost disappeared. Only a few lanterns still
burned in the streets. He joined the travelers on the road that led
out of Asakusa. One hundred and nineteen years past, Lord Oda's
army had clashed with Lord Asakura and the traitor Asai. But in
the here and now, would the man he sought to kill fall before his
sword tonight? Would he win another trophy to satisfy the debt of
honor that had gone unfulfilled for so long?

For a moment, he pondered the practical difficulties of finding
his next victim and avoiding capture. Then, with a giddy, ecstatic
rush, he relinquished his hold on the ordinary world and slid into
his dream realm.

Spring had given way to hot, humid summer. Lord Oda's army
had survived Asai's ambush and returned safely to Kyōto, thanks
to the Bundori Killer's masterful deployment of the rear guard.
Now the time had come to crush Asai and Lord Asakura for good.
Lord Oda's troops were on the march again, moving quietly by
night, on horseback and on foot, beneath a swollen yellow moon,
toward Asakura's headquarters.

The Bundori Killer led his unit. Inside his armor, sweat trickled
down his back and chest. Scouts had just brought news that Asai
and Asakura had marshaled twenty thousand troops across the
Anegawa River. His metal helmet amplified the pounding of his
heart, almost drowning out the sounds of the army's hoofbeats
and footsteps, and the insect chants from the woods around them.

Under his command he had the troops levied from among Oda's conquered foes. Had they really transferred their allegiance to their new lord? Could he trust them?

He hid his doubt and his youth behind the imperious bearing of a seasoned general who expects and receives obedience. The army marched on toward glory, or death. The moon reached its zenith and began to descend.

"Listen!" someone murmured.

From a distance came the faint pulse of war drums. Oda's drummers struck up a thunderous counterthreat. The army increased its pace. Hooves pounded; thousands of swords rasped free of their scabbards. The troops took up positions on the riverbank, gunners and archers in the forefront, then swordsmen and spear fighters, with the generals in the rear.

Suddenly the drumming stopped. As the Bundori Killer gazed across the dark water at the waiting enemy host, his anxiety disappeared; he knew no fear or doubt. It was every samurai's duty to win his lord's battles, or to die trying. With stoic resignation, he awaited Lord Oda's command.

The menacing silence lasted an eternity. The hot night was perfectly still. Then Lord Oda's cry shattered the calm.

From the river's opposite bank came Lord Asakura's answering challenge.

Amid murderous shouts and deafening gunfire, both armies plunged across the water.

7

"What has your search turned up?" Sano asked Hirata from
astride his horse when they met that evening on the wide boulevard that fronted Edo Castle's moat.

Hirata spread his hands in despair. "*Gomen nasai*—I'm sorry,
but we went to every building within two gates of the murder
scene, and didn't find any witnesses, anyone who acted suspicious, or any blood. One gate sentry reported seeing Kaibara last
night, alone. Another saw a man in a cloak and hat who might
have been carrying a basket. But he didn't get a good look at the
man's face."

He stared gloomily at the bridge that led across the moat to the
main gate. Above the towering stone walls, the castle's guardtow-
ers and keep loomed blackly against the star-flecked sky. Torches
burned on the hill, flickering in the darkness.

"We'd hoped to cover a wider area today, but it was slow going
with just the four of us."

"You've done well nevertheless," Sano told Hirata, who straightened his shoulders and managed a smile. The young *doshin* had
at least spared him the tedious footwork. "And we have a new
lead." Sano explained about the *eta* murder. "While your men continue the search, meet me tomorrow morning at the hour of the

dragon at Kaibara's house in the *banchō*"—the district west of the castle, where the Tokugawa *hatamoto* lived.

"And Hirata, this earlier murder means that until we catch the killer, no one is safe. On my way here, I stopped at every gate and told each sentry to detain, search, and note everyone who passes after dark. I ordered every neighborhood headman to have armed citizens patrol the streets between dusk and dawn. I want you to do the same in as much of southwest Nihonbashi as you can before the gates close. We don't want to panic the townspeople, but we must warn and protect them."

If Hirata minded following a hard day's work with a busy night, he didn't show it. He nodded briskly and said, "Yes, *sōsakan-sama*."

They made their farewells, and Sano watched him sprint away through crowds of homebound samurai. Across the boulevard rose the high stone walls of the great daimyo estates. Was the killer behind them? Or was he prowling the streets in search of another victim? Sano's hunter's instinct stirred despite the inconclusive end to the day's inquiries. Beneath the surface of Edo's controlled, orderly life, he sensed an evil presence, ready to wreak violence at any moment.

"Wherever you are, I'll find you," he vowed aloud.

As he crossed the bridge and entered the castle gate, bound for his meeting with the shogun, and, later, his rendezvous with Aoi, he wished he could believe his own words.

Armed guards admitted Sano to the shogun's private reception room, where lanterns lit lavish gilded murals of blooming plum trees and blue rivers, brilliant floral designs filled the spaces between the ceiling's cedar beams, and sunken charcoal braziers dispelled the evening chill.

"Ahh, *Sōsakan* Sano," Tokugawa Tsunayoshi said from the dais where he reclined upon silk cushions. In the soft light, his rich robes gleamed, and his face looked younger and more animated. "Come, rest from your labors. This spring air can be as, ahh, fatiguing as it is exhilarating."

"Yes, Your Excellency."

Sano knelt before the dais, awed and disconcerted to find himself alone with Tsunayoshi, except for three bodyguards who stood like silent shadows by the doors, and three equally quiet servants who awaited their master's orders. Still, Sano recognized a unique opportunity to further his acquaintance with the lord who controlled his fortune. And Tsunayoshi's conversation proved that he, too, welcomed the chance to develop their personal relationship.

"You are a scholar, are you not?" At Sano's assent, the shogun went on to ask, "With whom did you study? And which subjects?"

"With the priests at Zōjō Temple, Your Excellency," Sano answered, relaxing. His father, despite extreme financial hardship, had given him the best education possible. And considering the value that the shogun placed on scholarship, how fortunate that he had! Sano offered a silent prayer of thanks to his father's spirit. "I studied literature, composition, mathematics, law, history, political theory, and the Chinese classics."

"Ahh, a truly educated samurai." Interest kindled in Tsunayoshi's eyes, and he leaned forward with an eager smile. "I presume you are familiar with the Book of Great Learning."

Having had long passages of it drilled into his memory by the strict priests, Sano could and did answer yes. He hadn't expected a literary discussion, but he must follow his master's lead. He'd heard tales of Tsunayoshi's temperamental nature. One misstep could result in disaster.

However, the shogun apparently decided that it was time for business. "We shall have an enjoyable discussion about the classics someday soon." He sat upright and assumed a stern expression. "Now. What progress have you made in your, ahh, investigation of Kaibara Tōju's murder?"

Just then, footsteps sounded in the corridor. At a command from someone outside, the guards opened the door. Sano turned and saw Chamberlain Yanagisawa enter the room. With him came a young samurai about fourteen years of age. He wore his hair in a style that signified that he hadn't yet had his manhood ceremony: the crown shaven, but with a long, dangling forelock tied back from his brow. His face was as delicate and lovely as a girl's.

"Please forgive my interruption, Your Excellency." Yanagisawa knelt beside the dais and bowed. The boy did the same, but kept his forehead to the floor and his arms extended while the chamberlain sat up and continued speaking. "But I took the liberty of assuming you wanted to see Shichisaburō tonight." He gestured toward the boy, adding, "I believe you once expressed an interest in him."

Sano had heard of Shichisaburō, current star of the Tokugawa No theater troupe. He came from a distinguished stage family, had great talent, and specialized in samurai roles, which explained his hairstyle. The shogun, an enthusiastic arts patron, would naturally want to meet him—but now? Surprised and disturbed by Chamberlain Yanagisawa's ill-timed intrusion, Sano looked toward the dais.

The shogun was gazing at Shichisaburō as if entranced, eyes aglow, lips parted. Even before he'd come to the castle, Sano had heard stories about Tsunayoshi's fondness for young men and boys, his harem of beautiful actors, peasants, and samurai. Now he saw the truth in those rumors. He felt a spasm of disgust, though not at the shogun's sexual preference. Manly love was practiced by many samurai, who considered it an expression of Bushido. Rather, he was disturbed to learn that another rumor was also true: Tsunayoshi allowed erotic pursuits to distract him from official business. Sano fought his unfilial emotions as his father's voice spoke from the past:

"A good samurai does not criticize his lord, even silently."

Tsunayoshi seemed to have forgotten all about the murder investigation. "Rise, Shichisaburō," he ordered huskily.

The boy stood, and the shogun looked him up and down. Prodded by a sharp glance from Yanagisawa, the young actor smiled tremulously. Tsunayoshi's breathing quickened, and his throat contracted as he swallowed. Sano looked at the floor, embarrassed to witness this naked display of lust. Then, to his relief, Yanagisawa beckoned a guard.

"Take Shichisaburō to His Excellency's chambers to wait until he finishes his business with *Sōsakan* Sano." This casual mention of his name was Yanagisawa's only acknowledgement of Sano's presence.

As the door closed behind Shichisaburō and the guard, disappointment creased Tsunayoshi's face. Sano squirmed inwardly until Yanagisawa's smooth voice filled the awkward silence.

"Are you discussing Kaibara's murder?"

"Murder? Ahh, yes." Tsunayoshi blinked, and his eyes refocused on Sano, but a wistful sigh betrayed his lingering regret over Shichisaburō's departure. "*Sōsakan* Sano was just about to report on his progress. Won't you join us? I am sure we will both benefit from your, ahh, insight."

Yanagisawa and Tsunayoshi exchanged a glance that Sano couldn't read. He detected an emotional bond between them, but he couldn't grasp the nature of their relationship. Were they really lovers? They didn't touch, or appear to desire physical contact; Yanagisawa remained seated below the dais to Tsunayoshi's right, turning sideways so he could see both the shogun and Sano. Beneath their formal manner, Sano sensed fond admiration on Tsunayoshi's part; on Yanagisawa's, something more intense and ambivalent. He must pay close attention to their every move, to the inflections of their speech when they addressed each other. If, as he'd begun to suspect, he must always deal with his two superiors as a team, then he wanted to understand the dynamics between them.

What he saw so far disturbed him. Did Yanagisawa deliberately encourage the shogun's overindulgence in pleasure?

Sano shut his mind against this disrespectful thought. "I'm honored by your presence, Chamberlain Yanagisawa," he said.

Yanagisawa nodded in bland acknowledgement. "Then inform us, *Sōsakan* Sano, of what you have learned today," he said, assuming the role of interrogator. "Have you found the killer yet?"

"Well, no," Sano faltered. There was no escaping the truth, but Yanagisawa's direct query made it hard for him to emphasize the progress he'd made. He glanced at the shogun. Surely Tsunayoshi didn't expect miracles after a single day's work?

But Tsunayoshi frowned in disappointment. "Ahh, how unfortunate." He seemed content to let Yanagisawa take over the meeting. Again his gaze wandered toward the door, and he shifted restlessly on his cushions.

"But I've interviewed the people who found Kaibara's remains," Sano said, hurrying to head off more leading questions from

Yanagisawa. He wished the chamberlain would leave, and that he hadn't brought Shichisaburō. The rapport between himself and Tsunayoshi had weakened, and, with the shogun preoccupied, he saw little chance to restore it. "The old couple who run a pharmacy, and the gate sentry who—"

"You received a description of the killer from them?" Yanagisawa interrupted.

"No, Honorable Chamberlain, I didn't." Once again forced to answer in the negative, Sano forgot what he'd planned to say next. His nervousness increased.

"Hmm." Yanagisawa's monosyllable conveyed disapproval, scorn, and satisfaction.

Suddenly Sano remembered the look Yanagisawa had given him that morning. Now it appeared as though the chamberlain was acting upon his inexplicable hostility. That Sano still couldn't fathom how he'd earned it put him at an extreme disadvantage. Since protocol prevented him from requesting an explanation which Yanagisawa was under no obligation to give, how could he make amends?

"I've learned that Kaibara frequented the pharmacists' district," Sano said, striving to sound confident and capable. "It's possible that the killer is an enemy of his, who knew his habits and lay in wait for him."

"Perhaps," Yanagisawa conceded grudgingly. Tsunayoshi looked up from his private reverie. Sano's spirits lifted. Then Yanagisawa said, "I suppose you have evidence to substantiate this . . . scenario?" Fantasy, his tone implied.

This time Sano didn't intend to let the chamberlain make him say the damning word "no." "Tomorrow, when I call on Kaibara's family—"

"Do you mean to say that you have not yet done so?" Yanagisawa's voice rose in surprise; his mouth quirked in a malevolent smile. "Really, sōsakan, I fear that you are formulating a theory without facts to support it."

Sano fought back a rising tide of anger and confusion. Why was Yanagisawa undermining him? He felt even worse when he saw Yanagisawa and Tsunayoshi exchange another glance, this time with perfect comprehension. This man is a fool, said Yanagisawa's headshake. I guess you're right, said Tsunayoshi's rueful shrug and smile.

Knowing he must act fast to salvage the shogun's good opinion of him, Sano blurted, "When I went to Edo Morgue to examine Kaibara's remains, I discovered that—"

"The morgue!" Yanagisawa's horrified exclamation stopped him. "To go to that place of death—and to mention it in His Excellency's presence, yet." He turned to the shogun. "Please forgive this man's offense. His birth and upbringing, and not he himself, are undoubtedly responsible for his deplorable lack of judgment."

He capped this sincere plea on Sano's behalf with a quick, icy glare that proved he didn't want Sano forgiven, and had deliberately insulted his family. Helpless anger incensed Sano. He hated Yanagisawa for putting him in the wrong.

"My apologies, Your Excellency." He forced the words out of his constricted throat.

Tsunayoshi roused himself. "Accepted," he muttered.

Choosing his words carefully, Sano said, "I only meant to say that I've discovered that Kaibara was not the Bundori Killer's first victim. Ten days ago, another man was murdered in exactly the same manner."

Relief filled him when the shogun sat up and stared. And Yanagisawa's nostrils quivered; his finely shaped mouth tightened in displeasure.

"Your Excellency, I believe that this earlier murder will provide clues to the killer's motive and identity," Sano said, pressing his point while he still held Tsunayoshi's attention.

"An astute, ahh, deduction." Tsunayoshi stroked his chin thoughtfully.

But Sano's triumph was short-lived. "Another murder," Yanagisawa said, his dark, liquid eyes alight with mischief. "Well, *Sōsakan* Sano, does this not invalidate your theory that the killer is an enemy of Kaibara's?" Unerringly he'd spotted the weakness in Sano's logic. "And it is amazing how, in just one day, you have managed to complicate a simple murder case so enormously." His scornful laugh sent a chill down Sano's spine. "Yes?"

"No!" Driven to his own defense, Sano threw caution aside. "This other murder has opened up a promising line of inquiry."

He started to outline tomorrow's plans, but his voice trailed off when he saw Tsunayoshi contemplating the door. Yanagisawa laughed again, sealing his defeat.

Beneath his anger, Sano felt the frightening, lost-at-sea sensation that had plagued him since his arrival at Edo Castle. This meeting had strange undercurrents that threatened to pull him down, or at least carry him in the wrong direction. The chamberlain obviously didn't want him to succeed in catching the Bundori Killer. But why not? And Yanagisawa must have deliberately timed his interruption of the meeting, bringing the young actor in order to distract Tsunayoshi. Now Sano experienced a sudden stab of dread.

"Your Excellency, in regards to the police," he began.

"Ah, yes," Yanagisawa said, frowning. "In view of all the assistance you are receiving, it is strange that you have achieved nothing." The wicked gleam in his eyes belied his simulated concern. "But I see no reason to discuss the police. I have personally given orders to ensure that their efforts will continue to be as satisfactory as they have been up until now."

Even as Sano's stomach contracted in dismay, he had to admire Yanagisawa's finesse. The chamberlain had prevented him from telling the shogun that the police hadn't received orders to help him, and had not done so. He'd also confirmed Sano's suspicion that it was he who had made sure they wouldn't. Sano's drowning sensation worsened when he saw the position in which Yanagisawa had put him.

To secure the police assistance he needed to solve the case, he must expose Yanagisawa's sabotage and ask Tsunayoshi to rectify it. But Bushido forbade him to do either. Again he heard his father's voice:

"Any criticism of a lord's senior official also implies criticism of the lord himself—blasphemy! And a samurai has no right to make demands upon his lord."

To practice the Way of the Warrior could mean sacrificing not only his immediate success, but ultimately his entire career. Sano was caught between the two promises to his father, which he'd never expected to conflict. How he longed for his father's counsel!

Yanagisawa's triumphant smile reflected his knowledge and enjoyment of Sano's dilemma. "Since you have so many new avenues of inquiry to pursue, you had better waste no more time on conversation," he said smoothly, then turned to the shogun. "Your Excellency?"

"What? Oh, yes." Tsunayoshi refocused dazed eyes on Sano. "I shall hold audience with the Council of Elders the day after tomorrow. At that time, you will report to us the latest results of your, ahh, investigation. Make sure you've made better progress by then." He waved his hand. "Dismissed."

Feeling terribly and unfairly disgraced, Sano had no choice but to make his farewell bows and rise. As he walked away from Tsunayoshi and Yanagisawa, the path to the door seemed the beginning of a road leading to certain failure. Still, he must walk it as he tried to fulfill both promises to his father—exemplifying Bushido and performing a heroic deed—virtually alone, in the face of obstacles that now included a new and powerful enemy.

Before the door closed behind him, Sano heard the shogun say to Yanagisawa, "I shall be in my, ahh, chambers for the rest of the night. See that I am not disturbed until tomorrow."

The Momijiyama—the Tokugawa ancestral shrine—formed Edo Castle's sacred, most private heart. There, high on the hilltop, shrouded in pine and cypress and surrounded by high stone walls, reposed the relics of the past Tokugawa shoguns: Ieyasu, Hidetada, Iemitsu, Ietsuna. Their spirits protected the castle to ensure that their line might continue into the infinite future.

Sano hesitated outside the shrine. On either side of the soaring torii gate, flames leapt inside huge stone lanterns. A pair of snarling Korean temple dogs flanked the flagstone path just inside the gate, warning off evil spirits and earthly intruders. Beyond them, the path led between rows of pines and ended at a steep stairway that climbed to the shrine's main precinct. Smaller lanterns lit the way, their flames winking bravely against the immense, star-studded night.

A primitive disquiet stirred in Sano as he entered the shrine. Here on the dark, deserted hill, in the cold, restless wind that rustled the pines and smelled faintly of incense, the spirit realm seemed very near. Sano imagined ghostly presences lurking in the trees, inhabiting the rocks, buildings, and land. Only his determination to keep his appointment with Aoi propelled him up the steps.

At the top, the wind was stronger, the darkness relieved only by the starlight that filtered through the trees. Sano paused at the ritual basin, a huge stone font sheltered under a thatched roof. The icy water chilled his hands as he washed them.

"Aoi?" he called.

The wind whipped his words away. He followed a path that zigzagged through the trees and between structures he couldn't identify in the darkness: drum house, bell tower, sutra repositories? He passed a pagoda whose intricate spire pierced the sky, then emerged into a large open courtyard. At its far end, lanterns burned before the main worship hall, where Aoi waited, a still, silent figure dressed in black, holding a small, glowing paper lantern.

Sano raised a tentative hand in greeting, reluctant to speak again. Everything about this meeting—the late hour, isolated location, and eerie atmosphere—suggested a clandestine rendezvous. As he crossed the courtyard toward Aoi, the shrine's monuments loomed around him: treasuries, ceremonial stage, mausoleums. His footsteps made a forlorn, lonely tapping on the flagstones; the wind pressed at his back, urging him forward.

Aoi gracefully descended the steps to meet him. The wind swirled her dark garments around her. Wordlessly she bowed, then waited for him to speak.

"I've brought the things you asked for," Sano said. "A pouch that belonged to Kaibara Tōju. A lock of hair from another murdered man. And the label from the trophy."

His words sounded flat and banal in this strange setting. Beyond them, the worship hall was a glittering architectural fantasy of gilt pillars and lattices, carved wood and stone, undulating gabled roofs, and brilliantly colored ornamentation. Floral and geometric paintings decorated the walls. Fierce demons climbed the pillars; dragons writhed over the door; Chinese lions glared from the eaves; phoenixes poised, wings spread for flight, on the roof's pinnacle. The Tokugawa had exercised no restraint in honoring their ancestors. In contrast, Aoi, with her dark hair and clothes and pale skin, had the stark drama of a black and white painting.

"Come with me," she said.

Her husky voice sent a shivery warmth vibrating through Sano. Intrigued, he followed Aoi out of the courtyard and into the woods. There her lantern barely pierced the darkness. Sano groped his way past trees, stumbling over stones as he hurried to match her swift, sure pace.

They stopped at a place where overhanging boughs made a natural shelter from the wind, but the night seemed even colder, as if the pines exuded a resinous chill. The sudden silence made Sano's ears ring. Aoi raised her lantern, and in its glow, Sano saw that they were in a sort of woodland shrine—a circular clearing carpeted with pine needles, with an altar in the middle and, at one edge, the moss-covered statue of a deity he couldn't identify.

Aoi knelt before the altar and used her lantern to light the candles and incense burners arranged in a circle there. Sano knelt opposite her. His curiosity about this enigmatic woman increased.

"Have you always lived at the castle?" he asked.

"Not always, master." In the candlelight, Aoi's skin glowed; he had an urge to feel its smoothness. The smoke from the incense, sweet and musky, veiled her in its thin tendrils.

Sano tried again. "How long have you tended the shrine?"

"Six years, master. Before that, I was a palace servant."

Was she trying to discourage his interest by reminding him of her low status? "Where are you from?" Sano persisted, guessing from the slow tempo of her speech that she was not an Edo native.

Having finished preparing the altar, Aoi folded her hands in her lap. "Iga Province, master." An unyielding quality in her polite manner brooked no further questions. "If you would please place the relics there."

Sano removed the pouch, the paper-wrapped hair, and the label from under his sash and laid them in the center of the circle as she'd indicated. The murder investigation was first priority now. Breaking through her reserve was a challenge he looked forward to meeting later.

Gazing down at the relics, Aoi sat motionless except for the deep breaths that expanded and contracted her chest. Her eyes focused inward, and her respiration gradually slowed until it seemed to cease altogether. She was apparently entering a trance state, similar to one of deep meditation. Time passed. Sano waited, himself entranced by the flickering candles, smoking incense, and Aoi's deathlike immobility. On the edge of his aware-

ness, he heard the wind whistling outside the shrine, and the barking of a dog somewhere down the hill. The cold permeated his
bones. A current of apprehension shot through him, and he felt
an almost irresistible impulse to touch Aoi and make sure she was
still alive.

Then her mouth opened, emitting a moan that wandered the
range from high notes to low, and back again. Sano stared, trans-
fixed by the ritual's powerful erotic quality. Aoi's moist lips, her
moans, the quickening rise and fall of her bosom, and the sheen
of sweat on her face all made him think of a woman succumbing
to sexual pleasure. He could even see her nipples, large and
erect, pressing through her kimono. Warm blood pooled in his
loins. His overwhelming desire to touch her increased. Then she
spoke.

". . . my son. Promise . . ."

The voice was that of an old man, weak and cracked with mortal sickness. Aoi's features took on a startlingly familiar cast. Sano
sat forward so quickly that he almost lost his balance and fell onto
the altar. Shock banished arousal as he recognized his father's
voice and visage.

"Be the living embodiment of Bushido. . . ."

Even as Sano reeled with the blow of hearing his father speak
through Aoi, his mind cast about for a rational explanation. At his
house, she must have noticed his father's memorial altar and
known of his recent bereavement. But how could she evoke the
essence of someone she'd never met, and speak words that he
alone had heard? All doubts about her mystical abilities vanished
in a flood of pure joy.

"Father," he whispered, eagerly reaching out to grasp his sire's
elusive, longed-for presence.

To his intense disappointment, Aoi's face became her own
again, and she lapsed back into the wordless moaning. She un-
clasped her hands and picked up Kaibara's pouch. Her eyelids
lowered. Pressing the pouch between her palms, she rubbed the
fabric against her nose and mouth and put her tongue to the dangling *netsuke,* as if physically extracting Kaibara's spirit from his
belongings. She lowered the pouch to her lap and spoke in a high,
querulous whine.

"In the last year of my life, I was plagued by great sorrow. Death came as a welcome release. Why must you now disturb my well-earned sleep?"

"I—I want to know who killed you," Sano faltered, startled by the fresh shock of having the spirit address him directly. And in a voice he could easily attribute to the frail, elderly Kaibara, whose remains he'd viewed in the morgue.

A long, tremulous sigh. "Why does it matter? What is done is done."

"Your murderer must be prevented from killing again," Sano said. "Please, Kaibara-*san,* tell me what happened last night. Did you see your killer?"

A long pause. Sano noticed with amazement that Aoi had assumed Kaibara's characteristics. Her body shrank into itself, her jaw slackened, her eyes dimmed. And were those new wrinkles creasing her face and neck? The candles sputtered. The incense smoke now filled the hollow with a thick, pungent haze that made Sano dizzy and his eyes water. The sound of more dogs barking echoed up and down the hill. Then Kaibara's voice issued again from Aoi's mouth:

"It was dark. Foggy. I could not see his face. But he was very tall. And he walked with a limp . . ."

"Which leg?" Sano demanded.

". . . the right . . ." As Kaibara's voice faded, the old-man cast fell away from Aoi, leaving her face blank of all personality.

"Kaibara!" Sano resisted his impulse to clutch at the departing spirit. "Come back!"

With the slow, deliberate movements of a priest during a sacred ceremony, Aoi replaced the pouch on the altar. She unfolded the paper from around the dead *eta*'s lock of hair, which she rubbed between her finger and thumb, then cupped in both palms and sniffed. Recovering from the disappointment of losing contact with Kaibara, Sano waited tensely for the *eta*'s spirit to appear.

Aoi's facial muscles tightened; her eyes darted from side to side with a feral wariness. Her shoulders hunched, and she held her arms close to her sides, hands clasped to her bosom. Sano gasped as he recognized the characteristic cringing posture of the *eta*.

A sudden gust of wind stirred the pine boughs overhead. The

candles flickered; one of them went out in a hiss of singed wax. Aoi's lips moved.

". . . sorry . . . please, master, I don't mean to offend you. Forgive me!" This time the voice was hoarse, guttural, and laced with fear. Aoi bobbed a series of rapid bows, while her gaze flitted from Sano's face to the swords at his waist.

"I won't hurt you," Sano hastened to assure the spirit. "I just want you to tell me who killed you."

"Samurai. Don't know his name."

"What did he look like? Describe him."

Aoi's eyes blurred in fearful remembrance. "Big. Strong. Bad leg. And he was scarred."

"A scar? Where?" That the Bundori Killer had a visible identifying mark seemed too good to be true.

She shook her head impatiently. "Not just one. All over. Face. Hands." Her mouth worked as the inarticulate spirit struggled to say what he meant.

Sano hazarded a guess: "He was scarred from the pox?"

A vigorous nod; a look of relief in the fearful eyes.

"What else? Tell me more."

But the spirit lapsed into an incoherent muttering that soon faded. Aoi shed the eta's feral guise and subservient posture. Sano watched with mounting excitement as she replaced the hair on the altar and picked up the label. Would he now learn the tall, lame, pockmarked samurai's identity?

Aoi fingered the label, and a deep shudder convulsed her body. Fixing her stricken gaze on some distant scene visible only to her, she whispered, "The soldiers are on the march again. Soon they will arrive at the destined battle site. He will draw his sword. And then—"

With a shriek, she hurled the label away from her. The paper swirled in brief flight, then drifted downward. Sano thrust his hand out to snatch it away from the candle flames.

"Look out!" he shouted as concern for the evidence overcame his fear of disrupting the ritual.

In a fumbling movement devoid of her customary grace, Aoi stood. Her knees upset the altar, scattering candles and incense burners across the clearing. Her groping hands knocked Sano's away before he could rescue the label or other relics.

"What do you think you're doing?" he demanded, angry as well as confused.

"Fire, fire!" she cried. Her trance had dissolved; her voice was clear and sharp, her face alert and filled with dismay.

Sano looked down and saw the fallen candles smoldering in the dried pine needles that covered the earth. He jumped up and started to stamp out the fires. In her haste to help, Aoi darted into his path. They collided full tilt, face to face, with a stunning crash. Instinctively Sano threw his arms around her to keep them both from falling.

He felt his insides turn to molten heat. Her body was warm, firm, and pliant, her breasts soft against his chest. His breath caught as a surge of desire hardened his manhood and intoxicated his senses. For the long moment during which he held her, he read in her wide eyes, parted lips, and rapid breathing a need that matched his own.

Then, with a quick wrench of her body, she broke his embrace. She knelt before the upset altar, face averted, arms hugging herself.

Sano finished extinguishing the fires. He righted the altar and reassembled the candles and burners on it, along with the label—charred on one end; the hair—a few strands missing; and the pouch. As he resumed his place, he found himself shaking. His heart thudded; his body still clamored with desire. The rapid succession of strong emotions he'd just experienced—the shock of hearing his father's voice, elation at getting the killer's description, and the excitement of the ritual's abrupt, chaotic end—had left him totally drained and exhausted.

"Are you all right?" he asked Aoi.

Without looking at him, she nodded.

"What happened?"

Now, when she faced him, he saw that although her face was paler, she'd regained her composure. "Forgive me for behaving so badly. Sometimes objects speak to me of the places they've been. The people who have touched them. The emotions they've absorbed. That paper made me see and feel disturbing things."

Judging from her cool manner, they might never have touched. "You talked about soldiers marching, and someone drawing a sword," Sano said, trying to vanquish his lingering arousal by concentrating on business. "Was it the Bundori Killer?"

Aoi shook her head. "I don't know. But I sensed a great battle lust in him."

A new thought distracted Sano from his body's need. "Maybe the killer considers the murders acts of war, like the shogun does," he mused. "But was Kaibara his enemy, or Araki Yojiemon?" The battle scenario fit Araki's time better than the present. "And if it was Kaibara, why not put that name on the label?"

"Maybe he wanted them both dead."

Sano realized that Aoi didn't know who Araki was. "General Araki died at least a hundred years ago," he explained.

"Then perhaps the killer connected the two men in his mind. And attacked the living one."

"It's a thought," Sano admitted, intrigued by her suggestion. The connection between Araki and Kaibara bore looking into when he questioned Kaibara's family tomorrow. "But then why kill the man whose hair I brought you? He was an *eta,* with no conceivable link to two high-ranking samurai."

Interest animated Aoi's features as she rose promptly to the challenge. "And who better than an *eta* for a samurai to kill when he wants to test a sword or practice his technique?"

"Of course!" Sano regarded her with growing admiration. "The killer wanted to murder Kaibara, but he'd never taken a man's head or prepared a trophy. So he practiced on a victim for whose murder he would never be punished, if caught."

Discovery of Aoi's perceptive intelligence increased Sano's attraction to this mystic whose shocking, erotic ritual had yielded valuable clues. And her shining eyes, the eager forward tilt of her body, reflected her enjoyment of their collaboration. Fleetingly Sano thought of his prospective bride, about whose character and appearance he knew nothing. Then he forgot her as he sought a way to further his relationship with Aoi.

"Let's meet again tomorrow night," he said, enthusiastic in his pleasure at having a beautiful partner with whom to discuss his work. "I think your ideas will help me understand and catch the killer."

But strangely, his enthusiasm caused Aoi to withdraw into her former calm, aloof stillness. "As you wish," she said remotely. She scooped up the pouch, lock of hair, and label, and held them out to him, bowing.

It was a dismissal. She wanted him gone. Though Sano knew that a man of his position could order her to do anything he wanted, he would honor her wish. He couldn't think of her as an inferior to be used at will. She'd already given him more than he'd expected: insight into the killer's motives; a description of the man for whom to search. Reaching out, he accepted the relics.

Their hands touched. Hers was warm despite the cold night. From the faint blush that colored her cheeks, Sano suspected that the brief contact had stirred her desire too. But although he turned to look back at her as he left the clearing, she wouldn't return his gaze.

Perhaps tomorrow he would begin to know her—and to draw from her the same response she awakened in him.

A low-lying fog veiled the city when Sano rode out through the castle's western gate early the next morning. Ahead, he could discern only the rooftops of the *banchō*. The district where the Kaibara clan and other Tokugawa *hatamoto* lived looked like a village in a painting, floating on a lake of mist against hills softened by white haze.

This pleasant impression quickly faded as he entered the *banchō*. Hundreds of small, ramshackle *yashiki* stood crammed together, each estate surrounded by a live bamboo fence. Thatched houses rose above the leafy stalks. The smells of horse dung and sewage permeated the air. These Tokugawa vassals, however long and faithfully they'd served their lord, were by no means Edo's richest citizens. Rising prices and the falling value of their stipends kept them poor compared with their landed superiors and the affluent merchant class. Signs of poverty abounded: half-timbered walls bare of whitewash or decoration; plain, roofless wooden gates, each with a single shack for a guardhouse; the simple cotton garments and unadorned leather armor tunics of the samurai who occupied the guardhouses and thronged streets barely wide enough for four men to walk side by side.

Sano stopped a passing samurai and asked the way to Kaibara's *yashiki*. But as he edged his horse through the crowds and down bumpy dirt roads, he quickly lost all sense of direction in the *banchō's* tangled maze. Sano remembered an old saying: "One born in the *banchō* might yet not know his way around it." Finally, after asking directions again and losing his way several more times, he arrived at the Kaibara estate. There, outside a gate hung with black mourning drapery, waited Hirata. His wide, suntanned face looked ruddy with health, and a boyish eagerness lit his eyes at the sight of Sano.

After they'd exchanged greetings, Sano said, "Find out if anyone saw Kaibara leave the *banchō* the night he was murdered, or saw anyone following him. Particularly a large, pockmarked samurai with a lame right leg."

As he explained how he'd gotten the suspect's description, last night's events seemed bizarre and dreamlike. But his belief in Aoi's powers remained. As the young *doshin* set off to do his bidding, Sano glanced eastward at the castle. Mist still clung to its foundations, as if the spirits evoked in the ritual hadn't yet ceased haunting it. Sano wondered what Aoi was doing now, and whether her sleep, like his, had been disturbed by the experience they'd shared . . .

Banishing this irrelevant thought, he dismounted, approached the Kaibara guardhouse, and identified himself to the elderly sentry posted there. "I must speak to Kaibara's family."

"Yes, master." The guard shuffled toward the gate.

Sano wondered how a man so feeble could be charged with protecting his master's estate. "Were you on duty the night before last?" he asked.

The guard opened the gate and stood aside for Sano to enter. "No," he said sadly, hanging his head. "If I had been, I would have kept my master inside and prevented his death."

This answer perplexed Sano. It sounded as though the gate had been unguarded—surely an unusual occurrence in the *banchō,* and one that eliminated a possible witness to Kaibara's departure. And why should a retainer think it necessary to make sure his master didn't leave home?

"I want to speak to the night sentry," Sano said. "But first, tell me why you didn't want Kaibara to go out."

Shame filled the man's eyes, and Sano understood: No one had been on duty, and the loyal retainer didn't want to expose the private affairs of the Kaibara family.

"That will be all, thank you," Sano said, leaving his horse with the guard and entering the gate. Perhaps the answers to these questions, and others, lay inside the house.

He got an inkling of the truth when he entered the bare, deserted courtyard. The house was fairly large, with a wide veranda and generous entry porch. But cracks veined the walls; broken window lattices rattled in the breeze; weeds sprouted up through the flagstones of the path. No servant came out to greet him, or announce his arrival to the Kaibara, whose failure to maintain their property suggested financial hardship, which would also explain why they lacked men to staff and protect the house.

Once inside, Sano had to pause and compose himself after removing his shoes in the entryway. The smell of incense, the sound of a woman weeping, the hollow drumbeats, the monotonous chanting, and the house's shuttered gloom all reminded him of his father's funeral vigil. He steeled himself to enter the main room and observe its occupants with professional detachment.

An orange-robed priest chanted Buddhist scriptures, punctuating them with strokes upon a gourd-shaped wooden drum. Before him stood the coffin—an upright wooden box painted white. A low altar held a funeral tablet bearing Kaibara's name, a vase of flowers, burning incense sticks and candles, and offerings of rice, fruit, and sake. Although Sano had expected to see many mourners, only two women, one white-haired and elderly, the other about fifty, knelt near the priest. Both wore white mourning robes; the younger one wept as she clutched the stoic older woman's hand. They looked up at the sound of Sano's footsteps, while the priest continued chanting and drumming.

Sano introduced himself, adding, "I'm sorry to disturb you at such a time, but since the shogun has charged me with the task of capturing Kaibara-*san*'s killer, I must ask you a few questions."

The room's hushed emptiness and musty odor saddened him. Cobwebs laced the ceiling corners, revealing the same neglect as the house's exterior. Sano sensed a desolation that predated the family's recent tragedy.

"You were his wife?" he asked the older woman, who nodded. She had a deeply lined face with downturned eyes and mouth, and a hairline so high that her knotted white hair resembled a samurai's, shaven crown and all.

"Whatever you wish to know, I will tell you if I can," she said. Her voice had the deep, sexless quality of old age. To the other woman, evidently her maid, she said, "Fetch our honored guest some tea." Then she fell silent, hands folded in dignified resignation.

Sano knelt opposite her and waited until the maid had placed a tray of tea and cakes before him and withdrawn. The memory of his father's funeral made it hard for him to swallow, but he managed a few polite bites and sips. Then he said, quietly, so as not to interrupt the rites, "I've brought you something that belonged to your husband."

From under his sash, he took Kaibara's pouch and gave it to the widow. "Have you any idea who could have wanted to kill him?"

Slowly she shook her head, stroking the worn pouch. "No. You see, my husband had been dead for a long time already."

Taken aback, Sano said, "I don't understand."

"Little by little, with each passing day, my husband's spirit had been leaving his body. He lost his memory. Sometimes he didn't recognize the servants, our friends, or even me." The widow gave a barely audible sigh. "He cried and babbled like a child, and I had to feed and wash and dress him as if he were one. When he went outside, he got lost. Sometimes the police brought him back. We tried to keep him inside . . ."

Her gaze wandered toward the door, and Sano now understood the guard's words. Senility had destroyed Kaibara's mind, leaving behind only a failing body: a common tragedy—

"I must apologize for receiving you so poorly," the widow added. "In recent years, we've discharged most of our servants and retainers."

—and one that had evidently brought such shame to the family that they had accepted reduced living conditions rather than expose it to the eyes of others. No wonder they had only one guard, not enough staff to tend the house, and few mourners at Kaibara's funeral.

"So you see, there was no reason for anyone to hate my husband enough to kill him. But until last year, he still had days when he was himself again. Then our only son died."

She looked toward the room's far end, where Sano saw another memorial altar. His skin rippled as he remembered the words that the spirit had spoken through Aoi. Was the son's death the "great sorrow" that had plagued Kaibara?

The widow closed her eyes and clamped her mouth into a tight line, as if the memory of her son's death had joined with the fresh shock of her husband's to inflict unbearable pain. She clutched the pouch, making no sound, but the priest's mournful chanting, and the sound of the maid weeping in the other room, echoed her grief. Hating to cause her more anguish, Sano asked gently, "What was your husband doing in the pharmacists' district the night he died?"

This brought tears coursing down her cheeks. Then she opened her eyes, dried them with her sleeve, and composed herself. "Our son served as a captain in the city's fire brigade, as did my husband in his day. Last year there was a terrible fire in Nihonbashi."

Sano remembered that some two hundred people had died in the blaze.

"Our son was killed when a burning house collapsed on him. Afterward, my husband returned again and again to the site. We tried to keep him home, but he always managed to sneak out." Her voice broke as she added, "In the end, his sly escapes were the only sign that he could still think."

Now Sano knew why Kaibara had gone to Nihonbashi, and why he'd been such easy prey for the killer. But the widow had failed to identify anyone with a motive for the murder.

"I'd like to speak with the other members of your family," he said. A needy relative might have killed in hopes of inheriting Kaibara's meager property, and arranged the crime so as to conceal the motive behind it.

A spasm of pain stiffened the widow's features. "There are no other family members. Most of them died in the Great Fire of Meireki. Others have died of fever, in accidents. And with our son's death, my husband was the last of his clan."

"I'm sorry." Sano allowed a moment of silence to lapse in respect for a venerable family line now ended. He was beginning to believe that the Bundori Killer had chosen his victims out of pure convenience. How tragic for the Kaibara clan! And how much harder for Sano to find the killer.

The widow was literally sagging under the weight of her grief, and Sano concluded the interview with a last question. "Does the name Araki Yojiemon mean anything to you?"

He didn't expect the name to have any connection with the Kaibara, or the old woman to possess a knowledge of history. So he was surprised when she said, "Why, yes. Araki Yojiemon was my husband's great-grandfather. He was head of the clan and served Tokugawa Ieyasu during the wars."

As a history scholar, Sano knew that tracing samurai lineages was complicated because members of his class frequently changed their names for various reasons: Perhaps Araki's son had done so to celebrate a rise in status, to mark an important family event, or because a more auspicious set of syllables might bring good luck. And the new names often bore little similarity to the originals.

"The family name was changed to Kaibara after the Battle of Sekigahara, when Ieyasu became shogun and the clan came to Edo with him," the widow explained, confirming Sano's guess. "But what has this to do with my husband's murder?"

That Sano couldn't answer, but he intended to find out. He thanked the widow for her help, repeated his condolences, and bid her farewell.

Out in the street again, he mounted his horse, glad to leave the gloomy estate. He breathed deeply, willing away grief's debilitating onslaught. Once more he prayed to his father's spirit, seeking the wisdom to understand the new mysteries he'd uncovered. Again the spirit remained silent. He slapped the reins and started down the street in search of Hirata.

He didn't have to look far. When he turned a corner, he saw Hirata running toward him, shouting and waving. Hard on his heels followed what looked like half the samurai in the *banchō*.

"*Sōsakan-sama!*" Hirata called. "There's been another murder! The Bundori Killer has struck again!"

10

The rouged, pigtailed, perfumed, and mounted head resting on the ground at Sano's feet had belonged to a man perhaps forty years of age. He had heavy jowls, thick, bristly eyebrows, a lumpy, large-pored nose, and the shaven crown of a samurai. His glazed eyes stared straight ahead, and his thick lips had parted to reveal broken teeth. Even in death his features reflected the shock he must have experienced when the killer attacked.

An hour's fast ride north out of the *banchō,* through the suburbs of Edo and the fields outside town, had brought Sano here to the Dike of Japan, a long, willow-shaded causeway that ran west from the Sumida River, paralleling the San'ya Canal, to the Yoshiwara pleasure quarter. News of the murder had spread along it via the men returning home to Edo after a night of revelry. Now, as Sano contemplated the trophy that the Bundori Killer had brazenly placed in the middle of the road, the bitter taste of guilt eclipsed his horror. There had been three murders, despite the extra security precautions he'd instituted. While no one could reasonably fault him for not solving the case in such a short time, or for not knowing where the killer would strike next, he berated himself for the poor service he'd rendered the shogun, and for costing this unknown man his life.

Deploring his naive assumption that his investigation would pose little risk to others, he addressed the man beside him: a member of Yoshiwara's civilian security force, who'd greeted him upon his arrival at the scene. "Who is he?" Sano asked, gesturing to the head.

"I don't know, *sōsakan-sama*." The officer, dressed in a short cotton kimono and trousers, was a burly peasant who wore a wooden club at his waist. Unlike the Edo police, he'd been obviously glad to cooperate. Breaking up fights and ejecting rowdy drunks from the quarter comprised most of the Yoshiwara force's work. They weren't trained to handle any murders except the uncomplicated sort that resulted from street brawls and disputes over women. "But I've learned that he visited the Great Joy last night."

The Great Joy was one of the quarter's largest pleasure houses. "Who discovered the remains?" Sano asked, fearing that a valuable witness might have escaped before his arrival.

To his relief, the officer said, "A visiting samurai found the head; he's down the road. He alerted the guards at the gate, who fetched us." The officer indicated himself, and his four colleagues who stood in a circle around Sano and the trophy, holding off the growing crowd of spectators. "We found the body."

Sano directed his attention to the surrounding scene. At this hour of the morning, the road to Yoshiwara was well traveled in both directions. Samurai and commoners moved toward the pleasure quarter, while last night's revelers still straggled homeward. To the southeast, beyond the fringe of willows at Sano's right where his horse stood, the San'ya Canal gleamed in the sunlight. Wild geese flew over the plowed but yet unplanted and unflooded rice fields on the opposite sides of the canal and the elevated dike where Sano stood. Ahead, tea stands lined the approach to Yoshiwara's gate. Beyond them rose the walls and rooftops of the pleasure quarter.

"Has anyone reported seeing the murder?" Sano asked.

"No, *sōsakan-sama*."

Anticipating another long search for witnesses, Sano wished he could have brought Hirata. But he'd left the young *doshin* to continue the as yet fruitless search for the suspect along the route leading from the *banchō* to the pharmacists' street. More than ever Sano felt the lack of manpower. A curse upon Chamberlain Yanagisawa!

"I'll talk to the man who discovered the head," he told the officer, "and then you can show me the body."

First, however, he bent to remove the label from the trophy's pigtail, and saw characters inked in the same hand as those from the one on Kaibara's head. " 'Endō Munetsugu,' " he read, disconcerted.

This new development weakened his theory that the killer bore a grudge against the Kaibara clan. Like Araki, Endō Munetsugu had lived during the Sengoku Jidai and fought under Oda Nobunaga. But as far as Sano knew, the Endō and Araki-Kaibara families were not related. Nor had they owed allegiance to the same lord—the Endō had served not Tokugawa Ieyasu, but Toyotomi Hideyoshi, the general who had succeeded to power after Oda's death. Despair replaced hope as Sano saw the scope of his case widen yet again. Another historical angle to complicate the investigation! Was the dead man Endō Munetsugu's descendant? Was the killer obsessed with samurai from the past, and if so, why?

Sano tucked the label in his sash for later contemplation. Then, leading his horse, he accompanied the officers along the causeway toward Yoshiwara. Soon they reached the tea stands, each of which displayed a red lantern bearing the name of a pleasure house. There customers waited in line to buy sake or arrange liaisons with their favorite courtesans. Against the rear wall of the last stand on the canal side, a figure slumped dejectedly. Sano left his horse in the officers' care and headed toward the samurai, who roused at his approach.

Dressed at the height of dandified fashion for a trip to Yoshiwara, he wore a white silk kimono and trousers, white surcoat, shoes, and wide-brimmed hat, and ivory-hilted swords. Beside him stood his white horse. But these affectations failed to evoke the intended glamour. The samurai looked much the worse for his experience.

"Ah, His Excellency's *sōsakan-sama*." Slurring his words, he lifted a glum face to Sano. "It's about time. I've been waiting for hours."

In his late twenties, he had a round, bleary-eyed face flushed by drink. He sat low on his spine with his legs sprawled awkwardly before him. A brown stain covered the front of his kimono; he'd evidently vomited on himself. Despite his sad condition, he held a sake decanter.

"Your name?" Sano asked.

"Nishimori Saburō. I serve Lord Kuroda." Nishimori attempted to sit upright, then moaned, clutched his stomach, and bobbed his head in lieu of bowing. "Forgive me, but I've had the most terrible time. That head . . ."

Shakily he gulped from the decanter, shuddered, coughed, and wiped his lips on his sleeve. "Have some?" he said, offering the decanter to Sano.

"No, thank you." Sano winced inwardly at the stench of liquor and vomit. "Tell me how you found the head."

Nishimori's queasy expression indicated his reluctance. Then his eyes focused on the Tokugawa crest on Sano's garments. "Oh, all right. Left Yoshiwara at dawn, first one out the gate. Had to get back to my post, and besides, my time was up." There was a two-day limit on customers' stays in Yoshiwara. "Glad to go, really. What money I didn't spend on those overpriced women, I lost gambling. Then I get out here, and I find a . . . Now I ask you: Could there be a worse way to end what was supposed to be a good time?" His wet mouth pouted.

"Did you recognize the man?" Sano asked patiently.

"Can't say as I did. One meets so many people, but not looking like that."

"Did you see anyone nearby when you found the head?"

Nishimori closed his eyes. Saliva dribbled down his chin. "No."

Sano deduced that the killer must have committed the murder and placed the *bundori* last night, after the Yoshiwara gates had closed. But what had the victim been doing on the road? Had the killer somehow lured him to his death? And from where had the killer come? Along the causeway from Edo, from a nearby village, or from Yoshiwara itself? Where had he prepared the *bundori?*

"I go looking for fun," Nishimori complained, "and look what happens. I'm broke. Sick. A witness in a murder case." With the decanter, he gestured toward Yoshiwara. "And they call that place lucky," he said bitterly.

Sano pondered the allusion. Yoshiwara had originally been dubbed "reedy plain" for the land it occupied, but someone had changed the characters of the name to read "lucky plain," because men went there hoping for luck. Now Sano wondered whether mere bad luck had situated the victim in the wrong place at the wrong time as the killer roamed in search of prey. Or had he been the target of a planned ambush?

Dismissing Nishimori, Sano rejoined the security force and continued toward Yoshiwara. Beyond the tea stands, before the road sloped down toward the pleasure quarter, stood the famous "Primping Willow," where visitors stopped to groom themselves after their journey. Today the men gathered under the tree weren't dusting off their garments or smoothing their hair. Avidly they peered into the field below the embankment.

"Here, *sōsakan-sama*," the lead officer said. He skidded down the steep slope into the field.

Sano secured his horse to the willow and followed. Tall grass whipped his legs. At the foot of the embankment he saw two more Yoshiwara officers standing guard over a blanket-covered form. Ravens, crows, and gulls, drawn to the fresh kill, swooped and screeched overhead, periodically alighting nearby. In the field, rough dirt clods crumbled under his feet. He stopped a few paces from the body.

Blood darkened the surrounding earth. Sano could smell the cloying odors of death masking those of fertile earth and night soil. His stomach spasmed when the men, grim faces averted, gingerly peeled back the blanket.

The paunchy, headless man lay on his back, knees bent, arms splayed. Drying blood reddened his kimono, leggings, split-toed socks, and straw sandals. Already insects swarmed over the corpse; flies seethed thickly upon the severed neck. The unclean feeling of defilement stole over Sano. As he bent to examine the cut, he found relief in envisioning Dr. Ito's face, and in imagining his friend at his side.

"A clean and expert single slash," he said, "just like the last."

Wondering how the killer had lured the man off the road, he caught a whiff of liquor. Had the man been drunk, and thus, like Kaibara, unable to defend himself? Sano examined the rest of the body and found no other wounds. But two unexpected sights surprised him.

"Where are his swords?" he asked the officers. Had the killer taken them? Would their presence among a suspect's possessions eventually establish his guilt?

When the officers professed ignorance, Sano turned his attention to the strip of unwound loincloth protruding from the man's kimono. Then he understood. The victim had left the road to defecate; the killer had seized the opportunity to attack. This murder, too, had the look of a bizarre but meaningless act of violence against a handy victim. Yet Sano couldn't believe that the killer had picked Endō Munetsugu's name at random, from among those of all Japan's great war heroes. He doubted that Kaibara's relationship with Araki Yojiemon was pure coincidence, either. Now he must prove this, first by exploring the connection between the new victim and Endō.

Sano told the officers, "Send the remains to Edo Morgue." Perhaps Dr. Ito would find clues he'd missed. "Now I want to question everyone who was at the Great Joy last night."

As they followed the dike's final, zigzagging slope down toward Yoshiwara's gates, reluctance dragged at Sano. In the pleasure quarter, prostitution of all kinds was legal; food, drink, and other diversions—music, gambling, and others less innocuous—were available in abundance for a price. Men went to have fun. But for Sano, Yoshiwara had painful associations.

A recent night of violence and death had colored his view of the quarter, obliterating pleasant memories. When he approached the armored guards stationed at the gate's roofed and ornamented portals, their polite greetings couldn't make him forget their primary function: to make sure no *yūjo* escaped. Most of the women had been sold into prostitution by impoverished families, or sentenced to Yoshiwara as punishment for crimes. Many, mistreated by cruel masters, tried to flee through the gates disguised as servants or boys. Sano swallowed his distaste as he addressed the jailers who enforced women's misery.

"The man who was murdered last night. Did you see him leave?"

"How could we have missed him?" one said. "He was so angry he cursed us and kicked the gates." But neither knew the reason for his early departure, or his anger.

"Did anyone follow him?" Sano asked.

"No. He was the last one out before closing."

Asking the guards whether they'd seen a tall, lame, pockmarked samurai brought another negative reply. Sano saw the futility of trying to establish an individual's presence in the busy quarter, where many men—including priests, daimyo, and high-ranking *bakufu* officials—came in disguise. Some did so in compliance with the seldom-enforced law that forbade samurai to visit the pleasure quarter. Others merely wanted to preserve their privacy. One furtive, cloaked figure would have attracted little attention.

Sano thanked the guards and entered Naka-no-cho, the quarter's main street. It, too, had suffered an unhappy alteration in his eyes. The wooden buildings, once picturesque, now looked shabby and sad. The bold signs advertising the teahouses, shops, restaurants, and brothels failed to stir anticipation. The pleasure houses' empty barred windows, where the courtesans sat and solicited customers at night, seemed less like showcases for female beauty than like cages for trapped animals. The lushly flowering potted cherry trees that decorated the street only reminded Sano of the transience of pleasure, of life.

And the murder had cast a pall over the quarter. Visitors clustered in nervous groups along the street and in the teahouses, their customary boisterousness restrained. Servants slunk about their business. Samurai strode warily, hands on their sword hilts. All seemed loath to meet one another's gazes, or Sano's. A palpable aura of fear and mutual suspicion hovered in the air. Sano felt an increasing pressure to conclude the investigation quickly, before violence could erupt in this place where men's passions were already overstimulated by drink and sex.

The Great Joy, located on a side street off Naka-no-cho, was one of the most prestigious pleasure houses. The wooden window lattices, walls, and pillars looked freshly scrubbed and polished. Scarlet paint brightened the balcony railing. Curtains of the same shade, emblazoned with the house's white floral crest, hung over the entrance. As Sano and his escorts reached the house, these parted and a man dressed in gaudy silk garments stepped out.

"Greetings, *sōsakan-sama*," he said, bowing. Of some indeterminate age between forty and sixty, he had a fattish, pear-shaped body and a head to match. His knotted hair was streaked with gray. Yet his face, with its flat nose and cheeks, was unlined, perhaps preserved by the oiliness of his complexion. "I'm Uesugi, proprietor of the Great Joy."

His bow-shaped mouth seemed fixed in a permanent smile, but his shiny black eyes were like the counting beads on an abacus— hard, cold, calculating. "This murder is a very serious matter. However, let me assure you that the Great Joy has played no part in it."

To Sano, Uesugi's hasty disclaimer indicated the opposite. Was he hiding something? His uneasiness might result from a combination of class consciousness and concern for his business. While prominent Yoshiwara brothel owners held high places in peasant society, samurai snubbed them as money-worshipping flesh merchants. Uesugi wouldn't welcome an encounter that could embarrass him. And his establishment would suffer from association with the Bundori Murders.

"I've no reason to believe that the Great Joy is at fault," Sano said mildly, wanting to put Uesugi at ease and off guard. "I only want to know who the murdered man was, and with whom he spent the time up until his death. Can you tell me?"

As a pointed hint, he directed his gaze to the curtained entrance, then back to the proprietor.

Uesugi's smile remained, but his eyes jittered back and forth as he assessed his options. In a flat voice stripped of its former unctuousness, he said, "Is this really necessary?"

Sano didn't bother arguing. Uesugi was just stalling; he knew he had no right to refuse a request from a *bakufu* official. "Your house will get less bad publicity if we talk inside," Sano said, gesturing toward the swelling crowd of gawkers in the street.

Admitting defeat with a curt nod, Uesugi stood aside and lifted the curtain for Sano. On the right side of the entrance hall the watchman's bench stood vacant. Uesugi opened a door in the lattice partition to the left and ushered Sano into the main parlor, where two maids were sweeping the floor mats. This room, the scene of many gay parties of courtesans and clients at night, looked drab and unwelcoming by day. Uesugi's smile grew strained, though whether only because he disliked having a potential customer see the house in this unglamorous light, Sano couldn't tell. He let the proprietor show him into an office behind the parlor's wall mural.

"Please be seated," Uesugi said stiffly.

Kneeling behind the low desk, he called a servant and ordered tea, which came almost immediately. While they drank, Sano studied the room and its owner. The office was not unlike that of any prosperous shopkeeper. Sunlight filtered through a wall of paper windows, opposite which stood wooden cabinets and fireproof iron chests for storing records and money. Uesugi seemed even more ill at ease here than in the street; he sat unnaturally still, and his gaze wouldn't quite meet Sano's. Was he ashamed of the sordid side of his business—or fearful that he might incriminate himself?

"Who was the dead man?" Sano asked.

Uesugi glanced toward a ledger on the desk, which he'd probably consulted before Sano's arrival. "His name was Tōzawa Jigori, and he'd just arrived from Omi Province. When the watchman questioned him at the door, he admitted he was a *rōnin*. He engaged the company of a courtesan named Sparrow."

The proprietor delivered these facts willingly enough, but his face now shone with nervous sweat as well as oil. Sano, remembering his examination of the corpse, thought he knew why. Anger stirred within him.

"When did Tōzawa arrive?" he asked evenly.

Uesugi hesitated. "The day before yesterday."

"Then he was entitled to stay in Yoshiwara until this morning. Why did he leave last night?"

The disappearance of the proprietor's smile validated Sano's suspicions. "I was only following standard procedure," Uesugi huffed.

"You searched his possessions and found out that he hadn't enough money to pay his bill. So you threw him out. After confiscating his swords, of course." Sano's ingrained disgust for the venal merchant class fed his anger. "You know there's a killer on the loose, and you sent an unarmed man to his death!"

Uesugi folded his arms in defiance. "I would go bankrupt if I let customers get away without paying. And how was I to know he would die?"

Self-revulsion sickened Sano. He could despise Uesugi for valuing money over a man's life, but the blame belonged to him alone. His failure to catch the killer had doomed Tōzawa—as it might others. And part of his rage stemmed from the fact that Uesugi's statement had weakened the scenario he'd begun to construct.

There had been no robbery; the missing swords would never prove a suspect's guilt. The penniless Tōzawa could have fallen prey to a predator who didn't care—or even know—whom he killed. Furthermore, the likelihood of a connection between Kaibara and Tōzawa seemed minimal. Tōzawa was a lowly *ronin*, far beneath Kaibara's status. Sano doubted whether Tōzawa's family records would reveal a relationship between two men from such different backgrounds, though they might link the *ronin* to Endō Munetsugu. But Sano had far too much work in Edo to make a long research trip to Omi Province.

Then he saw a way to eke value from this interview, punish Uesugi, and protect Yoshiwara's guests.

"Give me Tōzawa's swords," he said.

"But, *sōsakan-sama*—"

"Now." He would take them to Aoi, who might be able to divine some clues from them—and whom he longed to see again.

Fury hardened Uesugi's eyes; his tongue rolled behind his compressed lips. Then he stood and opened a cabinet with an angry jerk that expressed his reluctance to part with valuable loot. From among at least twenty confiscated swords, he selected a pair and thrust them at Sano.

"Thank you," Sano said. "Also, you'll convey this order to your Board of Administrators." This governing body was composed of all the Yoshiwara pleasure house proprietors. "Until the Bundori Killer is caught, no swords will be confiscated as payment for debts. No guests will be forced to leave the quarter after dark. If you and your colleagues don't comply, you'll pay a large fine for each violation. Is that understood?"

"Yes, *sōsakan-sama*." Uesugi spoke politely enough, but his angry glance toward the door made clear his wish to throw Sano through it.

"Good. Now I'll speak to everyone in the house who was here last night, starting with the courtesan who entertained Tōzawa. As to those guests who've already left, give me their names."

"That's impossible!" Uesugi sputtered, his controlled courtesy shattered. "The privacy of the *yūjo* and guests—"

"Is more important than catching the killer? I don't think so."

In a rapid about-face, Uesugi's smile returned, and he conceded, "As you wish. I'll write out the names for you. Then I'll bring everyone to the parlor."

Sano realized that Uesugi planned to give him phony names and smuggle the clients out the back door. "Excuse me a moment," he said.

He walked to the front door and called to the security officers waiting in the street: "See that no one leaves this house." Returning to Uesugi, he picked up the ledger from the proprietor's desk and tucked it under his arm with Tōzawa's swords, then said, "Now I'll help you collect your employees and their clients."

His anger and frustration somewhat relieved by his exercise of authority, Sano accompanied the glowering proprietor on a tour of the Great Joy's private rooms. These occupied the rear ground floor and the entire upper level of the house, forming a square around the garden, with servants' quarters facing the alley. Sano covered every corridor, knocked on every door. Cries of surprise greeted his summons. Frantic scufflings followed. Doors slid open, and a disheveled parade of sleepy-eyed, hastily dressed, frightened men and women straggled toward the parlor.

In Uesugi's office, which he'd appropriated for his interviews, Sano beheld with surprise the woman who knelt opposite him. Sparrow, Tōzawa's companion of last night, was clearly one of the house's second-class courtesans, and hardly the delicate creature that her name suggested. Long past her prime, she'd lost whatever physical charms she'd once possessed. Her figure was heavy and shapeless under the blue and white cotton kimono, the skin beneath her eyes puffy. White strands dulled the hair piled sloppily on her head, and she had a double chin. The Great Joy certainly offered its clients a wide range of female attractions.

"You entertained Tōzawa last night and the night before?" he asked.

"Yes, master, that's right."

Smiling, Sparrow arranged her skirts around her like a hen settling on a nest. Sano suddenly understood the allure Sparrow held for men, and why Uesugi considered her well worth keeping. She exuded maternal kindness. A client in need of solace could pillow his head on that soft bosom, take comfort from that warm, reassuring voice and smile, and sleep like a child in those cushiony arms. All for the same high price as the wildest sex. Sano was glad to find Tōzawa's last companion such a woman.

"Did Tōzawa talk to you?" he asked her.

"Oh, my, yes. All my men do." A cozy chuckle jiggled her body. "Because I like to listen."

Just as he'd guessed. "What did Tōzawa talk about?"

"Losing his position when his lord fell upon hard times and had to let many retainers go. The hardships and shame he'd faced. How he hoped he could find work in Edo." Sadness clouded Sparrow's eyes: She, unlike the Great Joy's proprietor, sympathized with the unfortunate Tōzawa. "He annoyed everyone with his loud clowning because he needed to make himself feel big and important. And when Uesugi told him to leave, he was angry, because everyone knew he was poor—that's why he started a fight with Uesugi's watchman and threw a tray of food against the wall." She clucked her tongue. "Poor man."

That her years as a courtesan had given her insight into men, her next words further proved: "And yourself, *sōsakan-sama.* You're troubled, aren't you? Would you like to tell me about it?"

Her query seemed like neither nosy impertinence nor an avaricious ploy, but genuine concern. Sano could see how she'd coaxed Tōzawa's life story from him. She would make an excellent police detective—or spy.

"No, thank you," he said, smiling to take the edge off his refusal. "Did Tōzawa mention having any enemies in Edo?"

Sparrow's chin wobbled as she shook her head. "He said he was quite alone here."

So much for the idea that the murderer had killed Tōzawa out of hatred. "Did he speak of his family background?" Sano asked without much hope. He hardly expected Tōzawa to have recited his lineage, complete with the names of ancestors going back four generations.

Therefore a shock of excitement ran through him when Sparrow said, "Oh, yes. He said that the disgrace of losing his master was even harder to bear because his ancestor was a great war hero. But then most samurai claim such ancestors, don't they?" Her fond smile took the sting out of her implication that they were lying braggarts.

In Sparrow's statement, Sano found supporting evidence for his theory that joined Tōzawa with Endō Munetsugu and drew a parallel between this murder and Kaibara's. Had both men been killed because of the murderer's animosity toward their ancestors? Sano entertained the theory that the killer, stalking Tōzawa, had seen the commotion at the Great Joy, guessed its outcome, and waited on the dark causeway for his victim. Sano put forth his next question in a deliberately nonchalant voice, as if by pretending indifference he could elicit the desired answer.

"The ancestor Tōzawa mentioned. Was it Endō Munetsugu?"

"No, Tōzawa-*san* didn't tell me his ancestor's name."

Sano clung to the fragile hope that Endō could still be Tōzawa's unnamed family hero. But he had no evidence to confirm it, and even if a link between the two men existed, it shed no immediate light on the murderer's identity—or his motive for killing the un- related Kaibara.

Evidently perceiving Sano's frustration, Sparrow leaned forward and placed a consoling hand on his arm. "Don't be sad, *sōsakan- sama*. Tōzawa told me other important things about his ancestor. He said he was a brave general who won many battles for Lord Oda Nobunaga."

11

Sano finished his inquiries in Yoshiwara, where the Great Joy's other occupants didn't supply any useful information, and a search of the quarter turned up no one who'd seen the lame, pockmarked suspect. Back in Edo, he traced and questioned the men listed in Uesugi's ledger with no better results. Still, these dead ends failed to discourage Sano.

Sparrow's statement supported his belief that the *rōnin* Tōzawa was descended from Endō Munetsugu, as the *hatamoto* Kaibara was from Araki Yojiemon. Endō's and Araki's lords, Tokugawa Ieyasu and Toyotomi Hideyoshi, had been generals and allies under Oda Nobunaga. The historical records might reveal a link between past events and the murders. Sano decided to search the castle archives for this link before his meeting with Aoi.

As he traveled through Nihonbashi, the day's brightness faded from the sky, drawing after it a ragged quilt of clouds that gradually immersed Edo in a gray twilight. The strengthening wind swept dust through the streets, and an odd, silvery light edged the castle's ramparts and the peaks of the western hills. Sano, walking beside his horse to rest it after the day's hard travels, observed with dismay the effect that the murders were having upon the city.

Although full darkness wouldn't arrive for another hour, all the shops had closed for the night. The usual crowds of homebound merchants, artisans, and laborers had already vanished, leaving the streets in the possession of Edo's worst rabble. Idle young samurai and townsmen roved in trouble-seeking gangs. Itinerant *rōnin* and other drifters loitered. Many frightened citizens, loath to leave the safety of their homes while a killer roamed, peered out from barred windows. But others catered to the menacing traffic and encouraged the depravity that could turn excitement into violence. Sake sellers did a brisk business, as did seedy teahouses—the only establishments still open. Illegal prostitutes flirted from doorways. On every corner, newssellers hawked broadsheets.

"The Bundori Killer claims his third victim! Will you be next?" they shouted.

At an intersection, a crowd gathered around an old crone with long, tangled white hair who squatted before a pile of smoking incense sticks. Eyes shut, hands raised heavenward, she keened, "The invisible ghost walks among us. Tonight another man will die!"

As Sano had feared, the ghost story had spread, borne on a wave of contagious superstition that swelled unchecked because no other explanation for the murders had been found, and no human culprit identified. An evil carnival atmosphere pervaded the always unruly merchant quarter while Edo faced a threat the like of which it had never before experienced. Appalled, Sano tried to defuse the volatile situation before it turned dangerous.

"Give me those!" He snatched the broadsheets from a newsseller and skimmed the sensationalized accounts of Kaibara's, the *eta's,* and Tōzawa's murders, accompanied by lurid drawings of the trophies. Outraged, he tore them up and scattered the pieces. "You're scaring people. Go home!"

Cutting through the crowd to the elderly mystic, he seized her arm. "Show's over. Get out of here." To the bystanders, he shouted, "Go home, all of you!"

But more newssellers and seers continued to spread panic. The crowds ignored Sano's pleas. He looked around in bewilderment. Where were the police?

A *doshin* and two assistants strode past him. The *doshin* escorted a wild-eyed samurai whose hands were bound behind his back, while the assistants carried between them another, this one bleeding from a wound on his shoulder and moaning in pain.

Sano hurried after the police. "What happened?"

"These fellows each thought the other was the Bundori Killer, and they fought," the *doshin* explained. To the gawking crowds: "Let us through!"

Sano grew increasingly disturbed when he came to a gate, where he found two guards following his orders by questioning pedestrians. But at least three slipped by for every one halted.

"You're supposed to stop everyone," Sano reproached the guards. "Do you want to let the killer get past?"

The guards only shrugged helplessly. "There are too many people," one said, "and they won't answer questions or let us search them without a fight."

In more haste than ever, Sano continued toward the castle. The police could control the mounting hysteria for just so long. Only catching the killer would end it.

As he hurried along the streets, leading his horse, he passed through deserted districts where dark warehouses and buildings razed by recent fires offered a hostile environment for the loitering crowds. A new thought took shape in his mind. He hadn't yet felt personally endangered by the killer, and he shouldn't now. Unlike Tōzawa, he was armed. Unlike Kaibara, he was young, strong, and capable of self-defense. And he firmly believed, albeit without proof, that the killer chose his victims because of who they were or what they represented to him.

But fear is contagious. The killer preyed on samurai who traveled alone at night, as he did now. Madness often confers a peculiar strength—enough, perhaps, for the Bundori Killer to conquer the most formidable, forewarned adversary. Was he pursuing a new trophy tonight? Memory served up images of the bloody, mutilated bodies and gruesome trophies Sano had seen. The gathering darkness added danger. Rational thought couldn't keep dread from taking root and growing within Sano.

He quickened his pace, forcing the horse to trot beside him. Did he hear footsteps coming down the side street he'd just passed, or see a shadow lurking in the ruin of that burned building? Ahead, he saw lanterns burning above a gate and heard voices and laughter from the district beyond it. Mocking his cowardice, he nevertheless started to swing himself onto his horse's back—when a man leapt out of an alley and into his path, sword raised.

"Sano Ichirō, prepare to die!" he called.

Surprise tore a yell from Sano's throat. His horse neighed, rearing before he could fling his leg over the saddle. The reins ripped free of his hands. He fell backward, landing hard on the base of his spine. The shattering jolt drove his teeth together and forced the breath from his lungs. Pain shot through his back. His swords clattered against the ground. Through the ringing in his ears, he heard his horse's hoofbeats receding into the distance. He saw his attacker advancing upon him.

Sano lurched to his feet. Dizzy and disoriented, he trod on the hems of his trousers, and nearly fell again. Only his years of training and swift natural reflexes allowed him to right himself and draw his sword. Not waiting for his assailant to strike first, he launched a wild diagonal slice. His blade met his opponent's in a resounding clash of steel. He couldn't see the man's face, hidden under a wide hat, or distinguish any details about him other than his medium height, short kimono, and tight leggings.

"Who are you?" he shouted.

Without answering, his attacker thrust his weight against their crossed blades. Sano jumped backward, avoiding a wicked upslash that would have slit him from groin to throat. The wall of a shop halted him with a shuddering slam. Fresh pain burst in his already sore back. He parried another cut the instant before it reached his chest. Now his attacker's face was almost touching his as they both struggled to free their blades. He heard and smelled the other's sour breath. Pushing away from the wall, he managed to shove the man aside and regain clear maneuvering space in the street.

He circled the crouched figure at a distance of several paces, delaying the next clash. As a samurai, he'd been born to fight, to kill, to die by the sword. Battle lust rose in him, fiery and intoxicating, his learned response after thirty-one years of conditioning.

Yet he'd had enough senseless violence and bloodshed to last a lifetime. And he wanted to know who this man was, why he'd attacked.

The man launched a fresh assault, forcing Sano to return strike for strike. Steel rang upon steel; echoes reverberated from the walls. They dodged and pivoted, rushed and retreated. Sano's recently injured left arm ached whenever he wielded the sword with both hands. A part of his mind registered distant sounds, growing closer. Shouts. Running footsteps. Doors screeching open. On the periphery of his vision, he saw lights moving toward him. But instead of fleeing, his attacker persisted.

Sano's inner energy, called forth by combat, flowed from his spiritual center, empowering him. But that perfect coordination of conscious thought and unconscious action, which he'd rarely approached and achieved only once before, eluded him. Forced to rely heavily on learned expertise, he must win this fight in a rational, rather than a spiritual way. As he parried strikes, he noted his opponent's bold strokes, flamboyant style, and aggressive risk taking. Shrewdly he encouraged these faults. He adopted an awkward crouching posture. He limited his cuts to defensive parries, yielding the offensive to his attacker. He slowed his movements by a carefully calculated instant. With these ploys, he achieved his aim of making himself seem less competent than he was, but also endangered his life. The whistling blade shredded his left sleeve; a line of pain burned his forearm. A low slice grazed his shins and left the hem of his kimono flapping. He dodged just in time to avoid a cruel cut to the temple.

Gradually he became aware that a crowd had gathered in the street, which was now almost as bright as day. He could see his attacker's fierce grimace beneath the concealing hat. The spectators, bearing lanterns and torches, surrounded them in a ragged, shifting circle. Now his lunging, darting opponent moved against a changing background of figures: excited samurai, cheering and hooting; two gate sentries, mouths open in awe, spears dangling idle in their hands, one holding the reins of Sano's horse, which must have tried to run past them in its wild flight; men who looked like shopkeepers, armed with clubs and sticks, eyes alight with vicarious excitement. Fragments of talk impinged on Sano's concentration:

"What's going on, why are they fighting?"

"It's the Bundori Killer!"

"But they're men, not ghosts, and that one wears the shogun's crest."

"It's just a duel."

Although any of them would have readily defended their own lives, families, and property, no one moved to help Sano. They knew better than to interfere when samurai fought. One stray cut could kill anyone who got in the way.

Now Sano saw that his ruse was working. He felt his opponent gaining false confidence, growing even bolder. At last, Sano seized his chance.

He took a weak swipe at his opponent, who parried easily. Sano dropped to his left knee, pretending that the stroke had downed him. The man raised his sword high in both hands. His grimace widened into a grin as he prepared to deliver the final killing cut.

Sano moved with all the speed and strength he'd held in reserve. Before the deadly blade reached him, he lashed out his own sword in a short horizontal arc.

The man screamed in agony as the blade cut deep into his belly. Dropping his sword, he crumpled to his knees, hands pressed against the front of his kimono. Blood and entrails spilled from between his fingers. He raised his head to gaze in shocked disbelief at Sano.

Rising and backing away, Sano saw the life fade from the man's eyes, and animation leave his features. The attacker opened his mouth as if to cry out again. A gout of blood spurted forth. Then he fell sideways and lay motionless, hands still clasped over the fatal wound.

Sano cleaned his bloody sword on his soiled, tattered garments and sheathed it. With the heady heat of the battle still pulsing through his veins, he stared down at his conquered enemy while the silent crowd watched and waited. His heart's agitated thudding slowed and stabilized. His lungs stopped heaving; the cold night air dried the sweat on his face as he tried to make sense of what had happened.

Believing that the key to the murders lay in the samurai victims' connections with Araki Yojiemon and Endō Munetsugu, Sano didn't think he'd slain the Bundori Killer. His own lineage disqualified him as a target; he had no family ties to Araki or Endō. And how, without a concealing cloak or a container of some kind, could his assailant have transported a severed head past the strolling crowds, gate sentries, and police? If only he could have spared the man's life and learned his name, his motives.

Sano knelt beside the body and pushed aside the wicker hat that had fallen over its owner's face. In the glow of the spectators' lanterns he saw small, sharp features and teeth; the youngish, fox-like visage of a total stranger. Gingerly he rummaged inside the dead man's blood-soaked garments, seeking a clue to his identity. His probing fingers touched a hard lump secreted between the under and outer kimonos. He pulled out a cloth pouch whose contents clinked as he loosened the drawstring. Into his hand he poured ten gold *koban* and a folded paper.

The shiny coins drew gasps from the crowd. Sano unfolded the paper. A handful of dried melon seeds trickled out. As he read the characters inked on the paper, revelation chilled him.

"What's going on here?"

Looking up at the sound of a familiar voice, Sano recognized his old foe, the *doshin* Tsuda.

"You again." Tsuda's gaze moved from Sano to the corpse, then back; he scowled. "*Sōsakan-sama* or not, you're under arrest. I'm taking you to police headquarters."

Sano got to his feet. Wiping his bloody hands on his ruined kimono, he said, "I killed him in self-defense. But I'll be glad to go to headquarters with you. I want to report that someone has hired this assassin to murder me."

Police headquarters occupied a site on the southern edge of the Hibiya administrative district, as far from the city officials' mansions and the castle as possible because of the spiritual pollution its association with executions and death conferred. Sano, escorted by the surly Tsuda, gained entry from the guards at the gate and left his horse with them. Inside the walled courtyard lined with *doshin* barracks, he stared in surprise.

The yard, which should have been empty at the day's end, was jammed with people. A crowd of young samurai, hands tied behind their backs and minus their swords, squatted on the ground. All sported bruises and bloody gashes. They glowered at a gang of young peasants in similar condition. *Doshin* and assistants stood watch over them all.

"What's going on here?" Tsuda asked a colleague.

"Those samurai got drunk and looted a shop," the other *doshin* said. "The townsmen tried to stop them, and a riot started. Two people were trampled to death."

Tsuda bent an accusing stare upon Sano. "The Bundori Murders have caused a lot of trouble," he said. "But not as much as they will if they go on."

Sano could neither disagree nor dodge the blame. This most recent incident in the age-old conflict between samurai and townsmen could burgeon into the full-scale warfare that had troubled Edo's early history. He'd seen the heightening tension that the murders had wrought. He'd experienced the fear himself. And now he knew he must stop the Bundori Killer soon—for the sake of the whole city, as much as to save individual lives and fulfill his own vows.

Tsuda led him into the main building. In the reception room, a large space broken by square pillars hung with lanterns, more *doshin* and their noisy prisoners had gathered. An emaciated man with long, matted hair, dressed in rags, harangued the clerks seated at desks on a raised platform.

"I am the Bundori Killer," he shouted. Two guards tried to drag him away, but he repelled them with wild kicks and punches. "Take me to the magistrate at once!"

"And just what proof is there that you have in fact committed murder, Jihei?" the chief clerk asked wearily.

"Proof? I need no proof! I am the Bundori Killer! I weave magic spells to strike down evil men with an invisible sword and make trophies of their heads!"

He whirled in a manic dance, and a glimpse of his haggard face and sunken, red-rimmed eyes gave Sano pause. Was this man really the Bundori Killer, turning himself in? Incredulous, he glanced at Tsuda.

The *doshin* grimaced. "He's a simpleton who lives under the Nihonbashi Bridge. He's confessed to all the murders, even though we know he couldn't have killed Kaibara because he was in jail then."

That anyone, even a simpleton, should want to confess to a crime he hadn't committed escaped Sano's understanding. Clearly the Bundori Murders had loosed a current of madness that ran just beneath Edo's surface.

"Come on," Tsuda growled. He ushered Sano into a bare, windowless cell that Sano recognized from his police days as the place where samurai criminals—in deference to their status—were interrogated instead of at the jail. He lit the lamps, called two guards to watch the door, and left.

Sano waited. After at least two hours had passed, the door opened, and in walked *Yoriki* Hayashi.

"So, *sōsakan-sama*." Hayashi's lips twisted in a sarcastic smile. "You've decided to contribute to the troubles the murders are causing?"

Sano refused to take the bait. Arguing that he'd only been on the case for two days, or that he wasn't responsible for the mass hysteria the murders had provoked, would only invite more insinuations and preclude the cooperation he wanted from Hayashi.

"If you're concerned about the disturbances in the city, then you should help me catch the killer," Sano said, trying to sound calm and reasonable. "I want five more *doshin* to conduct inquiries, while their assistants perform door-to-door searches. And I want clerks to solicit and take statements from citizens who might have information about the murders."

Hayashi's response was a burst of derisive laughter. "You expect me to defy Chamberlain Yanagisawa's orders—for you? Never!" His bold sneer and aggressive posture bespoke the secure knowledge that his rude, unaccommodating behavior had Yanagisawa's sanction. "We the police can control the townspeople—but I doubt you will have as much success in finding the Bundori Killer."

Seeing the futility of trying to gain Hayashi's agreement in the face of Chamberlain Yanagisawa's opposition, Sano changed the subject.

"Tonight a man tried to kill me," he said, holding down the anger that had its roots in past injustices Hayashi had inflicted upon him. He described the attack, the sword fight, and his own necessary victory. "I found this on the body," he finished, handing over the dead man's pouch. "I believe he was a hired assassin, paid to keep me from investigating the murders."

Hayashi's slim hands lovingly counted the gold coins, but he snapped, "*Muimi*—nonsense! So the man died with money on him. You say there were no witnesses to the attack. Why should I believe that this . . . assassination attempt was not just a common street brawl?"

Sano took back the pouch and removed the paper that Hayashi had missed. "Because of this," he said, unfolding and proffering it.

Ripped from a larger sheet, it had characters inked on both sides. On one, the name "Junnosuke" and a date; on the other, the disjointed words:

caution	usual method
highly skilled at *kenjutsu*	as soon as possible
usual terms	

"The killer called me by name," Sano explained. "The letter is dated the day I took charge of the investigation. I don't claim to be highly skilled at swordsmanship, but anyone who attacks me should use caution. And the usual terms?" He pointed at the gold coins now resting in Hayashi's palm. "Partial payment upon accepting the job; the rest after my death."

"And why would an assassin retain a compromising document such as a letter ordering him to kill?" Hayashi asked skeptically. "Assuming that this is such a letter—which I cannot."

"He'd torn off the incriminating passages and used the rest to wrap some dried melon seeds."

For some reason, mention of the seeds caused Hayashi's derisive smile to slip, a muscle to twitch in his jaw.

"You know this man," Sano challenged. "Who is he?"

But Hayashi had himself under control now. "*Okashii*—ridiculous! He was probably someone you offended."

Sano had considered the possibility. He knew that many of his colleagues resented his promotion. Chamberlain Yanagisawa disliked him. But assassination was an extreme way to redress a minor grievance; its timing too coincidental. And Hayashi's involuntary reaction had strengthened his conviction.

"I want the police to find out who the assassin was, and who hired him," Sano said. "I believe it was the Bundori Killer, who considers me a threat, but doesn't want to attack me himself, either because of my skill or status, or because he's busy stalking other victims. If you investigate the attempt on my life as a new case, separate from the murders, you needn't fear going against Chamberlain Yanagisawa's orders."

"But you've given me insufficient justification for diverting the efforts of our already overworked police force to the task of investigating a common ruffian who is already dead." Hayashi's mocking manner returned. "You are nowhere near catching the killer; why should he deem you a threat? And remember: I have received no orders to assist you—with anything."

He replaced the coins and paper in the pouch, which he handed back to Sano. "And now, if you will excuse me, I have many criminals to attend to. As I would not, if you had caught the Bundori Killer by now."

He opened the door and told the guards, "Get a clerk to take the *sōsakan-sama*'s statement." To Sano: "Afterward, you will be free to go. But if you continue to engage in brawls, not even your status will protect you from the law. His Excellency does not condone such unseemly behavior."

As Sano sat down to wait, the new threat of the shogun's disapproval only compounded his problems. For despite the lack of solid proof, he was sure of several things.

His assailant wasn't just a common Edo street brawler, or a jealous rival. Someone wanted to stop his inquiry into the Bundori Murders. Probing the assassin's background could lead him to the killer. In the meantime, to pursue the investigation would mean risking his own life.

12

It was nearly midnight when Sano finished with the police, much too late for him to meet Aoi. When he reached the castle, he dispatched a messenger to the shrine with his apologies. But it wasn't too late to consult the Edo Castle historical archives. Chief Archivist Noguchi was an avid scholar who didn't confine his studies to the daytime. Often Sano and the other clerks had stayed up with him until dawn, copying, restoring, and poring over old scrolls by lamplight until their eyes ached.

Inside the castle's Official Quarter, Sano dismounted outside the mansion that housed the archives. The guards, accustomed to their master's irregular hours, took charge of Sano's horse and bowed him through the gate. At the door, a manservant met him and led him into the study.

"Sano-*san!*" Noguchi, working alone tonight, knelt in his alcove behind a desk cluttered with scrolls, burning oil lamps, and writing materials. "What brings you here?" When he saw Sano's condition, his frown lifted the wrinkles on his forehead into his shaven crown. "My friend, what has happened to you?"

Upon hearing about the attack, he left his desk and bustled in fretful circles around Sano, assessing the damage. "Oh, no. Oh my! Shall I call a doctor?"

"I'm fine," Sano assured Noguchi. His cuts stung, but they weren't serious, and he could tend them when he got home.

"Some refreshment, then."

"No, thank you, I've already eaten," Sano said, hoping the polite formula would discourage Noguchi from pressing hospitality on him. He hadn't eaten since noon, but he wanted to get to the purpose of his visit.

After assuring himself that Sano was indeed all right, Noguchi relaxed and said, "Well, at any rate, I'm glad you've come. I have good news for you. The Ueda have set a time and location for the *miai* between you and Miss Reiko."

"That's good," Sano said, trying to sound enthusiastic. His marriage negotiations had taken second place to the murders. "Thank you, Noguchi-*san*."

"It will be an afternoon meeting at the Kannei Temple the day after tomorrow," Noguchi continued. "If that is suitable to you and your honorable mother, of course."

When Sano pictured this first important acquaintance with his prospective bride, he found that his imagination had endowed the yet-unseen Ueda Reiko with Aoi's face and figure. Alarmed, he said, "Those arrangements will be fine," and reiterated his thanks. "Now I need your help with something else." Quickly he explained that he wanted information about Araki Yojiemon and Endō Munetsugu, and why.

Noguchi puffed his cheeks and blew them out. Then he said, "Sano-*san* . . . I've heard rumors that you have somehow earned Chamberlain Yanagisawa's disfavor. Of course, I expect that these rumors are unfounded." His blinking eyes begged Sano to agree.

Sano realized that word of his conflict with Yanagisawa had spread. The guards and servants present at his meeting with the shogun must have fed choice excerpts into the castle's rumor mill. Yanagisawa himself, seeking for whatever reason to blacken his reputation, had no doubt dropped disparaging remarks about him in all the right places. Sano knew his downfall had begun.

His face must have reflected his dismay, because Noguchi wailed, "Oh, no, the rumors are true, then! Sano-*san*, what have you done?"

"Nothing to offend Chamberlain Yanagisawa, at least that I can see." In his agitation, Sano began pacing the room. He succumbed to his impulse to confide in the only friend he had at Edo Castle. "But the chamberlain seems determined that I not catch the Bundori Killer."

Noguchi's head swiveled back and forth, following Sano's movements. "Then you must not," he said, as though this were the most reasonable course of action in the world.

Sano stopped in his tracks and stared in disbelief. When he began to protest, Noguchi cried, "No, wait! Allow me to explain!"

He hurried over and clutched Sano's arm. "You've not been in the shogun's service long enough to understand the way of things." Although they were alone, he glanced around furtively and lowered his voice to a whisper. "His Excellency's condition is on the decline. He grows weaker and more self-indulgent with each passing year. Someday soon he will abandon the practice of government and devote himself entirely to the theater, Confucianism, religion, and boys, leaving Yanagisawa to rule the land."

Sano pulled free of Noguchi's grasp and went to stand by the window. Arms folded, he stared at the opaque paper panes. "Tokugawa Tsunayoshi is still our lord, no matter what his character," he said, although having his own suspicions about the shogun confirmed dealt him a severe blow. For what future had he if abandoned to Yanagisawa's mercy? "The shogun wants the killer caught. I can't disobey his orders. And besides, this might be my only chance to distinguish myself and to make a name for my family."

Back and forth he paced, on a path that led nowhere, as did any course that involved opposing Chamberlain Yanagisawa.

Noguchi followed him like a small, persistent shadow. "My friend, what you don't understand is that if you defy Yanagisawa, you will not even keep your position, let alone distinguish yourself in it." He paused for breath, then said, "Saigo Kazuo, Miyagi Kojirō, and Fusei Matsugae. You have heard of these men?"

"Yes. They were all His Excellency's advisers when he became shogun ten years ago."

"They *were*. Each had considerable influence with His Excellency, but lost it when Yanagisawa rose to power. Saigo ended his days as a highway inspector in the far north."

Noguchi stopped trying to keep up with Sano, but his loud whisper followed, irritating as a mosquito's buzz. "Miyagi supposedly died of a fever. But many say Yanagisawa ordered his murder.

"And Fusei. Officially he committed *seppuku* because he was caught embezzling funds from the treasury. What really happened is that after much harassment by Yanagisawa, he went mad and drew his sword on Yanagisawa in the council chamber. He claimed that his dead mother's spirit told him to do it."

Noguchi didn't need to add that compulsory suicide was the penalty for drawing a weapon inside Edo Castle. "The chamberlain ruthlessly eliminated all these men whom he perceived as obstacles in his path to supremacy, without the shogun's lifting a hand to save them."

Sano's steps faltered. He'd heard rumors of Yanagisawa's machinations, but none as bad as these. "I accept the possibility that what happened to those men could happen to me, too," he said, trying to sound braver than he felt. "And it's my duty to catch the Bundori Killer."

Heaving a mournful sigh, Noguchi knelt, easing his body to the floor. "Sano-*san*. Please listen to reason. Do not ruin yourself over this murder investigation. When you see the shogun, convey to him that he should turn the job over to the police. You are intelligent; you can find a way to do this without a loss of face on your part or his. And Chamberlain Yanagisawa will help you—perhaps even reward you for yielding to him. Then leave the job to the police. They have the men. The expertise. Yanagisawa's sanction."

He gestured for Sano to sit opposite him. "Come. Save yourself before it is too late."

Sano remained standing.

Then Noguchi said timidly, "Have you considered the full consequences of your rash behavior, Sano-*san?* While you toil alone at the murder investigation, the Bundori Killer remains free to kill again. How many lives might be saved if you conceded?"

As this last remark hit home, Sano hid his discomposure by turning his back to Noguchi. He might accept the danger to himself, but could he sacrifice innocent people to his goals and principles? When he'd begun this assignment, he'd thought only of the good he could do. But now he found himself in the exact situation that he'd hoped his new status would allow him to avoid: Because of him, others might die. The nightmare of his first murder investigation was beginning again. Slowly he turned to face Noguchi.

"Oh, you see now." Noguchi's smile anticipated his capitulation.

"No." Sano had started to say yes, but the negative slipped out, spoken by that inquiring, truth-seeking part of his nature that he'd never been able to control. "I have to find out who the Bundori Killer is and why he kills, then bring him to justice."

With a sense of incredulity, he felt the familiar pull between practical wisdom and personal desire within him. For what conflict could he have expected to encounter while obeying his lord's orders? And how could he have foreseen that anyone would want to prevent his catching a multiple murderer who was terrorizing the city?

Even as he saw the futility of perseverance, he made one last appeal to Noguchi. "Will you help me?"

Noguchi looked away, and Sano understood that the meek, kindly archivist wanted to help a comrade, but feared punishment from Yanagisawa. Sano said nothing, hoping Noguchi's love of scholarly research would sway him.

Patience won out. Sighing, Noguchi rose clumsily. "Oh, well. Come along. But please, for my sake, do not tell anyone that I came to your assistance."

Noguchi picked up a lamp and led Sano out the back door, along a sheltered walkway through a garden scented with night-blooming jasmine, to a huge, windowless storehouse. Its thick, whitewashed earthen walls and heavy tile roof protected precious original documents from fire. Sano helped Noguchi swing back the massive, ironclad door.

The storehouse's dark interior exuded a musty, metallic odor. As they entered, the wavering flame of Noguchi's lamp revealed hundreds of iron chests, labeled with painted characters, stacked against the walls. As far as Sano could tell, they weren't in any particular order. "Shimabara Rebellion," about a peasant uprising that had taken place fifty years ago, sat wedged between "The Ashikaga Regime," of some two hundred years past, and "Nobuo," the name of a poet who had died last month. Never having understood the archival filing system, Sano was glad of Noguchi's assistance.

"This one, I think," Noguchi said. He tapped a chest labeled "Oda Nobunaga." "And these."

The last two both bore the unpromising notation "To Be Sorted." Sano helped shift the heavy chests, free the relevant ones, and carry them into the study.

With the reverent air of a priest conducting a sacred ritual, Noguchi knelt beside the chest labeled "Oda Nobunaga" and lifted the lid. His little eyes glowed. Sano, kneeling beside him, saw scrolls stacked to the brim, some clean and intact, others stained and crumbling. He smelled old paper and mildew: the odors of the past, which never failed to stir his intellectual curiosity. Feeling privileged to touch the old documents and read the words of witnesses to historic events, he'd disliked his assignment to the archives only because it offered no chance to distinguish himself. Now Sano's love of history reclaimed him. As he and Noguchi scanned the records of Oda Nobunaga's life, seeking any mention of his two allies, Araki Yojiemon and Endō Munetsugu, neither could resist reading irrelevant but fascinating passages.

"Oh, my, here are the writings of the Buddhist priest Miwa," Noguchi exclaimed. Untying a faded silk cord, he opened the scroll and intoned:

"Lord Oda Nobunaga was a beast such as the world had never before seen. In his quest for power, he destroyed his own family to gain the territories of Matsuda and Fukada Provinces. He forced one uncle to commit suicide and had another murdered. He killed his younger brother, whom their mother plotted to install as head of the family in his place. Later he slaughtered another brother to become the ruler of Owari Province. In savage battles, he destroyed the Imagawa, Takeda, and Saitō clans and hundreds of thousands of their troops. By the time of his death at age forty-nine, he had strewn countless severed heads and rotting corpses across the countryside and conquered half the nation's provinces."

"Described that way, Oda Nobunaga sounds more like evil incarnate than like a great lord," Sano said.

Noguchi laid the scroll aside. "You must remember that the clergy had no love for Oda Nobunaga. When the Ikko sect rebelled against him, he burned their temples and killed over forty thousand men, women, and children. But he was the quintessential warlord of his time—a master of *gekokujō*."

The low overcoming the high: the process by which a warrior rose to power by overthrowing his superiors. Few had practiced it as effectively as Oda Nobunaga.

"But one might imagine that the clergy found much satisfaction in the manner of Oda Nobunaga's death," Noguchi continued. "For as he lived by treachery and violence, so did he die by it. Here is the account of what happened one hundred seven years ago." Opening another scroll, he read:

"While Lord Oda was enjoying a holiday at the Honno Temple in Kyōto with but a small force to guard him, he was besieged by the army of an ally turned traitor, General Akechi Mitsuhide. Lord Oda's troops died in the attempt to defend their master. Lord Oda fought the attackers alone. An arquebus ball shattered his arm. With no hope of survival, he retired within the temple hall and committed *seppuku* to avoid capture. His body was destroyed in the flames of the burning temple."

"An unspeakable act, the murder of one's lord," Sano said, feeling the horror that this transgression of Bushido always inspired in him.

"And one for which Akechi received just punishment," Noguchi reminded him. "Lord Oda's loyal allies, Toyotomi Hideyoshi and Tokugawa Ieyasu, fared much better."

Sano quoted an old and apt saying: " 'Nobunaga quarried the stones to build the country's foundations, Hideyoshi shaped the stones, and Ieyasu laid them in place.' "

"Or: 'Nobunaga ground the flour, Hideyoshi baked the cake, and Ieyasu ate it.' Heh, heh, heh."

"Yes." Sano smiled, appreciating Noguchi's joke. No one could deny that Tokugawa Ieyasu and Toyotomi Hideyoshi had benefitted from Oda's ruthlessness—and his murder. Hideyoshi, Oda's direct successor, had consolidated the domains he'd inherited.

Ieyasu had eventually become the first shogun to rule over the unified nation whose construction his predecessors had begun. If not for Akechi Mitsuhide's treason, neither might have achieved military supremacy.

Noguchi read aloud the account of the aftermath of Oda Nobunaga's death.

"Yamazaki. General Toyotomi Hideyoshi, having received the news of Lord Oda's death, immediately embarked on a seven-day march through wind and rain to seek vengeance upon the traitorous Akechi Mitsuhide."

"Oh, my," Noguchi interrupted himself. "Here is one of the names you seek."

"Let me see!" Impatient with the archivist's slow, ritualistic reading, Sano took the scroll from Noguchi.

"Among the force accompanying Hideyoshi were his commander, Endō Munetsugu, and General Fujiwara, one of Lord Oda's most loyal retainers. The retribution they dealt Akechi was swift. After destroying Akechi's small army, they killed Akechi as he fled, pleading in vain for mercy, through the fields.

"Then, on the crest of their glorious victory, General Fujiwara suddenly turned his troops upon Endō Munetsugu. Wielding his two swords, which had guards wrought in the image of death's-heads, the great General Fujiwara cut down Endō's soldiers, leaving carnage in his wake, and suffered grievous losses in turn. These two allies had become bitter enemies because—"

Here, to Sano's distress, the scroll had deteriorated. Bits of moldy paper, covered with faded, fragmented characters, flaked away in his hands. He unrolled the scroll's intact lower portion, only to find that subsequent passages contained no mention of General Fujiwara, Endō Munetsugu, or Araki Yojiemon. He and Noguchi checked the other scrolls in the chest and found references to the three men—all mere short entries that listed them as participants in various battles.

"I believe I remember seeing something in here . . ." Noguchi opened a "To Be Sorted" chest, handling each scroll as if it were a fragile living thing. Sano opened the other. A thorough search yielded a single but intriguing find, dated a year and a half after the last.

Kyōto. The twentieth day of the twelfth month was one of heavy snow and bitter wind. As midnight approached, General Fujiwara and thirty of his men advanced on Araki Yojiemon's mansion. They smashed the gate's heavy timbers with a huge mallet. Then, as half his men scaled the estate's back and side walls, General Fujiwara led the rest on a frontal assault, storming through the gate like a legion of avenging gods.

Araki's retainers awoke from their slumbers and engaged General Fujiwara's force in a violent battle. Walls splintered, windows tore, and beams toppled. Blood flowed and cries pierced the night as fighters on both sides fell dead.

But although the Fujiwara contingent fought bravely, alas, they were sadly outnumbered. They never penetrated Araki's private chamber. Forced to retreat, General Fujiwara fled the house into the snowy night to his waiting horse, barely escaping with his life. General Fujiwara vowed to slay Araki, but never did. He took ill the following month, and died.

"General Fujiwara evidently bore a grudge against both Endō and Araki," Sano said thoughtfully. "Could the Bundori Killer be one of his descendants, who has resumed the feud by killing Araki and Endō?"

"But why now, after so many years?" Noguchi's forehead wrinkles climbed his scalp.

Sano pondered the question. "Maybe none of Fujiwara's sons cared enough about the feud to jeopardize their own positions or risk their own lives by committing murder. Maybe the present-day Fujiwara is braver than his forebears, or has a stronger sense of filial duty. Or perhaps he's mad."

"Perhaps. But if he's not mad, then what grievance could be so important? What could Araki and Endō have done to earn the Fujiwara clan's permanent animosity?"

Sano ran a hand over the scroll, as if by doing so he could divine the answers. Without them, his theory lacked substance. It linked Araki Yojiemon and Endō Munetsugu to a man who had

wanted them both dead. It offered an explanation for why someone might have wanted to kill Kaibara and Tōzawa. But the
records gave no motive sufficient to justify the gruesome murders—or the assassination attempt on himself—committed more
than a hundred years after General Fujiwara's death. Still, the theory was the best Sano had.

"I must locate General Fujiwara's descendants who now live in
or near Edo," he said. "Until proven otherwise, they're all murder
suspects. Will you help me find them?"

Noguchi cringed, obviously wanting no further involvement
with the murder investigation. Sano waited. Then, as he'd hoped,
the archivist's eyes began to shine.

"That would be a formidable task," Noguchi said with cautious
relish. "Examining the old family lineages, then searching the cen-
sus records at the Ministry of Temples and Shrines . . . Oh, my."
Eagerly he rubbed his hands together.

Sano smiled in relief and affection. The thrill of the hunt had
overcome Noguchi's fear of Chamberlain Yanagisawa. "I know it's
asking a lot, but can you get the names for me by tomorrow?"
Sano asked, rising to go. "Lives are at stake." His own included,
he thought.

Face alight with zeal, Noguchi rose and drew his pudgy body
up to its full, insignificant height. "Tomorrow, if it is humanly possible, I will have them for you." For once he exhibited a hint of
samurai steel as he girded himself for battle in his chosen arena.

As Noguchi saw him out the door, Sano felt, for the first time
since he'd begun the investigation, the fire of certainty. He was
finally making progress that he could report to the shogun, the
elders, and Chamberlain Yanagisawa at the council meeting tomorrow. He only regretted that the evening's unexpected, time-
consuming events had prevented his meeting with Aoi.

Then, before he'd reached the gate, Noguchi called his name.
Sano turned.

"*Gambatte kudasai*," Noguchi said solemnly. Do your best, and
good luck. "But know this: Yanagisawa will almost certainly make
sure that you do not succeed. And the shogun, who does not tolerate failure, will distance himself from you. If you persist, you
may find yourself a *rōnin* again—or worse—in no time at all."

When Sano didn't answer, Noguchi continued, "Sometimes the truth is dangerous to seek, and even more dangerous to know. Unfortunately that is a lesson some men must learn over and over again. But I fear that this time you will suffer enough to fix it in your mind permanently. Good night, Sano-*san*."

13

At Sano's mansion, the guards bowed and opened the gate for
him. A yawning stableboy led his horse away. Inside, a lantern
burned in the entryway, but the rest of the house was dark, silent.
As Sano walked toward his bedchamber, carrying Tōzawa's
swords to put away for safekeeping, the creak of the floor under
his feet echoed in the chill, deserted corridor. Where were the servants? Not that he required their attentions; he wasn't hungry, and
he could prepare his own bath and bed. But he always dreaded
this solitary homecoming. And tonight his melancholy went
deeper because of his disappointment over not seeing Aoi, which
he tried to dismiss as purely professional. He didn't want to admit
he'd been looking forward to her company all day.

Then he stopped when he reached the main reception room
and saw its paper walls aglow with light. Curious, he slid open the
door.

Inside, Aoi knelt before her altar, where candles burned and the
smoking incense saturated the air with its musky sweetness.
Sunken charcoal braziers sent up warm fumes. As Aoi returned his
gaze with one solemn and serene, her odd beauty caught at Sano's
heart. His depression disappeared; suddenly, he felt extraordinar-
ily alive. A dark thrill of excitement prickled his skin. His house

had been transformed into a temple, with Aoi enthroned as a living goddess ready to receive his prayers or offerings. His rational, intellectual self withdrew into slumber. He didn't question how Aoi had known to come to him, or how she'd gotten into his house. He simply responded to her implicit invitation.

He moved forward and knelt before the altar, placing Tōzawa's swords upon it. The world shrank to a hazy, glowing space that contained only this room, himself, and Aoi. Breathlessly he awaited her response.

She picked up the long killing-sword first, stroking its worn hilt and scabbard with gentle, probing fingers. Sano involuntarily imagined her hands caressing him. When she slowly unsheathed the blade, his manhood grew erect inside his loincloth. A pulse of desire drove hot blood through his veins as she brought the sword to her mouth and licked the gleaming steel. She repeated the process with the short sword, and Sano stared. Eyes half-closed in concentration, throat arched, she looked as though she shared his pleasure.

Now Aoi returned the swords to their scabbards and balanced them both on her palms. Her inarticulate moans intensified Sano's excitement. Then came laughter—hearty, male, and startling.

"By the gods!" She stared from side to side. "Yoshiwara is all they say it is. Look at those beauties in the windows!"

Everything about her was completely samurai. Her brash voice; the swagger of her shoulders as she pantomimed walking; the insolent leer she aimed at the imaginary courtesans. Tōzawa's spirit inhabited her body. Sano could almost see the *rōnin* walking toward him. Like an expert actor, Aoi somehow even managed to evoke the pleasure quarter's bustling gaiety.

Aoi laughed Tōzawa's laugh again. Her body jiggled like the stout *rōnin's* must have. "Oh, yes, this is the right place for a man to end a long journey!"

Long journey: Tōzawa's trip from his native province to Edo. Aoi's evocation of the murdered man reaffirmed Sano's belief in her powers.

"And the woman I had in Yoshiwara was the right one to be my last." Aoi's face lost its masculine cast to take on a new and disturbingly familiar aspect. She smiled in a maternal, yet flirtatious fashion. Her body seemed to gain a heavy ripeness of flesh. With a jolt, Sano recognized Sparrow, the prostitute he'd interviewed.

"You're troubled, aren't you? Would you like to tell me about it?"

Given his past experience with Aoi's powers, hearing the words Sparrow had spoken to him shouldn't have surprised Sano. But the rational part of his mind rebelled against this new assault by the supernatural. The incense choked his lungs. *Enough!* he wanted to cry.

Aoi replaced the swords on the altar. Cupping her bosom in both hands, she kneaded the full breasts; her fingers teased the nipples.

"Come," she murmured, smiling in fond encouragement. "Suckle at my breasts, master. Take your pleasure and your comfort from me." Her kimono rustled as she parted her knees. "Enter my heavenly chamber." Her voice dropped to a soothing, yet seductive whisper. "Forget your cares for one night. Come to me now."

A fresh onslaught of desire overrode Sano's urge to stop the ritual. As his carnal self goaded him to sweep aside the altar and take Aoi, he fought physical need and addressed the spirit.

"Tōzawa-*san*. After you left Yoshiwara, what happened?"

Sparrow's look left Aoi's face. Her hands dropped from her breasts and took up the swords again. Tōzawa's visage returned, distorted with anger and outrage.

"I started walking toward Edo," Tōzawa's voice said. "I was tired. Drunk. He caught me while I was undoing my loincloth to make dung. I went for my swords, but that miserable thief at the Great Joy had stolen them from me. And then I—a poor, defenseless *rōnin*—lost my life, all that I had left in the world after my lord dismissed me."

Aoi's face crumpled, and her chest heaved with a man's wrenching, tortured sobs.

How could she speak of Tōzawa's loosened loincloth, confiscated swords, and masterless status except through a mystical bond with the spirit world? Awe and fear sharpened Sano's desire even as he recoiled from her. His groin pounded with his need for her. What must it be like to possess a woman of such powers?

"Did you see your killer?" he asked.

A shake of the head; more sobs. "No. Too dark."

"Wait. Don't go yet!"

For Aoi's sobs were diminishing, her face becoming once again calm, serene, and female as Tōzawa's spirit left her body.

Sano watched, disappointed but nevertheless relieved, as she laid down the swords. How undisciplined he was to experience sexual arousal when he should have been concentrating on the investigation! Now, remembering last night's debacle, he took the label from his sash and cautiously handed it to Aoi.

When the paper touched her palm, she closed her eyes; her body swayed. But she had herself under control.

"I see a five-petaled flower," she whispered. "Painted on banners on the walls of a castle on a riverbank."

Filled with awe, her eyes gazed into the distance. "The castle is under siege. Bombs explode beneath the walls. The enemy troops fire guns from rafts on the river, from tall wooden towers on the banks. From inside the castle walls, the defenders shoot back, killing many."

Reflected in her eyes, the flickering candle flames mimicked the explosions and gunfires. "But the enemy has blockaded the castle; they will starve the defenders into defeat. That night, a brave scout leaves the castle and swims the river to seek help. Will he succeed?"

Enlightenment burst upon Sano as he recognized the scenario as the Battle of Nagashino, and the five-petaled flower as Oda Nobunaga's crest. As one of Oda's trusted men, General Fujiwara had surely fought at Nagashino. Aoi's vision linked the murderer with him and that violent past, lending credence to Sano's theory.

"But that was long ago." Aoi's hand trembled beneath the label as if under a great weight. "Now I see a man crossing a high bridge over a wide river. He passes great piles of wood, and canals with logs floating in them. He continues through fields and marshes. He carries a basket with a head in it. He reaches his house and goes inside. He washes the head, drives a spike through it, paints its face."

Sano realized with a flare of jubilation that she was seeing the Bundori Killer. "Where is this house?" he demanded.

Her eyes scanned the distance. "In the marshes. Where two canals meet. It looks . . . like a samurai's helmet."

Sano saw her vision clearing, her trance dissolving. "Wait!" he pleaded. "Is the killer there now? Can you see his face? Whose head is it?" In his urgency, he leaned across the altar toward Aoi.

"Tomorrow . . ." She spoke the barely audible word on a sigh. "He will go to the house tomorrow night. At the hour of the dog . . ."

She laid the label on the altar, and her own persona gazed calmly out from her luminous eyes. Sano sat back as his galloping heartbeat subsided. The hand he passed over his face came away damp with sweat. His loins ached dully with unsatisfied desire; his mind clamored with unanswered questions. Still, he'd gained more facts to report to the Council of Elders tomorrow, and another lead to pursue.

"Hirata and I will search for the house and try to capture the killer there tomorrow night," he said, striving for nonchalance in the face of Aoi's aloof poise.

"Do you wish to discuss what you've learned about the murders today?"

Aoi's husky murmur posed an irresistible invitation. Gladly Sano described his discoveries—as much to extend his time with her as to seek new insights. Her unwavering attention and apparently genuine interest drew every detail from him. And while his desire lost its edge as he warmed to his recital, he felt the current of attraction flowing between them.

"I think General Fujiwara's feud is the key to the murders," he finished. "But I couldn't find a reason for his attacks on Araki and Endō, or any explanation why the killer should choose to satisfy a blood score after all this time."

Aoi interrupted eagerly on his last phrase. "Kaibara was an old man, and the last of his family."

"So if the killer hadn't acted soon enough, Kaibara would have died a natural death, and the Fujiwara clan would have lost forever the chance to take revenge on the Araki. Then, having tasted victory, the killer took the next logical step by attacking the Endō clan." Sano followed Aoi's line of thought to its conclusion, once again impressed by her deductive ability. But for her, would he have ever seen the significance of Kaibara's age and status? Spontaneously he said, "Thank you, Aoi. You're the best partner a man could ask for."

To his astonishment, she looked as though he'd hit her: hurt, and somehow ashamed.

"What's wrong?" he asked.

She bowed her head, and he felt her withdraw from him as before. What caused her strange mood shifts? Fearing that she would retreat farther into herself, he didn't press for an explanation. "I think you were right when you said that the killer wanted to destroy both Kaibara and his ancestor," he said, eager to reestablish their rapport. "If you have more ideas, I want to hear them."

"I'm sorry, I have none." Aoi's low voice was strained. She removed the swords and label from the altar, placing them on the floor. "May I go now?"

"Wait." Sano sensed she was withholding something—and he didn't want her to leave him alone.

She stayed, but only out of obedience, he could tell, her reserve impenetrable in its polite blankness. He decided he'd wrongly perceived a mutual attraction between them. Out of pride—and respect for her wishes—he wouldn't force her to stay. But the late hour, the quiet house, and his own loneliness fostered in him an overpowering urge to confide in someone.

"Aoi. I need whatever help you can give. This investigation is important to me, and not just because the Bundori Killer must be captured and brought to justice."

He detected a glimmer of response in her eyes: She was not indifferent to his plight. Encouraged, he continued.

"Before my father died, I—" His voice broke on the grief that always overwhelmed him when he spoke of his father. He paused while his tears blurred the flickering candles and he struggled to contain his emotions. "I promised him that I would perform a heroic act that would secure our family a place of honor in history. But now I'm afraid of bringing disgrace upon our name, instead of glory."

Then his face went hot with shame. A proper samurai stoically hid private thoughts. Somehow Aoi had inspired him to voice his, and how wonderful the release of it! But wouldn't she despise him for his cowardice? Yet the deep empathy he saw in her eyes surprised and warmed him.

"We make commitments that are hard to keep," she said quietly. "And sometimes the biggest obstacles are within ourselves. Can we ever be strong enough to overcome them?"

Behind her enigmatic facade, Sano glimpsed a woman capable of understanding the conflict between duty and self that warred in him. She'd experienced it, too. And the cautious wonder in her eyes mirrored his dawning recognition of a kindred soul. For a timeless interval, they contemplated one another in *ishin-denshin:* the wordless, heart-to-heart communication so prized in a society that left deep feelings unspoken. A wild mixture of elation and dread swelled Sano's heart. What he felt for Aoi, he'd never felt for any woman before. It went beyond sexual desire and inflamed his spirit with a fierce joy; it obliterated all considerations of rank and class.

And terrified him. Because although love affairs were common for members of his class, he knew that many a samurai had let an unwise romantic infatuation wreak havoc with his finances, distract him from duty, and weaken his character, thereby ruining his future prospects. Sano thought of all the financial and political advantages of marrying into the Ueda family. That these seemed less attractive than the thought of taking Aoi to his bed, of knowing her in every way, signaled the danger of giving his emotions free rein.

Then Aoi stood. Before she bolted for the door, Sano saw her eyes turn glassy with horror. That she seemed to welcome their changed relationship even less than he both hurt and reassured him. For the sake of the investigation, he must see her again; but for his own good, they must never cross the boundary between work and love.

14

"I hereby call to order this meeting of the, ahh, Council of Elders." With an air of regal authority, the shogun spoke from the head of Edo Castle's great audience hall, where he sat upon the dais. At his back, a landscape mural rich with gold leaf set off his brilliant silk robes.

The floor before him formed two descending levels. On the higher, Chamberlain Yanagisawa knelt nearest the shogun, at his left and turned so that he could see both his lord and the rest of the assembly. The five elders knelt in two rows on the same level, at right angles to the shogun and facing each other. Hereditary Tokugawa vassals who advised the Tokugawa on national policy, they comprised the *bakufu*'s highest echelon. Servants unobtrusively refilled the tea bowls on standing trays before them and supplied tobacco and metal baskets of lit coals for their pipes.

The lower level belonged to lesser officials scheduled to present reports. Sano, cold and tense with anxiety, knelt among these. He tried to review his speech, but nervousness ruined his concentration. His thoughts strayed to last night, and Aoi.

Tokugawa Tsunayoshi concluded his opening remarks, then nodded to his chief secretary, who headed a battery of clerks seated at desks beneath windows that ran the length of the room. "Proceed."

"The first item on the agenda," the secretary announced, "is *Sōsakan* Sano Ichirō's report on his inquiry into the Bundori Murders."

Interest enlivened Tokugawa Tsunayoshi's features. "So, ahh, *sōsakan,* what have you to tell us?" he asked.

Sano's heart did a quickening drumbeat inside his chest; as he rose, walked to the front of the assembly, and knelt, he held his body rigid to still its trembling. "Your Excellency, it is my privilege to present my progress report," he said, praying that his voice wouldn't waver. "I hope my unworthy efforts will meet with your approval."

Conscious of all the eyes focused on him, Sano summarized the results of his investigation, encouraged by the fact that the shogun, not Chamberlain Yanagisawa, had opened the discussion. The chamberlain smoked his pipe in attentive silence, his expression neutral. The elders followed his example. The shogun leaned forward, eyes alight with the same enjoyment with which he viewed theatrical auditions. His face showed surprise at each new clue, excitement over the assassination attempt, and satisfaction when Sano presented his theory about the murders and his plans to interrogate General Fujiwara's descendants if he couldn't trap the killer at the house where Aoi claimed he would be tonight. Finishing his recital in a tentative glow of success, Sano held his breath, awaiting the shogun's response.

"Ahh, splendid!" Tokugawa Tsunayoshi exclaimed. "Well done, *Sōsakan* Sano."

He clapped his hands in hearty applause. After a moment, everyone else did, too. The elders' stern faces betrayed hints of approval—here a faint smile, there a raised eyebrow. Yanagisawa's features had hardened into a rigid mask that moved only when he parted his lips to remove his pipe. But Sano, almost giddy with relief, didn't care. The shogun had rescued him from Yanagisawa's conniving. Now he could pursue his investigation with the greater chance of success that his lord's favor would surely bring.

"*Sōsakan* Sano does indeed deserve Your Excellency's praise,"

Chamberlain Yanagisawa said with warm sincerity. His stony expression altered to one of pleased surprise. Sano breathed even more easily. The shogun's approval meant that Yanagisawa must put aside whatever grudge he held.

Then the chamberlain said with a delicate shrug, "It does not really matter that the suspect has not been located yet. Although it seems as if a lame, pockmarked man should be easy enough to find . . . Nor should we chastise *Sōsakan* Sano for failing to prevent another murder, or to control the resulting unrest in the city."

"No . . ." The shogun's enthusiasm faded visibly; doubt pursed his mouth. "After all, not much time has passed since the first murder, has it?"

Silk robes rustled as the elders shifted position and set down their pipes in response to the changed atmosphere. The assembly stirred. An iron band of dread closed around Sano's throat as he fathomed Chamberlain Yanagisawa's intent.

"Only two days, Your Excellency." Yanagisawa's inflection made it sound like years.

In the No theater, Sano had watched Yanagisawa dominate the shogun by possessing knowledge, which conferred power. During their private audience, Yanagisawa had manipulated Tokugawa Tsunayoshi by catering to his desires. Now Sano saw another way in which the chamberlain usurped the shogun's authority. Tokugawa Tsunayoshi was a natural follower who craved approval. Yanagisawa—with all the ruthless strength of character absent in his lord—undermined the shogun's weak self-confidence by playing upon this need.

"Nor should we attribute importance to the fact that *Sōsakan* Sano has presented no evidence to support his theory about the murders," Yanagisawa continued. "Although without such proof, the theory seems . . ." Ridiculous, said his quick glance skyward.

The shogun frowned and nodded. And Sano, locked into silence by Bushido's code of unwavering, unquestioning submission to his superiors, couldn't expose Yanagisawa's ploy, or prevent Yanagisawa from emphasizing the faults in his report. The incredible irony of the situation! While his own adherence to Bushido seemed likely to ruin him, the chamberlain, by defying its tenets, had risen to a position of unchallenged power. Helpless outrage erupted within Sano. To maintain the required, respectful silence took all his self-discipline.

Now Senior Elder Makino took up the chamberlain's argument. "I would like to know what motive of General Fujiwara's could possibly survive his death and induce a descendant to commit murder a hundred years later." Makino laughed, an obscene cackle. "The notion seems fantastic."

"Yes, Makino-*san*," the shogun said humbly, "I must agree that it does."

"Well, then." Yanagisawa shot Sano a triumphant glance, drawing on his pipe and exhaling smoke with an air of finality.

Everyone else turned to look at Sano, most with hostility, a few others sadly; none offered support. Fear of punishment held them in Chamberlain Yanagisawa's thrall. Sano's chest constricted in terror as before his eyes the hall turned into a battlefield. He could almost smell acrid gunpowder and burning castles. Yanagisawa had declared open war on him, and had among his allies the most powerful men in the *bakufu*.

"Furthermore," Yanagisawa continued, "*Sōsakan* Sano has exhibited a most disturbing character trait." Having swayed the shogun to his viewpoint, he didn't bother hiding his contempt. "He has refused the police's help, working alone in an attempt to win all the credit for solving the case. Obviously, self-aggrandizement is more important to him than saving lives."

Sano could restrain himself no longer. "That's a lie!" he blurted. "The police were ordered not to help me. And—"

Absolute silence. The elders toyed with tea bowls and pipes. An uncomfortable tension gripped the assembly. The shogun frowned at the floor. Chamberlain Yanagisawa alone looked directly at Sano.

And smiled. Too late Sano realized that the elders were more shocked by his contradiction of their superior than interested in learning the truth. He'd lost favor with Tokugawa Tsunayoshi, who had a ruler's dislike of direct challenge and a refined man's abhorrence of open argument. Yanagisawa had set him up. He'd taken the bait and fallen headlong into the trap.

As if nothing had happened, Chamberlain Yanagisawa turned to the shogun. "In view of *Sōsakan* Sano's incompetence, I recommend that he be relegated to a position in which he is less likely to endanger national security."

Tokugawa Tsunayoshi's brow furrowed. "Such as?"

Don't condemn me yet! Sano clenched his teeth to hold back another outburst that would only worsen his predicament.

Makino cleared his throat with a repulsive, death-rattle sound. "With all the troubles on Sado Island, we could use a new administrator there."

Yanagisawa's dark eyes sparkled with malevolent delight. "A splendid suggestion. What do you think, Your Excellency?"

A spasm of horror clutched Sano's heart. Sado Island was a cold, hellish prison colony far from the mainland, many days' journey over troubled northern seas. Violent criminals were exiled there to labor in underground mines. Sano knew what would happen if he went to Sado Island: Yanagisawa would make sure he never came back. If he didn't get killed during one of the frequent insurrections, he would surely fall victim to famine or disease. In any case, his spirit would die of disgrace long before his body did. He would lose his chance to fulfill his promise to his father, and he would never see Aoi again. Father, he prayed silently, help me save myself! He sent the shogun a wordless plea for the rescue he surely deserved.

"Well, ahh, Chamberlain Yanagisawa," said the shogun hesitantly, "something must be done about Sado Island."

He returned Sano's gaze with one both stern and apologetic. Apparently he hadn't forgotten the service Sano had rendered him, but lacked the energy and courage to oppose Yanagisawa and his cronies. Sano could already feel the motion of the ship carrying him across the sea; he sensed the other men in the room recoiling from him, as if to avoid the taint of disgrace. His stomach rolled with nausea and shame.

Then the shogun said, "*Sōsakan* Sano, your performance has been disappointing thus far." He lowered his eyes, perhaps ashamed of his weakness. "But I am a generous man."

Sano's heart leapt at the hope of reprieve.

"I give you five more days to catch the Bundori Killer. If you fail to do so within that time, then you can try your hand at, ahh, prison administration. Dismissed."

Five more days to catch the killer, to restore peace to the city, and to save himself from utter disgrace.

In a panic, Sano rushed from the audience hall to the castle archives to see if Noguchi had located General Fujiwara's descendants. But the archivist's clerks said he was still researching at the Ministry of Shrines; he'd sent back no message for Sano, and given no indication of when he might return. Sano then hurried to the police compound, taking his own horse and another from his stable, both saddled and provisioned for a journey. Aoi's new lead was the only one that promised quick success. He would need help finding the house and capturing the killer, and didn't know if Hirata, as a low-ranking samurai, owned a horse.

"In her vision, Aoi saw the killer crossing a high bridge over a wide river," Sano told Hirata as they rode across the Ryōgoku Bridge. The great wooden arch spanned the Sumida River, connecting Edo with the rural districts of Honjo and Fukagawa on the eastern banks.

Hirata followed at a trot, bouncing only a little in the saddle. The awkwardness with which he'd first mounted and handled the horse attested to his lack of riding experience. Yet he seemed a natural horseman, learning by instinct as well as by observation.

When he spoke, however, his abashed tone didn't reflect his growing equestrian confidence.

"*Gomen nasai*—I'm sorry for not being able to find the suspect or any more witnesses," he said.

"Hopefully, after tonight, that won't matter."

As they crested the bridge's arch, Sano darted wary glances at the other travelers streaming past them. A more immediate threat than the shogun's punishment haunted him. Someone wanted him dead—and likely wouldn't stop after one failed attempt. When would the next assault come? Was that hatted and cloaked samurai following them, awaiting the right moment to attack?

Sano peered between the bridge's railings. Far below, ferries, barges, and fishing boats floated on the swiftly flowing brown water. A ferryman lifted an oar in greeting. Sano looked away. Overnight, all of Edo had turned sinister. Every stranger was possibly the agent of an unknown enemy; every encounter promised danger. Hirata, whom Sano had told about the attack, stuck close by, hand on his short sword, ready to defend his superior. His protectiveness touched Sano, but Hirata's presence posed another dilemma. Remembering another young assistant he'd once had, who had been murdered while accompanying him on an investigation, he would rather face danger alone than risk Hirata's safety.

They reached the river's eastern bank, where warehouses, piers, and docks lined the water's edge. Beyond these, a jumble of houses, shops, and open markets comprised a flourishing suburb. To the north rose the E-ko-in—Temple of Helplessness—built upon the burial site of the victims of the Great Fire thirty-three years ago. Sano led the way south along a road that ran past the warehouses and paralleled the river.

"Aoi saw the killer pass piles of wood and canals with logs floating in them," he explained.

Hirata nodded. "The Honjo lumberyards."

The road ended at the Tatekawa River, a small tributary of the Sumida. In the lumberyards lining its banks, laborers cut and planed timbers, and stacked finished boards on barges bound for the city. The clear morning air rang with men's shouts and the rasp of saws and scrapers. Sunlight filtered through a golden haze of sawdust that bore the winy scent of freshly cut wood. A network of canals branched off the Tatekawa River, all choked with logs transported from the eastern forests. Burly men walked along the logs as easily as on land, guiding them with poles.

While Hirata stood watch for assailants, Sano asked the lumbermen if they knew of an abandoned house in the marshes, at the intersection of two canals, that somehow resembled a samurai's helmet.

"Nothing like that on our route," said the foreman of a log transport team.

"No. But then, I don't go out in the marshes much." This answer came from woodworkers, porters, and sweepers.

Giving up, Sano said to Hirata, "If the killer travels often between the house and the city, at least it can't be far."

Beyond the lumberyards lay open marshland, through which they headed east on a narrow road bordered by lilies, ginger, ginseng, and other spring flowers. The high blue sky reflected in standing pools that broke the expanses of lush green grasses. Willows drooped graceful boughs hazy with spring foliage. As humans grew scarce, wildlife abounded. Geese honked and gulls screeched overhead. Fish jumped in ponds, where water rats prowled, turtles sunned themselves, and white cranes fed on frogs and water insects. Butterflies flitted through the air; bees droned. Although the stinging flies and mosquitoes wouldn't swarm in full force for some months yet, the weather was as balmy as summer.

Spaced at wide intervals along the road, tiny shacks stood on stilts above the marshes. Sano stopped at one.

"We'll ask for directions," he told Hirata.

The marsh people eked out a meager living by collecting fish, shellfish, eels, frogs, and wild herbs to sell in the city. They would, out of necessity, range farther into the marshes than the lumbermen. In response to Sano's call, a weathered brown woman dressed in faded cotton kimono and headcloth came to the door. When asked about the house, she said, "I've heard about a hunting lodge that a rich samurai built a long time ago and doesn't use anymore. I've never seen it myself, but I think it's that way." She waved a hand in a vague gesture to the northeast.

Raising a hand to shield his eyes from the sun, Sano squinted into the distance, but saw only more marshes. "How far?"

"Oh, a few hours' walk."

Encouraged, Sano led Hirata off the main road and onto a narrow northeast-bound branch. This trail meandered, veered, and repeatedly doubled back on itself. The sun climbed higher in the sky. Noon came and went, and still they did not find the abandoned house. They passed no other travelers, and no other shacks where they could ask for directions. Sano grew increasingly worried. Would they reach their destination by the hour of the dog, when Aoi had said the killer would arrive?

"The house is out here somewhere," he said, as much to reassure himself as Hirata. "We should find it soon."

Doubt shadowed the young *doshin*'s eyes, but he neither questioned nor complained. Sano was grateful for his tact. Grim and determined, they pushed on.

All too soon, the day began its inevitable decline. The sun dropped lower in the west. The fleecy white clouds turned first pink, then violet against a flame-orange sky. The grasses darkened to murky gray. Waterfowl ceased flight to clamor beside the ponds. Every tree held a twittering orchestra of birds. The air grew chill; a thin vapor that smelled of fish and rotting vegetation rose from the marshes. Soon it would be too dark to search anymore. Less than three hours remained before the killer's expected arrival at the house.

Then Sano spied a building in the distance to the north. "There!" He pointed. "Look!

With no time to waste on looking for a road to the house, they dismounted and plunged into the marsh, leading their horses. The shoulder-high grasses closed around them. Icy water soaked them to the knees; mud sucked at the horses' hooves. Small creatures fled at their approach. Striking a straight line toward their target soon proved impossible. Deep pools and impenetrable reed thickets constantly forced them to detour. Keeping the house in view grew increasingly difficult as the darkness deepened. Only one thought consoled Sano: following them secretly would be impossible for an assassin. At last, after an hour's tedious trudge, they emerged on solid ground, at the junction where two shallow, weed-choked ditches merged to form a wider one that meandered off into the distance. Perhaps two hundred paces beyond the junction rose the structure they'd seen.

"Come on," Sano said, freshly energetic in his eagerness.

He jumped a ditch and urged his horse across it. Leaving Hirata to follow, he mounted and rode the remaining distance. The ground, though as overgrown with grasses as the surrounding terrain, was higher and firmer here. As he neared the house, its features grew apparent.

The house was a *minka,* the sort of dwelling found throughout rural Japan. A crumbling earthen wall surrounded it, also enclosing a ruined barn. The house had three stories counting the attic, with a few tiny barred windows set into half-timbered, unplastered mud walls. Sano dismounted outside a gap in the wall where rough wooden pillars marked the place where a gate had once hung. He drew and expelled a long breath of recognition.

"See the roof," he said to Hirata, who'd caught up with him. "Doesn't it look like a samurai's helmet?"

Made of thick, shaggy thatch, the roof jutted out between the first and second levels in wings that resembled the side flaps on a warrior's helmet. From the second story, it ascended to a flat portion over the attic before tapering to a narrow point. Exposed beams on either side of the ridgepole crisscrossed, forming long projections like horns crowning a general's headgear. But the place looked deserted, with an aura of complete abandonment. Sano's inner sense told him that no one had made consistent use of the house in ages. He felt a momentary prick of doubt, which he dismissed.

Hirata cleared his throat and said, "*Sumimasen.* Forgive my forwardness in speaking, *sōsakan-sama.* If the killer owns the house, the property records might tell us who he is."

Sano regarded his assistant with new respect. He'd guessed that the killer had simply taken over the old house, but Hirata's alternative made sense.

"That's a good idea," he said. "If we don't catch him tonight, we'll check the records when we get back to town." But he fervently hoped that they would, and that a long search wouldn't be necessary. "Now let's look around."

Tethering their horses inside the wall, they circled the property. At the house's rear, an overgrown trail ran west, probably to link up with a road leading toward the city. It bore no visible foot- or hoofprints or any other signs of travel. Around them, as far as Sano could see, stretched the marshes: a vast level spread of land, accented by occasional trees. The only sound was the wind rustling through the grasses.

"Let's go inside," Sano said, swallowing his misgivings.

From their saddlebags, they fetched candles and matches, then crossed a jagged flagstone path through an earthen courtyard that sprouted knee-high grass as the marshes slowly reclaimed it. The front door was unlocked, but the wooden planks had swollen in the damp climate, and opening it took their combined strength. Lighting their candles, they cautiously stepped inside the house.

The candle flames illuminated a single large room with earth floor and mud walls. Gaps between the ends of the ceiling's exposed beams admitted light and air. Walls, beams, and the rough pillars that supported the upper stories were blackened by smoke from past fires in the clay hearth that stood near one wall. The room was empty, almost as cold and damp as the outdoors, and showed no signs of recent occupation. Sano conjectured that the killer needed more than one hideaway, each near enough to a murder site for him to bring the head back, make the trophy, and take it to its final resting spot. Such a scheme bespoke the killer's intelligence and forethought. If this was the lair he meant to use for a murder in Honjo tonight, wouldn't he have prepared it better? Again Sano experienced doubts.

"Maybe he uses the upstairs." Hirata's voice echoed Sano's hope as he raised his candle to a ladder that ascended to a square opening in the ceiling.

Sano examined the ladder. Finding it sturdy, he climbed to the second story, holding his candle above him. At the top he found himself in a small empty room, probably a bedchamber, with a plank ceiling and floor, and one tiny window. A doorway in a wall of torn paper and broken wooden mullions led to more rooms.

Another ladder rose to the attic. Sano waited for Hirata to emerge through the hole.

"Search these rooms," he said. "I'll check the attic." A perverse reluctance kept him from assigning his subordinate the more hazardous, less promising task. By doing so, did he think he could ensure that they would find the evidence he sought? Shaking his head at his foolish attempt to manipulate fate, Sano mounted the second ladder. With his head and shoulders in the attic, he paused and lifted his candle, looking around the tent-shaped space.

On the attic floor, exposed wooden joists formed a neat pattern of intersecting strips. The ceiling sloped steeply upward to the roof's apex. From the thatch between the beams came sinister squeaks and rustlings: The roof was full of vermin. Gingerly Sano raised the rest of himself into the attic. He began to explore, testing the joists with each step before putting his whole weight on them.

Panning his candle from side to side, he saw a latticed vent window in the peak of the roof's far gable. Below this, a pile of objects lay on the floor. Restraining his eagerness, Sano carefully moved toward the pile.

Suddenly a loud squeal split the silence. A huge rat dropped from the thatch and landed with a thump at Sano's feet.

He cried out in surprise and instinctively reached for his sword. But even as his mind dismissed the threat as insignificant, he made an involuntary jump backward. His feet left the joist. With a loud, splintering crack, they burst through the unreinforced ceiling of the room beneath. He was falling. In a desperate effort to save himself, Sano threw out his arms, experiencing a shattering jolt as his elbows caught on the joists that framed the hole he'd made.

"Sōsakan-sama!" From below him, Sano heard Hirata's shout, and running footsteps. "What happened? Are you hurt?"

Braced on his arms, Sano hung with his upper half still in the attic, legs and feet dangling. He closed his eyes, gasping as panic subsided, feeling ridiculous.

"I'm all right," he called. "Just give me a boost up, will you?"

With Hirata pushing on his feet, Sano raised himself through the hole. He winced as the splintered boards scraped his already abraded legs. Inside the attic once again, he saw his candle, still lit, lying in a small bonfire of thatch. Sano hastily retrieved the candle and stamped out the fire. Then he said to Hirata, "I think I've found something. Go to the ladder and help me bring it down."

He walked carefully over to the pile he'd seen: two large hemp sacks containing hard, heavy objects, which he hauled to the ladder for Hirata to lower to the second level. Then he descended and gave Hirata his candle to hold while he upended the first sack.

Two square boards the length of his forearm clattered onto the floor, along with two sharp, flat-headed iron spikes long enough to penetrate a board and hold a human head severed at the neck.

"These are his. He's been here!" Sano could hardly contain his jubilance as he and Hirata exchanged grins. He wanted to shout for joy and dance around the room. Refraining from such an unseemly display of emotion, he said, "Let's see what else we have."

The second sack held a wooden bucket and toolbox. In the box Sano found a saw, an iron mallet, incense sticks, a sanding block, and a jar of rouge.

"His trophy-making equipment." Sano breathed.

Hirata cleared his throat. "I found something, too, *sōsakan-sama*."

He led the way to the adjacent room. On the floor lay a blue and white cotton bedroll. The cloth looked too new, unfaded, and intact to have lain in the damp house for long. The Bundori Killer must have brought it recently, in anticipation of an upcoming murder.

"Good work," Sano complimented his assistant. Hirata's boyish smile flashed. "We'll take these things back to Edo as evidence. Now let's get ready for him."

They repacked the Bundori Killer's paraphernalia and carried it downstairs. Then they went outside. Only a faint orange luminescence hazed the western horizon. Stars shone in the cobalt blue sky; the moon's waxing crescent soared amid them. The marsh winds carried a cold, bitter edge. Sano and Hirata brought the horses inside the house, both to shelter the animals and to prevent the killer's discovering them. Then they set up camp near the door and unpacked their provisions: *mochi*—hard, sticky cakes of compressed rice—pickled vegetables, dried fish, flasks of water. They ate ravenously by candlelight, sitting on the floor with heavy quilts

draped over their padded garments to ward off the chill. Then
Sano extinguished the candles and they settled down to await the
Bundori Killer's arrival.

The silence was oppressive; the damp cold bone-numbing. To
pass the time, and to satisfy his curiosity, Sano decided to get better acquainted with the young subordinate whose able, steadfast
service had favorably impressed him.

"How long have you served on the police force?" he asked.

"Three years, *sōsakan-sama*. Since my father, who held the position before me, retired."

So Hirata wasn't as inexperienced as Sano had assumed. Now
he remembered an incident that had occurred during his own
brief stint with the police department, although not in the district
he'd commanded.

"Aren't you the *doshin* who broke up the gang that was extort-
ing money from merchants in the Nihonbashi vegetable market?"
he asked. The gang had beaten to death a man who had refused
to pay, and eluded the police for months.

"Yes, *sōsakan-sama*."

In the darkness, Sano couldn't see Hirata's expression. Nor
could he detect in the young *doshin*'s voice any hint of boasting.
Even more curious, he said, "Do you enjoy your work?"

"Yes, of course." Now Hirata sounded resigned. "It's my duty. I
was born to it." A pause. Then he blurted, "But if I had my choice,
I'd rather serve you, *sōsakan-sama!*"

This uncharacteristically bold declaration surprised Sano. Then
he remembered their first meeting, when Hirata had told him he
wouldn't be sorry for letting him assist with the investigation. "Because this assignment offers more chance for advancement, you
mean?"

Hirata's quilt rustled. "Well, yes. But that's not the only reason."
After another pause, he spoke hesitantly. "You may not know this,
sōsakan-sama, but the police force is not as it should be. Many of
the other *doshin* take bribes in exchange for letting criminals go
free. They let the rich escape punishment and send the poor to
the executioner. They arrest innocent men just to close cases and
improve their records. The law is corrupt, dishonorable. But
you—you're different."

The hero worship in Hirata's voice disturbed Sano. Although he knew that in his new position he might eventually acquire personal retainers, he must, for Hirata's sake, discourage the young man's attachment to him.

"We've only worked together three days, Hirata," he said. "You don't know me at all."

"Forgive my presumptuousness, *sōsakan-sama!*" There were more rustlings as Hirata bowed, even though they couldn't see each other. "But I know your reputation. You have the honor and integrity that others lack." Hirata's voice grew agitated. "Please. If I prove I'm worthy, let me devote my life to your service!"

Sano was not unmoved by Hirata's earnest plea. Such an expression of loyalty to one's superior evoked all the stern beauty of Bushido. Unfortunately, if they failed to catch the Bundori Killer, then Hirata, as Sano's retainer, would be punished along with him. Sano couldn't let this happen.

"Your offer is much appreciated, Hirata-*san*," Sano said as coldly and formally as he could. "But the shogun may have plans for me that can't include you." For fear that the ardent Hirata might decide to share his fate, good or bad, Sano didn't elaborate. "You shall consider our association temporary."

Hirata made no reply, but his disappointment and humiliation sharpened the silence. That Sano had prevented a future, greater injury to Hirata did not ease his guilt.

The new awkwardness between them precluded further conversation. Huddled under their quilts, they sat in silence, periodically rising to stretch their stiff muscles and peer outside. Time slowed. Sano's elation over the discovery of the house and its incriminating evidence faded as anticipation grew. When would the Bundori Killer come, and what would happen when he did? Would there be a quick capture, or a fight? Would he have to kill again? And was a second assassin lurking in the marshes, waiting to attack? Uncertainty made waiting an ordeal.

When nothing happened, uncertainty turned to doubt. Even allowing a generous margin of error in estimating the time, Sano was soon forced to conclude that the hour of the dog had passed. What if Aoi was wrong? What if the Bundori Killer didn't show up? He would have wasted one of the precious five days left to complete his assignment and achieve the everlasting honor that his father had desired. And what if he then failed to find General Fujiwara's descendants, or tie them to the murders?

The hours stretched to an eternity. Making perhaps his hundredth trip outside, Sano guessed from the position of the moon that it must be nearing midnight. For the killer to come here from Edo—as Aoi's vision of him crossing the Ryōgoku Bridge had implied he would—he would have had to leave the city before the gates closed two hours ago. And with better knowledge of the marshes, he would have traveled more quickly than Sano and Hirata, and arrived by now.

A terrible sense of futility washed over Sano. The Bundori Killer wasn't coming. Sano stood outside the door, arms folded against the cold, staring down the trail, as the bitter marsh wind tore away his last shred of hope. After a long while, he turned to go back inside, where at least now he and Hirata could build a fire so that warmth and sleep might speed the hours until dawn and their return to Edo.

Then he lifted his head in sudden confused alarm as a bell's deep, sonorous peals, coming from the city, boomed across the marshes.

Hirata came hurrying out of the house to stand beside him. "It's the Zōjō Temple bell," he said. "But why would the priests ring it now?"

"I don't know," Sano said. The bells were sounded to mark Buddhist rituals that occurred at set times during the day or year. Only rarely did the priests depart from this schedule—to celebrate an unusual event, or to signal a fire, typhoon, earthquake, or other disaster.

A disaster such as murder?

Sano's gaze met Hirata's in sudden, unspoken understanding as they both guessed why the Bundori Killer hadn't arrived as expected. Together they dashed into the house to collect their possessions and load their horses for a midnight journey to Zōjō Temple.

16

Long after the Zōjō Temple bell ceased to toll, the Bundori Killer heard its relentless voice echoing in his mind as he sped down the dark country road toward the sanctuary of his lodgings.

No escape, the imaginary peals called. *No escape!*

Panting, he burst through the door of the secluded hut in an isolated village near the temple, then closed and latched the door. In the darkness, he threw his sword to the floor and tore off his bloodstained garments. Then he dived into bed. Terror gripped him like a great, nauseating sickness. Moaning, he thrashed under the quilts. This night, which should have been one of great triumph, had brought disaster.

Tonight he'd committed his fourth murder. With the confidence born of practice and a growing sense of invincibility, he'd expected it to be easier than the others, the satisfaction keener. He'd even dared the grave risk of leaving the trophy in the prominent place of honor that it deserved. But fate had conspired against him, and he'd made a mistake that could cost him his freedom, his life, and his chance to finish the mission he'd only begun. Tonight he'd left precious, dangerous evidence at the death scene.

The Bundori Killer drew his knees to his chest and balled his hands into fists so tight that his fingernails dug into his palms. His clenched teeth clamped the tender flesh inside his mouth, drawing blood. He endured the pain as a punishment for his stupidity and cowardice—traits alien to Lord Oda, who had planned and executed his battles brilliantly, and feared nothing.

Far more serious than leaving evidence at Zōjō Temple was the fact that tonight someone had seen him, someone who could possibly identify him. If only he hadn't returned to the temple again! He should have taken his earlier, unexpected difficulties as a warning against stubbornly adhering to his original plan. Now he must risk a different sort of murder, one he had no time to plan as meticulously as his others. Because he couldn't allow the witness to live.

Yet tonight's disaster wasn't his only worry. The shogun's *sōsakan* had strengthened security within Edo, making free movement through the city difficult. He'd discovered the *eta's* murder, the supposedly "safe" one. Heedless of all threats, including the assassin the Bundori Killer had hired to free himself for carrying out the other, more important murders, Sano was uncovering dangerous secrets. The Bundori Killer could feel the net tightening around him.

Rest now, he exhorted himself; replenish your courage and energy for tomorrow's battles. He shut his eyes and forced himself to concentrate. At last, the blessed heat of war lust burned away panic and dread; the beloved past came alive . . .

Summer, one hundred fifteen years ago. Nagashino Castle was under siege by the Takeda clan. Lord Oda's gunners knelt in ranks before a nearby palisade. Ahead of them stood wings of foot soldiers and mounted fighters: bait for the Takeda. Behind the palisade, the Bundori Killer waited with the main army. One of Lord Oda's top generals now, he commanded a regiment of crack troops. Although no one spoke or moved, he could sense the desire for victory consuming each and every man. The hoofbeats of the approaching Takeda army grew louder every moment. He felt no fear, only a passionate anticipation.

Then the Takeda burst upon them, engaging the decoy troops in fierce man-to-man battles. Impatiently the Bundori Killer listened to the shouts, the sword clashes, the horses' stomps and whinnies. He braced himself for what must come next.

The battle raged nearer as the decoy troops retreated. The enemy troops stampeded the palisade. Suddenly the boom of gunfire rent the heavens. Now the enemy's hoofbeats faltered; their cries changed to screams. The Takeda had fallen into the trap.

Another round of gunfire immediately echoed the first. More screams; thuds as men and their mounts fell dead. The Bundori Killer laughed in exultation. Lord Oda had ordered the gunners to fire in volleys when the enemy drew near, thus overcoming the arquebus's inherent disadvantages—short range and long loading time—and ushering in a new era of warfare.

Now, from behind the ranks, the war trumpet blared. The Bundori Killer galloped out from behind the palisade amid the main fighting force. Yelling orders to his troops, he steered his mount and wielded his sword. Scores of enemy soldiers fell before him, adding to the carnage that littered the field. The gunners continued blasting the Takeda to eternity. By the time the Nagashino Castle garrison sallied out to attack the fleeing Takeda from the rear, he was hoarse from shouting and delirious with joy.

With his help, Lord Oda had vanquished the Takeda, his chief rivals. Now nothing stood between him and his goal of dominating the entire nation.

17

Zōjō Temple, founded as the Tokugawa family temple nearly a hundred years earlier, occupied a vast area of land in Shiba, south of the city proper. The domain of three thousand priests and their attendants, its halls, pagodas, tombs, dormitories, and gardens nestled among hills shrouded in dense pine forest.

As he and Hirata neared Zōjō Temple, Sano felt a sense of homecoming that the late hour and unusual circumstances of their visit didn't diminish. Like other Edo citizens, he'd worshipped at the temple and attended ceremonies there. He'd also spent nine years of his life at the temple's school for boys. He knew every stretch of this country road, and found himself checking off familiar landmarks. There was the Iigura Shinmei Shrine; here was the bend in the road. In a moment they would reach the bridge leading across the Sakuragawa Canal, and then Zōjō Temple's main gate. As he rode, Sano dreaded what the temple might hold for him now—not the welcome of his boyhood friends and teachers, but another murder scene. Created by the killer he'd expected to catch tonight.

They rounded the bend. Hirata, riding beside him, exclaimed, "Look!"

Flaming stone lanterns lit the towering, two-story main gate. Beyond this, more lanterns climbed the hill alongside steep steps leading to the temple's main precinct. High above the road, the roofs of the temple's monuments, illuminated by lights in the courtyards below, floated atop the forest like rafts on dark waves. The priests had lit the temple as if for some weird nocturnal festival.

But the reception Sano and Hirata received when they arrived at the gate was anything but festive. Three grim priests, dressed in flowing saffron robes and armed with spears, greeted them.

"The Bundori Killer has struck here, hasn't he?" Sano asked the leader.

The priest only bowed and said, "His Holiness the abbot is expecting you, *sōsakan-sama*." His words confirmed Sano's fears, but he obviously had orders to let his superior do the talking. "If you'll please wait here?"

One of the other priests took charge of the horses. The leader ushered Sano and Hirata into the dim gatehouse, where, under the watchful eyes of an enshrined Buddha, statues of Manjusri and Samantabhadra mounted on white elephants, and the sixteen apostles, they waited for the third priest to fetch the abbot.

Apprehension's steel fist tightened within Sano's stomach as he wondered how best to approach an inquiry centered on sacred ground to which he had strong emotional ties. In what seemed like no time at all, the door on the temple side of the gatehouse opened.

"His Holiness," the messenger priest announced.

Down the torchlit path walked the abbot of Zōjō Temple, followed by a retinue of four priests. The abbot's shaven head rose above those of his subordinates; the silk brocade stole of his exalted office glittered. Seeing him again evoked in Sano his childhood fear and awe of the man who had once represented the highest authority. Bowing deeply in respect, he fought the resurgence of those emotions. To display the awkward uncertainty of youth would jeopardize the investigation.

"Sano Ichirō." The abbot's deep voice had a humming quality imparted by years of chanting sutras. "It has been a long time since last we met."

Sano straightened, tilting his head back to look into the taller man's eyes. "It has, Your Honorable Holiness," he agreed, before introducing Hirata.

He'd spoken with the abbot exactly twice before: at age six, during his admission interview, and again upon completing his studies. Now he saw with surprise that the passage of sixteen more years had scarcely altered the abbot.

Age spots marked the shaven head, and the thick eyebrows had turned white, but although he must be in his seventies now, the abbot retained an air of youthful vigor. His full-fleshed body was still firm; his oval face virtually unlined. The prominent features hadn't lost their resolute strength. Nor had time dimmed the serene light of his eyes. Benevolent and all-knowing, they contemplated Sano. Suddenly he remembered the abbot's parting words to him:

"You have an inquisitive spirit and a talent for uncovering truth, my son. This talent can be a blessing, or a curse. Will the truths you uncover bring darkness and trouble to you and the world, or light and serenity?"

Now Sano wondered if the abbot remembered their conversation. With the arrogance of youth, he'd disregarded his elder's insightful remark. Never had he imagined that he would one day appreciate the danger in his dubious talent.

Having acknowledged their past association, the abbot dispensed with refreshing their acquaintance. As much canny politician as spiritual leader, he undoubtedly knew as much about the shogun's *sōsakan* as anyone in the *bakufu,* and had probably reviewed Sano's school records in preparation for this encounter.

"I thought it best to await your arrival before attending to the remains of our brother, Endō Azumanaru, who was murdered tonight," he said. "You will, of course, have our full cooperation in apprehending his killer."

Endō.

Sano's excitement overrode his relief at learning that the abbot meant to facilitate his investigation. As the abbot and his retinue ushered them up the path toward the temple's inner precinct, Sano asked, "Was the dead priest a descendant of Endō Munetsugu?"

"Why, yes. Brother Endō took orders after retiring from the

bakufu service." Many samurai sought a contemplative life in their old age. "He was very proud of his ancestry. But how did you know of it?" Displeasure brought a transient frown to his serene face. "Did the guards tell you that the name Endō Munetsugu appeared on the label fastened to Brother Endō's head?"

Sano and Hirata exchanged glances of suppressed elation. This fourth victim proved the theory.

"No," Sano said, hastening to exonerate the guards of disobedience by explaining how this tragedy had brought enlightenment.

They passed beneath a torii gate at the end of the path, then climbed the steps.

"What was Brother Endō doing outside after dark?" Sano asked. Priests, who rose at dawn, usually retired by sunset.

"He was the security officer who led the night patrol."

Now Sano knew that the Bundori Killer chose his victims deliberately, familiarizing himself with their habits, then selecting the right time and place for their murders. Anyone in the *banchō* could have told him of Kaibara's visits to the pharmacists' district, but he must have paid informers to tell him the *rōnin* Tōzawa's whereabouts. To learn of Brother Endō's job, he must have questioned someone living at the temple. The thought of such elaborate calculation froze Sano's blood.

At the top of the steps, an enclosed corridor with a tile roof formed the temple's inner wall. Through its narrow windows, Sano saw frightened faces looking out at him, and heard whispered conversation. Even before he entered the main precinct, he could feel the atmosphere of fear, shock, and horror that pervaded the temple.

The precinct blazed with the light of flames that leapt within stone lanterns and flared from torches planted in the vast courtyard. The massive architecture, with its carved columns and doors, and undulating thatched roofs supported on complex wooden bracketry, dwarfed the priests who stood around the Buddha Hall, five-story pagoda, octagonal sutra repository, and the temple bell in its wooden cage. On the hill outside the wall, Sano could see the roofs of the temple's other buildings: abbots' residence; priests', novices', and servants' dormitories; refectory; the tombs of past shoguns. Stripped of the animating panorama of pilgrims and ritual, the temple seemed like a stage set where the minor players waited, motionless and silent, for the principals to arrive.

"This way." The abbot led Sano and Hirata around the main hall. There, outside the rear door, seven priests stood in an out-ward-facing circle, shielding something at the center. "Out of re-spect for our brother, we have retrieved his head, which the killer left outside the main gate, and placed it by the body. Otherwise, the scene is undisturbed." At the abbot's command, the priests fol-lowed him to the courtyard, leaving Sano and Hirata to their task.

Even the Bundori Killer's earlier atrocities could not have pre-pared Sano for his first sight of the priest's remains. Horror-stricken, he sucked air through his teeth. He heard Hirata moan.

Blood covered the white gravel in a lurid crimson stain. At its center, the priest's headless corpse lay on its back. Sword wounds covered his body. The torn fabric of his saffron robe framed a deep gash in his right side. Minor cuts on his calves showed be-neath the hiked-up hem of his cloak. And he'd lost his left hand, which lay several paces from where he'd fallen. This victim, un-like the others, had fought back. Still clenched in his bloody right hand was the spear he'd wielded in vain against his attacker's sword. More splashes of blood on the gravel defined the area where the fight had taken place.

Sano glanced at the trophy head just long enough to note the rouged face and square mounting board that proclaimed it the work of the Bundori Killer, who had nailed the name label to Brother Endō's shaven scalp. He surveyed the murder scene with a sinking feeling due only partially to his failure to prevent an-other death.

From behind him, Hirata voiced the troubling question in his mind. "*Sōsakan-sama,* why did the shogun's shrine attendant send us to that house in the marshes, instead of here?"

"I don't know, Hirata," Sano answered wearily.

And he wouldn't, until he saw Aoi again. But for the first time, he doubted the woman who had gained his trust, aroused his senses, and touched his spirit.

"Search the area and see if you can find any trace of the killer," he told Hirata. "Footprints. Blood—the priest may have wounded him." Brother Endō's spear was covered with blood, perhaps not only from his own wounds. "Maybe he left a trail showing which way he went after he left the temple."

While Hirata strolled and stooped in widening circles around the murder scene, Sano rejoined the abbot in the courtyard. "Please send Brother Endō's remains to Edo Morgue," he said. "Now I need to speak with each member of your community, starting with the person who found the body."

An incredulous smile touched the abbot's mouth. "That's hardly necessary. I can tell you whatever you need to know. The night patrol discovered Brother Endō. They report having seen no one and nothing out of the ordinary, either before or after. Everyone else was in their quarters, where they are now: all safe and accounted for. I and my assistants have questioned them and ascertained that no one saw anything relevant to the murder. And you surely don't think one of us is the killer?"

"No," Sano admitted, having no evidence to tie the other murders to the temple.

He realized that the abbot's cooperation didn't extend to independent interrogation of his subjects, which would breach their seclusion and challenge his authority. Much as he hated to overrule this man whom he revered, Sano knew he must, or endanger his chances of success.

"But I must insist that you bring your people to me, one at a time, in a place where we can talk in privacy."

The abbot's frown forced him to back his request with a veiled threat. "The murders have thrown the city into a panic that can only worsen until the killer is caught. I wonder what effect it would have upon the faithful to learn that their spiritual leader had actually obstructed justice?"

He didn't have to hint at the reduced donations and the mass defections to other temples that would result should such news spread. The abbot conceded with a wounded dignity that hurt Sano more than open reproach. "As you wish, *sōsakan-sama*." He ordered his aides to prepare a room and assemble the community. "But you are wasting your time. No one can help you." He paused. "With the possible exception of one individual."

Sano's spirits lifted. A witness, at last?

"A woman came to the temple early yesterday evening seeking

shelter," the abbot explained. "She said she wished to renounce her worldly life and become a nun. I gave her a room in the guest quarters, pending her transfer to one of our sect's nunneries. I believe it was she who discovered the murder and rang the bell. None of the priests, novices, or servants were outdoors after evening rites."

Sano took a deep breath to still the thudding of his heart. "Then I must speak to her. Where is she?"

"I'm afraid she has disappeared."

"Disappeared?" Sano echoed in dismay.

The abbot spread his hands in a calming, beneficent gesture. "When the security patrol searched the premises after discovering Brother Endō's body, they found the guest quarters vacant and the woman gone. She must have fled after ringing the bell."

"Well, then," Sano said, adjusting his plans, "give me her name and address so I can find her."

The abbot shook his head. "I am sorry to say that she gave no information about herself."

"She wouldn't tell you who she was or where she came from? And you took her in anyway?" Sano's disappointment turned to anger at the abbot. "She might have been a runaway wife or daughter—or a fugitive from the law!"

"*Sōsakan-sama.*" Annoyance tightened the abbot's smooth features. "We don't turn away those who come to us seeking sanctuary. Your criticism shows a deplorable lack of understanding of the charity and mercy that we practice in our faith."

"My apologies, Your Holiness." Inwardly Sano berated himself for letting the pressures of the investigation make him behave like an ignorant boor. "Perhaps if you describe this woman and tell me what she said, I can trace her."

"Certainly." Mollified, the abbot unfocused his gaze, remembering. "She was rather small, and not young. She wore a plain black kimono with no crest. She said she wanted to enter a nunnery because she was unhappy in her marriage."

"Unhappy in what way?" Sano prompted. "Did her husband beat her? Was he a drunk, or a lecher, or a miser? Were her in-laws cruel?"

The abbot shook his head. "She didn't say, and I didn't press for an explanation. After all, she was leaving those problems behind by coming here."

"What about her face? How did she dress her hair? Did she speak like a lady, or a peasant?"

"I'm sorry, *sōsakan-sama*. Her hair and face were veiled, and I spent only a moment with her. We get many women seeking shelter. I remember little about this one."

Sano refused to give up. "Did anyone else see her?"

"No. She acted as if she didn't want to be seen—she wouldn't allow the servants into her room to serve her meal; they had to leave it outside the door."

A witness who had seen something terrible enough to make her ring the huge bell—no small feat for a woman—and flee the temple. And no one knew who she was, or where she could be found. Sano cursed his luck.

"Did she leave any possessions behind?" he asked.

"Yes. A pair of kimonos."

Sometimes, owning nothing else of value, women entering nunneries brought their best clothes as dowries to pay for their room and board. Perhaps this woman's would provide a clue to her identity. "May I please see them?" Sano asked.

"Certainly. They are in my office."

The abbot led the way to another, smaller precinct, where they followed a path between two dormitories—long, narrow buildings with barred windows, plastered walls, plank doors, and narrow verandas. A sound from the left-hand dormitory's second floor caught Sano's attention. He looked up and saw a window open and the shaven head of a boy perhaps ten years old appear. On his face, Sano saw the curiosity and excitement one might expect in a child under the circumstances—but something more. Shame? Guilt?

"Who is that boy?" he asked the abbot, pointing.

The abbot glanced toward the window. "That's Kenji, one of our novices. A farmer's son who came to Edo to seek his fortune when the family crops failed. One of our brethren found him dying in the street and rescued him."

Catching sight of them, Kenji gaped, then slammed the shutters and disappeared. On impulse, Sano excused himself and returned to the main precinct. "Hirata," he called.

Hirata left his examination of the ground around the bell cage and hurried over to Sano.

"There's a novice named Kenji in the upper floor of the left-hand dormitory," Sano said. "I think he knows something about the murder. See if you can find out what it is."

The frightened peasant child might speak more freely to the young *doshin* than to him. Besides, Sano suspected that Hirata possessed abilities as yet untested, which perhaps included interviewing witnesses.

Inside the temple office—a spacious study with an elaborate coffered ceiling, and built-in cabinets and shelves containing books and scrolls—Sano examined the mystery woman's kimonos. Both were made of fine, expensive silk. One was crimson, with a lavish embroidered design of white cranes and snowflakes, green pine boughs, and orange suns—appropriate for the New Year season. The other was a gray fall kimono printed with blue-bells, patrinia, autumn grasses, bamboo, yellow clover, and wild carnations. Sano noted the hip-length sleeve panels typically worn by married women, or those past their youth. Both garments were in excellent condition, but he knew little about fashion, and he couldn't tell if they were new outfits, or old ones worn only on special occasions. Nor could he tell whether they belonged to a samurai lady or a wealthy merchant's woman.

Sano folded the garments and tucked them under his arm. "I'll take these with me, and return them as soon as possible." Maybe the Edo Castle tailors could tell him who had made the kimonos.

They left the office and started down the path. Sano saw Hirata coming to meet him, bringing a small, shaven-headed figure in a hemp robe: the novice Kenji.

"*Sōsakan-sama,* Kenji has something to tell you," Hirata announced.

The novice, seeing the abbot, backed away, his eyes round with terror. Sano guessed that he didn't want his superior to hear what he had to say. Turning to the abbot, Sano said, "I'd like to talk to Kenji alone, please."

The abbot nodded. "I will be in my office if you need me." His eloquent parting glance made it clear that he would allow the novice an unsupervised conversation with an outsider only because he feared adverse publicity.

"All right, he's gone," Hirata said to the novice. "Now tell the *sōsakan-sama* what you saw."

Kenji gulped. His lips trembled. Sano squatted, placing himself at Kenji's eye level, and gave the boy an encouraging smile. "Don't be afraid," he said.

Hirata's method of eliciting speech was more aggressive. With a rough but affectionate gesture, he cuffed one of the ears that stuck out from Kenji's head like jug handles. "Go on, talk! He won't hurt you."

Looking somewhat reassured but still wary, Kenji spoke in a rapid mumble. "Yesterday I went begging in the city." He had been collecting alms to support the temple, as did the other young clergy. "I stayed too late, and it was dark when I started walking home. When I got back, the others were already asleep. I climbed in the dormitory window. The priests didn't miss me, because my friends had fixed my bed to look like I was in it. I didn't mean to be late, honest. Please, master, you won't tell the abbot, will you?" Hands wringing the front of his robe, he raised beseeching eyes to Sano.

"It'll be our secret," Sano said gravely.

"Oh, thank you, master!" Kenji's radiant smile transformed him from a picture of abject misery to a happy, high-spirited child. "You see, master, I was late because I stopped to watch a juggler in Nihonbashi. He was amazing! He juggled knives, and flaming torches, and live mice—"

"The *sōsakan-sama* doesn't want to hear about that!" Hirata interrupted. "Tell him what you saw on the road leading from Edo back to the temple."

Sano's heart skipped, then began a strengthening pulse in his throat. Was he looking at his first murder witness? "What did you see, Kenji?"

"A palanquin," the novice said. "With four big men carrying it. I noticed them because all the pilgrims who come to the temple are gone by dark. When I'm out that late, I usually don't meet any—"

Kenji clapped his hands over his mouth. "I've only been late a few times before, master. Honest!" He clasped his hands in penitence, but his eyes danced with mischief.

"Did you see who was in the palanquin?" Sano asked patiently.

"No. The doors and windows were shut."

"Did you see the bearers' faces?"

Kenji shook his head. "It was dark, and they wore big hats. And I was running to get back to the dormitory before anyone noticed I wasn't there."

Disappointment descended over Sano. Grasping at the receding vestiges of hope, he asked, "Can you remember anything at all about the palanquin or the bearers?"

"I'm sorry, master." Then Kenji's drooping head snapped alert; his eyes brightened. "Wait—I remember now. The moon was shining on the palanquin. And I saw a big dragon painted on the side!"

This information was better than none, but not much. Elaborate decoration signified a private, rather than a hired vehicle. If the palanquin had, as Sano suspected, conveyed the Bundori Killer to and from the temple, he need only call on the several thousand Edo citizens rich enough to own personal transportation.

"What color was the dragon?" he asked, seeking to narrow the field.

Kenji shrugged. "It was too dark to tell."

"Would you recognize it if you saw it again?" Hirata interjected.

"I don't know. Maybe." The novice shivered, beating his hands against his arms. "Can I go now? I'm cold."

After ascertaining that Kenji remembered nothing more about the palanquin and had seen nothing and no one else in or outside the temple complex the previous night, Sano dismissed him.

"I'm sorry he couldn't tell us more, *sōsakan-sama,*" Hirata said. "I wanted to bring you evidence to make up for not having done you any good so far." Self-contempt laced his voice.

"Don't underestimate your achievement, Hirata," Sano said, fighting his own disappointment. "Kenji's testimony might eventually place a suspect near the crime scene. You're a talented investigator. You got facts from the boy that I might not have." Then, seeing Hirata flush with pleasure, he regretted his impulsive praise. He mustn't encourage the young *doshin*'s attachment to him.

"Keep searching the grounds," he ordered. "I'll join you after I've finished questioning . . . three thousand possible witnesses and suspects."

Sano spent the next hours in the temple's assembly hall, interrogating an endless parade of frightened, shocked clergy and servants. Some priests he recognized as former teachers, or classmates who had taken orders and stayed at the temple. By the time he finished, he'd verified the abbot's statement. No one but Kenji had seen anything. And Brother Endō himself had publicized his occupation. A gregarious man, he'd often stationed himself at the main gate to greet and chat with visitors. Any pilgrim—the killer included—could have learned his schedule directly from him.

Afterward Sano joined Hirata and a horde of priests in searching the temple for evidence. Carrying torches, they inspected paths, gardens, monuments, stairways, graveyards, the ground around every building and gate, the forest . . .

And found nothing.

At dawn, Sano and Hirata mounted their horses for the ride back to Edo. In addition to the killer's boards, spikes, and tools, Sano's saddlebags held the mystery woman's two kimonos—the sole tangible reward for their labors.

This night had forever changed his personal vision of Zōjō Temple. Now, when he thought of it, he would no longer picture a sunlit haven of prayer and learning, or recall the happy and sad times of his childhood. Instead he would see Brother Endō's mutilated corpse, and remember his friends and teachers as potential witnesses and suspects. The investigation not only dominated his present and future; it had also damaged cherished memories.

"We got more from this murder scene than from any of the others," Hirata said, as though trying to bolster his own spirits as well as Sano's.

But what did they have? Confirmation of a theory that had as yet led nowhere. The description of a possible suspect's palanquin. A missing witness, and only a pair of kimonos as clues to her identity.

And just four more days to catch the Bundori Killer.

18

Back in Edo, Sano and Hirata parted ways outside the Nihon-bashi produce market, a sprawling complex of stalls, where vendors haggled with customers and porters carried baskets of vegetables, fruit, and grain on their backs. Maneuvering his horse into a quiet side street, Sano gave Hirata orders for the day.

"After you've rested, visit all the palanquin builders in town and find out who made a palanquin with a dragon design on it. Ask who bought it, but don't say why you want to know. If that really was the killer Kenji spotted last night, we don't want him to know he's been seen and destroy the palanquin before we can use it as evidence."

He paused to stop a newsseller who was trudging toward the market with a stack of broadsheets under his arm. "Here's some news for you: 'The shogun's *sōsakan* says that the Bundori Killer seeks to destroy only the descendants of Endō Munetsugu, who should beware.' "

As the newsseller hurried away shouting the words, Sano said to Hirata, "While you make your rounds, spread that message to everyone you can. We want as many people as possible informed before another night falls." If they didn't catch the killer, at least the potential victims would be forewarned, and the citizens calmed.

"I'll start now," Hirata said. "I'm not tired."

Indeed he did look fresh and lively, as if he, like Sano himself, was functioning on the peculiar energy that sleeplessness can induce. Wistfully stroking his mount's mane, he said, "I guess you want your horse back."

"Keep her for now," Sano said. "I'll pay her board at the police stables."

Amazement and gratitude lit Hirata's face. "Thank you, *sōsakan-sama!*"

Sano realized that while he'd merely intended the horse's loan as a means of allowing Hirata to cover more ground faster, the young *doshin* interpreted it as an expression of trust and a deepening of their relationship. Now he couldn't retract the offer without hurting Hirata.

"Should I keep looking for the tall, lame suspect with the pock-marked face?" Hirata asked.

While he pondered the question, Sano let his gaze wander to the market. The morning was unseasonably warm, with a humidity that intensified the odors of vegetable refuse and open drains. Beneath a bright, hazy sky that presaged the summer to come, the market seemed quieter and less crowded than usual, its atmosphere of cheerful commerce conspicuously absent. How long before news of the latest murder spread throughout the city? Would his own message be enough to counteract it? Sano dreaded the escalation of civil unrest more than the threat to his own life.

"Forget about the suspect for now," he said finally.

He still believed in Aoi's mystical powers, and intelligence. Her evocation of his father's spirit and the courtesan Sparrow, her knowledge of the *hatamoto* Kaibara's sorrow, and the circumstances of the *rōnin* Tōzawa's death had convinced him that she could communicate with the spirit world. She'd identified the *eta* murder as a practice killing, and Kaibara's status as last surviving clan member as a reason for the killer to revive General Fujiwara's feud. So Sano had to consider the possibility that she'd deliberately misled him by failing to predict the murder at Zōjō Temple, and sending him to the marshes instead. He also began to doubt her description of the killer. With alarm, he discovered that although he no longer trusted Aoi, neither could he think of her without experiencing a desire that clenched his heart as it warmed his body.

"What should I have my assistants do?" Hirata asked.

Remembering the young *doshin*'s performance at the temple gave Sano an idea for making better use of Hirata's time. "Have you any good informants that you use in your work?"

"A few." The gleam in Hirata's eyes belied his modest disclaimer.

"Then have your men look for the dragon palanquin. You ask your contacts if they can identify the man who attacked me. You have his description. Leave a message for me at the castle gate if you learn anything. I'll send word to the police compound if I need you for anything else."

"Yes, *sōsakan-sama*."

As Sano watched his assistant go, a rueful smile tugged at his mouth. Hirata rode like an expert now, his posture confident as he steered the horse down the crowded street. He wore his pride like a battle flag attached to a soldier's back. Sano was glad that the investigation was bringing happiness to one of them.

He headed for the castle to see whether Noguchi had located General Fujiwara's descendants and show the mystery witness's kimonos to the tailors. So many paths to follow, any or none of which might lead to the killer before the four days were up. But one thing was certain: He would see Aoi tonight, and demand an explanation from her.

In the Edo Castle archives, Noguchi ushered Sano past the main study, where clerks and apprentices pored over documents, and down the corridor to his private office. Inside, chests, stacked shoulder-high and three deep, lined the walls, partially obscuring the windows. Piles of paper occupied every shelf and most of the floor. Noguchi's desk, cluttered with writing materials, formed a small island in the middle. With foreboding, Sano wondered what Noguchi had to say that he couldn't in one of the mansion's more comfortable public areas.

Noguchi cleared a space on the floor, knelt, and motioned for Sano to do the same. "I hope you are well?"

Sano recognized the formality as a stalling tactic: Noguchi didn't want to get down to business—either his, or Sano's. A furtive wariness had shadowed the archivist's open, friendly manner.

"As well as can be expected," Sano replied, explaining about the murder at Zōjō Temple.

"Oh, my, oh, no," Noguchi murmured. Then he cringed and said, "Sano-*san,* I regret to tell you that I can no longer associate myself with you professionally. I think you can understand why not?"

Sano looked away to hide his hurt. He could see that Noguchi had heard about the council meeting and wanted to sever their ties to avoid sharing Sano's misfortunes. He was losing the only friend he had at Edo Castle, when he most needed sympathy and support.

"However," Noguchi continued, "you need not fear that I mean to end our personal relationship before you can arrange for someone to take my place. I will act on your behalf on this day, which is so crucial to you."

Sano could have argued that every one of the next four days was crucial to him. "What do you mean?" he asked.

"Today is your *miai.*" Noguchi's forehead wrinkles began their ascent up his scalp. "Surely you've not forgotten?"

Sano had. Entirely. The event, to which he'd once looked forward so eagerly, couldn't have come at a worse time. How could he interrupt his investigation to pursue a marriage that would never happen if he didn't catch the killer by the shogun's deadline?

"At the Kannei Temple this afternoon," Noguchi reminded him anxiously. "Everything is arranged. The Ueda are coming. Castle palanquins will convey your mother and her maid to the temple. You will be there, won't you?"

Sano longed to postpone the *miai,* but his father had wanted this marriage for him; it was an essential factor in their family's rise to prominence. Sano couldn't offend the Ueda by cancelling on such short notice.

"I'll be there," he said.

"Good." Noguchi looked relieved. "Afterward you can engage a new go-between."

Sano had no time to worry about finding someone to replace Noguchi. The *miai* would consume the afternoon. In more of a hurry than ever now, he turned the conversation to the reason for his visit. "Have you managed to locate General Fujiwara's descendants?"

Noguchi dropped his gaze and suddenly became very busy fidgeting with an inkstone on his desk. Without looking at Sano, he said, "I am afraid you will have to discard your theory for lack of sufficient validity."

"Discard it?" Sano echoed, bewildered. "But tonight's murder confirmed my theory." Then a disturbing thought struck him. "You couldn't find the names."

Now Noguchi met his gaze with one full of pity and chagrin. "I have the list here." He removed a folded paper from his sash, then said with a sigh, "Oh, my. The role of harbinger of bad news is a thankless one. I hope you will not blame me for your disappointment."

Sano snatched the list and eagerly unfolded it. As he read the names, disbelief and despair flooded him. Now he understood what Noguchi meant.

He recognized all four names, even without the descriptions Noguchi had included. All the suspects were prominent citizens— none of whom he could imagine as the Bundori Killer:

Matsui Minoru. Edo's foremost merchant; financial agent to the Tokugawa.

Chūgo Gichin. Captain of the Guard; one of Edo Castle's highest-ranking officers.

O-tama. Concubine to the commissioner of highways; subject of a famous scandal ten years ago.

To the last name, Noguchi hadn't bothered to append a description. And he'd written it in smaller characters, as if reluctant to include it at all:

Yanagisawa Yoshiyasu.

19

In the seclusion of his private quarters, Chamberlain Yanagisawa held Aoi's coded letter to the lamp flame and watched it burn. His shaking hands scattered ash onto the lacquer table. Shock and dread blurred his vision until he could no longer see the room's carved chests and cabinets, painted murals, embroidered silk floor cushions, or the garden of boulders and raked sand outside his open window. As he absorbed the full import of his spy's message, which he'd just received, prickly tendrils of fear spread from his heart into his throat and stomach.

He'd thought that his plan to thwart *Sōsakan* Sano's investigation was working very well. From Aoi's last report, he knew she had Sano looking all over Edo for a suspect who didn't exist. He'd believed that Sano stood little chance of capturing the Bundori Killer.

True, Sano's revelations at the council meeting had shaken him badly; he alone had recognized the merit of Sano's theory, which he'd been unable to completely discredit. He'd failed to detach the shogun's fancy from Sano, and therefore couldn't simply banish or execute the troublesome *sōsakan*. Nor had he managed to relieve Sano of the murder case so that he could give it to the police, whom he controlled. But still he'd believed he would eventually prevail.

Until now.

In her message, Aoi reported the failure of her plan to sabotage Sano by sending him to an abandoned house in which her agents had planted fake evidence. Because of the priest's murder, he must now know she'd misled him, and would cease to trust her guidance. And the witnesses from Zōjō Temple could bring Sano dangerously closer to identifying the killer.

Worse yet, according to Aoi's informants in the castle archives, Sano's pursuit of his theory had yielded suspects. Yanagisawa didn't need to wait for her to collect and send the list of names to know it would include his own. In a haze of terror, he imagined his destruction at the hands of the most serious adversary he'd ever faced. The success of Sano's investigation would mean his own ruin.

The paper burned away, obliterating Aoi's words, but not Chamberlain Yanagisawa's woes. He got to his feet and crossed the room. Opening the door, he shouted for his manservant, who appeared immediately.

"Yes, master?"

Yanagisawa gave his orders. After the servant had hurried off to obey, he began to pace the floor. A bitter, self-deprecating laugh burst from him.

To his subordinates, he always managed to appear the suave, confident chamberlain, always in control of himself, of everyone, and of every situation. But sometimes his terrors and passions held him in a virtual paralysis of indecision and inactivity. He doubted his own judgment, but couldn't seek counsel from others for fear of losing face and power. He would pace, as he did now, like a man trapped inside the prison of himself.

Impatiently Yanagisawa went to the door and looked down the corridor. Why was that fool servant taking so long to deliver what he'd requested?

Yanagisawa resumed pacing. Sweat dampened his garments; panic shot flares through his body until he felt weak, dizzy. The hated Sano Ichirō had brought him to this miserable state. He must devise a plan to wreck Sano's investigation once and for all, to eliminate the threat it posed to him. But first he needed the release that he could achieve in only one way.

Behind him the door opened, then closed as someone entered the room. Yanagisawa turned. Anticipation warmed his blood. Worry and fear dissipated; he smiled.

There stood the shogun's favorite boy actor, Shichisaburō, who knelt and bowed. "I await your orders, master," he said.

Instead of his elaborate theatrical costume, he wore a plain brown cotton kimono and a wooden sword like those carried by samurai boys. As Yanagisawa himself had upon his eighth birthday, when Lord Takei had first summoned him to his private chambers. The simple garb only enhanced Shichisaburō's delicate, striking beauty, as it must have done Yanagisawa's own. The beauty that had attracted the lecherous daimyo.

His father had been Lord Takei's chamberlain, a cold, calculating, ambitious man who had sought to further his family's status by sending the young Yanagisawa to be a page in the daimyo's service. Yanagisawa, just as ambitious, but pitifully naive, had gone willingly enough, expecting to run the daimyo's errands and advance himself in the world. How could he have known, as his father must have, about Lord Takei's tastes? How could he have known that any handsome boy who entered the daimyo's service could expect to be used as an object of physical gratification?

Against a rising swell of memory and an accompanying sensual excitement, Yanagisawa spoke the words that had once been spoken to him: "Rise, young samurai, and let me see your face." He heard his own smooth voice assume the remembered gruffness of Lord Takei's. "Don't be afraid. I mean you no harm."

Shichisaburō obeyed. Yanagisawa studied him with approval. The boy's eyes were round, solemn. His lips trembled, but he held himself tall and proud.

"My only wish is to serve you, master," he said.

Yanagisawa sighed in satisfaction. The boy wasn't really afraid. They'd done this before; he knew what to expect. But his acting was no less inspired than on stage. Shichisaburō knew and accepted that his fate depended on complete cooperation with his superiors. At the first sign of rebellion he would find himself expelled from the castle, stripped of his status as a theatrical star, and working in some squalid roadside brothel. With Shichisaburō, Yanagisawa had come to appreciate the value of a professional.

He'd lost his taste for the castle's pages—inexperienced country boys who sometimes wept or soiled themselves in fright.

"Turn around," he commanded. As Shichisaburō pivoted, Yanagisawa savored the heady rush of arousal in his groin. He sighed again.

As he'd matured, Yanagisawa had learned that the exploitation of boys was common in other daimyo households besides Lord Takei's. Yanagisawa, though, had suffered more than his peers seemed to; he never recovered as they did. When his sexuality bloomed, some compulsion drove him to reenact that first encounter with Lord Takei. Promiscuous in his youthful lust, he'd experimented with men and women, singly and in combinations, in countless situations. But nothing else satisfied him as much as following this script, which had become ritual.

"I invited you here because I've heard reports that you are the most brilliant of all my pages," he said to the boy, "and I wanted to meet you."

Shichisaburō's response was prompt and sincere. "Your attention does me great honor, master!" He flashed his lovely smile, his fear overcome by happiness at being singled out by his lord. How amazing that he could blush at will.

Yanagisawa's heartbeat quickened; his manhood hardened. "Now that I've seen you, I have decided that you will be my personal assistant. You'll serve me well. And I . . ." He paused to enjoy his burgeoning erection ". . . have so much to teach you."

"It would be an honor to learn from you, master." Shichisaburō recited his line with convincing ardor.

"Then we will begin your first lesson now." Yanagisawa towered over the boy, reveling in his own masculinity, his superiority. As Lord Takei must have.

"An understanding of the human body is essential to mastery of the martial arts." Slowly Yanagisawa loosened his sash. "I will use my own as an example for your education." His garments parted to reveal the body he perfected every day with strenuous martial arts training: sculpted chest; strong legs; and the bulge beneath the tight wrappings of his white silk loincloth.

With ceremonial dignity, Yanagisawa unwound the loincloth and let it drop. He took his erection in his hand, offering it for

Shichisaburō's scrutiny. "See how large it is, how potent," he murmured, caressing himself.

As if mesmerized, Shichisaburō gazed upon the organ, eyes blank with uncomprehending fascination.

Lord Takei had made sure that none of his men had already used the young page Yanagisawa—although they would later. He'd reserved the first turn for himself. Yanagisawa had reacted to Lord Takei's self-exposure just as Shichisaburō was doing now.

"This," Yanagisawa intoned, "is manhood in its most beautiful form."

Wounded and disillusioned by his encounter with Lord Takei, the young Yanagisawa had wept every night when the other pages couldn't see him. With the stoicism of his samurai upbringing, he'd suffered the humiliation and pain of subsequent abuse. But gradually he'd begun to see how he could use Lord Takei's obsession with him. Soon he'd risen to the post of chief page. His precocious intelligence had enabled him to assume duties normally entrusted to the daimyo's adult retainers. As a young man he'd quickly advanced through the ranks of these. So when, at age twenty-two, word of his beauty and talent reached Tsunayoshi, the young shogun-to-be, Yanagisawa was ready for greater opportunities.

"This is the glory and the power you must aspire to." Yanagisawa moved closer to Shichisaburō. "Touch me."

He shuddered with pleasure as the boy's delicate hands stroked his shaft, fondled his scrotum. Shichisaburō was better than he, in his inexperienced awkwardness, must have been with Lord Takei.

But not as good as he'd been with the shogun.

Tokugawa Tsunayoshi—weak, trusting, sensual—had quickly fallen under Yanagisawa's control. As he enjoyed Yanagisawa's company in the bedchamber, so did he depend on his counsel. With Tsunayoshi's ascension to the position of shogun, Yanagisawa became chamberlain. He exacted tribute from the daimyo, the Tokugawa vassals and retainers, and anyone else who sought the shogun's favor. His fortune grew. But money wasn't enough. Always he craved greater wealth, higher status. He wanted to be a daimyo—a landowning lord—himself. He wanted to rise above those who had once been his superiors. He yearned to be rid of the fear that the capricious shogun might suddenly transfer his favor to Sano. And he would do anything to achieve the absolute power and freedom to fulfill all desires that the past had instilled in him.

"Take me in your mouth," he gasped now.

Shichisaburō knelt and lowered his head. His warm, wet lips closed over Yanagisawa's organ, sucking and licking. Yanagisawa forced himself to keep his eyes from closing in rapture. Watching someone else submit, as he once had, was the best part of the ritual. Knowing that now it was not he but his victim who suffered humiliation.

To Yanagisawa, humiliation was an integral component of sexual gratification. In his youth it had aroused him even as it withered his self-respect. Now he craved the cruel joy of abasing his partners. Especially the shogun. Oh, he felt a certain condescending affection for Tokugawa Tsunayoshi. They shared many interests—religion, theater, Confucian studies. The shogun doted on him, showered him with gifts and compliments. Sex between them was still pleasurable—although they both preferred boys—and allowed Yanagisawa to maintain his hold on the shogun. But in his deepest soul, Yanagisawa hated Tsunayoshi as an authority figure who dominated him as Lord Takei had.

And how he hated *Sōsakan* Sano, who had not only garnered the shogun's attention, but was also free from the demons of compulsion, and as honorable, well-intentioned, and as full of integrity as he himself should have been.

Yanagisawa banished the thought of Sano. He moaned, giving himself over to pleasure. At the brink of climax, he withdrew from Shichisaburō's mouth. It was time for the next step in the ritual.

"Rise, Shichisaburō," he ordered hoarsely. "Turn."

His hands on his docile victim's shoulders, Yanagisawa walked Shichisaburō to a low table against the wall. He smiled at the terrified, bewildered glances that Shichisaburō threw over his shoulder. Such perfect acting.

"Now I will initiate you into the rites of manhood."

He lifted Shichisaburō onto the table. He raised the boy's kimono, and gasped at the sight and feel of the soft, naked buttocks. He moved his hands around to caress the boy's small organ, which stiffened at his touch.

Like his own had, under Lord Takei's hands.

Then, with a groan like that of a wounded animal—his imitation of Lord Takei's—he drove his organ into the hot, tight mouth of Shichisaburō's anus.

Shichisaburō screamed in simulated fear and pain. "No, master! No!" His hands clawed the wall, leaving scratches among the others already there.

"How dare you defy me?" Yanagisawa demanded.

Jaws clenched, he plunged in and out, excitement mounting. Across the distance of twenty-four years, he heard his own childish screams, felt his own hands against rough plaster, felt the tearing pain as Lord Takei violated his body. And he remembered the sublime moment when he'd first penetrated Tokugawa Tsunayoshi after a year together, finally reversing their roles to become the dominant partner. Since then, no one had ever taken him. He was the taker now.

Shichisaburō's cries turned to whimpers; his body went limp. These cues nearly drove Yanagisawa mad with arousal, but he held back, awaiting the boy's final response, the one that would bring the ritual to its climax.

". . . please . . ." A tearful plea.

Yanagisawa's excitement peaked in a cataclysm of pleasure. He shouted out his orgasm. But as always, he experienced a triumph infinitely more satisfying than any physical sensation.

Never again would anyone dominate him, punish him, or make him suffer the humiliation he feared above all else. It was he who dominated, punished, and humiliated others.

No one must interfere with his rise to power. He would rule the land, if not as shogun, then as the next best thing. No one would ever relegate him to his former status as powerless victim.

Especially not *Sōsakan* Sano Ichirō, whom he must and somehow would destroy.

20

The Hinokiya Drapery Store—one of Edo's best-known shops, and centerpiece of the suspect Matsui Minoru's business empire—stood in the newer merchant district north of Nihonbashi. Sano followed the main approach to the store, urging his horse up the steep slope of Suruga Hill toward the famous view of Mount Fuji that adorned its crest. Around him, porters hauled goods to and from the shops that lined the broad thoroughfare. Food sellers staggered beneath loaded trays; water vendors swung buckets; browsers loitered before the storefronts. But these ordinary sights failed to reassure Sano. He rode with his hand on his sword, eyes alert, and with a growing sense of unease. Danger still lay in wait for him. And he could see that news of the priest's murder had spread faster than his calming message.

Newssellers shouted, "Read the latest! After killing a *hatamoto*, a *rōnin*, and an *eta*, the ghost has now slain a holy man. No one is safe!"

And the unrest had worsened: "Eight samurai killed in drunken duels. Twenty peasants wounded in gang brawl!"

Customers snatched the broadsheets; money changed hands. Eager listeners clustered around a storyteller who acted out the killings in melodramatic speech and gestures. Mystics moaned and wailed over lit candles and incense, trying to invoke the spirits of the victims, or the protection of the gods, while onlookers tossed coins in encouragement.

"O Inari, great goddess, please keep us safe from evil!" one ragged old woman keened.

Watching her, Sano thought of Aoi, and a spark of anger kindled within him. Not only had her last prophecy proved false, but her description of the killer fit none of the suspects. He was beginning to harbor suspicions about her, that he must eventually allay, or confirm. With all the spies in Edo, and more than one person who wanted his investigation to fail, had he been wrong to trust a stranger—even one recommended by the shogun? Now Sano remembered Noguchi telling him about an official forced to commit suicide because his mother's spirit had compelled him to attack Chamberlain Yanagisawa. Had Aoi, with her rituals, played a part in the man's demise? But for now, more pressing problems demanded Sano's flagging energy.

He had his *miai* to attend this afternoon, and four suspects to investigate in less than as many days. And he saw all too well the difficulties inherent to the last task.

Matsui Minoru's, Chūgo Gichin's, O-tama's, and Chamberlain Yanagisawa's status accorded them considerable protection from the law, and greater credibility than his. He couldn't jail them and order the truth tortured out of them, as with common criminals. He must back any accusations he made against any of them with hard evidence—gathered without offending the innocent.

With little time to plan and less expertise to guide him, Sano had left the archives and gone home, where he'd hoped to receive news from Dr. Ito, but the doctor's message said that he'd found no clues on the *rōnin's* remains. Sano had dispatched his servants and messengers to post notices warning Endō's descendants at the castle's checkpoints, on the city's notice boards, and at the gates of the daimyo and *hatamoto* estates. Then he'd prayed briefly at his father's altar for inspiration. Receiving none, he'd formulated a strategy based more upon emotion and expedience than logic.

He'd decided to leave O-tama, the least likely suspect, until last. His samurai spirit rebelled against challenging Chūgo, his superior officer, whose exalted position also posed unique obstacles. And as for Yanagisawa . . .

Any pleasure Sano might have taken from imagining his adversary exposed as a murderer fell before his fear of what he would have to do if he found evidence of Yanagisawa's guilt—which the chamberlain's attempts to thwart him already supported. A black abyss of terror yawned inside Sano whenever he thought of it, so he relegated Chamberlain Yanagisawa to the back of his mind. Instead he concentrated on Matsui, who was neither more nor less likely a killer than the other men, but whose situation presented an easy opportunity. He would go to the merchant's businesses, and, via discreet questioning of his staff, determine Matsui's whereabouts during the murders and probe for rumors of madness or violence on his part. He would investigate Chūgo and Yanagisawa only if this effort failed. Now he reviewed what everyone knew about his first suspect.

For generations, Matsui's clan had lived humbly as low-ranking samurai in the Kantō. Then, some thirty years ago, the young, ambitious Minoru had become head of the family. He'd relinquished his samurai status to enter trade, establishing a small sake brewery near Ise Shrine. Modest success had whetted his appetite for more. He'd moved to Edo and opened a drapery shop in Nihonbashi, where he introduced the revolutionary practices that made him a fortune, as well as many enemies. He advertised widely, and welcomed small customers as well as the great warrior clans. His prices were fixed, instead of negotiable, and he demanded cash upon sale, instead of at the end of the year. In exchange, his customers paid 20 percent less than elsewhere. This had so enraged his competitors that, to escape their hostility, Matsui had moved his shop to Suruga.

However, the change hadn't hurt the Hinokiya, or stopped Matsui's expansion into other business ventures. Now, at age fifty, he held controlling interest in the national shipping firm run by the great merchants. He operated rice plantations. He was one of the country's thirty principal money changers. He also served as financial agent and banker to the Tokugawa and several major daimyo, who considered the handling of money beneath their samurai dignity. These last ventures had made him another fortune in commissions, interest, and fees. He was the wealthiest and arguably the most famous commoner in Japan. And his achievements had regained him the samurai privilege of wearing swords.

The weapons he'd used to murder four men?

Reaching his destination, Sano dismounted and secured his horse outside the Hinokiya. Beneath the deep eaves of its stately tile roof, carved wooden doors stood open, exposing the store to the street. The indigo entrance curtains bore the store's crest in white: a cypress tree, for Hinokiya—Cypress House. From the eaves dangled paper lanterns painted with advertisements: "Cotton and Silk Cloth," "Readymade Clothing," "No Padded Prices!"

Lifting a curtain, Sano peered inside. The store was divided lengthwise into two sections. On the left, clerks wrote up orders and calculated prices on their abacuses at desks ranged along an aisle that extended to the back of the building. Separated from this aisle by a wall of cabinets was the showroom, where shelves held rolls of colorful cloth, sample garments hung from the ceiling, and clerks conferred with customers. Sano decided he would pretend to browse until the senior clerk, an elderly white-haired hunchback, became available. Renowned for his gossip and garrulity, he would be the most likely employee to know and report on his master's doings.

"*Sōsakan-sama.* Wait!"

Already inside the shop, Sano winced at the sound of his title, shouted from down the street. He hoped that his pursuer wouldn't follow, and that his plain garments and lack of response would preserve his anonymity. But to his dismay, the man rushed in after him, demanding loudly, "Is it true that there were witnesses to the Zōjō Temple murder?" A young newsseller dressed in cotton kimono and headband, he wore at his waist a pouch that bulged with coins from the sale of the broadsheets he carried. "Has someone actually seen the ghost?"

"Go away!" Sano hissed. "And stop spreading ghost stories—you're scaring people."

The newsseller stood his ground. "It's my job to bring my customers the news."

Sano touched his sword, and the newsseller hurried out the

door. But the damage was done. Business ceased as clerks and customers stared at him; he saw recognition on their faces, heard his title murmured. And then the street crowd, alerted to his presence, burst into the store. Sano found himself surrounded by frightened faces and grabbing hands. Hysterical voices assailed him.

"These murders are ruining my business . . . gangs own the streets . . . for two *zeni,* I'll perform an exorcism . . . stop the ghost before he kills us all!"

Sano realized with chagrin that he'd become a public figure. No longer able to conduct a covert inquiry at the Hinokiya, he decided to try one of Matsui's other businesses in hopes that he could maintain his cover long enough to get some answers.

"Get away!" he ordered.

The crowd pushed him farther into the store. "Please, save us!"

Sano saw clerks frantically lugging merchandise to safety, trying in vain to close the doors against the horde. Then an angry male voice bellowed, "What's going on here? Everyone out. Now!"

The mob's cries turned to screams. Bodies hurtled into the street, shoved, kicked, and thrown by two huge, grim samurai who had appeared from the back of the store. In no time at all, the doors slammed shut; the Hinokiya was empty except for its staff, Sano—and the man he'd come to spy on.

Matsui Minoru. The man whose business empire spanned the nation. Flanked by the two *rōnin* who served as his bodyguards, accompanied him everywhere, and had cleared the store at his orders, he presented an intriguing and contradictory array of merchant and samurai qualities.

His round, bald head, full cheeks, and eyes that closed into slits when he smiled at Sano could have belonged to any middle-aged, well-fed commoner. He wore a cotton kimono patterned with brown, black, and cream stripes, probably from the Hinokiya's least expensive inventory. Of medium height, he had a stout but firm body whose thick, muscular neck, shoulders, and arms bespoke a life spent lifting heavy sake vats and bolts of cloth.

Matsui bowed. "So, *sōsakan-sama.* Have you taken a break from your work to shop in my humble establishment?"

His direct gaze belied his words, betraying a wholly samurai arrogance. A luxuriant silk lining showed at his kimono's cuffs and hem: the wealthy merchant's circumvention of the sumptuary laws that forbade commoners to wear silk. And he'd not erased the samurai swagger from his posture. This lent his two swords an air of authenticity usually missing in merchants who wore weapons as status symbols. It was common knowledge that he employed a private *kenjutsu* master to tutor him. Matsui gave the impression of a man straddling two classes. Had spiritual conflict caused this former samurai to yearn for the simpler, nobler days of his ancestors? To continue General Fujiwara's deadly mission? Sano studied the merchant carefully as he framed a reply. Despite Matsui's genial welcome, this man of shrewd intelligence surely knew why Sano had come. With subterfuge impossible, he decided on a direct approach.

"I'm here to ask your assistance in apprehending the Bundori Killer," he said.

There was a collective gasp, then silence from the clerks. Matsui's smile widened; his eyes almost disappeared in creases of flesh. "I would be honored to assist you," he said blandly, "but I don't see how I can."

Sano smiled back, feeling like a novice trader entering negotiations with an acknowledged master. Matsui's profession of ignorance forced him to play a card he'd hoped to keep in reserve.

"You can help by explaining the relationship between Araki Yojiemon and Endō Munetsugu, the men whose names appeared on the trophy heads, and . . ."

He paused; Matsui waited him out. The guards tensed; the clerks stirred uneasily. Sano conceded temporary defeat.

"And a certain General Fujiwara," he finished.

To his delight, Matsui's face stiffened: The tentative probe had found its target. Then Matsui laughed, as if proclaiming his own victory in this first round.

"Well, that's definitely worth discussing. I invite you to my house. Come, it isn't far."

He clapped Sano's shoulder and nodded to the guards. Was he showing his innocence—or escaping his audience?

Outside the shop, the crowd engulfed them. Waving their

swords, Matsui's guards forced it back. Their threats and glares discouraged followers. Sano and Matsui continued down Suruga Hill unhindered, Sano on horseback, Matsui and his escorts on foot. Yet the guards' presence didn't relieve Sano's fear of attack. If it was Matsui who wanted him dead, then they were not his protectors.

"Your guards seem very competent," he remarked, wondering if they'd assisted their master with the murders. One had fresh cuts on his face and hands—from Brother Endō's spear? "What services do they perform for you?"

Matsui's knowing smile showed that he understood Sano's intent. "They keep my enemies away. And since I carry lots of money, I'm a target for thieves." He pointed at his guard's cut face. "The man who did that looks much worse."

"A thief?" Sano asked, remembering the priest's wounds.

"If you wish."

Sano realized that Matsui wanted to provoke an open accusation that he could deny, forcing Sano to either give up—or arrest the Tokugawa banker and disrupt the *bakufu*'s finances. Sano switched subjects.

"Do you know a fox-faced mercenary swordsman who eats melon seeds?"

Matsui shrugged. "Edo is full of mercenaries."

Suppressing his impatience, Sano tried still another tack. "I often see you traveling on foot. Don't you own a palanquin?" One with a dragon on it, like the one Kenji had seen outside Zōjō Temple?

"I have three." If this question disturbed Matsui, he didn't let on; he'd probably had plenty of practice hiding his emotions during business negotiations. "But I leave them for my family's use. I myself prefer walking. It's good for the body. Ah, here we are. Welcome to my miserable home, *sōsakan-sama*."

Matsui's house was a large, two-story structure with weathered wooden walls, plain brown tile roof, and unadorned entryway, separated from the street and the neighboring merchant dwellings by a small, bare yard and bamboo fence. An open shed held the three palanquins—all black, with no decoration. However, the dragon palanquin hadn't necessarily carried the killer, who could have traveled by other means. Matsui was still a suspect. And even if this interview cleared him, Sano had three others.

The house's drab exterior didn't prepare Sano for the treasure trove he found inside. Elaborate coffered and gilt ceilings decorated the long corridor they followed past rooms crammed with lacquer chests and cabinets, painted scrolls, embroidered silk cushions, life-size statues, tables and shelves crowded with ceramic vases and ivory and gold carvings. Each room had two maids and an armed guard. In a parlor, women dressed in gaudy, expensive kimonos played cards, smoked silver pipes, drank tea, and ate cakes made to resemble flowers. Windows overlooked a verdant garden and a miniature temple complete with halls, bell house, and pagoda. The whole place reeked of incense and perfume, and personified the vulgarity of the merchant class that earned them the samurai's disdain and jealousy.

"I hope my poor little house pleases you, *sōsakan-sama*." Matsui's voice held a hint of mockery. The guards snickered.

Sano wondered what Matsui's willingness to display his house meant. Nothing to hide? Aside from this obvious possibility, Sano glimpsed a more sinister one. The sumptuary laws prohibited merchants from flaunting their wealth; hence, the house's simple exterior. Breaking the laws could result in confiscation of all an offender's money and property. Last year, the *bakufu* had seized the Yodoya family fortune, including houses, rice fields, gold and silver artifacts, and 300,000 *koku* in cash. Yet Matsui had allowed him to see his outrageous hoard. His expert management of the Tokugawa finances must give him understandable faith in their continued protection.

Did he also have the audacity to believe he could get away with murder?

"Now I'll show you something that should interest you very much," Matsui said.

He slid aside a panel in what had appeared to be solid wall, revealing a short, narrow corridor that led to an iron-clad door. "Extra security precautions," he explained as he opened the door, "for my most prized possessions."

Wondering what could be more valuable than the things he'd

already seen, Sano followed Matsui into a small, windowless room. The bodyguards stationed themselves outside the door. Matsui summoned a servant, who lit a ceiling lantern, then left. The lantern's light illuminated the clay walls of what looked to be a fireproof storehouse connected to the main building. The full-length portrait of a seated man covered the back wall. He wore armor, with his head bare and the helmet resting on his knee.

"My ancestor, General Fujiwara," Matsui announced proudly.

Shocked, Sano stared at his host, then around the room, which he now realized was a shrine to the general. Beneath the portrait, an altar held incense burners, oil lamps, a cup of sake, oranges, and a bowl of rice. Low pedestals placed against the side walls held artifacts that Sano couldn't identify in the dim light. But he could see the soot that blackened the walls. The lamp wicks were burnt, the food fresh. Matsui, with all the luxurious rooms at his disposal, spent much time in this small, dark chamber, communing with his ancestor's spirit.

Matsui's hearty voice overlaid Sano's thoughts. "Just because I'm no longer samurai doesn't mean I've renounced my heritage, *sōsakan-sama*. What's in the blood can never be lost." He gestured to the portrait. "See the resemblance between us?"

Sano did. General Fujiwara's stylized face bore Matsui's features. Only the expression was different: stern, rigid, befitting a great warrior.

Matsui circled the room, lifting items from the pedestals for Sano's inspection. "These are the general's relics that I've inherited. And I'll spend whatever's necessary to acquire those which have become lost over the years. This is his helmet." Tenderly he stroked its battered metal surface. "And this is his war fan." It was a gold disk, mounted on an iron shaft, bearing a crescent-moon crest in flaking red paint. "These scrolls tell of his heroic deeds. And this . . ."

As Matsui extended to Sano a metal handguard with attached chain-mail sleeve, his voice dropped to a reverent whisper. "This is the armor he wore in the Battle of Anegawa. He was wounded; that dark stain is his blood."

A shiver rippled Sano's skin when he saw that Matsui's smile had vanished. His eyes, fixed on his grisly relic, shone with fierce obsession. In that moment he looked strikingly like General Fujiwara.

Like a warrior capable of killing his enemies.

Cautiously Sano said, "You pay respect to your ancestor. Do you also wish you could live his life?"

"Often." A sigh gusted from Matsui; his hands caressed the armor. "After a day spent making deals, counting money, and plotting against my rivals, I long for the simplicity of Bushido. Absolute loyalty and obedience to one's lord. Dying in battle for him. What could be cleaner or more noble?" Matsui chuckled wryly. "So unlike the filthy business of making money. Do you know that my own cousins severed ties with me when I became a merchant?"

Either the shrine induced in Matsui an urge to confide, or he was displaying a show of candor to absolve himself of suspicion. Sano couldn't tell which, but he nevertheless encouraged Matsui's revelations.

"Your family's rejection must have hurt you," he remarked.

"Oh, yes," Matsui said sadly. He returned the armor to its pedestal and knelt before the altar. "I like to think that I could have been a great general. But it seems my fate to lead others in the pursuit of making money. Still, my cousins' disapproval hurts less than the thought of his"—Matsui bowed to the portrait—"had he known how I would disgrace our family."

"You want to deserve General Fujiwara's respect, then?"

A sigh; a worshipful glance at the portrait. "Sometimes I think I would give everything I own for it."

"What do you know of the general's feud with the Araki and Endō clans?" Sano asked, quietly so as not to jolt Matsui out of his introspective mood.

He'd expected the merchant to deny knowledge of the feud, but Matsui answered without hesitation. "My grandfather, the family historian, considered the feud a puzzling but trivial epilogue to an exemplary life. General Fujiwara was ill when he began the attacks on Araki and Endō. His grievances against them may have been the product of a failing mind. But I believe he had a good reason for his actions, and I wish I knew what it was."

Although Matsui's tone and manner hadn't changed when he uttered the last sentence, Sano's extra sense told him the merchant was lying. Still, Matsui had given him an opening.

Phrasing his question carefully, he said, "Would your reviving the feud against Araki's and Endō's descendants appease the general's spirit?"

Matsui slowly turned from the portrait. Sano dared not breathe. Every instinct told him Matsui was capable of killing to ensure General Fujiwara a posthumous victory over his enemies. Now he need only elicit a confession.

Softly he said, "Where were you last night, Matsui? And on the nights of Kaibara's and the *rōnin* Tōzawa's deaths? Did you kill them?"

Visions of the shogun's approval, fulfilling his promise to his father, and the city delivered from evil hovered at the periphery of Sano's consciousness as Matsui lifted haunted eyes to his.

Then Matsui threw back his head and laughed, completely shattering the fragile structure of Sano's interrogation. "You're very good, *sōsakan-sama*," he said, standing. He waggled a playful finger at Sano. "But not good enough to trick old Matsui Minoru. Consider me a murderer, if you will. But remember this."

He faced Sano, arms folded, stance firm: once again the hard-driving merchant who refused to yield concessions. "Would I have shown you this shrine if I were the killer you seek? I certainly wouldn't have let you in my house if I had a blood-spattered trophy workshop to hide. I invite you to search my other houses, my store, my banks and moneylending shops, and my offices at the shipping firm. You'll find nothing there, either. You can question my staff, who will tell you that I'm a good, respectable citizen."

His brazen declaration left Sano speechless. Had Matsui's "confidences" been nothing but a joke at his expense? Or was Matsui bluffing now, to repair the damage they'd done?

"As for the nights of the murders," Matsui continued in the same recalcitrant tone, "I was here at home, in this very room." Pointing at the men outside the door, he added, "My guards will vouch for me. I never go anywhere without them.

"And now you must excuse me, *sōsakan-sama*; I have business to conduct. If you have any more questions, you'll have to arrest me. But think hard before you do. Should the shogun's gold cease to multiply and flow, I doubt if he would thank you."

21

Sano returned to Edo Castle at noon, feeling rushed and discouraged. Now he rode through the main gate to seek Chūgo
Gichin, captain of the guard and second suspect, before attending
his *miai*. Since he couldn't conduct a secret inquiry in the castle,
where spies would undoubtedly report his activities to Chūgo, he
hoped a surprise confrontation might prove more satisfactory than
his clash with Matsui.

He couldn't eliminate Matsui as a strong suspect, despite the
merchant's denials and the common sense that told him such a
man wouldn't risk his wealth and position to revive a dead feud.
He believed in Matsui's sinister obsession with General Fujiwara,
and had sensed his capacity for violence. During their short encounter, he'd grasped Matsui's essential nature: bold, ruthless,
with a grandiose self-importance that could easily inspire a sense
of invincibility. That Matsui's associates would attest to his good
character and his bodyguards to his whereabouts didn't convince
Sano of the merchant's innocence. All those people were in Matsui's pay. Still Sano appreciated the difficulty of establishing Matsui's guilt.

Matsui was far too clever to leave incriminating evidence in his
places of residence or work. Sano thought he could probably per-

suade Matsui's enemies to contradict the good references from friends and underlings, but he doubted whether he could break Matsui's alibi. If the bodyguards had taken part in the murders, they would lie to protect themselves.

This next interview would either offer a better suspect, or eliminate Chūgo Gichin and give him more time to incriminate Matsui. Of Chamberlain Yanagisawa, he could not bear to think, because Yanagisawa's guilt would mean his own destruction. For once, Sano closed his mind to his father's voice, which would force him to acknowledge the possibility he didn't want to face.

Inside the castle, Sano entered the main guard compound, where a thousand samurai occupied the huge, stone-walled courtyard shadowed by the towering keep. Some were mounted, others on foot; all wore swords and armor tunics. The long wooden sheds that bordered the compound held an arsenal of swords, spears, bows, polearms, arquebuses, cannon, and ammunition. This was the mighty heart of the Tokugawa military regime. Through it, like an emperor surveying his domain, strode Chūgo Gichin.

Accompanied by three lieutenants, he alone wore full battle regalia. A black metal helmet with deep side flaps and a pair of carved golden pine boughs adorning its crown sat proudly on his head. An elaborate armor tunic, its many plates laced with red and gold silk cord, hung from his high, square shoulders. Chain-mail sleeve guards covered his long arms. His kimono hem was tucked into metal shin guards that covered legs as slender and straight as wooden pillars. His erect, rigid posture emphasized his spare muscularity. As he made his inspection tour, he carried the weight of his armor without visible effort. His voice, barking orders and questions at his ranks, rose above the sounds of footsteps, hoofbeats, and muted conversation.

Sano watched the captain of the guard and tried without success to imagine him a murderer. This man's family had loyally served the Tokugawa for generations. Chūgo had worked his way up through the military ranks, even doing a stint in the navy. Now he was responsible for the castle's security during his duty shift. It was his job to protect the shogun, his family, and their multitude of officials, retainers, and attendants; to maintain order and peace.

How could he also be the person who had killed four men and thrown the city into turmoil?

Then Chūgo headed toward his command post, passing the armory sheds, whose red curtains bore his crest: a white octagon with the Fujiwara crescent moon in the center.

Sano dismounted and started after Chūgo. Before he'd moved ten steps, a pair of guards accosted him.

"May we be of assistance, *sōsakan-sama?*" one asked. A touch of insolence tainted his courteous bow and greeting. Just three days ago, these men would have treated Sano with fawning subservience. He marveled at how quickly news of his downfall had reached even the *bakufu*'s lower echelons.

"I must speak with Captain Chūgo Gichin," he said.

Scornfully looking him up and down, they advanced until he was forced to move backward toward the gate.

"It concerns a matter of vital importance to castle security," Sano added.

The two guards stopped, exchanged glances, shrugged. "Come with me," the spokesman said.

Sano offered a silent prayer of thanks for underlings who preferred to shift responsibility to their superiors. Shadowed by his escort, he followed Chūgo's steps to a large shed in the compound's corner, built under a tall watchtower. He braced himself, hoping his arrival would startle the captain into betraying guilt. But as they entered the command post, the guard shot an arm across Sano's chest.

"Wait," he ordered.

The post's anteroom was unfurnished, earth-floored. An open door at the rear showed the captain's office, which contained a desk, cabinets, chests, pieces of armor and weaponry. The walls were covered with duty rosters and maps of the castle. Sano's attention flew to the room's center, where Chūgo Gichin knelt on a straw mat, profile to the door, fists balled on his thighs. He'd removed his armor and helmet; now, a black hood completely covered his head. An attendant was positioning four man-size straw dummies around Chūgo. Finishing, he came to stand beside Sano at the door. He raised a finger to his lips for silence. Sano nodded agreement, eyes riveted on Chūgo. Anticipation tightened his stomach. He was about to witness a demonstration of the martial arts skill for which Chūgo had achieved nationwide fame: *iaijutsu,* the art of simultaneously drawing and cutting with the sword.

Chūgo sat perfectly still; he appeared not to breathe. But Sano sensed the mental energy flowing from him as his trained perception divined the positions of the unseen targets. While Sano waited in suspense for Chūgo to draw his sword, he wondered what the captain's proficiency at *iaijutsu* said about him.

Iaijutsu was a discipline particularly suited to peacetime, when samurai kept their weapons sheathed, instead of drawn as in battle. The techniques could be used defensively, or to secure the opening move in a duel. Hence, most reputable *kenjutsu* masters trained their students in them. But *iaijutsu* had a treacherous, and therefore dishonorable aspect. Too often it was used against unwary opponents or unarmed peasants. Many of the latter had died in "crossroad cuttings," or "practice murders," when a samurai merely wanted to test a new sword.

Had Chūgo used his deadly skill to strike down Kaibara Tōju, the *rōnin* Tōzawa, and the *eta* before they'd perceived the danger? Did his choice of discipline imply a willingness to attack helpless or unsuspecting victims? One thing Sano knew: Extreme devotion to the martial arts often indicated an obsessive adherence to Bushido. Had its credo of ancestor worship driven Chūgo to murder?

In a single fluid motion, Chūgo leapt to his feet and whisked his sword free of its scabbard. The blade's blurred white arc whistled sideways through the air, slicing off the first dummy's head. Without a pause, Chūgo whirled. He severed the second, third, and fourth heads before the first hit the ground.

Sano's breath caught at the beauty and precision of Chūgo's performance. Then a premonition of danger licked at him like an icy flame. He gave an involuntary shout and sprang backward. Heedless of the law that prohibited his drawing a weapon upon another man inside the castle, his hand instinctively sought his sword.

Because instead of sheathing his blade and kneeling again as the exercise dictated, Chūgo came hurtling straight toward Sano, swinging his sword upward in both hands for an overhead killing cut.

Sano had his sword free and ready to parry the blow. Then, at the last instant, the guard and Chūgo's attendant realized what was happening.

"No, Chūgo-*san!* Stop!"

Seizing Chūgo's arms, they arrested his attack. He froze, sword at the peak of its deadly ascent.

Sano froze, too, then slowly sheathed his weapon as he saw Chūgo's body relax and felt the captain's murderous impulse subside. With his heart hammering and combat energy still surging through his body, he watched Chūgo step free of his men. He let out his breath as Chūgo calmly returned his sword to its scabbard, then removed the black hood.

"Sōsakan-sama."

Chūgo spoke in a gruff monotone that betrayed little interest and no surprise. His long face conformed to his body's linearity. Thick, horizontal eyebrows crossed the bridge of his thin nose. His narrow eyes, dark, unblinking, and so devoid of emotion as to appear lifeless, looked out from deep, rectangular gashes set above knife-edge cheekbones. Vertical creases etched his skin from the nostrils to a thin, almost lipless mouth. From the jawline, his chin tapered to a sharp point. Only one feature deviated from this geometric theme: the puckered scar that snaked across his shaven crown.

Encompassing both Sano and the other two men in his death-like gaze, he said, "We won't speak of this accident."

Obviously he meant that no one would report the incident, and therefore neither he nor Sano would suffer the suicide penalty dictated by law. Sano, badly shaken by the violent encounter, could only nod as he tried to match Chūgo's stoic calm and organize the torrent of thoughts that flooded his mind.

Blindfolded, Chūgo had decapitated all four dummies in the time it would take an ordinary swordsman to sight a target and draw his weapon. Aside from Chūgo's obvious skill at swordsmanship, however, Sano had another reason to believe he'd cut down four men in the dark of night.

Chūgo had meant to kill him. This Sano knew with every particle of his being, despite the captain's claim of an "accident." Had

Chūgo lashed out in reaction to the vague threat of a stranger's arrival? Or because he'd instinctively recognized the man who might expose him as the Bundori Killer?

"Practice is over. Put the targets away," Chūgo told his attendant. To Sano: "What do you want?"

He dismissed Sano's escort and moved into his office, where he scrutinized the castle maps whose colored pins represented troop positions. Sano followed. He watched Chūgo shift pins like a general planning a battle. The minimal chance of a siege didn't seem to affect his dedication to his job.

"Well?" Chūgo asked.

Sano found himself sorting and grouping questions in his mind, much as Chūgo was doing with the pins. "You probably know that the shogun has assigned me to catch the Bundori Killer," he said, feeling his way.

"So?"

Apparently uninterested, Chūgo strode out of the command post, where he addressed his lieutenants. "The coverage of the eastern perimeter is too thin," Sano heard him say. "Dispatch another unit there at once."

Then he returned to the office to peruse the duty rosters. His movements had an impatient jerkiness that contrasted with the fluid grace of his swordplay. Intent on his duties, he seemed not to care if Sano ever stated the purpose of his visit.

"The labels on the heads of the killer's victims bore the names Araki Yojiemon and Endō Munetsugu," Sano said. "Two men who had a troubled relationship with your ancestor, General Fujiwara."

The captain's hand remained steady as he ran his finger along the columns of names on the roster. His lips compressed in irritation, but not surprise or dismay. "What of it?"

Sano tried to see the thoughts behind Chūgo's opaque eyes. If he was the Bundori Killer, he revealed no fear of exposure. But then Chūgo, as a martial arts master, would have trained himself to suppress all signs of emotion.

"General Fujiwara had a grudge against Araki and Endō," Sano said. "He risked his life trying to destroy them. Whoever killed Kaibara Tōju, the *rōnin* Tōzawa, and the priest Endō seems to have revived the feud by attacking Araki's and Endō's descendants. I believe the killer is a descendant of General Fujiwara's, out to complete his blood score."

"Pah!" Chūgo's snort conveyed all the contempt that his face didn't. Before he could speak, his attendant entered the office, bearing a lacquer box.

"Your meal, Honorable Captain."

"Set it there." Chūgo knelt on the mat and pointed to the space before him. The office was warm, and he opened his kimono and rolled up the sleeves. No wounds marked his limbs or torso; he'd either evaded Brother Endō's spear during combat, worn armor, or never fought at all. To Sano, he said, "If you're asking me if I'm a murderer, I'm not. And my ancestors are none of your business. Besides, the past is dead."

But was it, Sano wondered as Chūgo unpacked the lunchbox. "Dried chestnuts, kelp, and abalone," he remarked as each item appeared. "Do you always choose the foods eaten by soldiers before battle?" Perhaps Chūgo wasn't so indifferent to the past as he pretended. He was certainly familiar with war rituals.

Chūgo shrugged. He ate like a man fueling his body for combat: grimly, washing down each mouthful with a gulp of sake from a battered metal flask. "I eat what I please."

Having gotten nowhere by subtly probing this impenetrable man, Sano tried a blunt query. "If you're not the Bundori Killer, then where were you last night?"

"That's none of your business, either. But I'll tell you anyway. I was here. At the castle. Where I've been for the past fifteen days. I never leave during my duty shift. Any of my men will tell you that."

Sano tilted a pained glance at the ceiling. Here was another alibi, just as dubious as Matsui's and even harder to break. The Edo Castle guards, including the gate sentries, owed allegiance to their captain. They would corroborate any story he told, take his side in any dispute, especially one with a retainer who'd lost the shogun's favor. Even if Sano managed to find a brave or disgruntled individual willing to say otherwise, thousands more would swear to Chūgo's presence in the castle during all four murders. No magistrate would convict him without more proof. Sano thought of the two kimonos, which he had yet to show the tailors, and of the mysterious missing woman. He wondered if Hirata was having any luck finding the dragon palanquin's maker, or learning the assassin's identity.

"Do you own a palanquin with a dragon design on it?" he asked.

"No. I use the castle's." These bore no ornamentation except the Tokugawa crest.

"Have you ever hired a mercenary swordsman?"

This time, one corner of Chūgo's mouth lifted in a sardonic smile. "If I wanted to kill someone, I'd do it myself."

"What would you say if I told you a witness saw you outside the castle last night?" Sano bluffed.

Chūgo chewed, swallowed, and wiped his mouth on his sleeve. "That you're lying. Or your witness is."

Sano's frustration mounted. Chūgo had betrayed neither concern, nor knowledge of the witness's gender.

Finishing his meal, Chūgo said, "Enough false accusations, *sōsakan-sama*. Time for you to go."

He rose and strode to the door. Cupping his hands around his mouth, he shouted for his lieutenants in a voice that could have carried across a battlefield. Suddenly the two men were dragging Sano out of the command post while Chūgo returned to his work.

"Let go!" Sano shouted. He managed to shake his captors loose, but more men came to their aid. They hoisted him onto their shoulders, carried him across the compound, and dumped him, stomach down, upon his horse. Someone slapped its rump. Sano barely managed to sit upright in the saddle before his mount bolted. The entire command provided a resounding send-off of cheers, hoots, and laughter.

Fuming, Sano rode away, plotting the revenge he would take by seeing Chūgo arrested, convicted, and executed for the Bundori Murders. The captain's character, swordsmanship skill, and knowledge of war rituals all warranted more suspicion than his alibi could dispel. But for now, Sano turned his horse toward the Official Quarter. He had no time to waste on thoughts of personal retribution. If he didn't hurry, he would be late for his *miai*.

In the passageway, he stopped a castle messenger. From his

sash he took the letter he'd written in a stationer's shop on Suruga Hill. It detailed his plan for tonight, a course of action he'd hoped would be unnecessary, but now deemed crucial—especially because it could eliminate the need for investigating Chamberlain Yanagisawa. He gave the letter to the messenger, along with a generous tip to ensure quick delivery.

"Take this to *doshin* Hirata at the police compound immediately," Sano said.

Then he hurried home to prepare for his *miai*.

Kannei Temple, located in the hilly, rural Ueno district north of the castle, was one of Edo's most popular sites for viewing cherry blossoms. Every spring, citizens flocked there to enjoy the lovely scenery while contemplating the transience of life, so poignantly symbolized by the short-lived flowers. Across the temple's grassy slopes, the luxuriant leafless blossom clusters hovered in masses of pink cloud beneath the pale sky. Petals fell like snowflakes upon the paths and grass, the heads of the strolling crowds, and wafted toward Shinobazu Pond's pine-fringed silver expanse.

Sano, having left his horse outside the temple's wall, barely noticed his surroundings as he hurried along the gravel paths, past halls, pagoda, and pavilions, and wove through the crowds. He was very late for his *miai*. He ignored the cries of Ueno's famous crows as they circled overhead, and the colorfully dressed picnickers: beautiful women; playing children; drunken men who danced, sang, and cavorted on the lawns. The pressures of his work and this all-important social rite drained all pleasure from the outing that so many others were enjoying.

At last the Kiyomizu Hall came into view, a stately structure painted bright red, with a blue tile roof and a balcony overlooking Shinobazu Pond. Sano followed the wide promenade along the lake. Muttering apologies, he squeezed past a procession of chattering women carrying identical green and white paper parasols. He dodged more pleasure seekers and sprinted down the promenade, then came to an abrupt stop at the grassy hill that sloped upward to the hall. He winced at the social gaffe he'd committed.

According to plan, he should have arrived early, joining his mother and Noguchi for a seemingly casual stroll along the promenade, then meeting Magistrate Ueda and his daughter as if by accident. The charade would have allowed both parties to pretend that a *miai* had never taken place, thus saving face, should the marriage negotiations fail. Sano's tardiness had made all pretense impossible.

Everyone had already assembled at the designated meeting place on the promenade, beneath the famous Moon Pine, named for the branch that looped in a perfect circle: His mother, leaning on her maid Hana's arm; Noguchi; Magistrate Ueda, a stout, middle-aged samurai dressed in black ceremonial robes decorated with gold family crests. And a slender young lady with silky black hair that fell to her knees, dressed in a lavish red and white kimono and accompanied by two female attendants: Ueda Reiko, the prospective bride. All of them, despite their natural poise, must be suffering agonies of embarrassment on Sano's account.

Arriving sweaty and breathless, Sano said, "Please excuse my late arrival. I meant no offense, and I'm sorry for any inconvenience you've suffered." He bowed to those he knew. "Noguchi-*san*. Mother. Hana."

His mother smiled a gentle rebuke. She looked thinner and weaker, but more placid than when he'd last seen her. Noguchi's frown-wrinkles slid up his scalp as he said with false joviality, "Well, you're here now, and that's what counts." He turned to the other man. "Magistrate Ueda, may I present Sano Ichirō, His Excellency's *sōsakan-sama*."

Magistrate Ueda's gaze took careful measure of Sano as he bowed. He had abundant gray hair, broad features, and a ruddy, youthful complexion. Heavy lids shadowed eyes bright with intelligence. The lines around his mouth suggested that he smiled often, though he didn't now.

"The honor is all mine, Sano-*san*," he said in response to Sano's professions of respect and gratitude. His voice was low but confident, that of a man with no need to flaunt his power. "And this is my daughter, Reiko."

Sano bowed, courteously not looking too hard or too long. And she, a proper young lady, kept her head inclined, the lower part of her face covered with her fan. He glimpsed only her long-lashed eyelids and white forehead with its high, thin, painted brows.

"Well," Noguchi said, rubbing his hands together in exaggerated enthusiasm. "Let's walk around Kiyomizu Hall, shall we? The cherry blossoms there are particularly fine."

They ascended the hill. Sano knew he should impress his prospective father-in-law with his intelligence and wit, but couldn't think of anything to say. Coming in the midst of his troubles, this ritual seemed unreal. Would he survive to marry?

Noguchi initiated the conversation with a poem appropriate for the occasion:

> *"They bloom only a short time—*
> *Ah, this life of ours . . ."*

Thankful for his friend's intervention, Sano recited the rest of the poem.

> *"But when four days have passed, where*
> *Are the cherry blossoms?"*

He quoted other similar poems to display his literary education, and inquired about the Ueda family's journey to the temple. But he couldn't hold up his end of the conversation. The poems reminded him of his deadline. Was his hope of success as ephemeral as the dying cherry blossoms?

Breaking an uncomfortable silence, Magistrate Ueda spoke. "Might I have a private word with you, Sano-*san?*"

Sano looked at him in uncomfortable surprise. Convention called for the two families to converse as a group. Before he could reply, Noguchi answered for him.

"Why, yes, of course, Honorable Magistrate," he said, obviously anxious to make amends for Sano's deplorable rudeness. "Go ahead. I will chaperone the ladies." Making shooing motions at Sano, he joined Sano's mother, Reiko, and the attendants.

Sano walked on ahead with Magistrate Ueda. Fearing that his earlier apologies had been inadequate, he said, "There was no excuse for my tardiness. I beg your forgiveness, and your daughter's, even though I have no right to expect it."

"No need for apologies, Sano-*san*." Magistrate Ueda's tone was grave, but not unkind. "The responsibility given you by the shogun must and should consume the major part of your time and attention. No, I have other concerns besides your late arrival. If I may speak frankly?"

Warily Sano nodded.

"My sources tell me you've somehow offended Chamberlain Yanagisawa, who has turned the shogun against you." As the path wound beneath more cherry trees around a small hollow, Magistrate Ueda contemplated a merry group of men toasting one another with sake. "And that if you don't solve the murder case, you'll be exiled to Sado Island. Is this true?"

Sano, familiar with the upper-class custom of employing investigators to check on prospective in-laws, had feared that Magistrate Ueda would learn he'd lost the shogun's favor before he could reclaim it. Now he owed an honest disclosure to this man who had entered negotiations for his daughter's hand in good faith.

"Yes," Sano said reluctantly. "It's true."

"Ah." Magistrate Ueda nodded, seeming disappointed but not surprised.

"But my investigation is progressing," Sano hastened to add, not wanting to lose this chance at the marriage his father had wanted for him. He summarized his findings, ending with: "I've identified four suspects, and one of them is the Bundori Killer."

The magistrate didn't reply immediately. In silence, they skirted a bevy of shrieking children. "I must say I've also heard much good about you, Sano-*san*," he said at last. "You've acquired a reputation for courage, intelligence, and an impressive dedication to truth and justice. What you've just told me confirms it. There are also rumors of a valuable service you performed for His Excellency."

Sano regretted that his pact with the shogun prevented his answering the magistrate's unspoken question, and perhaps forestalling what he knew would come next.

"Because of these favorable reports—and Noguchi's recommendation," Magistrate Ueda said, "I agreed to this *miai*. And, I must admit, because of my daughter."

An affectionate smile touched his lips as he glanced over his shoulder. Sano, following his gaze, saw that Reiko had abandoned her prim reserve to laugh at something Noguchi was saying. Her eyes met Sano's for a moment. Before she again hid her face behind her fan, Sano saw that her beauty was different from Aoi's: delicate and classic. But she was a more suitable match . . .

"Reiko overheard Noguchi telling me about you," Magistrate Ueda continued. "She's never before expressed interest in any marriage proposal, but she insisted on meeting you, despite my reservations. Sometimes she displays a most unfeminine strength of will."

The pride in his voice softened his critical words. Then the smile left his face. "I love my daughter, Sano-*san*. She's my only child, and the very image of my deceased wife. Her happiness means much to me. For that reason, I consented to the *miai* and gave you a chance to speak for yourself. But I can't allow the marriage and let Reiko share your uncertain fate. I'm sorry, Sano-*san*."

That Sano had anticipated rejection didn't lessen his shame and disappointment. Suddenly he could no longer bear the beauty of the landscape, the laughter of happy revelers. Would the failure of his investigation follow this one?

Woodenly he said, "I understand, Magistrate Ueda."

He found that he regretted more than the lost hope of an advantageous marriage with an attractive lady. He knew Magistrate Ueda's reputation for fairness, which his willingness to hear both sides of a story had just proved. He meted out harsh sentences to the criminals he convicted, but showed mercy in extenuating circumstances; his mention of both the good and bad reports, as well as his considerate rejection, demonstrated his compassion. He was above bribery, untouched by scandal, and apparently incorruptible. Sano would have felt honored to deserve a family connection with a man of such character.

To hide his humiliation, he focused on his surroundings. They'd made a complete circuit of Kiyomizu Hall and reached the side overlooking the lake. And they'd gotten far ahead of Noguchi and the women.

Magistrate Ueda put a hand on Sano's arm. "I wish you success in your investigation, and the best of luck in the future."

The words were spoken with genuine sincerity, but Sano barely heard them. For just then, a familiar figure, standing on the hall's balcony, caught his eye.

Dressed in brilliant robes, Chamberlain Yanagisawa contemplated the blossoming cherry trees below him. As Sano watched, he turned and spoke to a group of similarly attired men beside him. Among them Sano recognized several important officials: This was a combination business meeting and pleasure jaunt. As Sano gazed at Yanagisawa's vivid figure, his muscles tightened and his mouth went dry.

Sooner or later he must confront Yanagisawa, if not to establish the chamberlain's guilt or innocence, then to settle their differences. He tried to rationalize his reluctance by listing the reasons Yanagisawa couldn't be the Bundori Killer. Despite his ancestry, character flaws, and attempts to halt Sano's progress, the chamberlain was Tsunayoshi's second-in-command, a respected *bakufu* official, and surely too occupied with government affairs to care about an ancient feud. But thoroughness, as well as Sano's desire for the truth, dictated that he treat Yanagisawa as a suspect until cleared, no matter how much he wished otherwise. And if the chamberlain wasn't the killer, Sano must propitiate him. Even if he solved the murder case and avoided exile, his future success depended on Yanagisawa.

"I'll wait for our party here," Magistrate Ueda said. "Perhaps you'd like to walk awhile?"

The magistrate was kindly allowing him time to recover from rejection before joining the others as if nothing had happened. Seeing Yanagisawa leave the veranda and disappear into the hall,

Sano realized that this might be his only chance to speak with the chamberlain, who might refuse him a formal private audience.

"Thank you, Honorable Magistrate," Sano said. No longer able to avoid the task that filled him with dread, he wandered down the path and waited.

Soon Yanagisawa came out of the hall and sailed down the steps. Leisurely he descended the hill and strode along the promenade. Sano followed him onto the narrow strip of land that extended into Shinobazu Pond. Yanagisawa walked between the teahouses that bordered it, toward the small island where the shrine to Benten, goddess of water, stood. With sinking heart and dragging footsteps, Sano trailed after him.

Chamberlain Yanagisawa reached the island and passed through the shrine's torii gate. Inside, a small pine grove sheltered the outer precinct, which was momentarily deserted. Sano caught up and drew a deep breath.

"Honorable Chamberlain Yanagisawa," he blurted. "May I speak with you?"

Yanagisawa turned. His half-smile vanished when he recognized Sano. His eyes began to smolder; hostility emanated from him in almost visible waves.

"I have nothing to say to you, *sōsakan*." Venom seeped through his suave tone. "How dare you intrude on my privacy in this brazen manner? Leave me at once!"

Sano's courage waned, but he held his ground. Dropping to his knees, he said in a rush. "Honorable Chamberlain, please tell me what I've done to offend you. Whatever it was, it was unintentional. And I want to make amends." If he did, then perhaps the chamberlain would agree to an interview that would undoubtedly clear him of all suspicion.

Instead of replying, Yanagisawa shot out his foot in a vicious kick. His thick-soled wooden sandal struck Sano's shoulder. Sano sprawled backward, uttering a cry of pained surprise. Anger erupted within him; he longed to take his sword to this man whom Bushido dictated that he revere as his lord's representative. He wished he could prove Yanagisawa the Bundori Killer . . . almost.

Yanagisawa stood over him, fists clenched at his sides. White lines of rage tightened the flesh around his mouth. "There is nothing you can say or do to compensate for trying to frame me for murder."

"I'm not trying to frame you," Sano protested, still shocked by the chamberlain's uncharacteristic display of temper. Away from the shogun, he apparently felt no need to maintain his suave poise. Sano stumbled to his feet, realizing that the castle spies must have told Yanagisawa about Noguchi's search for General Fujiwara's descendants. "I was only investigating a lead. I had no way of knowing that your ancestry connected you to the murders. Any inquiries I make about you will be strictly formalities, for the sake of a thorough investigation. I haven't told anyone that you're a suspect, or tried to incriminate you. Because I can't believe you're the Bundori Killer."

Even as he spoke, he tasted the doubt underlying his denial. Was Yanagisawa angry for the stated reason, or out of fear of exposure?

Yanagisawa appeared not to hear his words. He advanced, backing Sano up against the gate. "You seek to ruin my reputation and turn the shogun against me by slandering my ancestors and spreading lies about me." His voice issued from his distorted mouth like spurts of corrosive steam. "Well, I won't tolerate it. Do you hear me?"

Sano could only stare, dumbfounded by Chamberlain Yanagisawa's allegations. Such a scheme had never entered his mind, although he suspected that other *bakufu* officials might discredit an adversary this way. Now he realized that whatever had initially set Yanagisawa against him was nothing compared to this perceived insult. With nothing left to lose, Sano decided to pursue his investigation.

"Honorable Chamberlain, you can prove your innocence by telling me where you were during the murders. If you have a satisfactory alibi, the matter will be dropped, and—"

Sano gasped as the chamberlain seized his collar and yanked him so close that their faces almost touched.

"Listen to me, *sōsakan,* and listen well," Yanagisawa hissed.

Fury drew his face into an ugly scowl. Sano tried to pull away, but Yanagisawa gripped him with a strength amazing for a man of such slender physique.

"I am His Excellency's highest official. You are merely his lackey for three more days. You have no right to interrogate me, and I am under no obligation to answer." Hot, sour spittle pelted Sano's face. "And if you persist in harassing me with impertinent questions and false accusations, I will—"

Yanagisawa stopped just short of an open threat. Did his refined sensibilities shun such crude behavior? Or did he fear antagonizing a man who could destroy him?

Whatever the reason, he released Sano, stepped back, inhaled and exhaled deeply. He smoothed his garments as his elegant features hardened into their customary smooth mask. But his eyes were dark, bottomless pools of hatred and anger. When he spoke again, he did so in low, deadly tones.

"Let us just say that I will not allow you to succeed in your mission. And before I am finished with you, *sōsakan,* you will beg for the privilege of boarding the exile ship for Sado Island."

He turned and swept out the torii gate. In despair, Sano stood and watched the retreating figure. The encounter with Yanagisawa hadn't produced any evidence of the chamberlain's guilt, but neither had it cleared him and allayed Sano's dread. And by forcing Yanagisawa's hostility into the open, Sano knew he'd only worsened their relations. What would he do now?

Sano squared his shoulders, forced a pleasant expression, and started toward shore, where he could see Noguchi, Magistrate Ueda, and the women waiting for him beside Kiyomizu Hall. But when he reached the promenade, he halted in his tracks. All thought of the failed *miai* fled his mind.

To his right, Chamberlain Yanagisawa's party was climbing into a line of palanquins attended by bearers ready to carry them back to Edo. Yanagisawa bowed to his colleagues, then entered the lead palanquin.

The one with a snarling dragon emblazoned in red, green, and gold across the black lacquer doors.

Sano gaped as the bearers lifted the palanquins and trotted past him. The clatter of their footsteps faded from his consciousness; his vision darkened. The dragon palanquin's image burned into his mind.

That quickly, Chamberlain Yanagisawa became his prime suspect. And Sano finally acknowledged his worst fear—the terrifying heroic act by which he might have to secure his family's place in history. Now he could not shut out his father's voice, speaking to him across the years:

"Sometimes an evil spirit, in the form of a corrupt councillor, enters the house of a great lord. Such a councillor leads the lord astray with misinformation, surrounds the lord with his own cronies, and removes any opposition against himself. The councillor procures women or entertainers to seduce the lord away from business and addict him to pleasure. He squanders the lord's money to further his own evil purposes. He causes the ruin of the lord's health and character, and ultimately, the regime."

"No," Sano whispered.

He'd watched Yanagisawa dominate the shogun, usurp his authority, cater to his vices, and steal his wealth. If Yanagisawa had also murdered four men, this would confirm him as the "evil spirit." Sano didn't want to recall Bushido's harshest lesson, but his father's relentless voice continued as he watched Yanagisawa's palanquin disappear around a curve.

"The evil spirit must be destroyed, but not through open confrontation, which could cause scandal or war. The most admirable deed a samurai can do is to sacrifice himself for his lord's sake. To rid the regime of corrupting influence, he must kill the evil spirit, then commit ritual suicide to escape capture and disgrace, and establish his clan's honor for all eternity."

23

Astride his horse, Sano followed Chūgo Gichin into the daimyo district. This morning, he'd assigned Hirata the dangerous task of following Matsui Minoru tonight. For himself he'd claimed the even more perilous undertaking of watching Chūgo, whose formidable swordsmanship skills made him a greater threat than Matsui and his bodyguards combined—and who could command the demotion, dismissal, beating, or death of an inferior officer caught trespassing upon him. Now Sano carried out his plan, despite the knowledge that his time would be better spent pursuing Chamberlain Yanagisawa.

He couldn't deny what he must do should Chamberlain Yanagisawa, his prime suspect, prove to be the killer. No one would believe Yanagisawa was guilty based on the word of a man who'd lost the shogun's favor, as Sano had. Yanagisawa controlled the *bakufu*. Sano could be condemned as a traitor for speaking against him. To guarantee justice and serve honor, Sano must slay the chamberlain, then commit suicide to escape the disgrace of arrest and execution.

Yet the thought of *seppuku* sent terror gusting through Sano's soul like a cold, ash-laden wind. He wasn't sure he possessed the courage to take his sword to himself. He'd risked his family's honor and his own career to pursue this investigation. Now his life depended on proving Chūgo's, Matsui's, or the woman O-tama's guilt, rather than Chamberlain Yanagisawa's.

Heading south, Chūgo kept his head down, his horse to the middle of the wide boulevard, and its pace brisk, as if he feared observation by the sentries at the gates of the great walled daimyo estates. Sano followed at a safe distance. So far so good: Chūgo didn't stop or turn his head. But when they entered Nihonbashi, the captain acted increasingly wary. He meandered and back-tracked through the streets, pausing at intervals to look over his shoulder. Each time, Sano stopped his horse so Chūgo wouldn't hear the telltale hoofbeats, because this section of the quarter was deserted, with no noise to provide cover. Sano focused half his concentration on avoiding Chūgo's notice.

The other half he devoted to watching his own back. Because the attack he feared could come at any time, and he was most vul-nerable now—alone, at night. His preoccupation cost him. Once, when he didn't stop in time, Chūgo's head snapped alert at the two extra hoofbeats that echoed his horse's. Later, when Sano turned to check behind him, he lost the captain. He galloped wildly around corners and almost ran into Chūgo at a neighbor-hood gate. Hastily retreating into an alley, he watched Chūgo re-spond to the sentries' interrogation.

"Otani Teruo, retainer of Lord Maeda," the captain said when asked his name. The sentries, obviously intimidated by his stern appearance, let him pass without searching or challenging him. At the next gate, Chūgo gave his credentials as "Iishino Saburō, re-tainer of Lord Kii," with identical results.

Anticipation made Sano's skin tingle. Was the captain traveling under a series of aliases so no one could report his absence from his post? Or because he meant to commit murder, and wanted no witnesses who could place him near the crime scene?

The captain's next move completely perplexed Sano. Chūgo turned down a deserted street of closed shops. From behind a public notice board, Sano watched him dismount and tie his horse outside the only lit building. Chūgo looked up and down the street, then walked up to the shop's door. Someone opened it at his knock, and he vanished inside.

Sano blinked at his quarry's abrupt disappearance. His doubts about Chūgo's guilt and Yanagisawa's innocence resurfaced. Had Chūgo befriended his next victim, thereby gaining admittance to the man's shop, where he could kill without fear of discovery by gate sentries or patrolling *doshin?* Or did Chūgo merely have a late business appointment? Sano dismounted and secured his horse to the notice board. He scanned the area, but saw no one lurking anywhere. Keeping close to the buildings across the street, he stealthily advanced on the shop until he was directly opposite it. Through the translucent paper windowpanes, he saw at least four shadowy figures moving around in the lighted room. If two were Chūgo and his victim, then who were the others? He had to see! But heavy bars secured the windows. The wooden door, plaster walls, and thatched roof appeared solid, with no apparent chinks he could use for peepholes.

Sano crept back down the block and led his horse around the corner to an alley that ran behind the shop. The alley was wide, but crowded with stinking wooden garbage containers, night-soil bins, and public privies. Darkness enveloped the buildings, whose overhanging balconies partially blocked the moonlit sky. Sano entered, restraining his horse and tiptoeing so as not to arouse the notice of anyone inside the living quarters over and behind the shops. After secreting his horse between two privy sheds, he looked in both directions, but saw no one. Counting doors, he reached the building Chūgo had entered. His frustration increased at the sight of the shuttered windows and iron-banded door.

He didn't see the figure creeping toward him down the alley until it was almost within touching distance.

Alarm blared inside him like a soundless scream. In an instant, he noted the man's sinister appearance: the wide hat worn low over the face; the hand under a baggy cloak that surely hid a weapon. And the abrupt pause that meant he'd seen Sano, too.

Sano didn't wait for the attack to come. He hurled himself at the assassin.

The impact of their collision jarred Sano's bones and forced a startled grunt from the assassin. Together they crashed to the ground, Sano on top. He struggled to subdue his adversary, who was heavier than he, and obviously a seasoned fighter. Conscious of Chūgo inside the shop just a few paces away, Sano bit back a cry as a fist struck his cheek. He swallowed the pain when his opponent drove a knee into his stomach. They rolled over, and Sano's head slammed against hard ground before a muscle-straining heave regained him the upper position. With his knee, he pinned the assassin's right hand, which was scrabbling for the sword he could feel under the man's cloak. At the same time, he fended off more blows. He managed to get both hands around the assassin's neck. Taking a deep breath, he squeezed.

The man gasped and coughed. His body bucked, trying to throw Sano off. His nails gouged Sano's fingers. Sano bore down steadily, but didn't exert enough pressure to kill. He wanted his foe alive, and talking.

"Who hired you?" he demanded in a loud whisper, panting with his effort to restrain the thrashing man.

Wheezing and gurgling beneath his hat, which had fallen over his face, the assassin continued to fight. His knee sought Sano's groin, almost dislodging him. Sano banged the man's head on the ground.

"Who sent you? Talk!"

He throttled the enemy until his struggles weakened. Then he eased the pressure. This time, the assassin went limp and spread his hands in a gesture of surrender.

"All right," he rasped. "Just please let me live."

Sano cautiously removed his hands from the man's throat and sat back on his knees. "Who—?"

He never saw the punch that exploded against his chin and sent him flying backward to smash against a wall. His ears rang; he saw angry red fireworks. As he lurched to his feet, he saw his opponent rushing at him, hat off, sword raised. Sano knew he might never learn the identity of assassin or employer; instead, he must kill or be killed. He drew his own sword.

The instant before the assassin let loose his first cut, a ray of moonlight caught his face. Surprised recognition arrested Sano's defensive parry.

"Hirata?"

The young *doshin* froze at the sound of Sano's voice. Shock and horror rounded his eyes and mouth. Then he dropped his sword. *"Sōsakan-sama?"*

"Shhh!" Sano put a finger to his lips. In their surprise, both of them had spoken loudly. "Hirata, I'm sorry I attacked you," he whispered. "But what are you doing here?"

Hirata fell to his knees and bowed. *"Sōsakan-sama, gomen nasai*—a thousand pardons for hitting you! I was just following your orders." Pointing, he raised his whisper to a loud, urgent hiss: "Matsui Minoru is in there!"

Stunned, Sano stared first at Hirata, then at the shop Chūgo had entered. What were the two suspects doing together?

24

Chūgo Gichin knelt on the floor of the moneylending shop, watching Matsui Minoru pour sake. The shop's lamplit main room was empty except for him and his host. Matsui's clerks had long since left; their scales for weighing gold stood idle on the shelves beside the abacuses they used to count it. The desks were clear of the ledgers, writing materials, and strings of coins that would litter them during the day. Matsui's two nightwatchmen had retreated to the back room to resume standing guard over money and records. Of Matsui's many customers, nothing remained except the lingering smell of tobacco smoke. To Chūgo, the stench symbolized the taint of money. He felt soiled, as if being here contaminated his warrior spirit. His stomach twisted with ingrained loathing for Matsui: merchant, ex-samurai, symbol of greed and dishonor. And, unfortunately, his blood relative.

"Isn't it strange how destiny once led us apart, only to bring us together again, my kinsman?" With a genial smile, Matsui offered Chūgo a cup of sake.

The remark, as well as Matsui's familiar manner, nettled Chūgo. "We ceased to be kinsmen when you abandoned the Way of the Warrior," he retorted. Reluctant to advertise his connection with Matsui, he'd taken pains to make sure no one had seen him come here. Now he accepted the cup, but only pretended to drink. "I don't consider you family. Even if we are cousins by birth."

Matsui's cheerful laugh had a dangerous edge. "Well, that was blunt . . . cousin." He tossed back his own drink and regarded Chūgo with a bright, challenging stare. "Perhaps we'll soon see which of us brings the family more honor. Or more disgrace."

"So you invited me here to insult me?" Chūgo demanded. "If I'd known, I wouldn't have come."

Anger's corrosive poison spread through his chest. But the acrimony between him and Matsui had not begun with them. It had deep roots in the past.

After Oda Nobunaga's murder, most of his retainers were redistributed between his chief generals, Toyotomi Hideyoshi and Tokugawa Ieyasu. But General Fujiwara had spent the short remainder of his life attacking the Araki and Endō clans instead of serving his lord's allies. After his death, three of his sons—Chūgo's great-grandfather included—had sworn allegiance to Tokugawa Ieyasu. Matsui's great-grandfather became a commander under Toyotomi Hideyoshi, surpassing his brothers because his master was Oda's direct successor. This coup had caused a serious rift between the competitive brothers, who'd broken off all contact.

Now the thought of that ancient rivalry stoked Chūgo's anger. Setting down his full cup, he started to rise. "Excuse me. I must get back to my post."

Matsui only laughed again. "You know why I asked you here, and that's why you came. That's why you're neglecting the duty you consider more noble than the pursuit of money—even if you are just a glorified watchman protecting your master from a nonexistent threat."

Chūgo's anger flamed into outrage. Clenching his jaws and fists, he yearned to draw his sword and slay the merchant. His great-grandfather must have felt the same animosity toward Matsui's. And with what satisfaction must he have greeted the next major event in the family saga.

The rift between General Fujiwara's sons had widened with Toyotomi Hideyoshi's death and Tokugawa Ieyasu's ascension. Chūgo's ancestor, having fought heroically under the victorious Ieyasu at the Battle of Sekigahara, had accompanied the new shogun to Edo Castle. Matsui's, and the other two brothers, received lesser posts throughout the Kantō, the rich agricultural provinces outside Edo. Thus the family became separated by physical distance as well as mutual resentment.

Chūgo forced himself to sit back and lift his cup again. He couldn't afford the luxury of venting his anger, because he'd indeed guessed that Matsui had summoned him for one of two reasons.

Seeking a quick end to their meeting, he broached the more innocuous, though not less serious topic. "You wish to discuss my loan?"

Matsui's eyebrows rose in feigned surprise. "Your loan? Oh, yes, now I remember. You did borrow a large sum of money. Last year, I believe."

No doubt he could name the exact date and amount if he chose, Chūgo thought as hatred's bitter swell filled his throat. The merchant paid scrupulous attention to every business detail. The knowledge that Matsui was toying with him added to his anger, as did Matsui's next remark.

"Even you, cousin, must admit that we merchants are of some use, no?"

The vulgar oaf would remind him of the shameful fact that while the samurai ruled the land, the merchants controlled its wealth. However, Chūgo's family hadn't forseen the double-edged consequences of Matsui's defection from the samurai ranks when they'd first received news of it.

Chūgo had been fourteen—a year short of manhood and his career with the Edo Castle guard. On that summer morning, he'd been practicing swordsmanship in the barracks with three other young samurai when a castle messenger ran up to his family's quarters. When his father came to the door to receive the scroll, Chūgo intensified the swordplay, battering mercilessly at the other boys with his wooden sword. He barely heard their cries or felt their counterblows. He knew only the desire to excel, to win, to show his father his worth.

Realizing that the game had turned deadly serious, Chūgo's opponents fled, screaming. Feeling like the great General Fujiwara, whose blood ran in his veins, Chūgo looked to his father for praise.

His father stood on the veranda. Having just gone off duty, he still wore full armor. The open scroll dangled from his hand. His troubled gaze passed straight through his son.

"Your cousin Minoru has abandoned his post as warden of His Excellency's estate in north Kantō and opened a sake brewery in Ise," he said.

Contempt harshened his voice, but his strange smile bespoke pleasure as well as distaste; his eyes gleamed with righteous satisfaction. "Out of some remaining vestige of decency, Minoru has dropped the Fujiwara name—for which we can be thankful—and now calls himself Matsui."

Chūgo's father had schooled him in Fujiwara clan history from an early age. He understood that his cousin's shameful act, while disgracing the clan, elevated his own branch within its hierarchy. He grinned, triumphant as though he'd won another victory.

Then his father's eyes focused on him, and Chūgo saw himself as the older man must: a lanky, barefoot youth with a silly wooden sword. Through the misery of his shame and inadequacy, he heard his father's voice.

"It's up to us to uphold the family honor. You'll have to do more than win children's games if you expect to match General Fujiwara's standard."

Chūgo heard similar admonitions with increasing frequency throughout his young manhood, because his clan's glee over Matsui's disgrace soured as they watched him grow ever richer and more influential. While they scrimped to meet rising expenses with their fixed stipends, Matsui lived extravagantly. The Chūgo, as guard captains, saw the shogun during large ceremonies and business meetings; Matsui enjoyed private audiences. His position as financial agent of the Tokugawa put him closer to the seat of power than Chūgo would ever get. With a mixture of fury and humiliation, he realized that his wayward cousin had bettered him.

Now Chūgo fumed, remembering the debts he and his lord owed Matsui. He usually sublimated his desire for battle—a samurai's rightful work—in the meticulous execution of his duties. But now, with keen pleasure, he felt the power that always flowed through his body the instant before he performed an *iaijutsu* exercise. He imagined his hand flashing to his sword. He saw the blade whip free of the scabbard and blur across space, yearned for the sensation of sharp steel against flesh and cartilage. In his mind, he saw Matsui fall dead, and himself the victorious warrior . . .

A needle of fear pierced Chūgo's fantasy as he studied the stout, smiling, and still-very-much-alive merchant. Was Matsui calling in his loan? He couldn't possibly pay now. He had heavy expenses and no ready cash.

"Oh, you're right on schedule with your payments, Chūgo-*san*. There's nothing to discuss . . . about that, anyway."

A spate of dread swept away Chūgo's relief. Only his samurai stoicism enabled him to feign indifference. "Then what do you want?"

Matsui's jovial manner fell away like a dropped screen, revealing the shrewd trader who had made fortunes for himself and his clients. "We must discuss the Bundori Murders, and how to protect ourselves."

"I don't understand," Chūgo stalled.

Suddenly his need for liquor almost overcame his distaste for Matsui's hospitality. He longed to gulp the heated sake: potent, heady. Because of course he understood Matsui's meaning.

"*Sōsakan* Sano has learned about General Fujiwara," Matsui said, "and about the feud that ties him—and us—to the murders. He's talked to you, too, hasn't he?"

"How did you know?" Chūgo demanded, alarmed both by Matsui's knowledge and the fact that Sano had spoken to the merchant. Sano must truly believe he would find the murderer among General Fujiwara's descendants. What a disaster, should this information become public! "Who told you?"

Matsui shrugged impatiently. "I have many clients in the castle, whose debts I forgive in exchange for favors. Who told me isn't important. This is: Did you tell *Sōsakan* Sano the family secret?"

Chūgo barely managed to contain his shock at this blatant mention of the secret, passed down through the generations since General Fujiwara's death. It was the one tie that bound their family's estranged branches. Chūgo could remember vividly the day his father had bequeathed it to him.

It was the first day of the seventh month, ten years ago. He'd succeeded to his retired father's post as captain of the guard five years previously. Inspecting the castle's outer perimeter on that hot, wet afternoon, he'd turned at the sound of his name to see his father hobbling toward him down the stone-walled passage.

"*Otōsan,* what is it?" Alarmed, Chūgo hurried to meet the old man, who had never before interrupted his duty.

His father waved aside the supporting hand Chūgo offered. "Son, you've followed the Way of the Warrior in a manner that does our clan proud. Now I must tell you something of great importance. Come."

Although consumed with anxious curiosity, Chūgo knew his father wouldn't speak until ready. They walked slowly along the ascending passage. The drizzle trickled off Chūgo's armor and the old man's cloak. Moisture steamed up from the ground. Low clouds hovered over the castle, weighty as Chūgo's father's unvoiced message. They stopped outside the northwest guardtower, the old man's favorite spot, and he spoke in hushed, somber tones.

The secret's immensity left Chūgo breathless with shock and outrage at the terrible wrong that General Fujiwara had sought so valiantly to redress. And, as his father continued, he sensed the huge responsibility that came with his new knowledge.

"As head of the family after my death, you must pass the secret on to your own eldest son before you die. Except for then, you must speak of it to no one, not even your cousins, who have also received the knowledge from their fathers. You must keep the secret alive so that some day, when the time is right, one of General Fujiwara's descendants will complete the noble mission that he began."

"Yes, *Otōsan.*"

Dazed, Chūgo answered automatically, wondering when the time would be right, and if it was he who would fulfill their clan's destiny. In the years that followed, he'd guarded the secret zealously, awaiting some signal to act. How dare Matsui suggest that he would reveal the secret to *Sōsakan* Sano?

"Of course I didn't tell him," Chūgo said sharply.

"Good." Matsui refilled his cup. "Now I want your promise that you'll continue to keep quiet. *Sōsakan* Sano has guessed that the murders originate in our family's past. But without knowing the motive behind them, he can't build a good case against us. As long as he never learns our secret, he can never harm us."

He added, "And if you're considering using it to divert his suspicion onto others, remember that the secret incriminates you as well."

The unjust accusation and the prospect of colluding with Matsui curdled Chūgo's stomach, even as he realized the necessity of a conspiracy. He knew he would never tell the secret, but he needed assurance that the dishonorable, untrustworthy merchant wouldn't, either.

"I have nothing to fear," he said in futile protest. "I have an alibi that no one will ever break. Are you afraid because you can't say the same?"

Matsui let loose a hearty peal of laughter. "Don't be ridiculous. My bodyguards can vouch for me. But I have another alibi that's even better: my innocence. I'm no murderer."

Chūgo stared, amazed that Matsui could lie with such perfect sincerity. He knew for a fact that the merchant had killed in the distant, if not the recent past. The incident, a culmination of all the offenses Matsui had inflicted upon Chūgo's family, had provided a shattering aftermath for Chūgo's greatest professional triumph.

By age thirty, Chūgo had served as gate sentry, patrol and palace guard, squadron commander in both the army and navy— all in preparation for someday assuming his father's post as captain of the guard—and had just achieved the rank of lieutenant. His first major task: conveying Shogun Tokugawa Iemitsu on a pilgrimage to Zōjō Temple.

The huge procession, a series of palanquins carrying the shogun and his party, attended by squadrons of armed guards, had snaked through Edo's winding streets. Chūgo, as the guards' superior, rode through the ranks, constantly on the lookout for the slightest breach of security. Proud of the mighty defense he'd planned and now directed, he'd wished General Fujiwara could see him.

He was riding with the advance guard when suddenly he heard shouts. Rushing straight toward the shogun's palanquin came a ragged, unshaven samurai, waving a sword. Chūgo didn't pause to wonder whether the attacker's blood lust was due to drink, madness, or anger at the regime. While his troops were still turning to assess the threat, he cut swiftly through their ranks. Before the samurai reached the procession, Chūgo intercepted him, sword drawn. One stroke of Chūgo's blade, and the attacker lay dead at his feet.

The procession reached the temple and returned home safely. The next day, the shogun rewarded Chūgo's valor, presenting him with a new sword. Chūgo had thought that by risking his life for his lord—a samurai's ultimate purpose—he'd at last paid adequate tribute to General Fujiwara.

The next day, shocking news swept the city. A rising young merchant had been stabbed to death at his hillside villa. Chūgo and his father stood in the guardtower, reading the broadsheet that described an attempted robbery that had turned to murder when the victim surprised the thieves.

Chūgo's father crumpled the paper. "It was no robbery. My sources tell me that Matsui murdered the man, who was his chief competitor."

That a blood relation could kill for mere financial gain mortified Chūgo and detracted from his own noble achievement.

"I shall atone for the disgrace to our clan," he said, drawing his new sword. "I, unlike my cousin, will prove myself worthy to claim General Fujiwara as an ancestor."

Now Chūgo forced his mind back to the present, and to the man whose moral depravity had inspired his own ambition almost as much as their ancestor had.

"I'm only concerned about the effect that being a murder suspect might have upon my business," Matsui was saying. "I could suffer a loss of customers, a run on my bank, complete social ruin. And in your circles, even unfounded rumors can cost a man his position."

How well Chūgo knew and feared this terrible disgrace!

Matsui's jovial smiled returned; he raised his cup. "So come, cousin, let's make a pledge of silence, for the good of us both. After all, don't we already have an understanding?"

In a lighter tone, as if to change the subject, he said, "Blood ties are unbreakable. Family connections bind even enemies—especially when they revere the same hero. When such is the case, betrayal is out of the question. Yes?"

So the vulgar creature hadn't lost all his manners when he revoked his samurai status. In perfectly refined speech, he'd just alluded to the fact that because of shared blood and loyalty to General Fujiwara, each of them would refrain from questioning the other's innocence. Neither would turn the other in for any crime, even murder.

"Yes," Chūgo agreed grimly. He needed Matsui's reciprocal discretion, and he had another crucial reason for resisting the urge to kill Matsui: Eliminating one of General Fujiwara's descendants would only focus *Sōsakan* Sano's attention on the other three.

Still, Chūgo made a last valiant attempt to reject Matsui's proposition. "But aren't you forgetting something? There are two other people who know the secret. What if they tell?"

Matsui frowned, though with less concern than Chūgo had expected. "The woman O-tama could be a problem. But the other . . ."

For a moment, Chūgo saw the specter of Chamberlain Yanagisawa hovering in the room; he knew Matsui did, too.

"I doubt if we need worry about him," Matsui said. "After all, the secret is more dangerous to him than us. But enough of your pointless stalling, Chūgo-*san*. Your promise?" He brought his cup to his smiling lips. "If you don't give it, I may be forced to call in your loan."

Chūgo glared at the foul, filthy creature to whom fate and blood so disgracefully bound him. Then he sighed. He lifted his cup and drank, swallowing his anger, hatred, and fear along with Matsui's excellent sake.

25

From the promenade outside Edo Castle, Sano watched Chūgo
Gichin enter the main gate. Defeat dragged heavily at his spirits as
he waited a safe interval, then followed.

He and Hirata hadn't found a way to see or hear what was going
on in the shop, so they'd waited outside and resumed pursuit
when Chūgo and Matsui emerged. But the imminent closing of the
gates left the suspects insufficient time to kill. Chūgo had ridden
straight back to the castle, and Sano expected that Matsui, too, had
gone home. Now Sano returned to his mansion, but only to leave
his horse before setting forth on the night's second mission.

As he walked through the dim, quiet passageways, physical exhaustion hit full force. He hadn't slept for two days, or eaten since
afternoon; his head ached, and his empty stomach burned; his
chin hurt where Hirata had hit him. Therefore he found great relief in being safe inside the castle's walls, where no assassin could
reach him. However, survival seemed his only victory in a day
fraught with failure.

He'd seen his hopes for a distinguished marriage destroyed. He
hadn't eliminated Chūgo or Matsui as suspects, but had failed to
gather evidence against them. Tonight's fiasco had merely tipped
the balance more heavily toward Yanagisawa's guilt.

As Sano made his way toward the Tokugawa ancestral shrine, submerged anger burned through his unhappiness. His upbringing forbade him to rage against the code that formed the parameters of his soul, so he turned his anger on a convenient target: Aoi. Tonight he would find out whether his suspicions about her were valid—and make her pay for misleading him. Unwillingly he remembered their last meeting: her beauty; the yearning he'd experienced and knew she had too. Now fresh desire heated his blood and turned his anger to raw fury at the betrayal of what they'd shared.

Focused inward, Sano belatedly registered the sound of footsteps following him through the passage. They synchronized with his own almost perfectly. When he paused, they ceased until he resumed walking. His extra sense flooded him with alarm that he at first dismissed. Inside the castle, he was safe. He was simply reacting to two days and nights on the alert for an assassin by imagining threats where none existed. Still, his skin tightened; his bones vibrated in unmistakable response to approaching danger. Quickening his pace, Sano glanced over his shoulder. A curve in the stone wall blocked his view. He couldn't make himself stop and let his follower pass, or turn back and challenge him. He couldn't overcome the defensive instinct instilled in him by a lifetime of training.

Sano broke into a run. As he tore through around the passage's winding curves, he heard his pursuers panting between his own labored breaths. Once the hunter himself, he was now the prey. Was this a game of idle castle samurai who sought entertainment by ganging up on a convenient victim whose humiliation—or injury—would bring them no punishment? Or was it connected with his investigation, and the earlier attack on him? He could sense the pursuers' malice like a pressure current along his nerves.

A checkpoint loomed ahead of him. All hope of aid died when he saw the abandoned gate standing open. Where were the guards? Once past the gate, with his pursuers hard on his heels, Sano made an even more disturbing discovery. The guardhouses that ran along the tops of the walls were dark, vacant. No troops patrolled the passage. He was unprotected, alone with his pursuers.

Sano shot past more deserted checkpoints and open gates, end-less lines of empty guardhouses and towers. Soon he began to tire. His heart felt ready to explode; his lungs heaved painfully; his body grew slick with sweat; his legs heavy as stone. An ache stabbed his side. And still the footsteps pursued him, forcing him higher into the castle's upper northwest reaches, farther from home, the palace, the guard compound, and other populated areas lower on the hill.

His cramp worsened as he pounded through the gate that led to the martial arts training ground. He heard the men closing on him while he skirted the pond and swerved around archery tar-gets. He dashed past sheds and stables, then across a road, into the Fukiage, the castle's forest preserve, where he could surely lose his pursuers.

The towering pines enclosed him in their dark, whispering hush. Spurning the gravel paths that led to gardens and picnic grounds, Sano wove his way between trees, trying to run softly on ground carpeted with pine needles. He'd reached the limit of his endurance; he must rest, or collapse entirely. Sagging against a tree trunk, he gasped for breath. Blood roared in his ears. He looked back toward the forest's edge. His runaway heartbeat ac-celerated. Fresh panic seized him.

Moving toward him through the trees came two wavery spots of light. As he watched, three more joined them, then fanned out to his right and left. The men had brought torches to hunt him. He'd lost the protection of darkness.

With a groan, Sano pushed himself away from the tree. Urgency won out over his need to keep quiet. Low branches whipped his chest as he ran; gravel crunched loudly underfoot when he crossed paths. A torch flame appeared to his right, and he darted away, only to spy another coming straight toward him. Soon he lost all sense of direction. He could only hope he was moving to-ward the gate at the forest's far side, through which he might es-cape.

Then, without warning, a small clearing opened before Sano—a woodland retreat furnished with two stone benches. He knew he should stay hidden in the woods, away from exposed spaces, but his lungs could no longer suck in enough air. The cramp bit him like iron spikes. As he tried to flee the clearing, he stumbled and fell to the ground.

Leaves rustled; branches snapped. Now the torches drew a tightening circle around Sano. Their fitful light and acrid smoke filled the clearing as the men's shadowy figures emerged from the forest. Sano realized that they'd deliberately driven him into the Fukiage, to corner him here. With the last of his strength, he managed to stand, but too late. The pursuers emerged into the clearing, and unknown terror took on solid form at last.

The five tall, strapping men all wore armor tunics, with dark kimonos tucked into leather shin guards: the uniform of low-ranking castle guards. Swords hung at the left of their waists, stout wooden clubs at the right. Instead of helmets, they wore black hoods that covered the lower halves of their faces.

"What do you want with me?" Swaying on legs gone weak from exertion, Sano looked from one man to the next. His heart fell when he saw the rapacious gleam in their eyes. "Why did you chase me?"

Silence, except for the crackling torches, the restless wind, and his captors' eager breaths. Then the leader, whose more elaborate armor marked his higher rank, spoke.

"You will stop hunting the Bundori Killer," he said, his voice muffled by the hood that didn't conceal its deadly seriousness.

Sano felt a trickle of cautious relief. Had they only run him down in order to deliver a warning?

Then the leader flung down his torch and advanced on Sano, unhooking the club from his sash. The others followed suit. There was no mistaking their intent: to maim, cripple, or kill him to prevent future inquiries. A rush of fresh energy readied Sano's body for combat; his hand sought his sword. Then he remembered the law against drawing a sword within the castle grounds. He hesitated before following his natural impulse to defend himself.

That moment's indecision doomed him. Before he could reach his weapon, the man on his right clubbed his forearm. Sano gasped as pain sped up the bone clear to his shoulder. Again he tried to unsheath his sword, but the blow had rendered his right hand numb and clumsy. With his left hand, he grasped the scabbard to separate it from the blade, but another attacker's club whacked his shoulder and sent him staggering across the clearing. Another grab at his sword earned him a crack against the thigh.

Now his attackers closed in and began showering blows upon him. A club to the chin snapped his head back and locked his tongue between his teeth. The earth rocked; he tasted blood. Then a swipe across the backs of his knees knocked his feet out from under him. The moon and trees careened across his vision as he pitched backward, but he didn't fall, because a jarring swat on the back sent him flying forward again.

Taking advantage of his momentum, Sano lowered his head and drove it into an attacker's armored stomach. The crash jarred his skull; the man grunted and fell. Sano threw himself upon the fallen body. Desperation gave him strength. While hands seized his collar and hauled him up, he wrested the club from his opponent. A smear of light on the ground nearby caught his attention. He snatched up the torch as the men dragged him to his feet.

With a savage wrench, he freed himself. Turning on his foes, he backhanded the club across a hooded face. He heard teeth crack, a howl of pain; the man dropped his club and clutched his mouth with both hands. Sano whipped the torch at the others. Three dodged, but it sent the other's sleeve up in a *woosh* of flame. Screaming, he collapsed to the ground, rolling to extinguish the fire.

"Look out! Get him!" The others, who had fallen back, now rushed forward. One smote the torch a mighty blow that splintered it in two, leaving a short, useless stump in Sano's hand.

Never an expert at combat without swords, Sano knew that his only hope of survival lay in speed, unpredictability, and all-out effort. In a whirlwind of motion, he flailed the club, alternately pivoting, lunging, and striking. He caught a shoulder here, a cheek there, always aiming for unarmored body parts. His strength burgeoned in the excitement of battle.

But his next strikes met solid wood as his opponents parried with their clubs. The gang, having recovered from his assault, landed more blows than he could dodge or deflect. Pain exploded on his shoulders, back, and face.

"Who ordered you to do this?" he demanded in a voice garbled by a mouthful of salty blood. "Was it Chūgo?"

The guard captain commanded all the castle's soldiers, including these. He could have ordered both the attack and the necessary relaxation of security measures. Sano's tormenters answered with only a cruel kick to the knee. He gasped his next question through a daze of agony:

"Was it Chamberlain Yanagisawa?"

As the real power behind the shogun, Yanagisawa ultimately controlled the entire castle and everyone in it. He hated Sano, and desired his downfall. And Yanagisawa was the prime suspect. Sano saw another blow coming, and instinctively flung up his arm to shield his face. He took the impact hard on his elbow, unable to stifle a cry of anguish. Through it, he heard one of the men yell, "Shut up, or suffer more!"

Sano, determined to learn the truth, persisted despite the pain and terror.

"Was it Matsui?"

The merchant must have many of the shogun's retainers in his debt, and he could afford to buy whatever services he needed. Had he ordered this attack?

At a stinging crack on his wrist, the club flew from Sano's hand. He heard a thunderclap when another blow hit his temple. His surroundings shattered into a crazed jumble of light and motion before his eyes. Gasping, he fell on his side. His tormenters' raucous laughter echoed in his ears.

"Look at the great *sōsakan!* Down on the ground where he belongs!"

Sano couldn't move. His muscles felt like pulped meat; blood and sweat soaked his clothes. His vision darkened; sounds faded. Finally he accepted defeat as he began the downward spiral into unconsciousness. They would beat him to death, and he was powerless to stop them.

Then a loud scream arrested his descent. A body crashed to the ground beside him. Shouted insults turned to yells of surprise.

"Who—? What—?"

Sano blinked in confusion as another of his tormenters flew backward as if yanked from behind. Then a slender figure, clad in black, appeared, and a puzzling scene unfolded. Amid the lurching, shouting attackers, the black, silent figure whirled and lunged. Its arms chopped the clubs from their hands; its kicks to their stomachs and groins doubled them over. A vicious swipe to the neck downed another man as he reached for his sword.

Sano closed his eyes to blot out what was surely a bizarre hallucination. His mind foundered in the black waves that washed over his consciousness. Time passed, but how much he didn't know. Gradually he became aware that the noise and activity around him had ceased. He forced his heavy eyelids open. Above him, the moon's image swelled and shrank in rhythm with the pulsing agony in every part of his body. Had his tormenters left him for dead? Then he heard footsteps, almost soundless, but magnified by his painfully acute senses.

They were coming back.

Panic restored Sano's fading lucidity. Groaning, he tried to stand, but couldn't move. A dark figure loomed over him, head turned and lifted, listening and watching in perfect stillness. For a moment, Sano saw moonlight silvering the curving line of a three-quarter profile. Then the figure bent. Firm hands grasped Sano's arms.

"No," he whispered, but lacked the strength to resist.

He felt himself hoisted across a strong back. The ground tilted sickeningly, then sank as the figure lifted him. With his last conscious thought, Sano wondered if this was his imaginary rescuer turned real, or one of his attackers bearing him off to a worse punishment than he'd already suffered.

Then another black wave absorbed all thought and external sensation. Sano tumbled into oblivion.

26

Warmth, gentle and enveloping.

The soft splash of water.

Pain, at first muted and remote, then gradually more intense and immediate.

Sano floated up from unconsciousness like a swimmer breaking the surface of a viscous ocean. His eyelids cracked open. A light, piercingly bright, formed a blazing sun in his field of vision. Sano groaned in fear and confusion. He couldn't remember what had happened; he didn't know where he was, except flat on his back and in danger. He must escape. His efforts to move caused excruciating pain that roused him further, and he sensed someone beside him, felt a soft touch against his chin. Panic focused his eyes. He gasped.

In the lantern's golden glow, Aoi's serene face hovered above him as she dabbed his face with a wet white cloth. The sleeves of her green and white kimono were rolled above her elbows. Meeting his gaze, she smiled faintly: a ripple of light across her somber features.

"You're awake. Good."

Sano sat up, wincing as his sore muscles strained and his head spun. When the world settled again, he recognized his own bedchamber, with its coffered ceiling, painted screen, lacquer chests and cabinets, and burning charcoal braziers. He looked down at himself and recoiled in horror.

He was naked, except for his loincloth. His body had been cleansed of dirt, sweat, and blood, but dark red and purple bruises stained his arms, legs, and chest. Raw scrapes marked his knees and palms. Memories came rushing back: the wild chase through the castle, the beating. Now he recalled that he'd been on his way to see Aoi.

Placing a hand on his chest, Aoi gently but firmly pushed him back down onto the futon on which he sat. "Lie still now, while I treat your wounds," she murmured.

Her husky voice soothed Sano's senses; her beauty stirred his desire despite the pain. But now he remembered why he had wanted to see her.

"How did I get home?" he demanded, sitting up again. "What are you doing here?"

"The guard patrol found you lying unconscious in the Fukiage and carried you home." Aoi's eyes met his with perfect candor. "Your servants called me because I have healing skills."

She gestured at the floor beside her, where Sano saw three trays holding assorted items: a stone mortar and pestle; ceramic cups and spoons; a steaming teapot; lacquer bowls filled with pungent, cooked green onions for placing on wounds to ease pain; saffron threads to be steeped in tea and used to treat shock; yellow turmeric powder for inflammation. The teapot gave off the spicy scent of ginseng—that venerated root, both tonic and sedative, that strengthened the body's resistance to illness and injury. All these Sano recognized as common herbal remedies. Others, however, were strange to him. His suspicions about Aoi grew.

"What's that?" He pointed to a bowl of slimy brown strips that stank like rotten fish.

Aoi's forehead puckered in a frown of apparently genuine bewilderment at his hostility. "Skin of the mudfish," she said. "To prevent festering. It won't hurt you. Please, rest now."

She extended the cloth to his face again, but Sano slapped it away. "And what's that?" He looked toward a cup of mashed leaves from which rose an acrid smell.

"Hellodindron leaves and vinegar. To heal bruises." Aoi folded her arms. In a tone of determined patience, she said, "I can't help you if you won't cooperate."

As she turned and bent to rinse her cloth in a wooden bucket beside the bed, her upper body moved between Sano and the lantern. Against its glow, her pale garments turned dark. Light edged her averted face, stimulating Sano's still hazy memory.

A dark figure. A moonlit profile . . .

Sano grabbed Aoi's wrist. He heard her sharp gasp as he yanked her around to face him.

"The guards didn't bring me home. They're the ones who beat me. And you weren't summoned by my servants, were you? What really happened? How did you come to be here?"

With an air of conceding, Aoi answered, "All right. I was walking in the Fukiage. I found you in the clearing. I called your servants to carry you home, and stayed to treat your wounds. I was afraid to tell you because you might think me too presumptuous. Now, please let me go so I can heal you."

Anger opened a yawning cavity inside Sano's chest, sucking his breath into its vacuum. Flinging Aoi's hand aside, he scattered the medicines with a wild swipe, ignoring her cry of protest.

"No more lies!" he shouted. "I remember everything now. You—a woman, alone—defeated five men. Then you carried me home, all by yourself. To poison me with your magic potions, as if you haven't done me enough harm already!"

Upon her he unleashed all his rage toward the men who'd beaten him; Magistrate Ueda for rejecting his proposal; Chūgo and Matsui for thwarting him tonight; Chamberlain Yanagisawa for his scheming; Tokugawa Tsunayoshi for his weakness. And himself, for his powerlessness to control his destiny.

"You tricked me with your rituals and your visions." And made me want you, he would not admit to her. "You sent me and my assistant chasing after a man who doesn't exist. All so that I would fail in my investigation!"

Loath to sit before his enemy like a helpless invalid, Sano struggled to his feet. He gasped at the pain in his legs, wobbled under a wave of dizziness. Sweat gushed from his pores. Still, his mind registered that his injuries weren't as serious as he'd feared, or as bad as they might have been, if not for Aoi's intervention. But reason didn't diminish his fury. Her combat skills, strength, and medical knowledge only confirmed what her lies, her origin in Iga Province, and her mystical powers had led him to suspect.

"Ninja!" he hurled at her. "Dirty saboteur! Who are you working for, you agent of evil and darkness?"

Aoi rose to face him, her eyes glinting with a fury that matched his. "Who are you to call me dirty?" she spat back. "I serve the same masters as you—the Tokugawa. They command my duty as they do yours. Yes, I sabotaged you. If they told you to do what I've done, you'd do it, too. Then call it honor, and blame your sins on your filthy Bushido."

She flung her cloth into the bucket with a force that splashed water onto the floor. "Ignorant, arrogant samurai!"

That a peasant should address him thus further enraged Sano. His classless affinity for her vanished. "How dare you insult me!"

Raised to believe that a decent, manly samurai should be above striking a woman, Sano nevertheless refused to let Aoi go unpunished. He grabbed for her shoulders, intending to shake fear and respect into her.

He never reached Aoi. With lightning speed, her arms flew up, knocking his away. He didn't see her kick until it landed in his stomach. The wind puffed out of him. He stumbled backward and crashed against the painted screen, which clattered to the floor.

"Attack me, will you?" he wheezed.

Now fear poured ice water over his heart, for he knew Aoi could kill him if she chose. A wild glance around the room failed to locate his swords. He was no match for her in unarmed combat. And what other deadly ninja weapons might she use against him? Hidden blades, blinding powders, the mysterious forces of darkness? Yet fear only honed Sano's anger. Across the futon, over the scattered medicines, he rushed at Aoi. She sidestepped, but her stockinged foot trod on a ceramic cup. A spasm of pain crossed her face; she instinctively looked down. Sano seized the advantage and threw himself upon her.

"Scum!" he shouted, slamming her against the wall. Outside he heard his servants' concerned murmurs, but knew they wouldn't enter without his permission. "Liar!"

Aoi writhed and twisted in his grasp. Her fingernails raked his face; her knees gouged his thighs. Pressing his body against hers to hold her still, Sano snatched for Aoi's flailing hands.

"So I lied!" she shouted. "I was practicing at the training ground. Like I do every night. I saw the guards chasing you. I followed them, and saved you. Because I liked and pitied you. For this you abuse me. I should have let you die!"

She ducked her head, sank her teeth into his shoulder, and spat his blood straight into his face.

Goaded beyond self-control, Sano raised his hand to hit her. Then he became aware of her breasts pushing against his chest, her hips crushing his loins. Desire surged up through his anger. His manhood sprang erect in a stunning bolt of pleasure. For the first time, he understood how fear and anger can invoke lust.

Heedless of Aoi's lethal hands, Sano reached down and jerked her sash loose. Thrusting against her, he yanked at her kimono. The garment came away, baring her body. The sight of her breasts—as round, full, and large of nipple as he'd imagined—drove him to thrust harder. By taking her, he wasn't just exacting revenge upon the woman who had duped him, but expressing his ingrained hatred toward her kind. The ninja: demonic, dishonorable mercenaries who chose the dark, evil, and secretive methods of attack, and who represented everything his samurai upbringing had taught him to abhor.

Savagely Sano twined his fingers in Aoi's hair and yanked. It tumbled down, scattering pins and combs. Forcing her head back, he brought his mouth to her breast. Ferociously he suckled, biting the nipple, experiencing an excitement he'd never known before.

Aoi screamed. Her elbows and knees jabbed his body, unerringly finding the bruises. Sano cried out, but less from pain than the shocked realization that she welcomed his abuse even as she returned it. She didn't repel his assault as he knew she could. The nipple in his mouth was hard. While one of her hands continued to strike him, the other was between their bodies, frantically tearing the loincloth away from his erection. Sano knew that for both of them, at this moment, hatred and pain were no less aphrodisiac than fear and anger.

Now Aoi's legs circled his waist in a crushing embrace. Sano released her hair, her breast. He carried her over to the futon and flung her down upon it, landing on top of her with a floor-shaking thud.

Without pausing to recover, Aoi seized his erection and brought it to her naked crotch. Sano moaned as he plunged into wet, silken heat. The exquisite sensation nearly brought him to climax. Resisting, he hammered his pelvis against hers, wanting to have, wanting to hurt. Aoi only arched her back, meeting his thrusts. Emitting harsh, breathy cries, she clamped her hands down on his buttocks, forcing him deeper. Sano let loose his control. He thrust harder. He felt her inner muscles tighten around him, saw her eyes close. His own shout joined her scream as his pleasure crested. Time stopped while his body shuddered with violent ecstasy; the world disappeared. Then, satiated and exhausted, he collapsed onto his elbows. He opened his eyes.

Beneath him, Aoi lay motionless. All the tension had gone from her body, all anger and hatred from her eyes, leaving only a wistful sadness. Even as he resisted her, Sano felt again that affinity for Aoi, the desire for *ishin-denshin,* the rare, heart-to-heart communion they'd shared, a connection that went deeper than the need for sexual possession. He saw that he'd achieved no revenge by taking Aoi. Aided by his traitorous heart, she had defeated him. He could no longer deny that he was in love with her.

Sano let the breath gust from him in a long, sorrowful sigh, then rolled off Aoi to lie on his back. A vast mental and physical exhaustion overwhelmed him. The pain in his spirit echoed that of his wounds. He hadn't realized how much warmth and promise Aoi's presence had lent his lonely existence. Now the promise was gone, destroyed by her treachery. Flinging an arm across his eyes, Sano succumbed to desolation.

"Just tell me something," he said wearily.

He heard a rustle; in his mind's eye, he saw Aoi rise and don her fallen kimono. The floor creaked as she knelt a few paces—an unbridgeable distance—from him.

"When we last met, you wanted me as much as I wanted you." Never having spoken his feelings so frankly to anyone, he forced the words past the barrier of his natural reticence. "And not just with your body, but . . ."

The phrase "with your soul" seemed embarrassingly sentimental and refused to leave his tongue. "Didn't you?"

No answer. Letting his arm drop, Sano turned his face and saw Aoi kneeling with her back toward him, saw her bow her head in silent, defeated assent.

"So then how could you try to ruin me?" Sano heard the hardness in his own voice.

Still Aoi didn't speak, but her shoulders trembled.

Sano sat up and put on his own kimono, which he found lying beside the bed; with the spurious intimacy of their coupling gone, the room seemed cold and nakedness shameful. Then, too sore to walk, he dragged himself across the floor to sit before her.

Her expressionless features had a rigidity that revealed an immense effort to maintain her composure. The tendons stood out in her throat; her eyelids quivered. Sano realized that she was weeping—soundlessly, tearlessly. Even after the bitter disappointment of her betrayal, he couldn't remain unmoved by this brave denial of grief that would do any samurai proud. He touched her cheek, his hand clumsy with unpracticed tenderness.

"What's wrong?"

Aoi's trembling ended in a violent spasm. Then she grew still, gazing into the distance.

"Sometimes, while I sleep in my hut outside the Momijiyama, I have dreams of running away," she said in a low, unsteady voice. "In them, I shave my head and dress in nun's robes. I leave the castle at daybreak and begin walking. Over the highways by day, begging alms from fellow travelers. By night, crossing fields and sleeping in caves and forests. Eating plants, nuts, and small game. For however long it takes to reach my home and family."

Sano imagined her moving across the countryside like a slim, anonymous shadow. His sympathy stirred in spite of himself. Once a fugitive, he'd known the same homesick yearning he saw in her.

"But then I wake up, and the dream ends," Aoi said dully. "I know I can never leave. The Tokugawa would send troops to kill me and my clan and burn our village. Just as samurai have always done to get cooperation from the ninja."

Now her eyes focused on Sano, and a hint of anger reappeared

in them. "We've fought your wars. We've assassinated your enemies, infiltrated their camps, risked our lives to bring you victory.
And now that there's no war, still you won't leave us in peace.

"You forced my father to send me, as a young girl of fourteen,
to spy on and ruin your rivals. You force me to spend my life in
enslavement. For me to abandon this duty, which you so despise,
would bring death to my people. And for my effort to protect my
family—as you would yours—you call me dirty. Dishonorable."

Sano shook his head as his perception shifted. Never before had
he considered what his class and hers had in common. The Tokugawa had subjugated them both. The ninja served less willingly,
because at greater personal cost for fewer rewards. They reaped
no glory for their deeds. But there was honor in Aoi's courage, her
devotion to her family, her stoic acceptance of suffering. And
there was good in her character: She'd saved his life.

"I'm sorry," Sano said, meaning the apology as an expression of
forgiveness and understanding as well.

When he took her hand, her fingers stiffened, then curled
around his for a moment before withdrawing. Her gaze dropped,
but his gesture and her acceptance of it affirmed a love that knew
no class barriers, observed no conventions, withheld no intimacy.
This, Sano thought with a passionate, joyful certainty, was what
he wanted with a woman.

Bitter irony tinged Aoi's husky laugh. "What would Chamberlain Yanagisawa say if he could see us together now—his agent,
and the man he seeks to destroy?"

Leaden dismay settled in Sano's stomach. "So it was the chamberlain who ordered you to ruin my investigation. More evidence
of his guilt."

"Chamberlain Yanagisawa is a murder suspect?"

Aoi's sharp query startled Sano out of his gloom. "Yes," he admitted, explaining how he'd reached that conclusion. Though he
still didn't trust her, it couldn't hurt to tell her what Yanagisawa already knew.

When he finished, Aoi sat perfectly still, but with an intensity to
her gaze that belied her calm demeanor.

"Then . . . if the chamberlain is guilty . . . he'll be executed?"
Dawning hope hushed her voice.

Sano knew what she was thinking: If Yanagisawa died, she would be free to go home, without threat of punishment from a government too busy reorganizing itself to care what happened to the dead chamberlain's spies. His heart contracted as he sensed the vast difference in understanding that separated them. She didn't know what Yanagisawa's guilt would mean he must do. And, knowing the hold Yanagisawa had on her, he couldn't tell her and risk the news of his plan reaching the chamberlain.

"Yes," Sano said finally. "If Chamberlain Yanagisawa is guilty, he will die."

Aoi's luminous eyes shone as she leaned forward and grasped his hands. "I can help you prove his guilt. So that neither of us, nor my people, need suffer his cruelty any longer."

Sano inwardly shrank from her eagerness to incriminate Yanagisawa. The embers of his anger began to smolder again when he remembered how she'd "helped" him before.

"What can you do?" Suddenly suspicious, he extricated his hands from hers. Her visions had revealed truths, but also lies. This woman he loved was by birth and profession a trickster, no matter how noble her basic character.

She frowned, hurt by his rejection, but drew herself proudly upright, palms against her knees. "Yes, I tricked you, the way my people have always tricked yours," she said, again demonstrating her uncanny ability to read his mind. "I can't foretell the future or communicate directly with the dead. But I can sometimes hear the thoughts of the living, as I heard yours. And the dead do speak— through the possessions they leave behind. Objects speak of the people who've owned them. And I can understand their language."

Moving closer, she stroked his chest and smiled eagerly into his eyes, bringing to bear upon his resistance the full persuasive force of her beauty, and her love. "If Chamberlain Yanagisawa is the Bundori Killer, I can use my powers to help you bring him to justice. To do good instead of evil, for once in my life. Please, let's work together to destroy our common enemy!"

Aghast, Sano stared at Aoi. How could he let her endanger herself and her family by plotting against the master who commanded her obedience? And he didn't want more proof of

Yanagisawa's guilt. Yet he must accept any help he could get, no matter how bizarre and unwelcome. Only three days remained until the shogun's deadline. His duty to his father and his lord demanded his best effort to catch the Bundori Killer, no matter what the cost to himself or others.

Besides, he knew exactly what task he should ask Aoi to undertake for him.

With a sigh, Sano gathered her into his arms, laying his face against her hair so she couldn't see his unhappiness. "All right, Aoi. Thank you. We'll work together."

And be together, for whatever time remained to them.

27

O-tama, General Fujiwara's female descendant and Sano's last suspect, lived in the Hibiya district south of the castle. Sano knew it well from his days as a police commander, but now, the morning after his night with Aoi, he rode through the familiar streets as through a world created anew.

After he'd told Aoi how she could help with his investigation, she'd prepared more medicines and treated his wounds. Then they'd talked of their families, childhoods, and schooling, their preferences in food, entertainment, people, and places—such things as new lovers find so fascinating to share. While he'd lain motionless with remedies over his wounds, the desire strengthened their bond. It was still with him when he awoke alone, with the sun streaming in the windows, already yearning for night, when they would meet again.

And now, as he embarked on the next stage of his investigation, he realized what Aoi had given him. Not the least were his life and health. Her skillful treatment had dramatically reduced his pain; his wounds had stopped throbbing, and the dizziness had passed. He'd eaten his morning meal with good appetite and could ride and walk without agony. But even this miracle couldn't compare to the vast improvement in his spirits.

For the first time, Sano experienced the exhilarating sense of power that love bestows. A bemused smile hovered on his lips as he beheld the city with an altered vision. The teeming streets belonged to him, as did the houses, shops, mansions and castle, the distant green hills, swelling brown river, and boundless sky. The warm sunshine, scudding clouds, fresh, blustery wind, and the blooming cherry trees mirrored the new spring season of his soul. Fear and doubt clouded his thoughts no more than the thin veil of smoke that lay over Nihonbashi, where a minor fire that must have started last night still burned. Owning everything, he could bend the world to his will. He could command the investigation's outcome and free Edo from the grip of terror. He would exonerate Yanagisawa and incriminate Matsui, Chūgo—or O-tama, whom he would soon meet. He would fulfill his promise to his father. And he would find a way for him and Aoi to be together, despite their opposing loyalties.

Already his luck had turned. A message from Hirata, received that morning, had read:

> Matsui went straight home last night. But I have a new lead. Meet me at the police compound at noon.

As he neared his destination, Sano put aside his thoughts of Aoi and speculations about Hirata's discovery while his curiosity about the final suspect began to stir. O-tama. Once a *yuna*—a courtesan in one of Edo's many bathhouses, where prostitution flourished despite laws that officially confined it to the Yoshiwara pleasure quarter—she had been the most notorious beauty at the Water Lily, known for its lovely women and prominent clientele. She'd also been the subject of a famous scandal that had rocked Edo ten years ago.

The then-eighteen-year-old O-tama had become the object of men's obsession, her affairs with countless merchants, samurai, and clergymen the subject of popular songs. A ripe yet dainty girl with a saucy smile, she'd reached the peak of her celebrity when she won the patronage of wealthy Highway Commissioner Mimaki Teinosuke, thirty-two years her senior.

The public had followed the affair's progress with great zest.

Everyone talked of the gifts Mimaki lavished upon her; his poetic love letters; his neglect of wife, family, and work while he spent hours in the Water Lily's private rooms with O-tama; and the huge sums he paid for the privilege. Their great love for each other had been so sure to end in tragedy, as forbidden romance always must, amid rumors of a government crackdown on bathhouse prostitution.

Sano reached Mimaki's house, a large office-mansion with an unusually high wall that concealed all but the tip of its tile roof. He gave his name and title to the guard at the gate and said, "I wish an official audience with Mistress O-tama."

The guard opened the gate, spoke to someone inside, and closed it again. "Please wait while your request is forwarded to Master Mimaki," he told Sano.

As Sano dismounted and waited, he recalled how the story of Mimaki and O-tama had ended. The crackdown on bathhouse prostitution had proved unnecessary, as had the public's sympathy for the doomed lovers. A fire had destroyed the Water Lily. Mimaki had sent his family to live in the country and taken O-tama into his home as his concubine. There, the gossips reported, he treated her like an empress, giving her everything she wanted. She did no work; servants waited on her hand and foot. Jealous of her beauty, wanting her all to himself, Mimaki shunned society. If an unavoidable visitor came, he placed a screen before her to hide her from view. The great love story having ended happily, the public's interest moved on to other matters. Sano had heard nothing of O-tama in years. He wondered what she was like now, and pondered the strangeness of having her resurface as a murder suspect. And who would have thought that the blood of a great warrior like General Fujiwara flowed in her veins?

The gate opened. A middle-aged female servant, probably the housekeeper, bowed to Sano. "Please come with me."

Sano followed her into the entryway to leave his swords. But instead of ushering him through the mansion's public rooms, she led the way down a path alongside the house, through another gate, and into the most unusual garden Sano had ever seen. Gravel paths wound around the usual boulders, pines, and flowering cherries, but other less typical features dominated. From the delicate gray boughs of lilac trees, purple blossoms exuded a sweet perfume. Jasmine and honeysuckle vines draped the fence and veranda. Countless wind chimes tinkled from the branches of a red maple; birds twittered in wooden houses in the plum trees. Red carp splashed in a small pond, near which stood an odd seat, like ones Sano had seen in pictures of the Dutch traders' quarters on Deshima, only with wooden wheels attached to its legs. Beside a bed of pungent mint knelt a gray-haired samurai in black kimono, weeding with a small spade.

The housekeeper led Sano to him. "Master Mimaki, here is *Sōsakan* Sano."

Mimaki rose. As they exchanged bows, Sano noted with surprise that Mimaki, at sixty, looked not at all like the impetuous lover of a courtesan young enough to be his daughter. He was stout and ordinary-looking, with eyes that drooped at the corners and a narrow mouth tucked tightly between fleshy cheeks and chin. His tanned skin and muddy hands gave him a peasantlike appearance despite his shaven crown and high rank.

"I understand you wish to see O-tama on official business," Mimaki said. His grave manner showed no jealousy.

"That's correct."

"Alone?"

Sano nodded. "I would prefer it, yes."

Now Mimaki's suspicious scrutiny, plus the fact that he was working in his garden instead of in his office, matched Sano's expectation of a man preoccupied with his private life, into which he welcomed no intruders. But then Mimaki nodded, perhaps dismissing Sano as a rival.

"Very well." He turned to the housekeeper. "Prepare Mistress O-tama for a visitor."

The housekeeper hurried into the house. Mimaki and Sano followed more slowly.

"You may address O-tama under the following conditions," Mimaki said as they walked down the corridor. "You will stay no less than ten paces from the screen. If you try to move the screen or step behind it, I'll kill you. Is that clear?"

Shocked at this threat, delivered with no change of expression, Sano could only nod.

A door opened as they reached it, and the housekeeper slipped out, bowing them into a room that was bare except for a large wooden screen with thin mullions framing diamond-shaped paper panels. Light from the windows silhouetted a shadowy figure behind it.

Sano knelt in his designated place. Mimaki stepped behind the screen. Now two shadows appeared on its translucent paper, and Sano heard whispered conversation. Then Mimaki emerged, his face transformed almost beyond recognition. His eyes glowed; his mouth had relaxed into a smile at once joyful, sensual, and secretive. When he turned to Sano, his former gravity returned.

"Remember what I said." Then Mimaki left the room.

Sano, uneasy about interrogating a suspect he couldn't see, hesitated before speaking. How would he know if O-tama was telling the truth?

From behind the screen, she spoke. "It's an honor and a pleasure to meet you, *sōsakan-sama*."

Hers was one of the loveliest voices Sano had ever heard. High and sweet, it lilted and sang, tickled and warmed the inside of his chest. Sano smiled, despite the seriousness of this interview. Even so fresh from Aoi and so sure about his feelings for her, he couldn't remain immune to O-tama's charm. Many a man must have fallen in love with her voice alone.

"The pleasure is mine," Sano replied, meaning it.

A maid appeared and set tea and cakes before him. "Do make yourself comfortable," O-tama said. "And don't let Mimaki-*san*'s rules bother you. He doesn't mean to insult you; he's just very protective of me. And I can tell from your voice that you're an honorable, decent man."

Her manner, though flirtatious, as Sano suspected it would be toward any male, showed genuine affection for her master. Mimaki needn't fear losing her, and probably for this reason had allowed the interview. So then why the screen, the threat?

"If you hadn't come today, I would have invited you," O-tama continued. "Because I've heard of your great talents, of course, but also because I have important information for you."

"You do?" Sano said, taken aback by this reception, so unlike

those he'd received from the other suspects. To give himself time
to think, he lifted his tea bowl and drank, letting her continue.

"I like peace and privacy, and usually ignore the world," O-tama
said. "My dear Mimaki-*san* is my life. But I've followed these terrible murders with great concern. After the first and second, I
guessed what was happening, and with the priest's murder, the
pattern became obvious to me. Yet still you, of whom I've heard
tales of great courage and ability, hadn't caught the killer. I decided I must come forth and tell you what I know.

"*Sōsakan-sama,* forgive my unwomanly boldness. I can't name
the Bundori Killer, but I can tell you why he kills—and why he
must be one of three men."

"Who are they?" Sano stalled, suppressing his eagerness. For a
murder suspect, she seemed too forthcoming. Was this a bluff, designed to divert his suspicion? If only he could see her!

He peered through the screen, but could discern only the sil-
houette of her head, hair piled on top, rising above what looked
to be heaped cushions. Age had probably filled out her face and
figure, perhaps coarsened her skin and hair, but her voice suggested that she'd retained youth's fresh vitality. Certainly her master's continuing possessiveness meant she must be lovely still.
Sano regretted more than just his inability to assess her honesty.

"These men are bound to me by our common history," O-tama
explained. "I know their motives as no one else can. Because
they're my cousins: Chūgo Gichin, Matsui Minoru, and Yanagisawa Yoshiyasu." O-tama's lilting voice danced over the names.
"You've met them?"

"I have," Sano said warily.

"You're not surprised, so I believe you already suspect my
cousins. How clever of you! But you've made no arrest. Does this
mean you don't have any evidence against them, and that's why
you came to me?"

The former *yuna* was intelligent as well as charming. Sano saw
no use in denying the obvious, or pretending another reason for
the call.

"Yes," he conceded. After his experiences with Chūgo, Matsui,
and Yanagisawa, he knew how little he could expect to gain from

direct interrogation. All the suspects were on their guard now. With O-tama, he decided to let the conversation go where she led it and hope she betrayed some sign of guilt or innocence.

O-tama's bubbly laugh evoked images of flowing water and sensuous frolic. "Then I'd be most delighted to give you at least part of the evidence you need to deliver the Bundori Killer to the execution ground. Shall I begin?"

Sano, awed by the contrast between her gaiety and the grim promise she offered, let his silence give his assent.

"The roots of the murders lie in events that took place more than one hundred years ago," O-tama began.

At last, a confirmation of his theory, albeit from a questionable source—a onetime prostitute, Fujiwara descendant, and murder suspect. "You mean General Fujiwara's attacks on the Araki and Endō clans," he prompted.

But O-tama's shadow shook its head. "No, *sōsakan-sama*. I'm speaking of Oda Nobunaga's murder."

Confused, Sano said, "I know the attacks occurred after Oda's death. But there's nothing in the archives to suggest that this was anything but a coincidence."

O-tama laughed again. "*Sōsakan-sama,* a man of your intelligence must know that much of history is never recorded. What I tell you comes not from moldy old scrolls, but from this secret legend handed down from General Fujiwara through our family: The general attacked Araki and Endō because he sought revenge on them for their part in Oda Nobunaga's murder."

A sense of incredulity provoked Sano's immediate protest. "But Araki and Endō didn't kill Oda; Akechi Mitsuhide did. The facts are documented and undisputed." Was this remarkable woman claiming that her family myths superseded the official historical record?

Evidently she was. "Our legend says that Akechi didn't act alone. Araki and Endō conspired with him to murder Oda so that their lords, Tokugawa Ieyasu and Toyotomi Hideyoshi, could seize power.

"Ah, I sense your doubt, *sōsakan-sama*. But even in the records, there are facts that support the legend. Such as this: Why was Oda alone in a temple on the night he died, with only a handful of men?"

"His allies, Hideyoshi and Ieyasu, were away at the time," Sano said impatiently, thinking this visit a waste of time. She wasn't the Bundori Killer, she knew nothing of the murders or the motive behind them, and he hadn't come to debate historical points with her. "There's no evidence of their complicity. Ieyasu was on holiday at Sakai. Hideyoshi was fighting the Mori clan at Takamatsu Castle. He'd asked Oda for reinforcement troops, which Oda sent . . ."

His voice trailed off as he saw the connection that the historians had missed, or ignored.

"Thereby reducing the number of men at hand for Oda's protection," O-tama finished for him. "But did Hideyoshi really need those troops? And why did Ieyasu take a holiday then? Was it a coincidence that Oda's allies were both gone when he needed them? And what could Akechi have hoped to gain by killing the most powerful man in the country?"

Stunned by this new version of history, Sano repeated the standard answer, which now sounded ridiculous. "Revenge. Oda had sent Akechi's mother-in-law to another clan as hostage for his good behavior. She died when he attacked them. And Oda ridiculed Akechi in front of their colleagues, banging on his bald head with an iron war fan as though it were a drum."

"Oh, *sōsakan-sama*. Such silly reasons!" O-tama laughed merrily; Sano imagined her sporting naked in a bathtub with a client, amid clouds of steam. "And why did Akechi stay in Kyōto after the murder, instead of running for his life?"

"He wanted to win the support of Oda's allies by distributing Oda's treasure among them." Having seen documents that proved Akechi had indeed tried this, Sano answered with more confidence.

O-tama countered, "Oh, no, *sōsakan-sama*. He was waiting for Generals Araki and Endō, who had arranged their lords' absences so he could kill Oda. They'd promised him money and a higher rank. But they never came. And Hideyoshi avenged Oda's death by killing Akechi."

"If this story is true, then why didn't Araki and Endō keep their promise?" Sano asked, striving to maintain his position, but only for objectivity's sake. For he needed a motive for the crimes.

"Because Araki and Endō had acted without their lords' consent. They didn't want news of the conspiracy to make Oda's retainers rise up against Hideyoshi and Ieyasu. Akechi was supposed to take the blame, alone. And he did; he was punished—but Araki and Endō weren't. General Fujiwara learned of the conspiracy and vowed revenge, but failed. Now one of his descendants has taken up the task. Chūgo? Matsui? Maybe. But only Chamberlain Yanagisawa is a direct descendant of General Fujiwara's eldest son. With him lies the main responsibility for fulfilling our ancestor's wish."

Sano's earlier optimism drained away in a trickle of icy horror. The murder of a samurai's lord was the ultimate offense—a blood score that could indeed transcend generations. O-tama's story, supported by circumstantial historical evidence, explained General Fujiwara's bizarre behavior, and the murders. And reaffirmed Yanagisawa as the prime suspect.

"There can't be any truth to this legend!" Sano blurted in vehement denial.

"It doesn't really matter if there is, does it, *sōsakan-sama?* All that matters is that someone—the killer—believes so."

Sano couldn't argue, but leapt to challenge O-tama's credibility. "Why did you break the silence and tell me a secret that has been kept for so many years? Why have you given me evidence that endangers your cousins?"

Satin garments rustled as the shadowy figure behind the screen stirred. "You may find this shocking and disgusting, *sōsakan-sama,* but I have no love for my family." Bitterness damped the lilt in O-tama's voice. "Their problems are not mine. I care nothing for the samurai heritage that binds us. And I'll tell you why."

She recited the Fujiwara family history, and Sano learned of the rivalry that had divided the general's sons after his death, the rises and declines in fortune experienced by the clan's different branches. O-tama's, he discovered, had fared worse than Matsui's, Chūgo's, or Yanagisawa's.

"My grandfather mismanaged the estate entrusted to him by Tokugawa Ieyasu," O-tama said. "He was demoted to the post of secretary. And my father, who inherited the post, was a drunk who lost it entirely. He became a wandering *rōnin,* hiring himself out as a guard to peasant villages. We ate millet and lived in huts. Money was scarce; my father couldn't afford a dowry for my marriage. He turned me out when I was eighteen."

O-tama leaned closer to the screen. Against the milky paper, Sano could just make out the oval of her face. "So I came to Edo, looking for work as a maid. But I couldn't find a lady willing to hire a girl like me, who would tempt the house's menfolk and make the women jealous. For even then I was beautiful."

A strange, sad note crept into her voice. She swallowed audibly, then continued. "Winter came. Living and begging in the streets, I was hungry and cold and desperate. All my life, I'd heard my father talk about our great cousins. So I went to ask their help.

"I tried Matsui first, at his moneylending shop. He gave me enough coins for a meal and sent me on my way, with orders never to return. Chūgo refused to see me at all. And Chamberlain Yanagisawa . . ."

Her sigh trembled like wind through dead leaves. This woman who lived in luxury hadn't forgotten her harsh past.

"He was the shogun's new plaything. He took me to his private chambers in the castle, where he gave me food and heard my story with great sympathy. I was so thankful I wept. He was so handsome, so kind. He was going to help me. But then—"

O-tama's voice broke. "He violated me," she whispered. "From behind. And then threw me out without a *zeni.* That same day, the Water Lily's proprietor saw me wandering the streets and offered me work as a *yuna.* I had no choice but to accept, and no pride left to prevent me doing so.

"And so you see, *sōsakan-sama,* why I have no loyalty toward those who would deny mercy to a helpless girl. My story has a happy ending, of course. But I've always dreamed of taking revenge on Matsui, Chūgo—and especially Chamberlain Yanagisawa. Now I have. One of them is the Bundori Killer. And by speaking the forbidden secret, I hope I've delivered him to you."

Despite the timbre of truth in O-tama's words, Sano grasped at the slim hope that she, not Yanagisawa, was the murderer. He knew women were capable of killing, and it was they who had traditionally prepared trophy heads after battles. O-tama bore her grudge and spoke of revenge with a keen relish that even General Fujiwara would have been hard pressed to match. And there was one other reason.

"The secret incriminates you, too," he reminded her.

O-tama laughed again, but this time mournfully. "*Sōsakan-sama,* I have nothing to fear."

"If that's so, then where were you on the nights of the murders?"

"Here at home, where I always am." A pause; her shadow tilted its head in thought. "You wish proof?"

"Please," Sano said.

He expected her to summon Mimaki to back her alibi, but O-tama called the maid and said to her, "Remove the screen."

"But my lady . . ." The maid gasped in alarm. "The master . . ."

O-tama's shadowy hand rose, silencing her protests. "Do as I say."

Casting a nervous glance toward the door, the maid dragged the screen aside.

Sano's jaw dropped. Revulsion followed shock.

Supported on piled silk cushions, O-tama's small, thin body was twisted like a gnarled tree. Her right arm, bent and drawn up against her side, ended in a leathery stump. Only one dainty stockinged foot protruded from beneath her rich red satin kimono. Most horrible was her face, a shocking contrast to the perfect black wig on her head. A mass of puckered, mottled scar tissue had obliterated the features of the right side. On the intact left side, the half-open eyelid revealed a cloudy, sightless eye.

Sano, glad that she couldn't see his reaction, bowed his head in pity and awe. The fire at the Water Lily had freed O-tama from a sordid profession, but had ravaged her body. The public had no idea just how great Mimaki's love for her had been. He'd taken the blind, disfigured, and crippled prostitute into his home, to cherish and care for, to live with her in seclusion not because of jealousy, but to hide her terrible secret. He'd planted the fragrant garden and hung the birdhouses and wind chimes so she could enjoy its smells and sounds, if not its sights. He pushed her in the strange wooden seat along paths she couldn't walk. And, from the way his face had looked after he'd spoken to her, he loved her still. No one could have imagined a more poignant ending for the scandalous romance.

Or a better alibi for the murders.

"So you see, *sōsakan-sama*." The charming voice that so richly evoked O-tama's lost beauty issued from her deformed mouth. "I couldn't possibly be the killer you seek."

"My informant claims he knows who the assassin was, *sōsakan-sama*," Hirata said. "*Gomen nasai*—I'm sorry to make you walk so far, but he wouldn't come to the police compound. He doesn't want anyone to know he works for me."

"That's all right, Hirata, you've done well," Sano said. After the interview with O-tama, he desperately needed any evidence that might identify the Bundori Killer as someone other than Chamberlain Yanagisawa.

They were walking through Nihonbashi, toward their noon rendezvous with Hirata's cautious informant, in hastily improvised disguise. They both wore wide wicker hats, and had left Sano's expensively equipped horses at the police stables. Sano wore an old cloak of Hirata's to hide the Tokugawa crests on his own garments. With his single short sword, shabby kimono, and no *jitte*, Hirata made a convincing *rōnin*. Beneath his hat, his eyes glowed; his white smile flashed in boyish delight at Sano's approval. Sano, in his excitement at receiving the news, had forgotten to discourage Hirata's attachment. Now, though hating to hurt the young *doshin* again, he tried to counteract his spontaneous praise.

"Let's just hope your informant is telling the truth," he said coldly.

Hirata turned his face away, but not before Sano saw his smile fade. "This way, *sōsakan-sama*," he said in chastened tones.

They cut through the woodworkers' district, where carpenters sawed, hammered, and nailed in open storefronts. Along with more wild tales about the murders, newssellers distributed reports on the continuing fire, whose smoke filtered the sunlight.

"The fire must have spread," Sano said, concerned despite his relief at seeing the fearmongers' attention focused on something besides the murders. Edo's fire brigades usually managed to contain and extinguish the frequent blazes with admirable efficiency. "I wonder why it hasn't been put out yet."

"There's trouble in that district," Hirata said. "People have been burning candles and incense, to drive away the ghost. Last night, a house caught fire. And some men formed a gang to patrol the streets. They killed what they thought was a ghost carrying a severed head. But it was an old man with a jar of pickles. His sons went looking for revenge. A riot started. The fire spread because the fire brigade can't get in to put it out."

His worst fears realized, Sano looked away, speechless. The simmering tensions caused by the murders had finally erupted. All because he hadn't caught the Bundori Killer soon enough. Sano knew that other factors had contributed to the disaster—Chamberlain Yanagisawa's sabotage; the townspeople's superstition and unruliness; the police's failure to maintain order. But Sano couldn't help feeling responsible. Guiltily he wondered whether, fearing what he must do if Yanagisawa was the killer, he was expending his best effort on the investigation.

He and Hirata followed an eerily quiet street that Sano couldn't remember ever seeing before. The open storefronts contained unappealing merchandise: cheap, mismatched crockery; trays of stale cakes. The few pedestrians—all disreputable-looking samurai and male commoners—eyed them warily. Outside empty teahouses, the proprietors sat smoking pipes and lazing in the sun. Instead of trying to entice Sano and Hirata inside, they glared.

"This is it." Hirata stopped before a teahouse. To the proprietor, he said, "Wild Boar is expecting us."

The proprietor scrutinized them, then waved them inside. Sano and Hirata ducked under the faded blue curtain and entered the empty room. Hirata led the way through a doorway at its rear, from which muffled voices and laughter issued. Then Sano understood the real purpose of the deserted stores and teahouses.

Kneeling men jammed the dim back room. Their pipes added more smoke to the already thick air. Spread on the floor before them lay tobacco boxes, metal baskets of burning coals, cups and decanters of sake, playing cards and stacked coins. Intent on their games, the men ignored Sano and Hirata as they muttered their plays and bets, hands moving cards and coins with expert rapidity. This, like its neighboring establishments, was one of Edo's illegal gambling dens: domain of the city's burgeoning underclass of thieves, con men, gangsters, and other outlaws. The "proprietors" outside were lookouts, on the watch for police or rival gangsters.

Hirata eased past the gamblers, motioning Sano to follow him through another curtained doorway. This led to a dank, urine-smelling passage. Shouts, laughter, and clanking noises echoed from its other end.

"*Sōsakan-sama,* I want you to know that this isn't my district," Hirata whispered, obviously shamed by this lapse in police control. "I don't like the practice of taking bribes to let these places operate. But they do have their uses!"

They entered a hot, stifling room, whose shuttered windows and flaring oil lamps gave it a sinister, nighttime look. The reek of vomit, smoke, sweat, and liquor assailed Sano. At the center of the large, low-ceilinged space, rough wooden railings defined a combat ring where two young men, clad only in loincloths and cotton headbands, circled each other, gazes locked in fierce concentration. Both held *kusari-gama*—short, sharp-bladed scythes with weighted chains attached to the ends of wooden handles. This was a weapon normally used by peasants to disarm maurauding swordsmen, but here employed in a perverted and dangerous form of combat. Each fighter gripped his weapon's handle in his left hand; with his right, he spun the deadly chain in accelerating circles. Sweat glistened upon the fighters' tensed muscles; their savage grimaces bared broken teeth. Old scars and fresh wounds crisscrossed their skin.

Cheering, hooting samurai and peasants crowded around the ring. Many of the latter had elaborate tattoos on their arms and torsos—a mark of the organized gangster clans. Sano had seen men like these before, but never in such numbers. Here must be where they hid out while honest men were at work. Hirata was right: What better source of information about illicit activities could there be than this?

Hirata led Sano to the ring's far side, where a short, bald, muscular man was taking coins from eager customers—bets on the fight, judging from their shouts:

"Ten coppers on Yoshi!"

"Twenty on Gorō!"

On closer inspection, Sano saw that the banker wasn't much older than himself, and not really bald. His hair was cut so close to his domed head that in the dim light he'd at first appeared to have none. He had a crooked, flattened nose, puffy eyes and mouth. His kimono hung open to reveal a spectacular tattoo: a beautiful naked woman with winged demons suckling at her breasts.

Hirata approached the banker, who was apparently the informant, Wild Boar. "I've come for the goods I ordered," he shouted over the audience's cheers.

All traces of his usual deference had disappeared; he sounded brusque and rough, befitting his disguise, and confident like a man who expects satisfaction. Sano felt a touch of admiration for his assistant, who'd already demonstrated his talent for detection. Once again, he regretted the probable short tenure of their partnership.

Wild Boar jerked his head at Sano. "Who's your friend?" He spoke out of one corner of his mouth. His half-closed eyes showed no whites; the dark irises watched the fighters.

"The goods are for him," Hirata said. "Before you get the other half of your money, they have to meet his approval."

In the ring, the tall fighter launched an assault on his opponent. The other man didn't parry soon enough. The chain slammed across his chest. Shouts erupted from the audience. Wild Boar's eyes followed the action as he retorted, "You said nothing about this when we made our deal. Who is he? Why should I trust him?"

Hirata shrugged and started to walk away. Sano, fighting the urge to protest, followed his bluff.

"Wait." The informant's hand shot out and grabbed Hirata's sleeve. "You win." Rancor closed his eyes still more as he positioned himself between Sano and Hirata. Keeping his gaze on the ring, where the second fighter flailed his chain and thrust his scythe in a series of counterattacks, he began to speak.

"The man of the melon seeds and the fox's face was a *rōnin* named Nango Junnosuke. A stranger to Edo, as snow is to summer." Wild Boar's speech had a poetic quality that contrasted sharply with his gruff voice. "He came here four nights ago. He said he was just arrived from the Kantō."

Because the overlapping of shogun's and daimyo's authority had undermined police power in the eight agricultural provinces outside Edo, they'd become a center of criminal activity. Sano wasn't surprised to learn that the assassin had come from there. And "Junnosuke" was the name on the torn note in his pouch.

"Daikoku, great god of fortune, didn't bless Nango," Wild Boar went on. "He lost much money on cards and fights, then begged for credit, saying he would soon have enough money to cover his debts."

"How much money, and how soon?" Sano interrupted.

"Ten *koban,* the next night."

The exact sum found on the assassin's body, at the designated time. Sano's excitement grew with the certainty that Nango was his man. "Did he say how he planned to get it?"

"Said he'd been hired by someone important to kill a high-ranking citizen. But the gang didn't trust him. He had eyes that darted like minnows in a stream. So they made him leave. Afterward, they thought he might have been telling the truth. Because he was good with his sword, he was. Took five men to throw the ugly little fox out. And he cut them all."

Wild Boar's description of Nango's behavior fit the assassin: a good fighter whose rashness had gotten him in trouble during his life, and, in the end, destroyed him.

"Did he say who hired him, or who his target was?" Sano asked.

The informant laughed in derision: a grunt not unlike his name-sake's. "If it was true, he was smart enough to keep his mouth shut. But I'll tell you this. I've seen his kind before. They blow into town like a typhoon, do their evil, and blow out to sea again. And their master is the man up there on the hill."

A typhoon of foreboding swirled around Sano's heart. "Which man?"

"People come to me for facts, not opinions. But if you want, I'll tell you what I think." Wild Boar paused, then leaned closer to Sano. His sour, liquor-scented whisper rasped against Sano's face. "It's the Second Dog."

The shogun, Chamberlain Yanagisawa, and Senior Elder Makino were nicknamed "The Three Dogs"—all born in the year of the dog; all associated with Tsunayoshi's Dog Protection Edicts. The shogun was First Dog by right of rank. Yanagisawa, the Second Dog, led the pack. The typhoon over Sano's heart sent its fierce winds gusting into his throat.

"The Second Dog hired Nango?" he asked, resisting belief.

"I'd lay odds on it, friend."

"Why?" Sano pressed.

The informant's ripe breath blew the answer into Sano's face. "Miyagi Kojirō. Attacked and killed by an unknown swordsman three years ago while traveling along the Tōkaidō. The killer was never found. But I've got friends at highway post stations who saw a seed-eating, fox-faced man tailing Miyagi. A man not unlike the one we speak of now."

Sano remembered Noguchi telling him about Miyagi, once the shogun's adviser and Chamberlain Yanagisawa's rival. Whose secret murder, rumor said, had been ordered by the chamberlain. "But couldn't someone else have hired Nango?" Sano persisted, forgetting caution in his need to dispute Wild Boar's statement. The informant seemed rather too knowledgeable. Was he telling the truth, or inventing stories to give value for his price? "Chūgo Gichin, for instance. Or Matsui Minoru. Men with money and influence."

Wild Boar grunted again. "Chūgo keeps to the castle like the emperor to his palace. Thinks he owns it. No connections to men of Nango's sort, or none I know of. Word on him is, if he wanted someone killed, he'd do it himself. And Matsui has other ways of getting his way."

The guard captain's own words agreed with Wild Boar's assessment of Chūgo, and Sano's impressions of the merchant supported the informant's statement about Matsui. Sano had no knowledge with which to contradict any of what he'd just heard. Suddenly he found the room's frenetic atmosphere unbearable. He watched the tall fighter lash out with the scythe's curved blade. It sliced his opponent's shoulder. Blood poured from the gash. Gasping, the man fell against the railing. Four men from the audience leapt into the ring and dragged him out. With the first drawing of blood, the fight was over. But Sano couldn't share the crowd's uproarious glee.

Father, he prayed silently, *let the truth be other than it appears now!* But reality didn't change. His father's spirit wouldn't come to him, and, to his dismay, he found he could no longer envision his father's face.

"Thank you, Wild Boar," he said abruptly. "Hirata, let's go."

Wild Boar ignored Sano's thanks. Turning to Hirata, he said, "I've delivered the goods. Now pay up."

Hirata pulled out his money pouch. Sano realized that his loyal assistant had bought the information with his own funds. Reaching across Wild Boar, he touched Hirata's arm.

"Let me. How much?"

"No," Hirata protested. "I made the deal, I'll pay."

Sano shot him a stern glance. From his own pouch he counted out the huge sum that Hirata reluctantly named, and paid for the knowledge that endangered his own life.

29

The shrine attendant's tiny thatched hut stood hidden in the forest surrounding the Momijiyama. A narrow path wound through the trees to the doorway, which in turn led into an entry porch filled with equipment necessary for maintaining the shrine—brooms, buckets, cleaning cloths, soap, candles, lamps, incense—all arranged neatly on shelves. Beyond this lay a single room with a clean tatami floor, a hearth for cooking, a tub for bathing, a rough wooden cabinet for possessions, and a small window looking out on the forest: the bare necessities of the shrine attendant's life and work.

In the middle of the room, Aoi knelt and carefully unfolded the two kimonos that Sano had given her last night. To her he'd entrusted the task of identifying his missing witness, the mysterious woman who had disappeared from Zōjō Temple after the priest's murder. Her fingers trembled with anticipation and anxiety. She must help Sano find evidence against Chamberlain Yanagisawa. To fail would mean sacrificing their chance for freedom and happiness.

She spread both kimonos on the floor before her, but did not immediately examine them. Instead she sat motionless for a long moment, letting her vision blur. Then she began to take slow, deep breaths. Her lungs expanded to their limit, then expelled the air, contracting to complete emptiness. In. Out. For inspiration, she summoned the memory of her father. She pictured his stern face, heard his quiet voice.

"The special ninja breathing exercise cleanses the body and blood, Aoi," he said. "It calms the mind and enhances concentration."

Soon Aoi felt the power radiating from her spiritual center in her abdomen: a great, erratic pulse that shuddered through her body. Over its thunder, her father's voice came to her across time and space:

"Fearful outsiders call the ninja's power the 'dark magic.' But it's not magic. It's the power that every human has within himself, but only we know how to tap."

And this turbulent, swirling energy wasn't dark, either, but shot through with sparks of light that exploded behind her eyes. She envisioned it as a deep, restless sea filled with luminescent living things. She could hear the waves roaring in her ears, crashing against the shores of her consciousness. Resisting the tide that could carry her into chaos and madness, she clasped her hands. Her trained fingers automatically arranged and rearranged themselves in a series of intricate positions, interlocking, weaving, twisting, pointing.

"Many a samurai, seeing a ninja adversary perform this exercise, has dropped dead from fright," her father had taught her. "Use their fear as you would any weapon. But remember that the hand positions aren't an evil magic curse, but a silent chant, a manual mantra designed to harness, focus, and direct your energy."

As Aoi's fingers flexed and laced, the turbulent sea within her grew quiet, its pulse slow and rhythmical. She floated in a cold, exhilarating atmosphere of heightened sensory perception. She could smell houses burning in the city below the castle, hear snow melting on distant mountains. She tasted the river's fishy water and experienced the pressure of her clothes against her skin as a crushing weight of layered stone. All these sensations, though, were extraneous. The last hand position banished them to the edges of her mind. Her father's image faded, as did his voice, saying "Now you are ready, my daughter."

Aoi picked up the first kimono. Its white cranes, snowflakes, and green pine boughs seared their images into her brain; the brilliant crimson background made her sensitized eyes water. As she moved her hands over the fabric, she almost swooned at the sensuous pleasure of touching the lush silk, the million tiny stitches of embroidery. Her fingertips probed every area of the garment, seeking the almost invisible thinning where the wearer's body had rubbed the fabric. With surreal clarity she saw tiny particles adhering to the neckline, cuffs, and hem. She found a single long black hair, which she stroked, sniffed, then ran along her tongue.

Last, Aoi lifted the kimono to her face. She closed her eyes to eliminate visual distractions. Then, concentrating on the underarm, breast, and crotch areas, she inhaled body odors left by the wearer: perfume, sweat, intimate secretions. With her tongue she tasted what information sight, smell, and touch hadn't given her. When she finally laid the kimono down, her heart was thudding, her body trembling from the profound sensory experience. She rested for a moment, then repeated the procedure on the second kimono, a gray one printed with autumn flowers and grasses. It confirmed what facts she'd gleaned from the first and yielded a few more. Finished, she lay on her back, exhausted and gasping, eyes closed. The energy sea receded; its pulsing tide ebbed. Gradually Aoi's heartbeat slowed, her breathing evened, and her body ceased to tremble. The world returned to its normal state—muted, colorless by comparison.

Aoi opened her eyes and sat up at the sound of soft footsteps outside the door.

"Enter," she called before the knock came. Even with her ordinary perception she could identify the caller as the person for whom she'd sent.

The young maid entered on her knees and bowed. A small woman with a pleasant face and quiet demeanor, she was one of the Edo Castle network's best agents, liked and trusted by her peers and superiors.

"I await your orders, my lady," she said.

"I want to know who owns these," Aoi said, showing her the kimonos. "Show them to all the women in the palace, Official Quarter, and attendants' quarters."

For who better to ask about the mystery witness than the castle women—confined and idle—who thrived on town gossip and fashion news brought them by their men and servants?

"The woman I'm looking for went to Zōjō Temple to become a nun," Aoi continued, "but she may have returned home."

Having filled her agent in on the bare facts Sano had given her, Aoi next fleshed them out with her own discoveries. "The woman is a wealthy commoner. Her husband is probably a rice broker. And she's unhappy because he has other women." There was no mistaking the expensive quality of the kimonos. Or the fine dusting of powdered rice hulls at the hems—too much for a rich woman with no need to enter the kitchen, but typical of one who lived near a brokerage, with someone who worked there. And Aoi had recognized the distinctive aura of heartbreak, a wife spurned.

"She's fat, past forty-five, and suffers from congestion in the nose and chest."

This from the strained seams, the faint wear patterns over the hips, buttocks, and breasts, the sour odor of a woman beyond her childbearing years, and the faint saltiness of dried mucus.

"But she tries hard to look young and pretty. She wears too much makeup."

Aoi had found numerous particles of white face powder and tiny smears of rouge on the kimonos' necklines. The fabric, bright and gaudy, was more appropriate for a young girl. And Aoi had tasted bitter dye on the long black hair.

"Ask everyone if they know this woman's name, and where she lives," Aoi finished. "Report to me by sunset."

"Yes, my lady." The maid took the kimonos, bowed, and left the hut.

Aoi gazed after her, thinking: That girl is young, but a good, obedient worker. She's careful to hide her loneliness and pain, as I once did. She would make as good a replacement for me as I did for Michiko . . .

Abruptly Aoi rose and left her hut, taking with her a whisk broom and dustpan. She hurried through the woods toward the shrine, as if by running toward duty she could escape the fact that meeting Sano had changed her life, that love had destroyed her carefully constructed defenses and made her vulnerable.

She'd vowed never to involve herself with a man again. Remembering her dead lover, Fusei Matsugae, she couldn't open herself to the pain and self-hatred that came of destroying that which was dearest to her. Yet now she'd done it again. She couldn't dismiss her union with Sano as a momentary yielding to lust, nor could she pretend that their collaboration was based solely on coinciding interests—his wish to please the shogun, hers to destroy Yanagisawa. Somehow their togetherness had become an integral part of her desire to succeed.

Aoi strode the paths of the shrine precinct, seeking any task that could occupy her thoughts and assist her denial of the truth. She turned down a path where a strip of garden formed a boundary between precinct and forest. Along this ran flagstones on which worshippers could stroll and view the cherry trees, shrubs, and flower beds. Aoi knelt on the path and industriously began sweeping up dirt, pebbles, twigs, and fallen blossoms. Sweat filmed her face. Sunshine, dappled by the swaying branches of a cherry tree above her, dazzled her eyes. The smells of damp earth and pungent pine filled her lungs. Despite her attempt to purge all thought and emotion from her mind, she succumbed to the magic of the warm spring day and the yearning voice of her own heart. Her hand slowed. She slipped into a daydream that blended past and present.

She was back in her village, standing at her favorite place on the mountainside, with the wind in her hair and her spirit at peace. How good and clean she felt, having used her mystical powers for good rather than evil! And working with Sano had given her a sense of community she'd not experienced since leaving home. The memory of last night made her body sing with desire. Now she saw Sano standing on the mountain beside her, with all the trappings of his class and rank miraculously stripped away. His hair had grown, covering his samurai's shaven crown. He wore no swords, no Tokugawa crest. Seeing him thus, Aoi gasped. She hadn't noticed until now his resemblance to her father. They didn't look alike, but the same inner essence of honor and integrity marked their faces.

Gazing at her, Sano didn't smile. Neither did she. They didn't embrace, or even touch. Free from the castle walls that imprisoned them, they walked up the mountain together, toward a shared future ambiguous in its particulars, but radiant with promise. Aoi's heart swelled with happiness.

Her extra sense, trained to remain alert even when her mind was occupied, detected the approach of evil first. In an instant, Aoi's dream evaporated. Her skin contracted, her nostrils quivered; her body stiffened as danger wafted toward her like a predator's spoor. The wild elixirs of fear and excitement began to flow in her blood. Her legs tensed instinctively, ready to run for cover. Then she recognized the person behind the aura that preceded him. Fear gave way to dread. Trapped, she stayed on her knees, head bent, hand still wielding the broom, while she frantically sought escape.

Now he entered the range of her ordinary senses. She heard his stealthy footsteps and the whisper of his satin robes on the path. She smelled his wintergreen hair oil and masculine body odor. He stopped just short of her, his presence a cold patch of night in the bright morning.

"Continue working. Don't look up," said Chamberlain Yanagi-sawa.

Aoi kept her eyes on the ground and her hand moving, though less out of obedience than from fear of meeting his gaze. Why had he come to her like this, in the open, where anyone could see them? Had he somehow learned of her defection? Her thoughts flew to her family. She must warn them of the danger. And Sano, too, who at this moment was out gathering evidence against the chamberlain.

Above her, a branch of the flowering cherry tree rustled, then snapped: Yanagisawa had picked a spray of blossoms. She felt him hold them to his nose and heard him sniff their fragrance—his ostensible reason for stopping, the pretense to hide their conversation.

"What have you to report about *Sōsakan* Sano's inquiries?" he asked.

Aoi relaxed a little. Maybe he'd found a spare moment in his busy schedule, had been passing by the shrine, and impulsively stopped to see her. Hastily she marshaled her thoughts.

"Yesterday Sano interviewed Chūgo Gichin and Matsui Minoru." She knew Yanagisawa had other spies, who might tell him even if she didn't, and the last thing she wanted was for him to doubt her efficiency or loyalty.

"Has he found evidence against any of the suspects?"

She heard an anxious tremor in the chamberlain's smooth voice. Were Sano's suspicions justified? Now Aoi longed to look into his eyes and read the truth there.

Instead, she arranged her sweepings of dirt, twigs, and dead blossoms into a neat pile. "No, Honorable Chamberlain," she replied evenly.

A beat passed. Then: "Did you see Sano last night?"

Panic rippled the surface of Aoi's nerves. Sano's servants knew she'd brought him home last night and stayed until dawn. How much else they knew—or would tell, if asked—she couldn't say. In addition, Sano's attackers might have recognized her. She must stay as close to the truth as possible.

"I saw him, Honorable Chamberlain," she said.

"How did he seem?"

He knew about the attack. Aoi could tell by the acceleration of his pulse, which she felt as a palpitation in her ears.

"He was badly beaten," she said cautiously. "I treated his wounds. I listened to his troubles. I left him asleep."

"Good. He will trust you all the more."

The satisfaction in Yanagisawa's voice chilled her. He was a suspect; he wanted Sano's investigation stopped. Had he ordered the beating? Was this proof of his guilt?

"And how is our invalid this morning?" Yanagisawa's hushed laugh made Aoi imagine a soft quilt stuffed with steel needles. "In bed, where he'll languish away the rest of his miserable life?"

Aoi wanted to tell him that Sano's body and spirit were broken, that the investigation was over—anything to cease Yanagisawa's interference and buy her and Sano time to destroy him. But she couldn't risk the possibility of his learning the truth elsewhere and discovering her lies.

"No, Honorable Chamberlain," she said, hating her role as a spy even more now that she'd renounced it. "Sano is a strong man.

And lucky that whoever beat him didn't hurt him permanently. He was well enough to leave the castle this morning to call on another suspect. A woman named O-tama."

Yanagisawa's robes rustled as he began to pace. His movements stirred up a cold draft that raised bumps on Aoi's skin. A net of terror fell over her heart: silk threads tightening, cutting. She could no longer pretend to work, because she knew what he was going to say.

"It's just as I feared. It's not enough to feed Sano false information, undermine his relationship with the shogun, threaten him with ruin, and hope he fails. He's too zealous in his duty. He's impervious to pain; he has incredible good fortune, and no regard for self-preservation. If he's interrogating Chūgo, Matsui, and O-tama, he's on the path to the truth. He must be stopped before he gets any farther."

Yanagisawa stopped pacing, but his anger, fear, and hatred coalesced around them like a gathering storm.

"At the earliest possible moment, you will kill Sano."

Aoi heard his robes swish as his arm moved. On top of her dirt pile landed the cherry branch he'd been holding. The broken end exposed the pale wood beneath the bark; the bright blossoms had already begun to wilt. Aoi's horror blurred its image into a vision of torn flesh and spilled blood. She couldn't speak, couldn't move, couldn't breathe. Through her mind's silent screams of protest, Yanagisawa spoke again.

"And make it look like a natural death."

Then he was gone.

When Sano returned to his mansion that evening, he was so stiff and sore he could barely move. Pain clothed him like a skintight suit of armor lined with spikes. At his gate he almost fell off his horse, then staggered through the courtyard and into the house. There he collapsed facedown in the corridor, thankful that no one had attacked him on his way home, for he wouldn't have been able to defend himself. He rested in the security of having stone walls and guarded gates between him and whoever wished him harm.

Then he heard soft footsteps coming down the corridor. He looked up to see Aoi kneel beside him, her lovely face grave with concern. In his joy at seeing her again, he almost forgot his pain.

"I've prepared a medicinal bath for you," she said. "Come."

With her strong arms, she helped him to his feet and supported him down the corridor. Sano wanted to rest in her embrace and drink in her beauty, but he could do neither.

"I can't stay," he said.

"You must. For the sake of your health."

He'd spent the afternoon in a futile attempt to establish the suspects' presences in the pharmacists' district, the *eta* settlement, Yoshiwara, and Zōjō Temple at the times of the murders. Now he should find out whether Aoi had identified the mystery witness from the temple, then begin surveillance on Chamberlain Yanagisawa. But the pain, coupled with his desire to be with her, overcame his resistance. He let her lead him to the bathchamber.

In the lamplit paneled room, a coal fire burned beneath the large, round wooden tub. From the heated water rose steam redolent with a sweet, pungent herb Sano couldn't identify. The open window framed the branches of a blooming cherry tree that trembled in the cool evening breeze, dropping petals like snow flurries.

Sano undressed, and saw that the bruises had darkened; he looked as bad as he felt. His happiness at being with Aoi turned to puzzlement. As she helped him scrub and rinse himself, her touch was gentle but impersonal. She didn't speak, and wouldn't meet his eyes. Last night's intimacy was gone, as if it had never existed.

"What's wrong?" he asked.

Still not looking at him, she shrugged and shook her head. "Get in. Before the water cools."

Wincing in pain, Sano climbed the short ladder into the tub and immersed himself. The heat seeped into his aching muscles; a blissful sigh escaped him. But even as the pain and tension slipped away, he examined Aoi with increasing concern.

She stood stiffly beside the tub, her face pensive. And why was his extra sense detecting the cold breath of danger emanating from her? His innate distrust of the ninja resurfaced.

"There is something wrong. What is it?"

"Nothing," she answered, too quickly.

A sick feeling spread through Sano's stomach, almost eclipsing his fear, as he guessed at the problem. "You weren't able to find out who the missing woman was?"

"Yes. I did." Her voice was flat, its huskiness turned hoarse. "Madam Shimizu, wife of an Edo rice broker, fits what you told me, and what I learned from her clothes. She's staying at her husband's summer villa." In the same lifeless voice, Aoi gave the woman's description, and directions for finding the house.

Sano received the news with less relief than he'd expected, because so far every inquiry had led to Yanagisawa. "Thank you,

Aoi," he said, trying to sound pleased. "I'll interview Madam Shimizu tomorrow morning." He hoped that whatever she'd seen wouldn't provide the final, incontrovertible evidence that would condemn him to death.

Hesitantly Aoi said, "What did you learn today?"

Sano told her, all the while wondering why she'd changed toward him. "O-tama's story strengthens Yanagisawa's motive," he finished. "Wild Boar's ties the assassin to him. And I didn't find any evidence against Chūgo or Matsui."

"Then you'll arrest Chamberlain Yanagisawa soon?"

Sano turned away from her innocent, hurtful eagerness. She didn't guess what form Yanagisawa's execution would take—and he couldn't tell her.

"Not until I have solid proof of his guilt," he said.

Although she didn't move, he felt her shrink from him. Disappointment darkened her eyes. He could forgive her for wishing Yanagisawa's downfall, and her freedom, but he couldn't deny the pain of knowing that both could only be bought with his own life. Yearning to bridge the barrier of heritage that separated them, he lifted his hand from the water. She stepped back before it touched her cheek. In the awkward silence, steam rose around them like a physical manifestation of their unhappiness. Then Sano understood the reason for her distant behavior.

She'd reconsidered the wisdom of helping him, and now regretted it. She realized the danger their relationship posed to her, with every day adding to the risk of Yanagisawa's learning about their collusion. Terrified for her family and herself, she wanted to end their liaison, but feared hurting him.

Guilt and sorrow flooded Sano. He knew what he must do, but couldn't bear to let her go. Perhaps unwisely, he let his heart voice the message his mind ordered him to deliver.

"My father followed the ancient samurai practice of familiarizing one's sons with the phenomenon of death, to desensitize them so that they would grow up unafraid of it and thus willing to die in battle for their lord. During my fifth year he began taking me to funerals to watch cremations. In my sixth year he instructed the priests at Zōjō Temple to let me spend nights alone in the cemetery. And when I was seven he started taking me to the execution ground to see the rotting corpses and severed heads. He did this until I reached manhood at fifteen.

" 'A samurai must keep constantly in mind the fact that he has to die,' he would tell me. 'And you must neither feel nor show fear of death.' "

Sano laughed grimly, remembering. "I got part of the lesson right. I never showed fear. My father was proud of what he thought was my courage. But I never told anyone that the funerals gave me nightmares about being burned alive, or that those nights in the cemetery were the longest of my life because I heard ghosts moaning in the trees and thought they would tear me to pieces. I never told anyone that after a trip to the execution ground I would wash myself over and over to remove the spiritual pollution that I believed would kill me. And I've never told anyone how much I still fear death—"

Sano caught himself. He hadn't meant to confess his cowardice. Yet, as before, Aoi had provoked in him the need to reveal thoughts that a samurai wasn't supposed to have. No one else listened with such understanding, or allowed him the emotional release he sought from the unbending stoicism he must show the world. Now he hastened to the point of his story.

"Aoi. It's a samurai's duty to deny fear and emotion, and to accept death. But it's not yours. You've risked your safety and your family's to do something for which I can never repay you, or forgive myself."

Dragging out the next words was like uprooting pieces of his soul. "You're free to go. Tell Yanagisawa I refused to see you. I'll never reveal what you did for me. I promise."

Because I love you. He averted his eyes to hide his sadness and avoid seeing the relief in hers. For both of them, duty must prevail over romance. His own personal code of honor wouldn't let him imperil her further. His only comfort came from knowing that he might not live to suffer long from her departure.

Then he heard a rustle; the tub's ladder creaked; the water rose to his chin. In surprise, he looked up to see that Aoi had undressed and climbed into the tub beside him.

"Hold me," she whispered.

She wasn't leaving him! Sano's sorrow rocketed into joy, but he knew he mustn't give in to it.

"Aoi, no," he said.

"Shh." She put a finger to his lips. Her own trembled; tears welled in her eyes.

"Tell me what's wrong," Sano pleaded.

Her only answer was a vehement shake of the head. She straddled him, and, yielding to desire, he let her. Buoyed by the water, she seemed almost weightless. He succumbed to the urge to run his hands over her shoulders, breasts, and hips, to draw her spread thighs closer around his waist. The warm, oily water gave her smooth skin a delicious slickness. With their bodies' contact, intimacy returned. Aoi's fingers traced his features with a tenderness she'd never expressed in words. She accepted his caresses with a passionate abandon that told him she was giving him her self, and not just her body. Sano's earlier fear and distrust evaporated like the steam around them. With a moan, he pulled her down onto his erection.

In a rush of intoxicating pleasure, he slid into her. The scented water made him dizzy; the beauty of her face against the lush backdrop of falling cherry blossoms swelled his throat. Restraining his urgency, he raised and lowered her with deliberate slowness; she sighed. This gentle, sensuous coupling couldn't possibly have been more different from last night's mutual assault. Sano realized that theirs was a union that could encompass the extremes of emotion—joy and sadness, pain and pleasure, love and hatred, tenderness and violence. His heart mourned as he remembered that it had to end.

Aoi seemed to share his bitter knowledge. She was weeping openly now, even as they moved ever faster together. Her final cry mingled grief with pleasure. Sano moaned in the rapture of his own climax. They clung to each other, and when she pressed her cheek to his, he couldn't distinguish her tears from his own. He tried to believe that as long as they remained together thus, the moment would last forever.

Too soon the water cooled, forcing Sano to acknowledge the passage of time. Reluctantly he released Aoi.

"I have to go," he said.

Climbing out of the tub, he dried himself on a towel, noting with relief that he could again move with ease.

"Wait." Aoi also clambered from the water, hastily drying and dressing herself. "You need your medicines first."

Once again Sano sensed that air of distracted tension about her. Distrust returned, stronger this time; but she was right. His bruises still ached; without treatment, he would again grow too stiff and sore to move, let alone complete his night's work.

"All right," he said. He accompanied her to the bedchamber and lay down on the futon. "But hurry."

"I'll make the room warm for you . . ." Aoi's voice was muffled as she turned her back to him and bent over the sunken charcoal brazier. Rising, she hurried to the door.

"Aoi. Wait. Don't go." Sano had to find out what was troubling her, and to reestablish contact.

Over her shoulder, she said, "Rest now, and I'll be right back with the herbs and potions . . ."

. . . and closed the door behind her, leaving Sano to worry about the future. Would he fulfill his duty and his promises? Would he catch Yanagisawa in the act of murder? Must he execute the chamberlain, then take his own life tonight? If not, would fate allow him to arrest Chūgo or Matsui for the murders before his two days were up? How many more nights would he and Aoi have together? Too anxious to relax, Sano stared up at the ceiling. But soon, to his surprise, his eyelids drooped. Realizing that he must have underestimated his fatigue, or the sedative effects of hot water and sex, he struggled to stay alert. But great, irresistible waves of drowsiness washed over him.

He gave in to sleep.

Outside Sano's door, Aoi stood, rigid with misery. Her mind resonated with the silent howl of anguish that had begun when Chamberlain Yanagisawa ordered her to kill Sano. It had intensified as she'd made love to him and denied anything was wrong. Now she closed her eyes and clenched her fists against the loneliness and despair that filled her heart like blood pooling in a wound. She forced herself to concentrate on the sounds emanating from Sano's room. His restless stirring ceased, and she waited for the change in his breathing that would mean he'd passed into deep sleep.

Before she'd left the room, she'd dropped into the brazier a secret ninja sleep potion—rare herbs, blood of mole, snake, and newt, absorbed into a piece of paper—that would give off sleep-inducing fumes as it burned. During wartime, her people had tossed this potion into guardhouse stoves to make the sentries drowsy so they could penetrate enemy castles. Now she was using it to put her lover to sleep so she could follow her master's orders and take his life.

All day long, her thoughts had chased endlessly over the same ground, like a wolf she'd once seen trapped in a mountain crevasse outside her village. Now her mind ached from trying desperately to find a way to disobey Chamberlain Yanagisawa's orders without endangering her family.

She'd considered delaying Sano's murder in the hope that he would discover incriminating evidence against Yanagisawa, but what if the chamberlain grew impatient? He would get someone else to kill Sano, and her family would be punished for her failure.

She'd thought of telling Sano about the plot against him. Together they could fake his death, then hide him someplace where he could live under a false identity. But she'd discarded this alternative even more quickly than the first. Despite their short acquaintance, she knew Sano well enough to understand that he would never abandon his post.

What if she were to destroy Chamberlain Yanagisawa, as she longed to do? She'd spent hours plotting how: poison; a thrown blade; a quick blow; an arrow. Yanagisawa, though, was careful, as is any man with many enemies. He employed food tasters and bodyguards. Even with her skill at stealth and combat, she would never get close enough to kill him, then manage to escape afterward. And she couldn't discredit him by reporting his scheme to the authorities. Yanagisawa controlled the *bakufu* and the shogun. No one would dare act against him to save her or Sano.

She'd even considered suicide, but that, although releasing her from responsibility, would ensure neither Sano's safety nor her family's.

Only one option remained: the most perilous, the one she could never choose.

Now Aoi cast aside these useless thoughts. The mountain wolf had finally starved to death. So must her dreams perish. Old loyalties took precedence over new; filial duty superseded love. Sano must die, by her hand, now.

Fighting tears, she put her ear to the door's paper panel and listened. The depth of Sano's breathing confirmed what her extra sense told her: He was fast asleep. She waited a moment to make sure all the sleep potion had burned away. Then, summoning all her courage, she opened the door.

He lay on his stomach, head pillowed on his folded arms. His face was turned toward her; sleep had smoothed away the worry, leaving him looking younger, more innocent, and less troubled than she'd ever seen him. She swallowed pity and self-hatred. Resisting the urge to shake him awake and warn him, she stepped into the room, closing the door quietly behind her. She crossed the floor and knelt beside Sano. The howling inside her rose to a deafening blare that sounded the same word over and over:

No—no—no—no—

Under the noise, Aoi heard Sano's soft, steady breathing quicken and catch, his pulse skip. She saw his eyelids flutter: He was dreaming. Still, she knew the potion wouldn't let him awaken. It was time.

No—no—no—

With unsteady hands, she removed from her hair a long wooden hairpin with a black lacquer head shaped like a lady's fan. She tugged on the blunt shaft of the pin. The hollow wooden sheath came away, exposing the steel prong inside: sharp, needle-thin, and deadly.

Aoi's tears spilled down her cheeks and over her lips. She wiped them away with her fingers. Her mind's silent scream vibrated in every muscle of her body. Clutching the hairpin in her trembling right hand, she laid her left on the base of Sano's neck. The feel of his warm, resilient flesh caused a rush of tenderness, which she choked down. As he writhed and moaned in his sleep, she felt the blood flowing beneath his skin, and the exuberant life force radiating from him. His heartbeat pounded up through her fingers, its quickening pulse matching her own. Slowly, gently, she moved her hand down his spine. Her fingers, wet with tears, left a damp trail on his skin.

Now, despite her anguish, the circumstances evoked a powerful contradictory response deep within Aoi. Her training had prepared her for this dreaded task. Her killing instinct stirred, like a dormant snake uncoiling. Even as her spirit sickened, reflex took over. Her fingers probed the bones and interstices of Sano's spine. The hand that held the lethal hairpin ceased to tremble. With her inner eye, she saw the great energy wave whose roar drowned out her mind's screams as it broke over her. She saw the colored lights. And her father's image.

He stood in the classroom of the village ninja academy. Upon a table before him, a naked man lay facedown, with female students clustered around. Aoi recognized the anatomy lesson she'd attended at age eight.

"Here, between the vertebrae," her father said, touching a spot on the young man's spine, "is where you insert your needle. Death is instantaneous, and the needle leaves no trace except a tiny hole where no one will find it."

One by one, the girls stepped forward to feel the spot, to memorize its position and texture. For a moment, Aoi inhabited her childhood body and world. She touched the man's back. Then she returned to the present, with her finger at the same spot on Sano's spine.

The wave's roar grew louder. Aoi lost contact with her humanity and became a mere vessel for the power coursing through her. The swirling energy focused at two points: her fingertip, pressed against Sano's flesh, and the hand holding the hairpin. Possessed by the irresistible force, the latter moved until the hairpin's tip was poised directly over Sano's back.

Faintly she heard her father's voice: "Killing is the last, least desirable alternative. But when the time comes, you must recognize it and act without hesitation. Because the safety of us all depends on you."

No . . .

Her conscious mind's weak protest quickly faded. Aoi's fingertip moved aside, baring the space between Sano's vertebrae. She lowered the hairpin as every impulse and instinct in her demanded satisfaction. Her heart pounded. The blood thundered in her head. Her breath came in gasps. Her fingers locked around the pin. Slowly she pressed down. The hairpin's point pierced the outer layer of Sano's skin. Aoi felt the dark strength gathering in her arm muscles in preparation for driving the weapon home—

Then some last vestige of her essential self rallied against the forces that possessed Aoi. Memory recalled her impossible vision of the future. Like a faded painting on transparent silk, the image of herself and Sano climbing the mountain together hung between her and the turbulent, luminous energy wave. But this time, black storm clouds boiled up over the distant peaks. The wind tossed the trees and rustled the grasses. Aoi saw herself smile and reach out to take the hand Sano offered her, with its promise of love and protection. Then his image shimmered and disappeared. She was alone on the mountain, in the storm.

"Come back!" Aoi pleaded.

At her cry, the dark energy abruptly dissipated. The wave receded. The roar ceased; the colored lights vanished. Her trance was broken.

Aghast at what she'd almost done, Aoi sat stiff and still for a long moment. Then her body went limp, spent of all strength by the effort of reaching the brink of murder. She let go the hairpin, which slid off Sano's back and onto the futon, leaving behind only a tiny, harmless pinprick. With a low moan, she collapsed against Sano, clinging to him as sobs wracked her body.

Sedated by the poison, Sano slept on, oblivious to her grief, and to the threat against his life. Her weakness had saved him—for now. But she owed her first loyalty to others, for whose protection she'd learned the deadly ninja skills she so dreaded using.

Tomorrow she must find the strength and courage to do what she could not tonight.

31

Sano steered his mount up a twisting road into Edo's western hills. Wild azalea bushes, vivid with red blossoms, crowned the stone embankments that shored the road's upper side; oak, laurel, cypress, chestnut, cedar, and flowering cherry trees adorned the grassy slopes that fell away on the lower. Narrow lanes branched off the main thoroughfare to picturesque, rustic summer villas. Small streams burbled beneath wooden bridges; birds darted and twittered. But Sano was virtually oblivious to the serene beauty of this place where Edo's wealthy citizens sought relief from summer's heat.

He could see the cloud of smoke hanging over the area of Nihonbashi where yesterday's fire still burned, its spread facilitated by the continuing riots and the weather, which was unseasonably warm and windy. Far to the east, dark storm clouds hovered; thunder rumbled. But the spring weather was unpredictable; rain might or might not come to extinguish the fire and disperse the rioters. And other doubts added to Sano's concerns.

If Madam Shimizu really was the mystery witness from Zōjō Temple, would he get from her the evidence he needed to identify the Bundori Killer? He couldn't shake the visions of suicide that had disturbed his sleep. He'd awakened at dawn to discover he'd missed his chance to shadow Chamberlain Yanagisawa—and that Aoi was gone. Had she decided to leave him after all?

Sano had resisted the temptation to hurry to the shrine in search of her. Much depended on what he learned today. By discovering evidence against someone besides Yanagisawa, he could save his life—but would Aoi cease to care for him?

The western hill country, like the rest of Edo, was divided according to social hierarchy, with the great daimyo villas occupying the loftiest peaks, and those of the rich merchants below. Halfway up this latter sector, Sano found the turnoff Aoi had described, where the road forked between two towering cypresses. He directed his horse down a narrow lane through oak and beech woods, over a short bridge that spanned a stream. A sharp curve left brought him to the Shimizu villa, composed of three attached buildings arranged on ascending levels of the hillside amid more woods.

He dismounted, secured his horse, and approached the tree-shaded front entrance. Before he reached it, the door flew open, and a sour-faced peasant woman dressed in a gray cotton kimono hurried out.

"No visitors allowed!" she shouted. "You will please leave!"

She showed none of the usual deference to his rank, and the two men who followed her lent weight to her order. Both were youngish samurai—brothers, apparently, with the same wide mouths and prominent ears. They wore shabby clothes and a look of angry desperation. Sano recognized them as *rōnin* who made a precarious living by working as security guards for wealthy commoners. They stopped a few paces short of him, legs planted wide, arms folded, gazes hostile.

Sano introduced himself to the woman, whom he took to be the servant in charge of the house. "I'm here on the shogun's official business. Take me to Madam Shimizu."

The servant didn't deny or confirm Madam Shimizu's presence in the villa, but her quick glance backward told Sano that she was here—probably hiding from the consequences of her visit to the temple, whatever they were. "No visitors," she repeated.

Her willingness to defy a *bakufu* official's order demonstrated a fierce loyalty to her mistress that exceeded prudence. The *rōnin* grasped their sword hilts, and Sano didn't like the message he read in their eyes. They were angry at the whole world and would welcome a fight, even with the shogun's retainer. They would be betting that he valued his life more than they did theirs, and would forsake his errand rather than oppose them.

And they were right—partially.

"Good day." Bowing politely, Sano turned and walked down the lane, retrieved his horse, and rode away. Then, once beyond the curve and out of sight from the house, he resecured his mount and doubled back through the forest, heading for the rear of Madam Shimizu's residence.

He scaled the steep hill, staying within the cover of the trees, until he came to the road behind the villa. The rear of the uppermost, largest building had few windows, all shuttered, and no balcony. High walls extended from it, enclosing the two lower wings and the garden. Sano could see no doors, but there must be others besides the front entrance, through which the residents could escape during a fire or earthquake.

Sano looked around and saw neither the servant nor the guards. Skidding down the hill, he waded through the thick grass around the villa. As he examined the head-high, stone-faced earthen wall around the garden, he heard from within it a woman's high, quavery voice, singing a slow, melancholy tune:

"The green woods fade to brown, alas
Frost withers the peony and the rose—"

Sano smiled. The singer must be Madam Shimizu. Quietly Sano tried the heavy, weathered plank gate. It was locked. But the wall was covered with a network of vines; some had woody stems as thick as his wrist. Using these as a ladder, he climbed the wall. Cautiously he peered over the top.

He formed a quick impression of an overgrown garden, bordered on left and right by the verandas of the upper and lower buildings, and on the far end by a covered walkway connecting the two wings. Then he spotted a pavilion at the garden's center.

Almost hidden by the vines that climbed the pavilion's lattice wall and up its thatched roof knelt a woman. Sano could discern no more than her bowed head and blue kimono, but her plaintive song continued:

> *"Summer's birds are flown,*
> *Love has gone—*
> *My heart dies, too."*

Sano took a hasty look behind him, then pulled himself atop the wall. He jumped, landing in an ivy-choked flower bed. Eagerly he started toward the pavilion. Then he halted as a door in the covered walkway banged open.

"Hey! What do you think you're doing?"

The *rōnin* guards ran toward him, drawing their swords. Sano's was already in his hand. He thought he could take these men without serious difficulty, but he wanted no more bloodshed. And if Madam Shimizu was terrified because she'd already witnessed one killing, then more wouldn't improve her willingness or ability to answer his questions. Keeping his eyes on the *rōnin*, he addressed the woman in the pavilion.

"Madam Shimizu, I'm Sano Ichirō, the shogun's *sōsakan*," he called. "I won't hurt you. I just want to talk to you."

Scuffles and whimpers came from the pavilion.

Swords raised, the guards circled Sano. The elder glared fiercely; the younger looked nervous.

"You're in trouble, aren't you, Madam Shimizu?" Sano called. "You're afraid; you're hiding from someone. I can help you—but only if you call off your guards."

Still no answer. Then the younger *rōnin* retreated a step. "He's the shogun's man—we can't kill him! I don't care how much she's paying us to protect her. I don't want to go to jail, or have my head cut off!"

"Shut up!" his brother shouted. "Do you want to go back to begging in the streets?" To Sano, he said, "Get out, or I cut you."

He lunged at Sano—then fell back as the woman's voice spoke softly but clearly:

"Stop. . . . It's all right. He can stay."

The guards shrugged, and went back into the house. Relieved, Sano sheathed his sword and looked toward the pavilion.

She stood in its arched entryway, a short, plump woman dressed in a vivid aqua kimono printed with butterflies. Sano's initial impression of youth and beauty quickly faded as he walked toward her. Her hair, though looped up at the sides and hanging long at the back in the style of a young lady, was an unnaturally dark, lusterless black: dyed. The heavy white face powder and bright rouge didn't hide the pouches under her eyes, or the slackness of her cheeks and jowls. Her bright, girlish clothes only emphasized her thick waist, double chin, and the empty space in the upper row of her blackened teeth. Sano's lingering distrust of Aoi melted away in a flood of gratitude as he stared, amazed to find the mystery witness just as she'd described: a fat, aging woman clinging desperately to youth.

"*Sōsakan-sama.*" Madam Shimizu bowed, then peered coyly at him from beneath lowered eyelids; but her smile was strained, her tone weary and resigned. "I've been expecting you. . . . I'm glad you're here at last."

"I went to Zōjō Temple because my husband no longer loves me," Madam Shimizu said.

Obviously distraught, she hadn't invited Sano into the house. Instead she wandered aimlessly around the garden, leaving him to follow.

"For the past ten years, he's never once looked at me . . . or spoken to me with affection." Her speech was filled with long pauses and trailing endings, perhaps in deliberate imitation of highborn samurai women. Now her voice dropped to a whisper. "And no matter how much I beg, he won't share my bed . . ."

Sano, embarrassed by this intimate confession, nevertheless recognized her urgent need to tell her troubles to someone, anyone. By simply listening, he would learn more than through formal interrogation. Considerately, he turned his gaze from her sad, ravaged face to the garden.

Like her, it must have once been lovely. A huge cherry tree blossomed beside a pond; elaborate stone lanterns and benches graced a bower of luxuriant plant life. But this paradise had fallen into neglect. Withered vines clung to the buildings. Dead branches stuck out from the cherry tree like black bones. Rotting leaves, fallen blossoms, and green scum covered the pond. Shrubs were unpruned, lanterns and benches coated with moss and lichen, flower beds and lawn choked with weeds. If Mimaki and O-tama's garden was a monument to love, this served as mute testimony to its loss.

Madam Shimizu's thoughts seemed to follow his. "Do you see this garden?" Her soft voice quivered with pain. "My husband once employed gardeners to keep it beautiful. When we were young . . . before I bore our seven children . . . we spent many happy hours here.

" 'I can't bear to be apart from you,' he would tell me. He praised my beauty, and made love to me . . . there." Madam Shimizu pointed to a spot beneath the cherry tree. Her plump hand was smooth and soft-looking, as if it had never done a day's work. "But now I'm old and ugly. . . . My health is poor; I suffer from congestion. My husband never comes here anymore." Sano saw tears tracing rivulets through the thick makeup on her cheeks. "He's brought two young concubines into our house in Edo, and often visits the courtesans in Yoshiwara, too.

"Ours was a marriage of love . . . that's rare, you know, in this world where marriages are arranged for the sake of money and family considerations. One doesn't expect to find love, and so it hurts all the more to lose it."

"I know," Sano said, wishing he could cut her story short. With his own romance threatened, he didn't want to hear about lost love. If he should lose Aoi . . . For the sake of the investigation, he let Madam Shimizu talk.

"In summer, we would take our pleasure boat out on the river to watch the fireworks. It's a big boat, with a comfortable cabin . . . We would drink wine and delight in each other's company." Madam Shimizu dabbed her face with her sleeve; it came away stained with powder and rouge. "But no more. The boat has been docked for ten seasons. I decided to become a nun because I could no longer bear living without my dearest one's love. . . ."

With relief, Sano turned the conversation to the night of the priest's murder. "So you went to Zōjō Temple and asked for sanctuary. What happened there?"

"I took my best clothes as a dowry for the priests. I hired a palanquin . . . and reached the temple at sunset." Madam Shimizu's narrative faltered. She ceased her stroll around the garden and dropped onto a bench. Her fingers picked at the lichen that encrusted it. "*Sōsakan-sama* . . . if I tell you what I saw, will you promise not to tell anyone else?" She raised pleading eyes to him. "Please . . . before you object, let me explain why I'm in hiding. Why I want no visitors, and have hired *rōnin* to protect me."

She shot a nervous glance around the garden as if she expected an attack at any moment. "After I left the temple, I went home to Nihonbashi. But the very next morning, three strange samurai came and asked to see me. They wouldn't say why, or who they were, so the servants told them I wasn't home. They left, but a few hours later, they came back. . . . I don't know who they were, but I know why they came. They were sent by the Bundori Killer. He must have recognized me at the temple, or somehow found out who I was. *Sōsakan-sama,* he's looking for me, he wants to kill me because he thinks I can identify him. Now do you understand why you mustn't let anyone know I spoke to you?"

Sano sat beside her, wondering if the strange callers were really the killer's minions, sent to eliminate a witness to the priest's murder. If so, then which suspect had sent them? Matsui, who moved in the same social sphere as the Shimizu and might have recognized Madam Shimizu because he'd met her before? Chūgo or Yanagisawa, both of whom had access to the *bakufu*'s intelligence network—which no doubt included spies inside Zōjō Temple—and its files on Edo's prominent citizens? Or was Madam Shimizu imagining threats where none existed? He would have to question her servants and try to trace the three samurai. But of one thing Sano was certain: If he wanted the Bundori Killer convicted, he couldn't keep Madam Shimizu's testimony a secret.

"If you'll sign a confidential statement that I can show the magistrate, you won't have to come forward as a witness," Sano proposed. After the killer's capture, she would have no reason for fear. He suspected she had other motives for shunning publicity, which this plan might satisfy.

After a long moment's thought, Madam Shimizu said, "Yes . . . all right." With a sigh, she resumed her story.

"The abbot at the temple accepted my dowry and gave me a room in the guest quarters . . . but I couldn't sleep. I missed my husband terribly, and wondered how he would feel when he found me gone. Would he be glad, or unhappy? I wondered if I was making a mistake. Might he come to love me again someday if I waited long enough? Finally I couldn't bear the thought of never seeing him again. . . . Around midnight, I sneaked out of the guest quarters. I didn't care if I had to walk all the way back to Nihonbashi, alone, in the dark. I just wanted to be near my husband . . . even when I knew him to be asleep in the arms of his concubines. And . . ."

Fresh tears spilled from her eyes, washing away more powder to reveal the sallow skin beneath. "I was too proud to let him know I'd tried to leave him, and couldn't," she whispered.

So here was her real reason for wanting confidentiality. Sano felt a burst of anger toward the faithless husband, and pity for the wife who still desired his respect even if she couldn't have his love.

"I understand," he said gently. He waited for her to compose herself, then prompted, "So you left the guest quarters. What then?"

"There were priests patrolling the grounds. I stayed in the shadows close to the buildings so they wouldn't see me." She pantomimed her furtive escape, hands groping, her expression fearful but determined. "I went into the main precinct . . . the moon was out, and there were a few lanterns burning, but it was still very dark, and I was afraid. And then . . ."

Madam Shimizu twisted her hands in her lap. "When I ran around the main hall on my way to the front gate, I tripped and fell on something. . . . It was a dead priest!" A strangled sob burst from her, and her plump body shivered. "I screamed and jumped up. His head was gone . . . there was blood on his robes . . . and a sword sticking out of his chest . . ."

Sano looked at her in surprise. He'd seen no sword in the priest's body, and no one at the temple had mentioned finding one. If Madam Shimizu was telling the truth, then what had become of it?

"I knew the Bundori Killer had killed the priest," she went on, wiping away more tears. "I was afraid he was somewhere in the temple grounds, and that he would kill me, too. I should have called for help, or run back to my room to hide. But all I could think of was how much I wanted to go home. . . . I needed a weapon to protect myself with, so I—I pulled the sword out of the priest's body."

With both hands, she grasped an imaginary sword hilt and yanked, averting her face and grimacing at the remembered friction between steel and flesh. "I stuck the sword under my sash. Then I went to the temple bell. I picked up the mallet and hit it as hard as I could. Then I ran to the gate."

So the abbot had correctly guessed that the mystery woman had rung the bell. The Bundori Killer, to overcome the priest's unexpected resistance, must have used both his swords in the fight—and then forgotten one when he left with the head. A small fire of hope lit inside Sano. Perhaps this was the clue he needed. He started to ask where the sword was now, but Madam Shimizu hadn't finished.

"And that was when I saw the killer," she said dully, drained of emotion now.

"You saw the Bundori Killer?" In his excitement, Sano almost forgot about the sword. Here at last was his murder witness.

Madam Shimizu nodded, sniffling. "He was outside the gate when I got there . . . unwrapping a bundle. I could see that it was a head. . . . The lanterns were burning beside the gate, and I was but ten paces from him. The bell was still ringing, and I could tell he was in a hurry to be gone. I screamed, but he didn't hear me, he couldn't have, the noise was so loud. Then he looked around and saw me."

"Madam Shimizu," Sano said, keeping his voice quiet, though his heart was pounding and his mouth had gone dry, "this is very important. What did the killer look like? Describe him as best you can. Take your time."

"I didn't get a good look. I think he was tall, but I'm not sure . . . it was dark . . . he wore a hooded cloak, and his face was in shadow. . . . And when he looked at me, I turned and ran." She grabbed Sano's arm; her nails bit into his flesh. "But he must have seen my face, sōsakan-sama. He thinks I can identify him. He's looking for me now. That's why you must protect me!"

Crushed by disappointment, Sano chastised himself for expecting too much. "What did you do then?" he asked.

"I should have gone back inside the temple . . . I could hear people running and shouting . . . I would have been safe with the priests. But I wasn't thinking clearly . . . so instead I ran into the forest. Oh. Forgive me."

She withdrew her hand and, with a pathetic attempt at dignity, sat up straight. "The killer chased me. I ran, and he almost caught me . . . but he fell over a rock, and I got away. I hid in a hollow tree. Then I saw lights coming through the forest and heard men calling. The killer ran away. I stayed hidden until dawn, and everyone was gone. Then I ran all the way home to Nihonbashi."

Sano shook his head in gloomy awe as he listened. His witness had been there all the while he'd been questioning the temple's residents and searching the forest. She'd inadvertently prevented the killer from retrieving the only clue he'd left at any of the crime scenes, then stolen it.

Bracing himself against further disappointment, Sano said, "What did you do with the sword?"

Madam Shimizu lifted her useless-looking hands, then let them plop into her lap. "I carried it with me on the way home, just in case I met the killer. Then I didn't know what to do with it. First I wanted to throw it away. Then I thought I should have my husband give it to you . . . but I didn't want him to know what had happened. So I brought it here with me."

"And you have it still? May I see it?" Too excited to remain seated, Sano stood.

"Yes. I'll get it for you." Madam Shimizu rose, but instead of entering the house, she walked to the big cherry tree and reached inside a hole in its gnarled trunk. "This was once our special hiding place," she said wistfully. "My husband would leave gifts and poems for me to find . . ." Blinking her tears away, she extracted a long, thin bundle wrapped in oiled silk, which she offered to Sano. "I didn't want this in the house . . . it's a wicked thing. So I put it here, where no one would ever look."

Sano stood perfectly still, the bundle balanced on his palms. Here at last was the physical evidence he'd sought. Prolonging both anticipation and dread, he didn't open it at once. To which suspect would the sword lead him? Then, unable to delay any longer, he undid the wrappings.

Dried blood encrusted the thin, curved blade of the short sword: Madam Shimizu hadn't bothered to clean it. Upon first examination, Sano felt a twinge of disappointment. The hilt was modern and ordinary, bound in black silk braid in an overlapping crisscrossed pattern with gold inlays in the diamond-shaped gaps. There were no identifying crests or other marks on either hilt or blade. Then Sano noticed the flat guard that separated them.

Made of black cast iron, this was shaped like the upper part of a human skull. The blade passed through the vertical nose opening; two smaller holes on either side formed empty eye sockets. The jawline sported five gold teeth. The artist's symbolic rendition of death was skillfully executed, grotesquely beautiful—and familiar. Sano's heart leapt as he remembered faded characters on a crumbling scroll:

> Wielding his two swords, which had guards wrought in the image of death's-heads, the great General Fujiwara cut down Endō's soldiers, leaving carnage in his wake . . .

Grasping the sword's hilt in one hand and the cloth-wrapped blade in the other, Sano forced them apart. There, on the exposed tang of the blade, he saw incised the tiny characters that confirmed this as General Fujiwara's sword. One of the matched pair he'd used against the Araki and Endō clans, handed down through the generations to his worthiest descendant—the Bundori Killer.

The sword's various possibilities flicked through Sano's mind. He might find witnesses who could establish the ownership of the unique, distinctive weapon. This evidence, combined with Madam Shimizu's signed statement, would be enough to convict Matsui or Chūgo in the magistrate's court. Such an investigation, however, might take longer than the two days left to Sano. And what if the killer was Chamberlain Yanagisawa, to whom the sword would most probably have passed, from General Fujiwara's eldest son?

Yanagisawa would never go to trial if neither shogun nor *bakufu* accepted his guilt. Sano would be executed as a traitor for acting against Yanagisawa, who would survive to kill and corrupt unchecked. Sano would bring everlasting disgrace instead of honor upon his family name, and lose his chance to slay the evil spirit.

Then an intriguing alternative occurred to Sano. The killer, whoever he was, would want his ancestor's precious, incriminating sword back—Chūgo or Matsui to avoid punishment, Yanagisawa to avoid scandal and bother. The killer seemed to know it was Madam Shimizu who had seen him, and to fear she would report him. Sano saw a way to use this knowledge, and the circumstances at hand.

"I need a favor from you," he said to Madam Shimizu as he rewrapped the sword.

Her plump chin trembled, and she looked at him fearfully. "Haven't I given you enough already? Why must I do you a favor?"

"Because if you don't, I won't keep silent about your trip to the temple and what you saw there. I'll make you testify at the killer's trial, and everyone—including your husband—will know what you did."

Even as he pressured Madam Shimizu, Sano hated his treatment of this miserable, helpless woman. With sudden frightening insight, he realized that this was how one rose within the *bakufu*. You used your knowledge and position to bend others to your will, to achieve your purposes. Until one day you ended up like Chamberlain Yanagisawa. . . . Sano's quest had brought him this understanding of his enemy, and of how much similarity existed between them. Now he swallowed his self-disgust, telling himself that his goal justified the means—as Yanagisawa probably did while he dominated the shogun, ruined lives, and squandered treasury funds.

"I see I have no choice but to honor your wishes," Madam Shimizu was saying.

Then, to Sano's surprise, she lifted her chin and smiled. She laid a hand on his arm, gazing coquettishly up at him. A strange mixture of fear and gratitude filled her eyes. Sano saw with pity that she thought he wanted her to service him sexually. Furthermore, she welcomed his request as proof of her desirability, and to assuage the pain of her husband's rejection.

"I'm sorry, Madam Shimizu, but I couldn't force myself on you," he said gently, putting her hand away from him in feigned regret.

And, while her expression changed from disappointment to surprised alarm, he told her how she could help him deliver the Bundori Killer to justice.

32

When he got back to town, Sano found Hirata riding back and forth along the promenade outside the castle gate.

"*Sumimasen*—I'm sorry to report that I couldn't follow Chamberlain Yanagisawa because he hasn't come out," Hirata said gloomily.

"Never mind. Let's go." Sano slapped his horse's reins.

Hirata hurried to catch up. "Where? Why?"

"We're going to set a trap for the Bundori Killer."

They rode through the daimyo district, into Nihonbashi. Sano told Hirata what he'd learned from Madam Shimizu, and about the sword now hidden in his saddlebag. But he couldn't specify the details of his plan until they'd scouted the location.

Once across the Nihonbashi Bridge, Sano led the way east, then north up the wide firebreak along the Sumida River, past warehouses and through the crowds around the teahouses, food stalls, and entertainment halls at the foot of the Ryōgoku Bridge, to the Kanda River—an aqueduct that emptied into the Sumida.

"Here," Sano said, turning left onto the path bordering the Kanda. Hirata, looking puzzled, followed.

The path sloped upward to run along the top of the river's vertical, stone-faced bank. On Sano's left rose affluent merchants' houses with balconies overlooking the river. To the right, a wooden rail shielded the drop to the water. Docks jutted out from the path. At the end of these floated pleasure boats, all of which faced east toward the Sumida, with sloping gangplanks lowered from their decks. A wooden bridge gave access to the Kanda's opposite side, which offered a similar scene.

"I don't understand," Hirata said.

By the fourth dock, Sano dismounted and tied the reins to the rail. "This is Madam Shimizu's boat," he explained. "We'll set the trap here."

At the villa, Madam Shimizu's mention of the romantic boat trips she'd once enjoyed with her husband had inspired Sano. The boat's location was near the city center, convenient to all three suspects, and yet relatively isolated, preventing interference from passersby. The layout, with its enclosed cabin and limited means of access and escape, would allow him to capture Chūgo or Matsui—or kill Yanagisawa and himself. He'd persuaded Madam Shimizu to let him set his trap on the boat, because if the Bundori Killer was indeed looking for her, then he would come here willingly to find her. Now Sano saw how well he'd chosen.

Made of cedarwood, the boat was perhaps fifty paces long. Both ends swooped gracefully up out of the water. At the stern, the deck tapered to a high viewing platform. The bow bore the boat's figurehead—a likeness of a younger, lovely Madam Shimizu, lips smiling, long hair rippling. The cabin had a red shingled roof with upturned eaves. A single sail, furled around its tall mast, rose from the foredeck. Along the railed gunwales stood poles for hanging lanterns or banners. With its shallow draft, single pair of oars, and open rudder chamber, the boat was not a seaworthy vessel—the *bakufu*, to keep citizens from leaving the country, forbade the building of private craft equipped for rough waters. But the boat would suit Sano's purpose admirably.

Sano turned his attention to the surroundings. Like Madam Shimizu's, most of the other vessels were deserted; the boating season wouldn't begin for another month or so. Sano squinted up at the sky, where the strengthening wind had blown more clouds in from the sea to the east.

"Not much chance of anyone setting sail tomorrow if this keeps up," Sano remarked with satisfaction.

He was equally glad to see only a few people about: a maid hanging laundry on a balcony; a street vendor carrying a load of baskets across the bridge, where an old man stood fishing. The Shimizu boat was far enough from the Sumida's heavy water traffic and the crowded firebreak so that any activity here would go unobserved.

"We'll come early tomorrow and clear the area," Sano told Hirata. "Your assistants can keep everyone away while we wait for the killer."

Hirata's face brightened with comprehension. "Aboard the boat."

"Right." Sano crossed the dock and ascended the creaking gangplank onto the boat, circling the deck. Not being a sailor, he made only a cursory inspection of the bow, where he found the anchor—a large, multipronged iron hook lying atop a heap of straw cable—near the sail. Then he more thoroughly examined the features of the boat that most concerned him. Beneath the hatch on the aft deck, in front of the tiller, he found coiled ropes, folded sails, a toolbox, lanterns, lamps, candles, water-tight metal containers of matches, and ceramic jars of water, oil, and sake. He opened the cabin door and entered a spacious, low-ceilinged compartment lined with silk-cushioned benches. Windows, equipped with slatted shutters that could be adjusted to let in light and air, overlooked the port and starboard decks. Sano's search of the cupboards turned up folded bedding and clothes. Drawers under the benches held dishware, napkins, chopsticks, chamberpots, soap, toiletries, and bundles of dried fish, seaweed, and fruits. Madam Shimizu, hoping in vain for her husband's love to return, had kept the boat provisioned for a trip they would probably never take.

Behind Sano, Hirata spoke. "What do we do if—when—the killer comes?"

Sano stalled by going to the window and opening the shutters.

He hated to involve Hirata in his dangerous quest for justice and honor, but he needed the *doshin's* help.

"If the killer is Matsui or Chūgo, you and your assistants will help me capture him—alive so he can be tried and punished for his crimes," he said, pretending an interest in the view. "We'll tie him with ropes from the hold and take him to Edo Jail."

"But we believe Chamberlain Yanagisawa is the killer." Hirata sounded puzzled. "What then?"

To delay voicing the inevitable, Sano walked out the door and stood on the windy deck, staring upriver. On the bridge, the old fisherman jerked his line out of the water. On its end, a large, glistening fish writhed.

"If it is the chamberlain," Sano said to Hirata, who had come to stand beside him, "then you and your men will do nothing. I will kill Yanagisawa, then commit *seppuku*." He forced himself to turn and face his assistant.

Eyes round and mouth agape, the young *doshin's* face presented a perfect picture of shock, horror, and reluctant admiration. He started to stammer in protest. But an order was an order; finally, his bleak nod and sigh signaled his acceptance. Then he squared his shoulders and said in a thin but brave voice, "Let me have the honor of acting as your *kaishaku*."

"No, Hirata. I can't let you be my second. It will be awhile before the shogun realizes he's better off without Chamberlain Yanagisawa. In the meantime, you would be punished for what he'll see as your role in the murder of his companion. If Yanagisawa comes tomorrow, you and your men must leave the scene and report to the authorities news of what I've done. I'll give you additional orders after we leave here."

Hirata shook his head, politely insistent. "It's my duty to help you. I don't care if I'm punished. You'll have your chance to prove your loyalty to your master. Let me have mine. Accept me as your retainer."

Sano was trapped. He couldn't refuse another samurai the right to serve honor, nor could he deny that he needed Hirata's help. He wasn't at all sure he could make the first cut to his abdomen, let alone the subsequent, fatal ones. He would need a helper to sever his head, ending his agony and his life. Against his wishes, he would have to pull an innocent young man down with him.

"All, right, Hirata-*san*." Sano bowed his appreciation. "Thank you."

The ardor in Hirata's eyes pierced Sano's heart. He was young, zealous; in his first joy at gaining his chosen master, he didn't yet comprehend the enormity of what he might have to do. Sano gazed with sorrow at his new retainer, whom he felt proud to have. Were the two of them doomed soldiers, destined to die without ever realizing the potential of their partnership?

Hirata spoke first, in a voice strong with new maturity and confidence. "Now we must lure the killer into the trap."

Sano nodded sadly. "Yes."

Duty and honor demanded they set into motion the events that would determine their fate.

Traveling through Nihonbashi, they entered the first stationer's shop they found, where the proprietor knelt amid his wares—rice paper, inkstones, brushes, carved seals, spools of cord, scroll cases—writing a letter dictated by an illiterate peasant. When he finished, his wife took the peasant's money while he greeted his two new customers.

Sano chose four sheets of paper, three of plain quality and one of the finest, four scroll cases, three of bamboo and one of decorated lacquer, and the appropriate grades of silk cord. "Can your wife write?" he asked.

The proprietor nodded, and Sano dictated his first message to the woman, whose feminine calligraphy he hoped the Bundori Killer would take for Madam Shimizu's.

If you want your sword back, bring five hundred *koban* to the Kanda River's south docks. Come at noon tomorrow, alone. Board the fourth pleasure boat from the mouth of the river. I will be waiting.

The Lady from the Temple

Sano had the woman prepare three copies on the plain paper. Then, taking the brush from her, he drew the sword's skull-shaped guard at the bottom of each copy. He blotted the ink, rolled and tied the scrolls, and sealed them inside the bamboo cases.

"Write 'Urgent and Personal,' " he instructed the woman, after telling her to put Matsui's, Chūgo's, and Yanagisawa's names on the address labels. Then he took her place at the writing desk and held the brush poised over the finest, smoothest paper as he sought the proper phrasing for what could be the last, most important message of his life.

Genroku Year 2, Month 3, Day 25

To His Excellency the Shogun Tokugawa Tsunayoshi:

To my great regret, I must inform you that my investigation has revealed that the Bundori Killer is none other than your own Chamberlain Yanagisawa.

Your Excellency, I have seen how Chamberlain Yanagisawa manipulates yourself and your government for his personal gain. Now he has revealed the true extent of his evil nature by coming to pay blackmail in exchange for the sword he left at Zōjō Temple when he murdered the priest, his most recent victim. Motivated not by loyalty to Your Excellency, but by his need to satisfy a blood score that his ancestor, General Fujiwara, swore against the Araki and Endō clans more than one hundred years ago, he has slain three descendants of those clans, and would likely have killed more if not stopped.

Rather than allow Chamberlain Yanagisawa to escape punishment by subverting the legal system he controls, I have appointed myself the agent of justice. I have executed Chamberlain Yanagisawa, and committed *seppuku* not only to avoid capture and disgrace, but to pledge my eternal loyalty to your person, and to honor a promise to my father that I make of myself the living embodiment of Bushido.

I hope history will remember me as the member of my clan who freed the Tokugawa regime from Chamberlain Yanagisawa's corrupting influence and restored Your Excellency as rightful ruler of the land.

Your humble servant, *Sōsakan* Sano Ichirō.

Sano stamped the letter with his personal seal, then enclosed the scroll inside the fine lacquer case and paid for his purchases. Outside in the street, he gave Matsui's bamboo scroll case to Hirata.

"Pay a messenger to deliver this immediately," he said, handing over the necessary coins. "I'll see that Chūgo and Yanagisawa get theirs." Then, with a heavy spirit, he gave Hirata the lacquer case. "If all goes . . . as expected tomorrow, give this to the authorities." He mounted his horse. "I'll meet you at the boat at daybreak."

"Yes, *sōsakan-sama*." Hirata cleared his throat. "*Sumimasen* . . . after the messages are delivered, would you please be my guest at dinner?"

Sano was touched by the offer. Hirata, kind as well as loyal, didn't want to leave his new master alone to dwell upon death, or let what might be the last night of his life pass without ritual.

"Thank you, Hirata-*san*," he said with sincere regret, "but I've urgent personal business to attend to."

In Hirata's eyes he saw understanding and sympathy. The young *doshin*, his fellow samurai, knew exactly what that business was.

33

When a samurai planned to commit ritual suicide, custom required him to bid farewell to the important people in his life and express gratitude for the services they'd done him, the kindnesses they'd shown him, and the privilege of associating with them.

Sano found Dr. Ito in the Edo Jail guard compound, practicing the medical skills he'd acquired before being sentenced to lifelong service as morgue custodian. There grim, dingy barracks formed a second enclosure within the jail's towering walls. Outside the barracks, a prison guard sat on a stool, with Dr. Ito bending over him. As Sano approached, Ito pulled down the man's lower lip, revealing a huge, ugly blood blister surrounded by pus-engorged flesh. Upon this Ito placed a shiny brown leech. The patient winced and closed his eyes as the leech sucked the poisoned blood.

"Sano-*san!* What a pleasant surprise." Dr. Ito's stern features relaxed in a smile as he looked up. "I presumed you had received my messages about finding no clues on the murder victims' remains, and so would have no reason to visit soon." Then his expression altered to concern when he saw Sano's face. "Something is wrong?"

For the first time, Sano felt awkward with his confidant and mentor. "I have to talk to you," he blurted.

"Of course. One moment."

Ito turned back to his patient. He waited until the leech swelled to twice its original size, and the blister had shrunk. Then he plucked the leech off the patient's lip and sealed it inside a small ceramic jar attached to his sash.

"Rinse your mouth with saltwater every hour to prevent further festering," he told the guard. He handed over a paper packet. "Drink this turmeric in your tea tonight, for the pain and swelling. You'll feel much better by tomorrow."

"Thank you, Ito-*san*," the patient mumbled.

Then, apparently recognizing Sano's need for privacy, Ito said, "Come. Let's go to my quarters."

They left the compound and entered a passage, where Sano stopped. He didn't want to cut short what might be their last meeting, but he must get this ordeal over with before he lost his resolve.

"I can't stay," he said abruptly. "I—I just want to thank you, Ito-*san*. For everything you've done for me."

Ignoring his friend's puzzled frown, Sano rushed on. "Your wisdom and support have guided me through times of trouble. Your courage, dedication, and integrity have been a source of inspiration to me." Used to expressing respect with formal rituals of bowing, gift-giving, and other oblique gestures, he found this blunt speaking unbearably gauche and melodramatic. But he forced himself to continue. "It's been an honor and a privilege to associate with you."

He bowed deeply, as if to a superior rather than the commoner and criminal that Ito was. "Now I—I must say good-bye," he ended in a breathless fever of shyness, embarrassment, and grief.

" 'Good-bye'?" Though he shook his head in confusion, Dr. Ito obviously recognized this as no ordinary parting. "Sano-*san*, what is the meaning of this?"

Sano compressed his lips against the outpouring of terror that threatened to spill from them: *I don't want to die! Please, save me!* If Ito offered any sympathy, he was lost. He longed to flee. But an explanation was the least he owed his friend. With frequent pauses to control his emotions, he related his plan, and its probable outcome. "I may die tomorrow, Ito-*san*. That's why I came to say good-bye, and say—what needed saying."

The lines in Dr. Ito's face deepened. His penetrating gaze lost its edge; his eyes were dark with shock. "But why must you even consider doing this—this thing?" he demanded.

"I promised my father I would exemplify Bushido and perform a heroic deed that would secure our family a place of honor in history," Sano recited woodenly. "When I began this investigation, I promised myself that I would deliver a killer to justice and save lives. Chamberlain Yanagisawa is corrupt, evil. If he's also the Bundori Killer—as I believe he is—then destroying him, ridding the regime of his influence, and taking my own life will satisfy all my aims."

Dr. Ito opened his mouth and closed it again. He raised his arms, then let them fall. For once he seemed at a loss for wisdom. Then he drew a deep breath and said, "Forgive me, Sano-*san*. Out of respect for you and your class, I would never say this under any other circumstances. But your Bushido is a cruel, destructive code. Can you not see that it carries honor, duty, loyalty, and filial piety to the extreme? Why, indeed, its ultimate expression is the annihilation of the self—of the very life force that harbors those virtues!"

He leaned closer, exerting upon Sano the whole force of his compelling personality. "Listen. When I became a physician, I dedicated myself to healing, to the preservation of life. Because life is precious; it makes all things possible. While you're alive, you have the potential to accomplish many miracles. All of these may well add up to more than this one final act you are contemplating. But if you kill yourself, then what?

"Your name in history books—an empty reward. Man has a short memory; yesterday's heroes are soon forgotten. Your body will be ashes in the wind; your soul will never live again—unless through rebirth, the occurrence of which I have seen no scientific proof. Please, Sano-*san*. Reconsider!"

Sano turned away from the argument that called to the questioning, rebellious part of his nature. "Bushido is absolute," he said, although he could see the truth in Dr. Ito's impassioned plea.

"I can't repudiate it and still call myself a samurai. A promise is a promise; duty is duty."

Dr. Ito hurried around to face him. "Your father should never have demanded such a sacrifice from you! That he did is an example of a dying man's selfishness." Ito's voice was harsh; his eyes blazed with desperation. "And that consummate fool, Tokugawa Tsunayoshi—who imprisoned me, who lets the foul Chamberlain Yanagisawa rule in his place—does not deserve your sacrifice!"

To hear his own secret thoughts voiced aloud shamed and horrified Sano to the point of rage. "How dare you criticize my father and my lord!"

Ito sighed. "Ah. I see that in my effort to save you from yourself, I've only angered you. My apologies. But I only have your welfare at heart—as no one else seems to. You won't listen to criticism of Bushido, or of those who command your loyalty. So I won't argue anymore. I will simply beg you, as a friend who values and esteems you: Please. Find another way. Don't do it."

The clasped hands he extended to Sano trembled; for once he seemed not an imposing symbol of scientific curiosity and personal commitment, but a feeble old man.

"I've made my decision," Sano said wearily. "I have no choice."

An expression of infinite sadness came over Dr. Ito's face as he nodded in defeat. "I'm not a samurai; therefore, I can't comprehend the forces that compel you. But I do know that a man must do what he believes is right. I've lived my own life according to that principle." He paused, then bowed. "I will miss you, Sano-*san*."

"And I you, Ito-*san*." Sano bowed with equal formality. He didn't want to leave his friend; he didn't want to die and forsake all life's wonderful possibilities. Unshed tears stung his eyes. Dr. Ito couldn't save him. Only fate could—and so far, fate looked to be favoring his death.

Flaming lanterns sent Sano's shadow leaping along the path before him as he raced wildly through the Momijiyama.

"Aoi!" he called. "Where are you?"

His voice echoed off the shrine's magnificent buildings. He was beyond caring that such crude behavior showed disrespect for his lord's ancestors. Nor could he fear another attack. All he cared about was finding Aoi. He ran up stone steps to pound on doors. From the rooftops, carved demons leered their disapproval.

"Aoi, answer me!" he shouted.

He'd imagined that she would be waiting for him when he returned to the castle. But he'd arrived home to find no one other than his servants, who said they'd neither seen her nor taken any message explaining her absence. Disappointment had overcome the self-control Sano had maintained with Hirata and Dr. Ito; stoicism gave way to desperation.

He must spend what was probably the last night of his life with Aoi, to cram into it all the years they wouldn't have together. He wanted to tell her that all the evidence he'd found today pointed to Chamberlain Yanagisawa's guilt, that in all likelihood Yanagisawa would die tomorrow, and she would be free. He wanted to carry the memory of her joy with him as a reward when he met his fate tomorrow. And, like a warrior before a battle, he felt the ancient yearning to lie with a woman, to celebrate life while he still had it, and to experience his body's last pleasure.

The shrine was deserted. Sano plunged into the pine forest. Rocks tripped him; boughs lashed his arms and legs. Remembering Aoi's mention of the cottage where she lived, he somehow managed to find it.

The hut's window was dark. No one answered his knock. He entered the single room to find it empty. Then he heard a rustle outside. Alarm prickled his skin; he sensed danger. Ignoring his instincts, he rushed heedlessly out the door, his heart lurching with gladness.

He heard and saw no one.

"Aoi," he whispered brokenly. "Aoi."

With the residual pain in his muscles underscoring his misery, Sano trudged home. There he knelt before his father's memorial altar. He lit the candles and incense, bowed to his father's portrait, and prayed:

"Father. Please give me courage to do what I must. Let me have the strength to bring the Bundori Killer to justice, even if it means my own death."

His tortured voice only echoed in the empty room. The portrait gazed back at him unseeingly. In his greatest hour of need, his father's spirit remained mute, unreachable.

Lonely to the core of his soul, Sano wept.

34

The fateful day had arrived. Only moments remained before the appointed time that would bring life and worldly glory, or death and eternal honor to Sano. Aboard Madam Shimizu's boat, he and Hirata concealed themselves in the cabin. The preparations had been made. Now all they could do was wait for the killer to appear.

From his place on the bench overlooking the starboard deck, Sano looked through the slatted window shutters, then out the open door. He saw two of Hirata's assistants occupying their designated positions. One, posing as a trash collector, loitered on the path. An easily removable bamboo tube had transformed his spear into a stick for skewering debris and placing it in his basket. The second assistant, equipped with a pole and bucket, fished from the bridge. His tackle box concealed a club and dagger. Sano had stationed these men in the open so that the area wouldn't seem unnaturally deserted and arouse the killer's suspicion, but he'd hidden a third assistant beneath the dock, as a surprise reserve. They all had their orders. As Sano watched, the man on the bridge chased away a genuine fisherman. He could almost hear the prearranged command:

"This area is closed by order of the police."

So far the weather gods had seen fit to cooperate with Sano's plan. The sky was a dark, curdled mass of gray-green rain clouds. A gusty southwest sea wind rocked the boat, creaked the mast, whistled through the shutters, and slapped waves against the hull. The warm air was damp, saturated with the odors of fish and brine. All morning there had been little traffic on land or water; the balconies and other boats remained empty. With luck, no innocent bystanders would inadvertently interfere with the killer's capture—or slaying.

Keeping his gaze riveted to the footpath, Sano stirred restlessly. He'd spent a sleepless night alone, waiting in vain for Aoi. Now his eyes burned with fatigue; his bruised body ached. Inside him, an invisible chain twisted around his stomach, lungs, and heart, its grip growing tighter by the moment. Panic kept rising in his throat as he imagined Chamberlain Yanagisawa walking up the gangplank. At the same time, he began to see in the ordinary, familiar world things he'd never noticed before. To ease the tense atmosphere, he spoke of his discoveries.

"Hirata, look how every cloud is made up of a thousand shades of gray. And how the wind blows them into everchanging skyscapes." Emotion lent his tongue eloquence, and his voice ardor. "Have you ever noticed how the rain smells so sweet you can taste it? Or how the birds sing a special song when they know it's coming? Or how even sadness and pain can be good, because when you feel them, you know you're alive?"

Sano's heart swelled with sorrowful love for the world. "I never noticed how beautiful life is."

He stopped, stricken with the realization that it had taken the threat of death to make him appreciate that beauty. Shame destroyed his brief exhilaration. He'd communicated his undignified reluctance to die to Hirata, who would only suffer on his account.

"Ignore what I just said," he ordered hastily.

Too late; the damage was done. Hirata, who'd by now realized how irrevocably tied his fate was to Sano's, looked green and terrified. He clapped a hand over his mouth. "Excuse me," he mumbled.

He dashed out the door. His footsteps pounded the deck as he stumbled around to the port side. Through the shutters, Sano could see him hunched over the railing, and hear him vomiting into the river. Sano wished he could vomit up his own fear, but his stomach was empty; he hadn't eaten since yesterday.

After a while, Hirata returned, paler but composed, his hair plastered against his sweaty forehead. "The rocking boat made me seasick," he lied valiantly.

They resumed their watch. The cabin's atmosphere grew closer, tenser, and ripe with the smell of the river. Distant thunder rumbled. While the wind sighed and moaned around the boat, the first raindrops pattered onto the cabin roof and stippled the water. Sano began to wonder whether the killer would show up at all.

Then, rolling across the city, came the peals of myriad temple bells, signaling noon. Suddenly the watcher on the path paused while collecting a bit of trash. He straightened, peering down the slope toward the firebreak. The fisherman laid aside his pole.

Sano's body went still and cold; his blood congealed. His last breath caught in his lungs. Hirata joined him on the bench, head close to his as they stared out the window together in paralyzed silence.

With exaggerated casualness, the watcher on the path lifted his hand to his head and scratched.

The signal for Chūgo.

Hirata moaned softly. The chains inside Sano released their grip. His heart pumped giddy relief through his veins. He expelled his breath as all of life's boundless possibilities clamored around him: once again, the future existed. Feeling reborn and invincible, Sano wanted to shout and dance and laugh, but even as he and Hirata exchanged gleeful smiles, they were taking their positions. Sano, his sword drawn, stood to the port side of the door. Opposite Hirata waited, *jitte* in one hand, a coiled rope in the other, ready to help capture their prisoner.

A small eternity passed. Then Chūgo's gaunt figure appeared on the path, moving with grim purpose, head down, through the rain that now pelted the city in fitful squalls. He reached the dock, turning to look in all directions before stepping onto it. Briefly he disappeared from view, hidden by the boat's hull. Then came the creak of his footsteps on the gangplank. The boat dipped slightly under his weight. His head loomed over the railing. Sano's heart lurched as he glimpsed Chūgo's face through the shutters. Stony and ruthless, it was the face of the Bundori Killer.

Sano gripped his sword tighter. Then a movement behind Chūgo distracted him.

Instead of moving onto the dock as planned, the signaler was still on the path, looking toward the firebreak. The "fisherman," who had left the bridge to join his companion, club and dagger in his hands, had stopped halfway there in obvious confusion. The man under the dock raised his head above it, but emerged no farther.

Chūgo's shoulders came into view as he slowly ascended the gangplank. He paused, trying to peer through the cabin's shutters. Sano and Hirata exchanged disturbed glances.

What? Hirata mouthed. Sano could only shake his head before looking back outside. Then, to his sheer amazement, he saw, coming down the path, a familiar trio.

Matsui Minoru carried a brightly colored umbrella. His two bodyguards, hunched beneath hooded cloaks, trooped along behind him.

Hirata turned disbelieving eyes to Sano. "Chūgo *and* Matsui?" he whispered. "What's going on? What do we do now?"

"I don't know! Let me think!"

One look at Chūgo had convinced Sano that the guard captain was the Bundori Killer. But why had Matsui come? Whatever the reason, the situation had altered drastically. Must they take four men instead of just the formidable Chūgo? If so, how would he communicate the change of plan to the outside team?

They had to act, fast. Chūgo was continuing up the gangplank. On the path, Matsui had passed the signaler and stopped just short of the dock.

Either the guard captain heard Matsui's voice or sensed his presence, because he turned, his shock evident in the sudden rigidity of his posture.

"Chūgo-*san!* Cousin!" As Matsui hurried onto the dock, his voice carried across the water. "Wait!"

Sano and Hirata abandoned their posts to hurl themselves onto the bench, faces pressed to the shutters. Matsui huffed his way up the gangplank, his guards trailing him.

"What are you doing here?" Sano heard Chūgo demand.

Matsui and the guards appeared below Chūgo's figure. Matsui was struggling to hang on to his umbrella, which the wind had inverted. "I got a letter from a woman who was at Zōjō Temple when the priest was murdered," he panted. "She said to come here if I wanted General Fujiwara's famed death's-head sword." He pulled Sano's scroll from his cloak; the wind blew it open. "See?"

Chūgo snatched the scroll. "You got this letter, too?" Though his back was turned, Sano read dawning comprehension in his slow headshake.

"Cousin, I suspected you were the killer all along," Matsui said. "I know how much you revere our ancestor. And I knew you owned the swords." Dropping his useless umbrella, the merchant clutched Chūgo's arm. "But I kept our bargain. I didn't turn you in before, and I won't now. I just want the sword. For my collection; for my shrine to General Fujiwara. I promise I'll never tell anyone how I got it. Please, cousin, let me have it!"

With an angry jerk that rocked the boat, Chūgo freed himself from Matsui's grasp, at the same time flinging away the scroll. "You fool! This is a trap!" Obviously he'd realized what Matsui, blinded by his desire for the sword, had failed to see. "The shogun's *sōsakan* has set us up!"

He started down the gangplank, but Matsui's guards blocked his way.

"Please," Matsui persisted, seeming not to have heard Chūgo's words. He pulled out a bulging coin pouch and waved it at the boat. "Madam! I've got five hundred *koban* here. You can have it all, if you'll just give me the sword!" Coins spilled from the pouch and clattered onto the gangplank along with the raindrops that now fell in torrents.

"Get out of my way!" Chūgo ordered.

"Please, Madam—" Matsui grunted in surprise as Chūgo shoved him sideways. There was a loud splash when he hit the water. "Help!" he screamed. "I can't swim!"

Sano made a decision. "We take Chūgo now."

"But—" Hirata motioned toward the bank, where his assistants stood in a helpless huddle. They'd been told to burst into the cabin after the killer had entered. Now one suspect was in the river and the other hurrying down the gangplank to freedom. "They don't know what to do!"

Sano was already out the door. The rain hit him like a curtain of water, drenching him to the skin. Over the wind that howled in his ears, he heard Matsui screaming and the bodyguards shouting. Clutching his sword, he lurched around the corner onto the starboard deck just in time to see one guard dive from the gangplank to save Matsui and the other face off against Chūgo.

In a blur of speed, Chūgo drew his sword. It cut the bodyguard's throat before he could even unsheath his weapon. With a gush of blood, he fell dead. Chūgo kicked the corpse into the river and hurtled down the gangplank.

"Chūgo!" Sano shouted. "Stop!" Awed and horrified by the swift, efficient murder he'd just witnessed, he pounded after Chūgo. His feet slipped on the wet, slick gangplank.

Hirata followed on his heels. "Catch him!" he shouted to his assistants.

The three men hurried onto the dock, waving spears, clubs, and daggers. Then, as Chūgo rushed them, bloody sword raised, they scattered and fled in panic. Chūgo was on the path now, running for the firebreak. Sano leaped from the gangplank and onto the dock, glad the assistants hadn't challenged Chūgo, who would have cut them down with one stroke. But how he dreaded chasing their quarry through the streets of Edo, where he might kill bystanders and escape into the crowds. Half blinded by the rain, Sano sprinted across the dock. His heart raced like runaway hoofbeats; determination powered his sore muscles. Chūgo passed the last dock. He reached the slope leading down to the Sumida River firebreak, but Sano was gaining on him, with Hirata panting at his elbow.

"Stop, Chūgo!" Sano shouted, brandishing his sword. A huge lightning bolt momentarily turned the dark world a blazing white; a thunderclap drowned out his words.

The guard captain started skidding sideways down the slope. With a burst of speed that nearly exploded his heart, Sano closed the distance between them to twenty paces. He must forget about taking Chūgo alive. In a moment, he would pit his fighting skills against those of perhaps the best swordsman in Edo—

Suddenly Chūgo slid to a halt. Sano stopped too, so abruptly that Hirata slammed into him. They stared in disbelief.

Rounding the corner from the firebreak and climbing up the slope toward them came a procession of at least fifty people—foot soldiers, mounted samurai, servants holding umbrellas over silk-garbed officials. At its head, six bearers carried a palanquin emblazoned with snarling dragons.

"Chamberlain Yanagisawa." Sano breathed. An incredulous laugh burst from him as he slicked the rain from his eyes. He'd set a trap for the killer—and caught all three suspects. What schemes or passions had brought Yanagisawa here? Sano crouched, sword ready. For Chūgo was backing away from the procession, obviously deciding that his two pursuers posed a lesser obstacle.

"Sano Ichirō!" The shout snatched Sano's attention from Chūgo, who faltered, also arrested by the familiar voice of authority. Chamberlain Yanagisawa's head protruded from the palanquin. "Sano Ichirō, listen to me, you miserable fool!"

Heedless of the wind that whipped his brilliant silk garments and the slanting rain that drenched them, Chamberlain Yanagisawa jumped out of the palanquin. He ran up the slope, his high wooden sandals sliding in the mud.

"So you think you're clever, do you?" he shouted at Sano. "You think that because a witness saw my palanquin near Zōjō Temple—where I went to worship on the night of the priest's death—that you can frame me for murder. You think you can trap me with a fake letter and a nonexistent sword." His streaming face twisted with anger and hatred. "I am the man who rules the land. I know everything; I'm all-powerful. You dare deem me a killer? You dare match wits with me?"

Yanagisawa slipped and went down on one knee. He righted himself, his fury undiminished. "Well, I'm here to ruin your transparent, pathetic little scheme. And to destroy you once and for all!" He pushed past Chūgo, whom he didn't appear to notice, and stood tall and regal on the path before Sano. "You won't catch the

Bundori Killer. And you will never, ever take my place as the shogun's favorite!"

The wind swirled the chamberlain's vivid garments; the rain swept around him. With lightning dazzling his angry face and thunder punctuating his words, he seemed like an avenging god. Belatedly Sano understood that jealousy, not guilt, had motivated Yanagisawa to sabotage him.

"I will see you dead before I let you seize my wealth, power, or position," Yanagisawa raged.

With sudden terrifying prescience, Sano knew what would happen the instant before it did. "Look out, Chamberlain Yanagisawa!" he shouted.

His warning came too late. Before the last syllable left his mouth, Chūgo was standing behind Yanagisawa, with one arm locked around the chamberlain's chest and the blade of his sword in front of Yanagisawa's shocked face.

"Nobody move!" Chūgo ordered. "Come any closer, and I'll kill him."

Sano froze in midstep, his mind a blank sheet of horror. Down the slope, the foot soldiers who had drawn their weapons and the horsemen who had leapt from their mounts halted in their rush to save their master. Lightning illuminated their stricken faces; thunder echoed their outraged shouts.

"What do you think you're doing?" Yanagisawa demanded. "Release me this instant!"

He twisted around to face his captor, and for the first time really seemed to see Chūgo. The anger on his face gave way to startled recognition, then fearful understanding. "Chūgo Gichin? The captain of the guard . . . the Bundori Killer? He caught you in his trap?"

Yanagisawa began to struggle, straining away from the sword by his face, trying to pry Chūgo's arm off his chest. "I'm your commanding officer, Chūgo. Let me go!" Panic robbed his order of authority. "Guards! Help!"

His thoughts in a hopeless tangle, Sano cast wildly about for a way to subdue Chūgo without harming Yanagisawa. He saw the reckless determination in Chūgo's eyes, and Chūgo's unwavering hand forcing the sword ever closer to Yanagisawa's face. He sensed the entourage's growing panic. Infusing his voice with a calm authority he didn't feel, he said, "Chūgo-*san*, he's your kin— a fellow descendant of General Fujiwara. He's not your enemy." Focusing his entire concentration on the captain, Sano was barely aware of the rain streaming over him, or the sudden hush that fell over his audience. "He's not responsible for Oda Nobunaga's murder—or for the trap you walked into."

Chūgo neither spoke nor changed expression, but Sano sensed an inner response to General Fujiwara's and Oda Nobunaga's names. Now if only no one would interfere.

"I'm the one who tried to prevent you from carrying out your ancestor's wishes. It's me you want, Chūgo-*san*." Sano thumped his chest. "We can settle this, you and I, alone. Kill me, and you're a free man. The case against you dies with me; the evidence goes with me to my grave."

Chūgo and everyone else remained silent. Blinding cracks of lightning split the heavens; more thunder rattled the ground. Rain fell in great sheets, blurring the city into the drowning sky. Choppy waves smacked the riverbank, and the tossing boats strained their moorings. Then Chūgo lowered the sword almost imperceptibly. Encouraged, Sano eased himself into a defensive posture, preparing for Chūgo's assault. *Spirit of my father, give me strength!*

Then Yanagisawa shouted, "This is all your fault, Sano Ichirō! Guards! Seize him!"

His cry, choked off by Chūgo's encircling grip, thwarted Sano's attempt to transfer the captain's malevolence from the chamberlain to himself. Chūgo jerked the sword closer to his captive's face. Yanagisawa screamed, and the entourage became a chaotic mob. Cries of "What shall we do?" and "Let's get him!" rose from its midst.

"Look out, *sōsakan-sama!*" Hirata stepped between Sano and the advancing horde.

Sano barely registered the threat to himself, for Chūgo, his intention unmistakable, was propelling the ranting, cursing Yanagisawa down the path. The bottom dropped out of Sano's stomach.

"Try to stop me, and I'll kill him," Chūgo spat.

"You'll die for this, Sano Ichirō!" Chamberlain Yanagisawa

howled, his face wild with anger and terror. "You impertinent lackey, you despicable fool, you—"

"Shut up!" Sano yelled.

The chamberlain did, his mouth agape as Chūgo continued to shove him along the path toward the boat. Sano didn't wait for Yanagisawa to recover from the shock of being addressed so rudely. "Chūgo. You can't escape," he said. "Soon everyone will know you're the Bundori Killer. You won't be safe anywhere."

He darted in front of Chūgo, running backward as the captain bore down at him and Yanagisawa glared in outrage. Beyond them, he could see Hirata trying to hold off Yanagisawa's shouting, sword-waving entourage.

"If you let the chamberlain go, you'll be allowed to commit *seppuku,* or even live under house arrest." Sano heard himself babbling whatever came into his head. "Endanger him, and you'll be tortured and executed like a common criminal. Surrender, Chūgo. It's over. Do you hear me? It's over!"

They reached the Shimizu dock, where Matsui, whom Sano had almost forgotten, lay while his surviving bodyguard pumped water from his lungs. Hastily the guard dragged him out of the way and into the river again.

Giving no sign that he'd heard Sano's pleas, Chūgo made for the gangplank. Frantic to avert disaster, Sano blocked the captain's way, but Chūgo only gripped Yanagisawa tighter. The chamberlain gasped, his hands locked on his captor's arm, eyes fixed on the blade in front of his face.

"Sheath your weapon," Chūgo ordered Sano. He thrust his sword against Yanagisawa's lip. The chamberlain screamed as blood welled from the cut and washed away in a flood of rain. "Now get out of my way, or I'll cut him again."

"Do as he says," Yanagisawa pleaded.

Sano sheathed his sword. "Chūgo—"

"Move!"

The chamberlain's retainers swarmed past Hirata and onto the dock. Their shouts rang above the thunder, wind, and rain. Chūgo spun around to face them, pulling his prisoner with him.

"Stand back, or he's a dead man."

Sano leaped forward, intending to grab Chūgo, wrest the sword away, and free Yanagisawa, but the chamberlain's shriek and the retainers' fresh outcry stopped him. When Chūgo turned back to him, he gasped.

The blade had slashed Yanagisawa's left eyelid. Blood poured over his face, which had gone completely white. He opened and closed his mouth, but no sounds came out. Then his eyeballs rolled up into his head. His hands let go of Chūgo's arm and dropped. His legs buckled.

"You can't hurt him, Chūgo-*san*. He's your lord's representative." In growing desperation, Sano appealed to the guard captain's samurai values. "You're honor-bound to protect him. Let him go. If you want a hostage, take me instead. Don't—"

"Move. *Now*." Chūgo's gruff command cut him off. The sword now pressed against the limp and unconscious Yanagisawa's throat.

"Do as he says!" The command issued from Yanagisawa's entourage.

"Chūgo, if you take the boat out in this storm, you'll both die. Please—"

The words froze on Sano's tongue when he saw from the captain's hard, merciless stare that he'd passed beyond reason. With defeat crushing his heart, Sano stepped off the gangplank and out of Chūgo's way. Helplessly he stood on the dock with Hirata and the stunned, silent crowd as Chūgo dragged Yanagisawa up the gangplank and aboard the boat. He'd failed in the shogun's mission; he'd failed to fulfill his promise to his father. The Bundori Killer was escaping, and Sano was responsible for Yanagisawa's certain death—a disgrace that would result in severe punishment and everlasting dishonor.

With Yanagisawa draped over his arm like a broken puppet, Chūgo slashed the boat's mooring ropes. It drifted free of the dock. He sheathed his sword, then pulled up the gangplank and unfurled the sail. The wind slapped the tall, rectangular hemp-cloth sheet open. The boat rocked and pitched, moving down the river.

Merciful gods, if Chūgo managed to get all the way down the Sumida into open sea . . . The flimsy pleasure craft would never survive the strong currents and rough waves. Not even the most expert crew could maneuver it around the treacherous reefs that had sunk many better ships.

The crowd surged down the path after the boat. Sano groaned as Yanagisawa's archers let fly a spate of arrows at Chūgo, who now stood in the stern, working the ropes stretched from the billowing sail and over the cabin roof. Killing the guard captain now wouldn't solve the problem: Without a sailor, the boat might founder and sink before they saved Yanagisawa. Sano ran after the entourage.

"No! Get help! The police, the navy—"

No one listened; more arrows flew. Sano saw that he must stop Chūgo and rescue Yanagisawa himself. He squeezed past the crowd. Through windblown sheets of rain, he ran down the farthest dock, which the boat was just passing. He heard Hirata yell, "Go, *sōsakan-sama!* I'll get help!"

Whispering a prayer for strength and courage, Sano gulped a deep breath, then dived headfirst into the river.

35

The icy water claimed Sano with a heart-stopping splash. Gasping, he swam through the choppy waves after the boat. His clothes hindered his movements; his swords weighed him down. The rain still poured from the sky; every time he raised his head for a breath, he inhaled as much water as air. His muscles ached, and the cold quickly penetrated to his bones. The tossing swells nauseated him. How different this was from the stylized exercises he'd practiced in the castle training pond, at which he'd never excelled anyway, even when in the best of health. The water, not his natural element, fought his every effort to conquer it. He forced his legs to keep kicking, his arms to keep stroking. A cramp gnawed his left side. The river burbled in his ears, louder than thunder, while lightning blazed around him.

Yet every time his eyes cleared the waves, he was closer to the boat. At last, his hands smacked the hull. But the smooth wood offered no way to climb up. Sano groaned. The boat was pulling away from him. Utterly exhausted, he could swim no more. The Bundori Killer would escape; Yanagisawa would die. Having failed in his duty to his father and his lord, Sano knew that Bushido demanded he die, allowing his disgrace to perish with him.

Then something rough slapped his cheek: one of the boat's mooring ropes, which Chūgo had cut before setting sail. Sano grabbed it. Too weak to climb aboard, he simply hung on.

Aboard the rocking, listing boat, Chūgo struggled to control the sail, whose lines the wind strained taut against his hands. Rain sluiced the deck and lashed his face. The boat heeled perilously. With all his strength, Chūgo heaved. The sail turned; the boat veered right, leaving the Kanda and sailing into the Sumida River, where the current carried it southwest, seaward.

Triumph roared inside Chūgo as he tacked, guiding the boat on a zigzagging course against the wind. He'd escaped the angry mob, and the foolish *sōsakan* who'd interfered with his mission for too long. Looking starboard, he saw only the rainswept warehouses and deserted docks that bordered the Sumida's west bank, and the distant misty marshes opposite. All other boats had taken shelter from the storm. The river was a wide-open channel to freedom. He would live to complete General Fujiwara's blood score. Filling his lungs with air, he shouted into the storm:

"Honorable ancestor! I will kill every last member of the Endō and Araki clans!"

For by a stroke of pure luck, he had a guarantee of continued survival.

Chūgo released the lines from his raw, bleeding hands and secured them, leaving the boat to move with the current. He strode into the cabin. The rain battered the roof like rounds of gunfire. Outside, the thunder boomed like mighty cannon. Water streamed off Chūgo and onto the floor around his hostage.

The great Chamberlain Yanagisawa lay on his side, eyes closed, arms and legs bent—a wet, pathetic heap of garish garments. Blood from his cut lip and eyelid still trickled down his white face. His knotted skein of hair had come undone; it dangled onto the floor like a dead black snake. Chūgo eyed the chamberlain with contempt. Such a disgrace to General Fujiwara, this coward who fainted because of two harmless little cuts! Who stole his lord's authority, and indulged his unseemly passions for wealth and sex. The very antithesis of Bushido! To acknowledge him as kin mortified Chūgo. Never had he foreseen the day when he would find value in the foul creature.

Yanagisawa groaned. Weakly, he flopped over on his back. His eyelids fluttered open. The dark, dazed eyes grew huge with fear as he stared up at Chūgo.

"Where—where am I?" he asked hoarsely. He tried to rise, but his twisted clothing held him down.

Chūgo snatched up a coil of rope that lay conveniently on a bench. In an instant, he had Yanagisawa's hands and ankles tied behind him.

Yanagisawa writhed and thrashed. "Chūgo! Are you mad? Untie me at once!"

A wave rocked the boat, and he rolled sideways, slamming his head against the bench. "Oh, no, the river . . ." Panic blurred his voice. "Where are you taking me?"

Chūgo ignored him. Quickly he searched the cupboards, then went outside and examined the hold. A grim smile touched his lips when he found plenty of provisions. He could sail down the coast—a dangerous journey, but he could make it; he was invincible. After dumping Yanagisawa at sea, he would put ashore at some distant province, where he could lie low, disguised as a *rōnin,* until the manhunt died down and the *bakufu* realized that the chamberlain was no great loss. Then he would make his way across the country, finishing his work. . . . Returning to the cabin, Chūgo closed his eyes, the better to anticipate his imminent victory.

From the floor, Yanagisawa spat a steady stream of threats: "Every soldier in the country will be looking for you, Chūgo. And when they find you, they'll crucify you, then cut off your head. They'll leave your remains on the execution ground to be gawked at by every lowly peasant who walks by!"

For Chūgo, the chamberlain's voice had less meaning than the buzz of an insect. His surroundings blurred as imagination and desire transported him into the past . . .

. . . to Oda Nobunaga's encampment, where the great warlord sat in his curtained enclosure. Today he'd won the Battle of Nagashino, his greatest victory. He had finally vanquished the Takeda clan, his most powerful foes, and added their territory to that which he already ruled.

Chūgo's spirit inhabited General Fujiwara's body; he wore the general's armor. Fierce pride ignited his blood as he knelt before Oda and spoke the words his ancestor must have spoken that night so long ago.

"Honorable Lord Oda, please accept these as my tribute to your supremacy, and proof of my loyalty and devotion."

As Lord Oda surveyed the severed heads that Chūgo–General Fujiwara had brought him, his gaze lingered most fondly on those of the *hatamoto*, Kaibara Tōju; the *rōnin*, Tōzawa Jigori; and the priest, Endō Azumanaru: trophies from the present that had accompanied Chūgo into the glorious past.

"You've done well, Fujiwara-*san*," Lord Oda said. "In recognition of your service, I shall reward you now."

Chūgo's spirit soared with his ancestor's. Now he would experience the culmination of General Fujiwara's career. He reached out to accept from Oda the two magnificent death's-head swords—

Suddenly a stabbing pain gripped Chūgo's ankle. He shouted in angry protest as his fantasy ended. He was back in the boat's cabin with the storm howling outside, and Chamberlain Yanagisawa's teeth sunk into his flesh. With a vicious kick, Chūgo shook Yanagisawa loose. How dare this scum interrupt his vision?

"If you think you can escape disgrace by committing *seppuku*, you're wrong, Chūgo," Yanagisawa shouted. "You'll die like a common criminal. You—owww!"

The chamberlain's body jerked when Chūgo kicked his ribs. His voice rose in shrill panic. "How dare you hurt me? You'll die for this, you will!"

Now Chūgo saw the man he'd always suspected lived behind the chamberlain's suave facade: weak, frightened, and small. Yet the discovery evoked no sympathy in him. He kicked Yanagisawa again and again—in the stomach, thighs, and groin.

"Stop, I beg you," Chamberlain Yanagisawa wailed. "Please

don't hurt me. I'll do anything, give you anything—money, women, a higher rank—name it. Just let me go!"

Chūgo ignored Yanagisawa's pleas and promises. His foot struck hard bone and soft tissue, eliciting screams from his victim. In the dark pleasure of venting his anger, he almost forgot the necessity of keeping Yanagisawa alive until they were far from Edo.

Desperately, Sano clung to his lifeline. The water swirled around him; the Sumida's current threatened to drag him under. He gulped air between waves that doused his head. The storm continued unabated—if the river didn't drown him, the rain would. With the boat ahead of him, he couldn't see downriver. The landscape streamed past at a frightening speed, and he guessed they must be halfway to the Ryōgoku Bridge. He couldn't see anyone following, either on land or water. Where were Hirata, the police, the navy? And what had become of Chamberlain Yanagisawa? He must get aboard the boat!

Clenching his teeth with the effort, Sano climbed the rope, hand over hand, knees and ankles grasping the rough straw cable. The hull slammed his sore body. Hand over hand. Finally he swung free of the water. Hand over hand he climbed, thumping against the boat, until finally his head cleared the deck and he locked his fingers around the railing.

"Please don't hurt me anymore!" Chamberlain Yanagisawa shrieked.

But Chūgo's anger had tapped the reservoir of deep rage that learning his family secret had instilled in him. That rage drew him into the past, making him a witness to the abominable act that had inspired General Fujiwara's blood score.

※

A summer night, one hundred and eight years ago, at the Honno Temple. In the guest cottage, Oda Nobunaga awakened, sensing danger. He jumped to his feet, sword in hand.

"Enemy attack!" he shouted to his guards.

Too late. The door burst open. Arrows flew, slaying the guards. Akechi Mitsuhide's army stormed into the cottage.

Oda lashed out at his attackers, downing two with one stroke of his sword. Spears slashed his arms and legs. Then, realizing he was doomed, he jumped out the window and fled, bleeding from his wounds. Akechi's troops loosed upon him a round of gunfire. A bullet struck his arm.

"Now you'll die for insulting me!" shouted the traitor Akechi. "Better men will rule in your place. I and Generals Araki and Endō have seen to that!"

Oda ran into the main hall to die by his own hand rather than suffer the disgrace of capture. Akechi and his troops set fire to the hall: a splendid funeral pyre for the greatest warlord who ever lived.

⁂

Wild with fury at that ancient catastrophe, Chūgo ground his foot against the screaming, sobbing chamberlain's face. The greatest sorrow of General Fujiwara's life had been his inability to save Lord Oda. Akechi, Araki, and Endō, knowing his loyalty, had persuaded Oda to send him to help Hideyoshi fight the Mori. Now Chūgo experienced the full force of his ancestor's grief and rage. He hauled the chamberlain to his feet and punched him square in the face.

The chamberlain flew backward, slamming up against the cabin door. "Please, Chūgo," he begged. Crumpling to the floor, he twisted in a futile attempt to free his hands and feet. Blood and saliva spattered from his mouth as he pleaded, "I'll make you a rich man. I'll promote you to chief of defense. Anything. Just have mercy!"

But Yanagisawa's status, power, and hostage value no longer mattered to Chūgo. Now he saw Yanagisawa as a symbol of all he hated—of today's weak, corrupt samurai, so inferior to past heros. A kinsman who had failed to venerate their ancestor as he did. A representative of the Tokugawa, who'd reaped the benefits of treachery, and were therefore just as responsible for Oda's murder as Akechi Mitsuhide, Araki Yojiemon, and Endō Munetsugu.

Chūgo backhanded a blow across Yanagisawa's mouth. Then he hit on a truly fitting punishment for the chamberlain, who so deserved a taste of his own evil.

Chūgo threw Yanagisawa facedown on the floor. He lifted the chamberlain's outer robes and yanked down his voluminous trousers. He tore away the loincloth whose band cleaved the naked buttocks. Then he hiked up his own kimono, loosened his loincloth, and rubbed his organ until it hardened. He straddled Yanagisawa and entered him with a brutal thrust.

"No, master!" screamed Yanagisawa. His body bucked; the fingers of his bound hands clawed the air. "Please!"

Five quick strokes, and Chūgo spurted. He felt potent, powerful, but physical satisfaction wasn't enough. He craved the ultimate release that slaying his ancestor's enemies always brought. Deep inside, he knew there was every chance that he would be captured. Killing the chamberlain might be his last chance for revenge.

"Please, have mercy," Yanagisawa blubbered. "Please!"

Rising, Chūgo straightened his garments. He threw the door open. Rain and wind blasted into the cabin. He dragged Yanagisawa onto the deck. He would have to live in the cabin for days or months while he sought a safe harbor, and didn't want to contaminate it with his enemy's death.

"No!" screamed Yanagisawa.

Dragging the chamberlain with him, Chūgo splashed through the ankle-deep water on the starboard deck. A jagged lightning streak seared his eyes; the simultaneous thunderclap shook the sky. The boat rolled. Spreading his legs to balance himself, Chūgo positioned Yanagisawa against the railing, head and shoulders hanging over the water.

"No, please, no!"

The sweet flame of anticipated victory leapt inside Chūgo. The thunder rumbled like war drums; the lightning blazed like a burning castle. The rain became soldiers' chants; the wind, the blaring of conch trumpets. Chūgo saw himself riding into battle, and presenting a new trophy to Lord Oda. Pinning the chamberlain still with his body, he grabbed Yanagisawa's hair and yanked his head back, exposing his throat. He drew his short sword.

Still clinging to the railing, Sano looked into the stern. Dread clutched his heart when he found it empty. Why wasn't Chūgo manning the sail's lines? Had he jumped overboard, leaving Yanagisawa to die? Then Sano heard hysterical screams coming from the starboard deck.

"No, master, spare me, I beg you!"

Sano hauled himself aboard the boat and collapsed on the waterlogged deck, where he fought to catch his breath and regain his strength. His chilled body shivered violently in the cold wind, and when he tried to rise, he fell twice before he gained his feet. Then, leaning against the cabin wall, he lurched toward the sound of Yanagisawa's voice.

Horror energized him when he saw Chūgo holding the chamberlain over the railing, blade to his throat. Sano drew his own sword. Though he wanted to take Chūgo alive, he would kill to save Yanagisawa.

"Chūgo!" he shouted above the wind and rain and the chamberlain's pleas. He lunged at the guard captain.

The chamberlain kept screaming. Chūgo's head snapped around. His eyes were fierce slits, his mouth a snarl like that of an armor mask. Sano raised his sword in both hands, but before he could bring it slashing downward across Chūgo's face and shoulder, the boat rocked. Sano lost his footing and stumbled sideways. The movement threw Chūgo and Yanagisawa free of the railing. The guard captain let his prisoner fall to the deck. In a motion so fast that Sano didn't see it, he sheathed his short sword and drew the long one. He rushed at Sano, slashing and thrusting.

Sano regained his balance, sidestepped and parried, but too late. Chūgo's blade sliced his left upper arm. A gush of blood warmed his cold skin. Darting backward just in time to avoid a cut to his neck, he launched an offensive, but his reflexes were dangerously slow. Spiritual energy couldn't entirely compensate for an exhausted body. Chūgo effortlessly parried every cut, inserting thrusts between each, driving Sano backward into the stern. The boat swayed as it careened downstream, hurling Sano at Chūgo. Ever more unsure that he could defeat the guard captain, Sano tried to reason with him.

"Give up, Chūgo," he urged between gasps. "Even if you kill me, you won't get away. Especially if you harm the chamberlain. The army will hunt you down. And without a hostage, they'll have no reason to spare your life."

Chūgo dealt a low cut that sliced Sano's calf. Sano's instinctive jump saved his leg from mortal damage, but his despair increased because he'd easily recognized Chūgo's maneuver as one he'd faced during practice sessions, yet had been too weak to react soon enough. He had only his wits to use against the madman's superior strength.

Chūgo's assault propelled him around the port deck and into the bow. Still parrying frantically, Sano circled the foredeck, noting how, as the boat tipped, the sail swung back and forth in an arc. With a sideways leap that strained his bursting lungs, Sano forced Chūgo to pivot and fight with his back to the sail. Sano lashed out at Chūgo and took a cut to his shoulder. Dodging, he tripped over the anchor. Then the wind whipped the sail around. The boom whacked Chūgo across the back; he stumbled. Sano sliced at Chūgo's sword hand. The tilting boat knocked him off balance again, and the blade only grazed Chūgo's knuckles, but the captain dropped his sword. Sano lunged at Chūgo. Then the boat lurched, throwing him backward.

Sano's feet skidded on the flooded deck. His arms instinctively shot out. As he hit the cabin, Chūgo was upon him, one hand gripping his throat, the other clamped around his wrist, immobilizing his sword. The boat rocked again. Together he and Chūgo pitched forward. Now Chūgo, in a deft maneuver, reversed their positions. Sano reeled backward, past the swinging sail, and into the bow. His back struck the railing as he grappled with Chūgo. The guard captain increased the pressure on his throat, bending his head back.

Sano coughed, struggling with his left hand to break Chūgo's hold, and with his right to free his sword. Back, back, he arched over the railing. Faintly, he heard Yanagisawa's screams. Rain filled his gaping mouth, splattered his eyes. Above him he saw the stormy sky, then a soaring arch of crossed and parallel wooden beams. They were passing beneath the Ryōgoku Bridge. Sano couldn't resist Chūgo any longer. His feet left the deck—

With a sudden, shuddering crash from the port side that Sano initially took for thunder, the boat stopped. He barely had time to register that it had struck one of the bridge's supports. Their forward momentum carried him and Chūgo over the railing. They were falling . . .

The resultant splash jarred Sano's bones. He gasped and gurgled when the cold water closed over his head. Kicking and thrashing, he tried to raise himself above the surface, but Chūgo kept hold of his wrist, twisting it. Pain shot through his arm; he let go the sword. Then Chūgo clasped both hands around his throat, throttling him, holding his head underwater.

The blood thundered in Sano's head while he tried to tear Chūgo's hands away. Seemingly made of steel, they didn't budge. Sano retched and wheezed. Through the water that swirled across his vision, he saw Chūgo's face: fierce, teeth bared, maniacal. The bridge seemed to sway above him, while the boat tossed beside it. Desperately Sano scissored his legs, pulling Chūgo down with him. At the same time, he grabbed for the short sword at his waist.

Obviously guessing his intention, the guard captain released Sano's neck and intercepted his hand. Together they shot above the surface. Sano gulped a breath of air before a wave hit his face. He reached the sword, but Chūgo's hand pinned his at his side. The captain's muscular legs locked around Sano's waist; his other hand pressed against Sano's face, gradually pushing him back underwater. Sano's strength was fading and his struggles weakened. Then despair brought inspiration. Behind Chūgo, the boat's rocking, curved bow rose. Sano thought of the obsession that had compelled Chūgo to commit four murders and embark on this perilous journey.

"Chūgo," he choked out, timing his words with the boat's movements, "General Fujiwara and Lord Oda Nobunaga command you to let me go!"

The guard captain's hold on him relaxed—just for an instant, but it was enough. With all his remaining strength, Sano threw his weight against Chūgo. Chūgo surged backward just as a wave

lifted the boat. Then the boat dropped, smashing its hull against
Chūgo's crown. The captain's face froze in an expression of puzzled surprise; his legs and hands fell away from Sano. Unconscious, he floated on his back amid rain and waves.

Sano wasted no time savoring his triumph. He had to get himself and his prisoner out of the river before they both drowned,
free Yanagisawa, and tie the boat to the bridge, so a rescue party
could reach them. Crooking his arm around Chūgo's neck, Sano
swam around to the stern and found the rope he'd climbed earlier. He tied it around Chūgo's chest, then pulled himself up the
rope and aboard the boat. Heaving and straining until his muscles
almost tore and tears came to his eyes, he got Chūgo onto the
deck . . .

. . . only to find that, while he was laboring, the boat had drifted
out of reach of the bridge and down the river. Waves washed over
the deck and dashed against the cabin. Sano used the rope to tie
Chūgo's hands and feet and lash him upright to a lantern pole. He
slumped against the railing in despair as he scanned the deserted
riverscape. Even if he anchored the boat, it might capsize before
help arrived. Sano staggered around to the starboard deck, where
Yanagisawa lay moaning and sobbing in a pool of water.

"Chamberlain Yanagisawa. Can you sail a boat?"

Yanagisawa abruptly quieted. Gulping in surprise, he raised his
head. Rain, tears, and blood drenched his face. His mouth trembled; his swollen eyes were wells of stark fear.

"*You,*" he croaked. "Where's Chūgo?"

Sano's animosity toward the chamberlain dissolved into pity,
leavened by a slight pang of satisfaction at seeing his enemy thus.
"I've tied him up. He can't hurt you. Chamberlain—"

Yanagisawa's features contorted into the familiar mask of hatred. "I order you to untie me, Sano Ichirō," he rasped. Safe from
Chūgo, he'd recovered his authority. He wriggled toward Sano,
spitting hoarse curses.

The boat was speeding down the river, smacking the waves.
Lightning forks stabbed the sky. Sano repeated, "Can you sail this
boat?"

"Of course not, you imbecile. I'm not a common sailor. Now
free me, so I can kill you!"

Sano grabbed Yanagisawa by the armpits and dragged him into the cabin. Then, leaving the chamberlain tied, Sano hurried out to the stern. He'd never sailed a boat before, but he would have to try. Through the rain, he squinted in dismay at the bewildering web of ropes that ran from the sail, over the cabin, and through wooden fittings on the gunwales. What to do?

Sano seized the tiller and tried to turn the boat shoreward. Nothing happened. The oars, designed for a team of rowers, were too heavy and too far apart for one man to operate alone. Sano grabbed the sail's lines and yanked, turning the flapping sheet at a diagonal. The headwind filled it, pushing the boat right—too hard. The boat heeled sharply. Sano's heart seized as he first let out the sail, then heaved the other way and tried to brace his feet on the slippery, tilting deck.

"I'll kill you!" Yanagisawa screamed from the cabin.

Just when Sano thought the boat would capsize, it bobbed upright. But his next attempt to change direction met with similar, near-disastrous results. He realized that he would have to correct the boat's course gradually. He turned the sail again, this time at a slighter angle to the wind. The boat heeled, but held stable. As it raced downstream, it continued to turn. The bow aimed west and shoreward. Soon Sano saw looming toward him Edo's docks and warehouses. Now he heard other shouts besides Yanagisawa's. He saw ahead the tiny figures of people waving from warehouse doors. One man separated himself from a group and ran out on the dock, jumping up and down. Recognizing Hirata, Sano laughed aloud in sheer, joyous relief. Now he was approaching his assistant on a diagonal. He waited until he neared the dock, then let loose the sail.

The boat turned downstream and drew up alongside the dock. Its bow crashed into small craft moored there; its hull scraped against the pilings. But the boat stopped. The storm still raged around Sano, yet the world stood still.

Suddenly the boat was swarming with men: a *doshin* and assistants; two boatmen in wide hats and straw rain cloaks; Yanagisawa's retainers. The boatmen secured the vessel to the dock and lowered the gangplank. The police untied Chūgo—conscious now, but dazed—and led him away. Yanagisawa's retainers rushed into the cabin.

"Sōsakan-sama!" Hirata ran up to Sano, his face radiant with joy and excitement. "You've done it, you've caught the Bundori Killer! Come on, let's go."

Suddenly too weak to stand, Sano let his assistant help him down the gangplank.

"Sano Ichirō!"

Turning, Sano saw Chamberlain Yanagisawa emerge from the cabin, leaning on his retainers.

"You'll pay for this, Sano Ichirō!" Yanagisawa shrilled, shaking his fist. Pale, disheveled, and furious, he looked like a mad demon from one of the shogun's No plays. "I swear you'll pay for this!"

Sano's mind closed against the chamberlain's threats as a temporarily forgotten longing swelled his heart.

"Aoi," he whispered.

36

One month after the Bundori Killer's capture, the shogun's banquet hall sparkled with noisy festivity. Lanterns brightened the huge room and the garden, visible through sliding doors opened to admit the warm, summer night breeze. Beautiful attendants, both male and female, served refreshments to gaudily robed men who reclined on silk cushions in laughing, joking clusters, or moved about the room to pour liquor for one another in the customary social ritual. On the veranda, musicians performed songs from the shogun's favorite plays. Tokugawa Tsunayoshi, seated on the dais, struck a dramatic pose and intoned:

"I am a wanderer in life's journey
I know not when it might end—"

Occupying places of honor just below the dais, the Council of Elders, Chamberlain Yanagisawa, and the boy actor Shichisaburō laughed and applauded.

Sano sat alone in a corner, isolated by the terrible devastation that had followed Chūgo's capture and destroyed much of the pleasure he'd derived from succeeding in his lord's task. Seeing Tsunayoshi's quizzical glance at him, he forced himself to approach the nearest group of guests, which included Hirata—his former assistant and now retainer—his former superior, Noguchi, and Magistrate Ueda. He poured them a round of sake and joined in their conversation. He must show gratitude and pretend enjoyment, even though his spirit was dying inside him.

"Silence!" Tokugawa Tsunayoshi clapped his hands.

The music ceased; conversation halted. The guests expectantly awaited their host's words.

"As you know, this, ahh, banquet is being held in honor of *Sōsakan* Sano," the shogun said, face flushed and speech slurred from the sake he'd consumed. "Tonight we officially celebrate two momentous events in the life of this most dedicated retainer, the first of which is, ahh, his capture of the Bundori Killer, who, I am glad to say, no longer terrorizes the city."

Everyone turned to Sano. Hirata beamed in vicarious triumph. Noguchi smiled and bobbed his head. Magistrate Ueda merely nodded approval, but Sano saw genuine admiration in his eyes. The elders bowed gravely; the other guests applauded. Only Chamberlain Yanagisawa made no gesture of respect or congratulation. Yanagisawa, who Sano guessed—but couldn't prove— was responsible for his beating. Yanagisawa, the "evil spirit" he might eventually have to destroy. Yanagisawa, powerless against him for only as long as he managed to retain the changeable Tokugawa Tsunayoshi's favor. From his place at the shogun's feet, he glared at Sano with undisguised hatred.

"*Sōsakan* Sano's deed required all the qualities most admirable in a samurai: courage, loyalty, intelligence, and, ahh, perseverance." The shogun's eyes twinkled. "Though I believe you had a little help from Chamberlain Yanagisawa?"

The shogun laughed heartily at his own quip. He'd received the news of Yanagisawa's role in Chūgo's capture with great amusement. He seemed unaware of the chamberlain's attempts to obstruct the investigation; Sano, prohibited from speaking ill of a superior, hadn't told him. The guests, except for the chamberlain, laughed too. Yanagisawa's gaze shot pure venom at Sano. With a fingertip, he touched the scars on his lip and eyelid.

"Now," continued Tsunayoshi, "I shall perform a song I have composed, describing the trial of Chūgo Gichin.

*"It was during the time of the cherry blossoms
That evil was vanquished—"*

The manner of Chūgo's demise had so tickled the shogun's fancy that he'd completely forgotten the doubts Chamberlain Yanagisawa had instilled in him and welcomed Sano back into his favor. He'd even come to the Court of Justice to watch Chūgo's trial. Now, as the shogun chanted his song, Sano relived the unforgettable experience.

Three days after the capture, Sano had appeared before Magistrate Ueda to present the evidence against the accused. While the shogun smiled delightedly and a curious crowd gathered outside the hall's barred windows, Sano described how he'd identified Chūgo as a suspect, then tricked him into revealing himself as the killer.

"A later search of Chūgo's house revealed a list of the names and whereabouts of Araki and Endō clan members," Sano continued. "I also found the mate to the death's-head sword given me by the witness whose confidential statement you just heard. And I found deeds to three houses—one in Nihonbashi, the others near Yoshiwara and Zōjō Temple—all under different aliases. Chūgo's financial records prove that he bought them with money borrowed from Matsui Minoru. When I searched the houses, I found boards, spikes, face paint, incense, and traces of blood."

Magistrate Ueda, dignified in his black garments, sat upon the dais, flanked by secretaries who recorded the proceedings. "The case seems sufficient," he said. To the courtroom attendants: "Bring in Chūgo Gichin."

Sano heard Chūgo coming before the guard captain reached the hall. From the mob outside came angry calls for the Bundori Killer's blood, and above the commotion rose Chūgo's wild rantings. The guard captain had gone completely mad during his stay in Edo Jail.

The main door flew open, and the attendants dragged in the cursing, thrashing defendant. The shogun, his retinue, and the rest of the audience gasped and murmured. Sano stared, amazed at the change in Chūgo.

Stripped of swords, armor, and Tokugawa crests, Chūgo wore a torn, filthy cotton kimono. His wrists were tied behind his back and iron shackles hobbled his legs. His eyes rolled; his teeth were bared in a fierce grimace.

"May demons destroy all you who would stop me from honoring my ancestor as a samurai should!" he shouted, trying to throw off his escorts.

The attendants dumped him on a mat on the *shirasu*—the "white sand of truth" that covered the floor before the magistrate's dais. Not until they'd administered several hard kicks did he kneel and cease cursing, and even then, an angry, animal growl rumbled in his throat. Though Sano couldn't forget Chūgo's terrible crimes, he could pity the once proud warrior.

"Chūgo Gichin, you are charged with the murders of four men: Kaibara Tōju, *hatamoto* to His Excellency; the *rōnin* Tōzawa Jigori; the priest Endō Azumanaru; and an *eta*," Magistrate Ueda said. "You are also accused of ordering two attacks on *Sōsakan* Sano: one by a mercenary swordsman in Nihonbashi; the other at Edo Castle. What have you to say in your own defense?"

"They were not murders," Chūgo snapped. "They were acts of war. Of vengeance. The Endō and the Araki killed my lord Oda Nobunaga, and for that they deserved death by my hand!"

Obviously unable to distinguish his victims from the long-dead traitors or himself from General Fujiwara, he flung a wild glance at Sano. "I had to act before Kaibara, the last member of the Araki clan, died. Then I decided to kill every last Endō. That cursed *sōsakan* tried to stop me, so I hired an assassin to kill him. And if someone else hadn't already had him beaten, I would have!"

Magistrate Ueda frowned. "Then you deny the last charge, but not the others?"

"Deny what I've done?" Chūgo's laugh resembled a dog's howl. "Why? I want the world to know that General Fujiwara is at last avenging his lord's murder!"

Exclamations swept the audience. Sano, though shocked by the extent of Chūgo's delusion, was relieved that his confession would shorten his path to justice.

"Silence." Magistrate Ueda's raised hand quieted the room. "Then, Chūgo, you do not repent of the crimes to which you have confessed?"

"Repent? Pah! A samurai doesn't apologize for doing his rightful duty by his master."

There was a fresh outcry from the audience, which Magistrate Ueda also silenced. "Then I am sorry to say that I must deny you the privilege of committing *seppuku* to which your rank entitles you. Instead you will be beheaded at the public execution ground immediately, and your remains displayed as a warning to would-be criminals."

Sano closed his eyes as the guards dragged Chūgo from the hall. The awful spectacle of disgrace poisoned his satisfaction at seeing his investigation successfully concluded, a killer brought to justice. Through his horror, he heard the shogun's high, excited voice:

"Ahh. A marvelous show. Well done, *sōsakan!*"

Now that same voice recalled Sano to the present. "Yes, this is an accomplishment that must be entered into the nation's official history." Tokugawa Tsunayoshi's face brightened with inspiration. "Since you are a historian, you yourself shall have the privilege of chronicling your, ahh, miraculous deeds for the castle archives."

Heads nodded; murmurs of approval came from the guests.

"This is a great honor, and I thank you, Your Excellency." Sano tried to infuse his voice with enthusiasm. Here at last was the fulfillment of his promise to his father. Sano took pride in his deed; his samurai spirit basked in the shogun's praise. But Sano still felt as though his heart had been torn from his chest, leaving behind a vast, aching emptiness that grew larger and hurt more with each passing day.

Aoi had vanished, apparently for good.

After conveying Chūgo to Edo Jail, giving statements to the police and magistrate, and reporting the success of his investigation to the shogun, Sano had rushed to the Momijiyama to see Aoi—only to find another woman installed as chief shrine attendant and unable to tell him more than that Aoi had disappeared, leaving no explanation.

Frantic with grief and bewilderment, Sano had spent the past month searching for her, to no avail. Then, this evening, as he dressed for the banquet, he'd found the note hidden among his ceremonial robes.

My dearest,

Please forgive me for leaving without saying good-bye. I had no choice. With each passing year, my enslavement to the Tokugawa has grown harder to bear. When we met, my spirit had been dying little by little. It would have gone on dying, if not for you, who restored my hope, happiness, and desire to live.

But now Chamberlain Yanagisawa has ordered me to kill you. Rather than obey, I have fled, in the hope that I can join my family and escape with them before the troops come for us. Perhaps fate will spare your life and mine, even if we can't spend them together.

I beg you not to pursue me, or tell anyone of our liaison. To reveal the full extent to which I've betrayed my master would only endanger me more.

Don't be angry with me, or blame yourself for what is entirely my own decision. Instead, remember me as I will you:

> With eternal love,
> Aoi

The message closed with the crude sketch of a veiled female figure facing a mountain range. Sano, remembering their conversation the night of his beating, understood that Aoi had taken the perilous step of making her dream a reality. Disguised as a nun, living on roots and nuts and the alms of strangers, she was making her way toward Iga Province. Despite her attempt to absolve him of guilt, Sano knew he'd provided the final impetus for her action.

He'd saved lives by stopping Chūgo's killing spree, but endangered the woman he loved by winning her affection and letting her forsake her duty. Guilt embittered Sano's misery. Despite the ninja's renowned ability to survive, he pictured Aoi hunted down, tortured, slain. And he could do nothing to prevent it. He couldn't even thank her for her help, to which he owed much of his success, or for the gift of his life, which she'd purchased with her own.

Then Sano gasped in surprise. The characters of the note were fading. Written in magic ninja ink, they vanished, withdrawing from him as their writer had. Soon Sano held a blank sheet of paper.

As blank as his life was without Aoi.

Now, as the shogun praised his courage, Sano faced the hard-est task of all: to stay at his post instead of following his heart and going after the woman he loved but couldn't save. He wanted to dash from the room, mount his horse, and gallop wildly into the night, shouting Aoi's name. He wanted to search every road, vil-lage, forest, and field between Edo and Iga Province until he found her. Yet her wishes and his own duty forbade him.

In his misery, Sano saw his life stripped of illusion. The castle was a luxurious prison. The shogun for whom he'd almost sacri-ficed his life, who now rambled drunkenly upon the dais, was merely the chamberlain's puppet. Bushido was cruel; a place in history an empty reward. Heartbreak had shown him the truth of Dr. Ito's words.

The shogun's high, merry voice cut into Sano's thoughts. "Ahh. Let us also rejoice in *Sōsakan* Sano's engagement to Magistrate Ueda's daughter."

Except for Chamberlain Yanagisawa, who narrowed his eyes and compressed his lips, the assembly cheered. Sano woodenly exchanged nods with Magistrate Ueda. His change in fortune had induced the magistrate to bestow upon him Reiko's hand. Sano valued the match that his father had desired for him, and an as-sociation with a man he respected. But he would gladly give it up for one brief moment with Aoi, to again know the exhilarating joy of *ishin-denshin*—their precious, unspoken soul-to-soul commu-nication.

The shogun spoke about the match's propriety and offered his blessings for its success. Then he said, "But enough of speeches." He laughed and clapped his hands. The music resumed. "Come, ahh, let us enjoy ourselves!"

Sano accepted a sake decanter from a servant and reluctantly rose to perform the courtesy he'd been avoiding all night. Ap-proaching Chamberlain Yanagisawa, he knelt, bowed, proffered the decanter, and said, "Honorable Chamberlain, please permit me."

Ritual dictated that the chamberlain raise his cup and bow. This Yanagisawa did with characteristic elegance, but his expression was frigid, and as Sano poured the liquor, Yanagisawa's hand trembled as though he longed to throw it in Sano's face.

"I won't forget, *sōsakan*," he said in a vicious murmur meant only for Sano's ears. He downed the sake, grimacing as if the taste sickened him, then bowed to the shogun. "If you will excuse me," he said, and swept from the room.

Sano knew the chamberlain would never forgive him for causing, albeit unintentionally, his terrifying abduction. Nor would he forget that because of Sano, the shogun had enjoyed a joke at his expense. Above all, Yanagisawa would never forgive him for witnessing his humiliation, or for rescuing him. These last had won Sano the powerful chamberlain's permanent enmity. From now on, whatever he did, Yanagisawa would thwart him at every turn. With his spirit broken over Aoi's departure, this prospect was more than Sano could stand. His position had lost its meaning for him and presented a challenge to which he no longer desired to rise.

The party dragged on and on. Sano's face grew stiff from the strain of smiling; his throat ached with grief as he forced polite conversation and false laughter from his mouth. Not even drink could numb his emotions. He took some pleasure from seeing Hirata, with an air of suppressed rapture, fill the shogun's cup.

Bringing happiness to someone he esteemed didn't ease the howling anguish inside Sano. When dawn came, he could bear his pretense of enjoyment no longer. The shogun was snoring on the dais; the few guests not also asleep were engaged in drunken, senseless merriment. No one would miss Sano. He went home, got his horse, and rode out through the castle gate. Where was Aoi? To go to her now . . . Imagining the joy of seeing her again, he forgot the prohibitions that kept them apart.

A cry disturbed the summer morning's humid hush: *"Sōsakan-sama!"*

Sano turned and saw Hirata galloping down the promenade after him. His senses returned. He couldn't leave his post, and he couldn't endanger Aoi further. Grief drew cords of pain tighter around his chest; the emptiness within yawned wider and blacker.

"Are you all right?" Hirata asked, catching up. "Where are you going?"

Sano rode faster to get away from him. "I just need some fresh air," he lied. "I'm going for a ride—alone."

"I'll go with you." Hirata obviously sensed that something was wrong, although he couldn't know what. Now he stuck by Sano, secure in his new status and concerned enough about his master's welfare to disobey an order.

Too tired and dispirited to argue, Sano let him come. Together they rode north out of the city, where the murders had ended with Chūgo's arrest, and the fire and riots in the accompanying storm. As they journeyed through the tranquil, awakening streets, Sano saw that the ravaged areas had already been rebuilt. The Bundori Killer might never have stalked the city.

In the Asakusa temple district, Sano dismounted outside a minor temple. "Wait here," he told Hirata.

Entering the gate, he crossed the small precinct and passed through another gate leading to the cemetery, where the cherry trees were in full leaf now. A sprinkling of dry, brown fallen blossoms mingled with the gravel on the paths. The air was heavy with summer's rich, fecund fragrance, but underneath it, Sano smelled autumn's incipient decay. The sounds of temple bells, priests' chants, and the clack of pilgrims' wooden shoes seemed muted, distant: part of the living world that encompassed this memorial to death.

Sano knelt before the grave monument, a square, upright stone shaft topped with a pagoda roof, where an urn hidden in the hollow pedestal held his father's ashes. Evidence of his own and his mother's faithful visits stood ranged around it: flowers; a decanter of sake and a bowl of dried fruits to nourish his father's spirit; prayers printed on wooden stakes. But even here, Sano felt no sense of his father's presence. In his despair, he spoke aloud:

"*Otōsan.* I've done what you asked." His voice shook with his effort not to weep, but he didn't care; there was no one to hear him. "Why isn't the fulfillment of duty enough to make me happy?"

Footsteps crunched on the path behind him. Sano started, then turned and saw a strange samurai.

"Who are you?" he blurted. "What do you want?"

The samurai regarded Sano with a sad smile. "Don't you recognize me, Ichirō?"

And now, with a staggering shock, Sano did. The voice—young and vibrant instead of old and quavery; the strong body not yet wasted by illness; the proud spirit not yet crushed under the hardship and shame of living as a *rōnin*. The features, so like his own. This stranger was his father—not old, sick, and feeble as Sano had last seen him, but with his life still ahead of him.

"*Otōsan!*" Awed, Sano bowed. "I've prayed so often for you to come. But you never did, until now. Why?"

The spirit's warm, firm hands grasped Sano's shoulders, raising him to his feet. Of equal height, they stood face to face, and in his father's eyes Sano saw the look of forbearing patience he remembered so well.

"My son, I never left you," the spirit said. "Haven't I spoken to you through the lessons you learned from me? Am I not present in your thoughts? Do I not live through you, my flesh and blood?"

Seeing the truth of his words, Sano had no answer. As they strolled the cemetery together, he again sought his father's wisdom. He told the spirit about his successful murder investigation, and the loss that had robbed his achievement of satisfaction and his existence of all joy.

"Father, what will I do, how can I live?"

"Your struggle is one that all samurai inevitably face, Ichirō." The spirit's far-gazing eyes contemplated the distance. "The struggle to understand right and wrong, good and evil. To do what is right and good and avoid doing that which is wrong and evil."

Somewhere in that oblique remark, Sano knew from experience, there was a message for him. "And how does a samurai know what's right?" he asked hesitantly, reduced to the role of ignorant young pupil by this spirit that appeared no older than he.

The spirit's reproachful glance told Sano he'd missed the point, as he had so often during childhood lessons. "Better you should ask how a samurai makes himself follow the path of right rather than the one that leads to wrong."

Sano waited, chastened but expectant.

"Although a samurai may at first be motivated to do right by the shame he feels when doing wrong, if he does that which is right often enough, then it will become a natural habit. In doing right, he will find the satisfaction of fulfilling his destiny, and of knowing he has mastered the most difficult part of Bushido."

They'd reached the cemetery gate, and the spirit halted. "This is where we part, my son. But I am always with you."

"*Otōsan!*" Sano clutched his father's arm. "Don't go!"

His hand closed on empty space. The spirit had vanished.

"*Sōsakan-sama?*"

Sano turned to see Hirata standing in the open gate. "*Gomen nasai*—I'm sorry to bother you," Hirata said with a trace of his old hesitancy, "but you were gone so long, and I was worried . . ."

"I'm fine." Sano spoke the lie through the fresh grief at his father's abrupt departure. The combination of liquor, exhaustion, and longing must have produced his waking dream, but now it was over, and he was more alone than ever. "Let's go."

Yet as they left the temple and mounted their horses, Sano felt more at peace than when he'd arrived. His father's elusive spirit had finally appeared to him, when he needed it most. The encounter hadn't removed his pain, but had given him insight that illuminated this troubled period of his life. He now saw the resemblance between his pledge to his father and lord and Chūgo Gichin's to General Fujiwara and Oda Nobunaga. Both represented attempts to do right, to embrace Bushido. Chūgo had avenged the betrayal of a ruthless warlord by committing crimes that had led to his own death. And Sano, who had risked his life serving a weak, self-indulgent despot, must continue to do so, no matter what the cost to himself. His own *bundori*—the war trophy he'd earned during the investigation—was his better understanding of what it meant to be a samurai. He had struggled, and despite his anguish, could admit he'd found satisfaction in performing well, in doing right. He must continue to do right—because the habit was already an integral part of him—until the act of doing right brought him happiness.

Someday.

Hirata was waiting beside him. "Where are we going now, *sōsakan-sama?*"

Sano sighed. "Back to the castle," he said.

Though his spirit might ache forever for Aoi and his thoughts range across land and water in pursuit of her, he must seek happiness in his work, his marriage, and his continuing loyal service to his lord.

Because someday began now.

ACKNOWLEDGMENTS

For their contributions to this book, I thank Pamela Gray
Ahern, Marie Goodwin, John McGhee, Craig Nelson,
and David Rosenthal.

ABOUT THE AUTHOR

LAURA JOH ROWLAND, the granddaughter of Chinese and Korean immigrants, was born in Michigan and is the author of *Shinjū*. She lives with her husband and two cats in New Orleans. *Bundori* is her second novel.